BROKEN

THE FOUNDER'S SEED BOOK 2

BROKEN

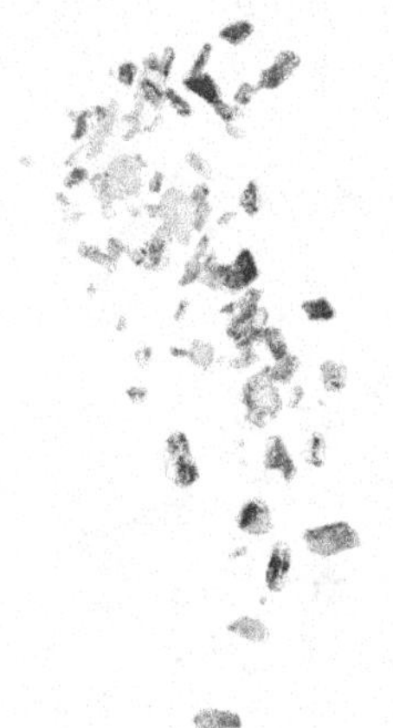

DREMA DEÒRAICH

NIVEYM ARTS LLC

Harajüd

Timatu
Malushta
Chaleda
Channel
Phoenix Islands
Kishnur
Straits
Miradu
Ocean
Mesataym
Straits of Guzan
Surian
Ocean
Syrinaia
New Canaan
Mari Bay
Shamashu
Shambu Straits
Nöbetchi
Mountains
Upasu
N
LEGEND
Ice, Snow
Inland Water
Land (undefined)
Marsh
Mountains
Open Water

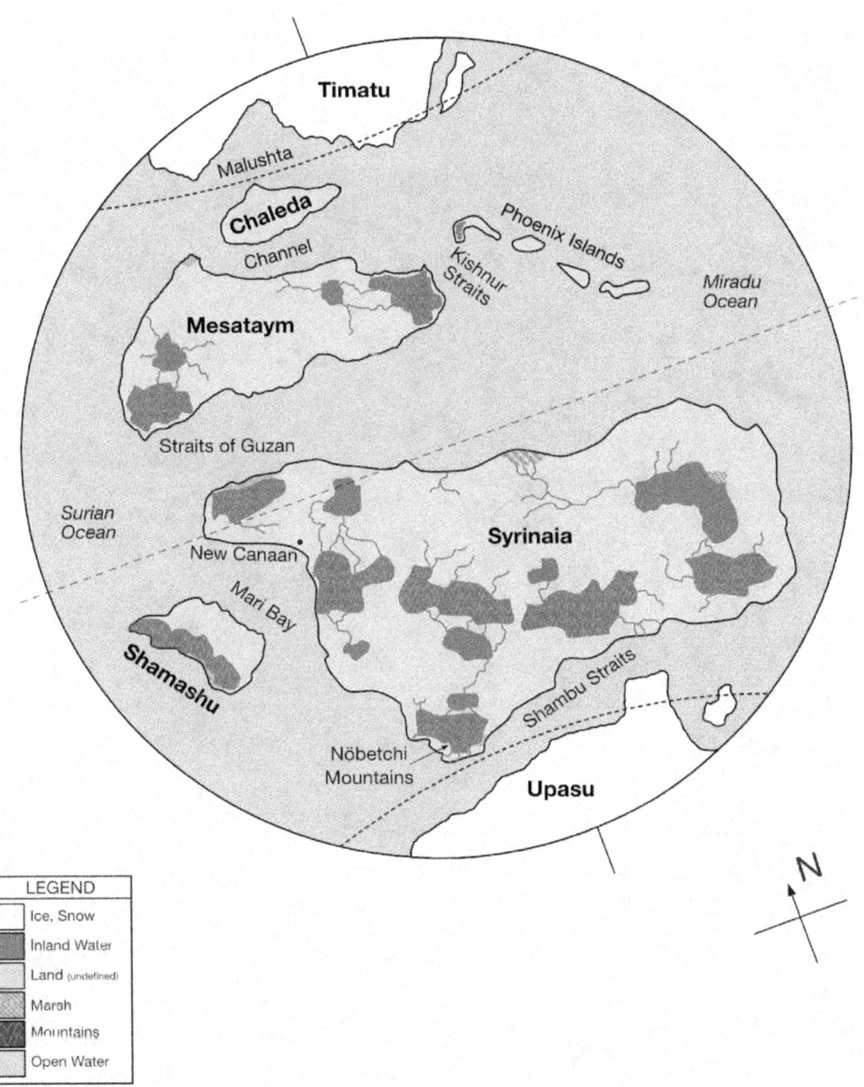

Zebalu

Daima Ocean
Utatikra
Binka
Batikri
Cara'antra Sea
Matakri
Bantali Sea
Pelarr
Duakela
Lapua
Achitina
Gulf of Busala
Kekalu Ocean
Seladik
N
LEGEND
Bog
Ice, Snow
Inland Water
Land (undefined)
Mountains
Mountains-Polar
Open Water

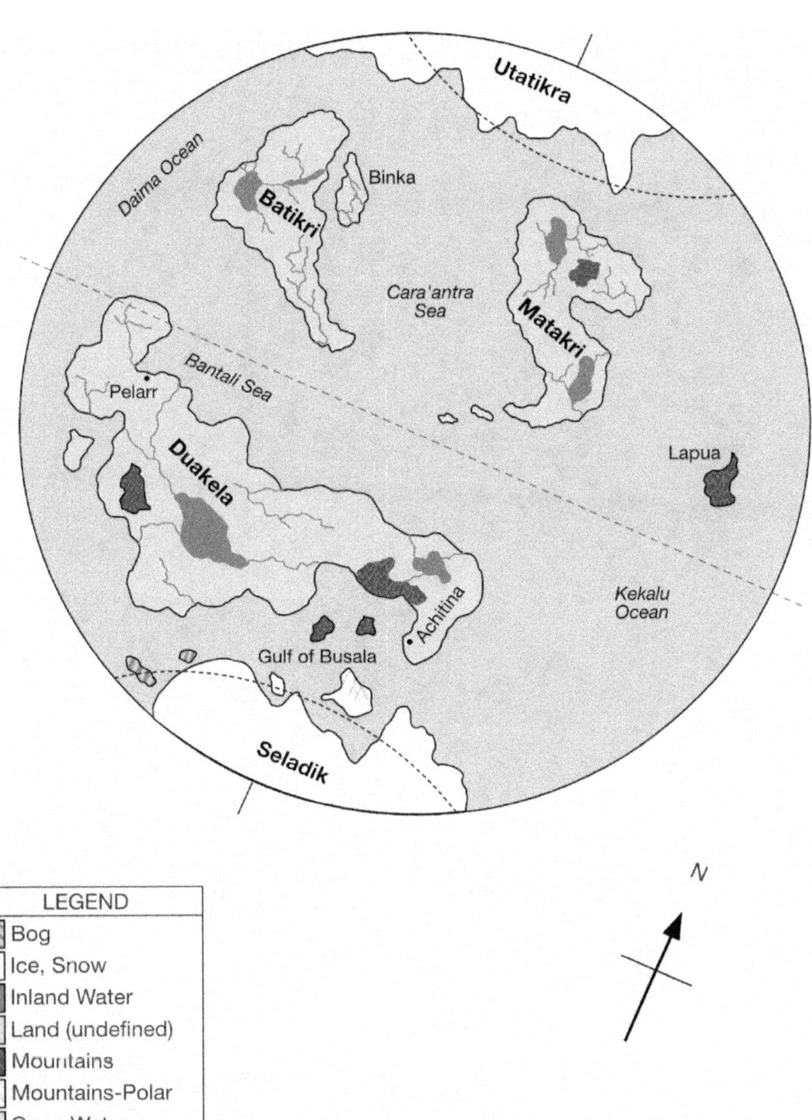

Saacharis

Gheatanor
Retraga Island Sanctuary
Tuneloras
Ezi Tributary & Wetlands
Apanordica Sea
Gauri Metalb
Apagroz Sea
Scarpre Ceri Mountains
Treican
Sulacran
Metaliven
Apasudica Sea
Sudighea
N
LEGEND
Ice, Snow, Glaciers
Inland Water
Land (undefined)
Marsh
Mountains
Open Water

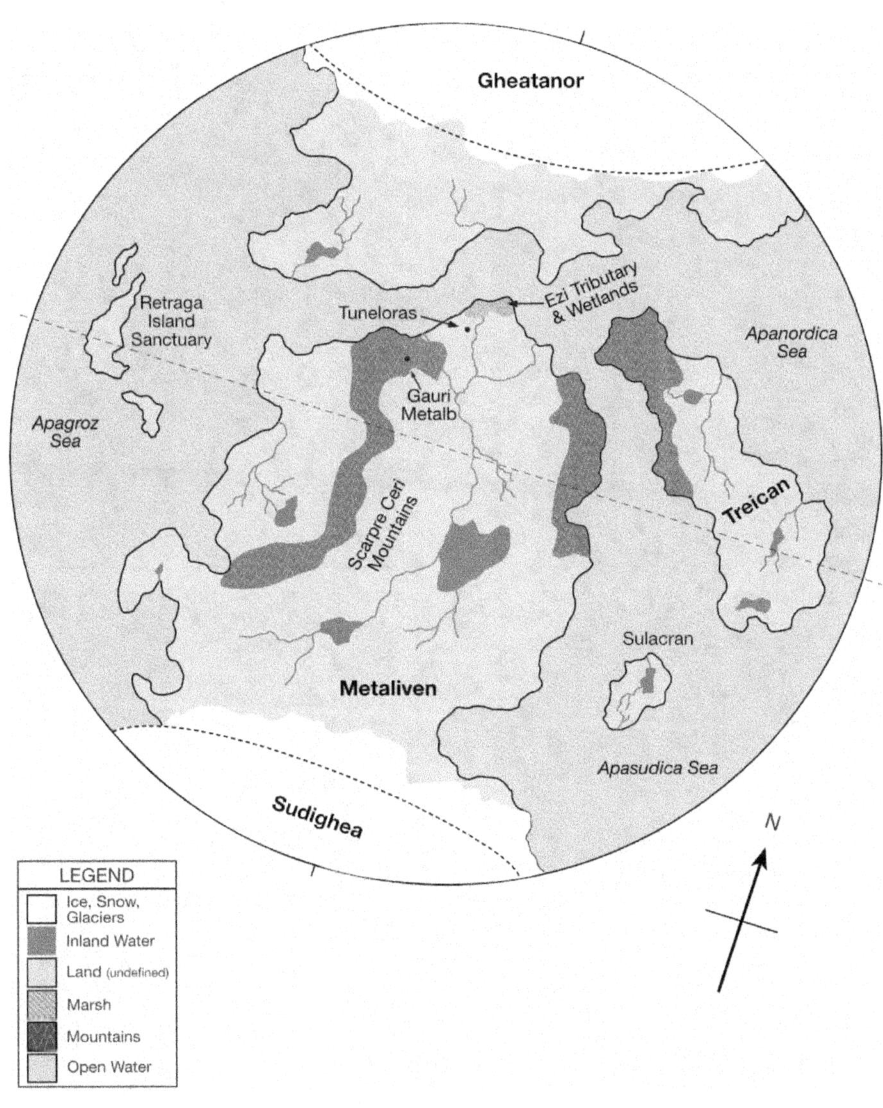

Danua

Nordislan
Smalvan Ocean
Bevgerlan
Caves
Storelandsør
Haven
Fjellet Isthmus
Utenende Tomrom Rift
Uendelvann Sea
Sørislan
N
LEGEND
Ice, Snow
Inland Water
Land (undefined)
Marsh
Mountains
Open Water

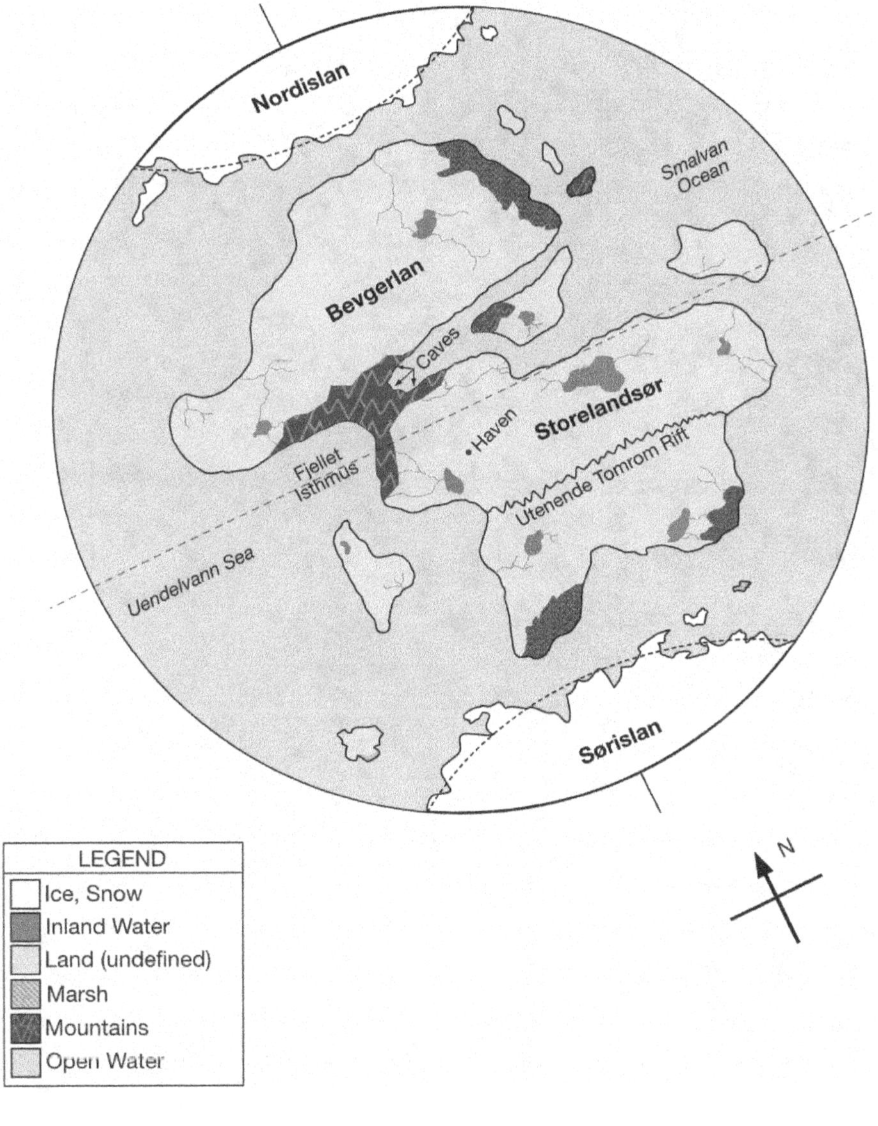

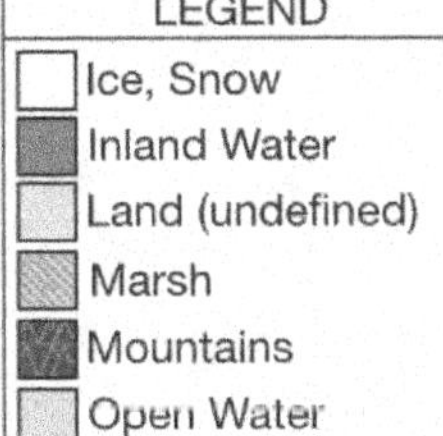

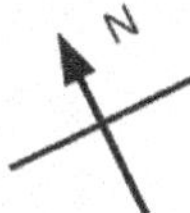

Part One

chapter 1

New Canaan, Harajüd
<u>Northeast Sector</u>

THRACE STOPPED HER SKIMMER BENEATH the trees, in the shadowy green space behind the arena. She left the vehicle and jogged through the dark toward the lights on the opposite side of the building where a noisy throng awaited the start of the games. Her informants said her latest targets would be there, attempting to hide from Admiral Malcolm Skalar, or Thrace Baldric, his captain. The admiral swore these unfortunates were two more enemies in a sea of people he needed yet did not trust. Thrace hated being his weapon, but better her than him. As long as Alira wore Skalar's skin, it would always be this way.

Nearer the front of the arena, light spilled into the surrounding shadows as Thrace slowed to a walk, rounding the corner to join the crowd as if she belonged there. As if no one would know who she was. Foolish hope, that, but perhaps these thrill-seekers were too caught up in the moment to notice.

In such close proximity, the crowd's excitement raised the hairs on her arms to full attention. She shook it off and eased between the gathered humans. Behind the mask of Thrace Baldric, Galen stretched tendrils of empathic awareness in all directions, searching for the targets, until—

There. Two additional members of the Consortium contingent that had challenged Skalar. Even without seeing their faces, their fear thrummed through Thrace as if it were her own. They knew their fates were sealed, and yet they dared hope for escape. She almost pitied them.

She worked her way closer, staying behind others in the crowd as she drew near, until one of the targets saw her closing in. The other locked eyes with Thrace before shoving through the crowd in the opposite direction, her cohort on her heels.

Eager arena fans ignored them, pushing ahead toward the opening gates. Thrace pursued her targets, following the stink of their fear as she elbowed her way through the horde that packed the lighted accessway. Beyond, the targets broke free and dove into the obscurity of surrounding woods.

Their mistake.

She shot after them into the gloom, her eyes shifting to their natural silver to track her prey. Just ahead, the pair dodged trees at high speed, no doubt on their way to Arzu Aslan. That brothel held no heroes, but it did house witnesses. Thrace almost snorted. The targets should have stayed where they were. Then again, she shouldn't have expected them to do the smart thing. If they hadn't been stupid enough to defy Skalar, they wouldn't need to elude Captain Baldric.

Her legs pumped faster, gaining slow ground. A few seconds later, she reached out and snarled her fingers in the fabric of the man's shirt, yanking him off his feet and down to the ground with a grunt. In a flash, she was on him, snapping his head around in a macabre angle, the grisly sound echoing off the trees even above the roar of crowds at the nearby arena. Then she was up again and racing toward the woman, but that few seconds had been enough for the other target to burst out of the arena's shadow and into the dappled clearing near the brothel. She was as good as gone.

Damn.

Thrace snatched her knife from its sheath and drew back an arm, then hesitated, extending her senses, feeling for others nearby. It felt safe, but what if she was wrong? If she struck an innocent…

While she deliberated, her target pulled ahead and Thrace cursed again, slammed her knife into her belt, and poured on more speed. As the woman burst into a wider patch of moonlight, the air before her shimmered and flowed in a thickening silvery sheen. Pieces of what had appeared to be trees, scrub, and hard-packed ground transformed into Alira's short, blue form, her skin pulsing in shades of red and pink patterns. The fleeing woman shrieked, lurched away from the sudden obstacle in her path, her feet skidding on the moist ground as she tried to change direction, but it was too late. She was dead before she could retreat three steps.

Thrace slowed to a walk, breathing hard, and approached while Alira blinked and shuddered with the harvest, absorbing the memories and personality of this latest "enemy" of the unammi.

The captain sighed. She thought Alira was going to watch from a greater distance, far enough away that she could avoid the reaping. Now there would be another passenger added to the growing multitude in Alira's head. How many could she take before they commandeered her own voice, her own actions and thoughts? How many would it take to tip her sanity over the edge?

When the harvest was complete, Alira's form shifted into Skalar's and he looked up.

"I thought you weren't going to do that again," Thrace said.

"And I thought you were going to take care of this yourself," Skalar said.

Tension prickled the air between them. Thrace sighed. "I would have. There was no need—"

Skalar shrugged. "Better here away from the cameras than out on the street. I couldn't risk her getting away. She knows too much."

"Knew." Thrace sounded dull, even to her own ears. "Past tense."

chapter 2

THRACE MADE IT SOUND SO easy, as if all Alira had to do was make a simple choice. But the truth was that when her throng of harvested souls began arguing, it was nearly impossible to do anything but act on impulse. Yesterday, in the early moments of her first full day in this charade, Alira had spent far too much time listening to those internal voices, questioning them, trying to hear them out, and wavering over every tiny decision. The real Skalar never would have done so. Even though she wore the admiral's face and body, spoke with his voice, commanded his faction, if she couldn't convince his crew she was the real thing, they'd mutiny. She couldn't allow that.

Already, hiding behind Skalar's eyes, she'd caught others in the faction giving her—him—strange looks that confused her

what does that mean?

so when her harvested nemesis, the one whose face she wore, began to push to the fore, shout louder than the others, she'd let him take control. Just a little. He would know best how to handle Consortium business.

But this? The killing? Even after all these humans had done, killing them sickened her.

him. stay in character, squib.

shut up, crow.

Unfortunately, it had to be done. Those targets were loyal to Commander Walker, who now sat stewing in the Consortium's brig. Skalar had enough to worry about without looking over his shoulder every moment of every day wondering when their blades would strike.

Galen had done all the necessary wetwork through Thrace Baldric's hands—until now—and Alira was glad to stay out of it. She'd watched from a safe distance, able to see enough to know it was done, but far enough away to avoid the inevitable harvest. All except this one. This target had run straight at her camouflaged body hiding in the shadows

the woman was going to escape.

and Thrace wasn't going to catch her in time, and the old Skalar whispered that if this one got away, his enemies would have time to spread the word, garner more support, make her task even harder than it already was.

If it was just Alira, or even just she and Galen, she would have let them all go, left this world and donned a new shape and a new name, in a new place. They could be happy. At peace. Right now.

But it wasn't just the two of them. The remaining unammi, sheltering and vulnerable in the caverns on Earth, depended on them. Alira had to follow through.

So she hadn't stopped to think. Instead, she'd done what she needed to do

galen is right, though.
you could'a stopped this one without killing—
gettin' kinda crowded in here, squib.
shut up, all of you.

even though the price was one more voice in her head

his head.
what the hell—
welcome to the club.
you did the right thing, netzyl. step aside, let me do the rest.

and, worse, the annoyance of Galen—*Thrace*...damn, this was confusing.

eli, where are you? i could use a little help.

In the expectant silence that followed, she turned Skalar's face away and surrendered control to the loudest of her reapings as she raised his wrist. "Sa'abah," she said, in Skalar's deep voice, "we're ready for cleanup. Just behind Arzu. Make it quick."

chapter 3

THRACE JOGGED BACK THE WAY she'd come. Might as well put all the cargo in one spot, make things easier for everyone. No telling what to expect from Alira—or Skalar, or Crow, or whoever she was—right now. In fact, Thrace no longer even recognized herself. Nothing had been the same since the incident on Bejami when the humans had confiscated Galen's ship and he had fled into Thrace's flesh. He'd been lucky to escape that fire, yet now here he was, embroiled in another, even hotter one. All because Alira had asked it of him.

Thrace sighed as she reached the first body and looked down at it. Seeing through Thrace's eyes, Galen almost felt sorry for the bastard. The man was just trying to live. So were the others Thrace had taken out since Galen and Alira had returned to Harajüd disguised as the Admiral and his new second and assumed command of the Consortium. So, too, were the unammi, but at what cost? In less than two months, Galen had acquired a new face, a new body, a new world, and a new, very dangerous life. In the last two days, he'd become an assassin, using his Thrace Baldric persona to hunt down anyone who posed a risk to the unammi's weak link.

Thrace sighed. She'd dealt enough harm in two days to last a lifetime. She didn't like it. Not at all. She'd done so before when there was a need but it was never easy or pleasant, especially given her empathic nature. Each of her targets dragged a small piece of her with them when they died. How much more of herself would she have to sacrifice to make this work? How much of the real Thrace—the real Galen—would be left when it was done?

She'd objected to this course of action at first, and argued that the crew would run, would force them to carry out Consortium business in the open, beyond the safety of the faction's walls. She'd been right, but Skalar had shrugged, commed Chairman Roucharde, and been granted limited free rein to see this through as long as there were no witnesses. Still, if someone stumbled across the two of them standing beside bodies out here in the wooded green…

Thrace swung the corpse up into her arms, retraced her steps to the tree where Skalar waited in the shadows, and laid her burden beside the other victim.

"I think that's the last of the security risks for now," she said, her tone carefully neutral, though she couldn't think why she bothered. Even if she suppressed her disapproval, Skalar would know. Alira would know.

"Good." He peered at her through the murk. "The others are loyal?"

Thrace nodded. "To Ronan, yes. Or to Sa'abah. If those two officers stay true to you, their people will follow their example. But this isn't going to be the end of it, you know."

"What do you mean?"

"There's talk. Some of the base crew know something weird is going on with the admiral. They can see you've changed. And they don't much like me. I'm not sure how to handle their near defiance."

"You must be brutal with them. You can't let them challenge your authority or they'll lose all respect and eventually kill you—and then they'll come for me."

"Alira—" She glanced around. "Admiral Skalar, *sir*," she whispered, "I trust you. I want to help you see this through, but I am not a Trader captain. Nor are you a Trader admiral. I don't want to be brutal. Neither do you. At least you didn't. Before…." Her voice faltered, and she coughed to cover the weakness. "You've set us on a precarious path. How far can we follow it before we are both changed beyond all recognition?"

Skalar's expression softened at the edges, and Thrace's heart stuttered across the tension between them. Even in the shadow, she could see the line of his jaw, the dark smudge of his beard against bronze skin, his sharp eyes, normally dark brown but silver now below that jet-black hair. Was Alira still in there?

"That, my dear Captain, is a fait accompli for me," Skalar said, almost to himself. He sighed and his gaze hardened once more. "You, however, may still be saved. These deaths couldn't be avoided. You know this. As for any others, I don't care how you handle them, provided that you remain in control. If you don't want to harm anyone, find some other way to deal with the problem. Just keep them off me. I have enough to manage."

Thrace nodded. "I know. What do you want me to do about the rumors?"

He waved a hand. "I don't care what they say about me. If they aren't talking about the outpost, they can speculate all they want."

Skalar's face twisted, as though he were frowning at someone Thrace couldn't see, and he turned away.

Alira must be hearing the voices again. Still. "You should care," Thrace said. "This isn't a game. It could take your life or mine or both at any moment with no warning. If that happens, the outpost is forfeit. The rest of the unammi are in danger."

chapter 4

THRACE'S COMMENTS PROVOKED A CLEAR response among Skalar's harvested passengers.

shut her up.

stupid squib, can't let her talk to you like that—

Heat rushed up the back of his neck. How dare she?

calm down, sister.

no, netzyl, calm won't fix this.

That last, loudest argument in his head overrode all reason and he rounded on Thrace. "You think I don't know? That I don't wrestle with that threat every single second? That I don't have others in there," his fingers wriggled at his own head, "repeatedly reminding me of this fact? I'm doing the best I can under very difficult circumstances and learning on the fly, so grant me some space, if you please."

Thrace stepped closer. "I can't do that. As long as we're in this mess, we each have a duty to keep the other on full alert at all times. If either of us slips even a little at the wrong moment...." She cleared her throat. "You know I'm right."

Skalar ground his teeth, glaring at the silver eyes in Thrace's dark face. Galen was Alira's i'shin. Her beloved. Behind the captain's facade,

Galen was trying to help. But oh Na'staani, when the voices clamored so, it was hard to tell the difference between reason and insubordination, even with his predecessor driving this shared body. Everything was so mixed up.

"You sound like Lurien," Skalar said, his voice tight.

Thrace watched him, as if she were searching his face for—what? Something in their shared history? Their personal connection, maybe? There was a time when he could read her just by her expressions, or the tilt of her head.

That seemed a long time ago.

"You miss your ama," Thrace said.

"Of course I do. Don't be ridiculous. Lurien would be the first one to say I should do what needs doing, even if it's hard. Especially if it's hard." He looked down at the dead targets. Thrace said this was the last of them. But how could he be sure others wouldn't come forward?

a trader admiral always has enemies, netzyl. can't be too careful.

Without knowing who they were, how could he stop them from harming the faction? Or, for that matter, the outpost? Maybe Tiral and the other outcasts there needed to be able to defend themselves.

yes…you can't always be there.

weapons would at least give them a chance.

He stepped over the bodies and peered through the darkness toward Arzu. "Where is Sa'abah? She should be here by now."

consortium industries could make the hardware, squib.

bad idea, netzyl…that would draw attention to you.

"Alira—"

"My name is Skalar," he said, distracted, then spun toward her. "I'm thinking of arming the outpost."

Thrace frowned. "I thought we wanted to make the place look deserted."

"We do."

"Arming it runs counter to that goal."

True. Skalar's human reapings whispered of other ways.

"Besides," Thrace said, "wouldn't that raise questions among the crew?"

He shrugged. "Skalar—the real Skalar—talked about improving the shields before we came along, but never got the chance. We could start with that and add a hologen to project an abandoned facade."

"That'll draw a lot of power from the generators. Won't it be detectable?"

Probably. But he didn't want to admit that. "I'll leave that detail to the techs. I just think that, given the fact we've spent two days chasing down potential threats, arming the base seems a good idea."

Thrace's features twisted.

"Think of it this way," Skalar said. "What if something happens to either or both of us? If Ronan or one of the other crew made a run for that base, the outpost could at least defend itself."

Thrace blinked. "To what end? If that happens, their best option would be to continue the charade. Come to New Canaan or whatever, until they can get free and flee to Earth. If they fight and lose, they're dead, which means they're discovered—unammi bodies curiously close to a potentially habitable world. Don't you think the humans would take a chance and check it out?"

"No. They're too afraid of whatever microbes chased their ancestors off Earth in the first place, especially Ronan. They'd be curious, yes, but I don't think they'd make the connection."

Thrace shook her head. "I fear you underestimate them."

"Remember," he said, tapping his forehead, "I have Skalar's memories. He knows these people better than you do."

Thrace frowned.

"When will Tiral be here?" Skalar said.

"Almost a month. Why?"

"I'll ask his opinion when he arrives." He stared into the darkness toward the road. Shadowy boles blocked them from casual view. A silhouette, some small nocturnal creature, leaped from one tree to its neighbor, followed by scuffling sounds of claws digging into bark as it climbed and leapt to yet another tree. "What's Tiral's human name again?"

"Spencer Kilbee. He's a merchant for HHU."

"I remembered that part," Skalar said, shooting Thrace a quick look. "Did you complete his employment transfer to the Consortium?"

"Not yet. It's in the works, though. The process takes a few weeks. He won't return before then."

Skalar shoved his hands in his pockets. "Very well. Keep in touch with him. Let me know when he's due. I'll want to meet with Mr. Kilbee immediately upon arrival."

Thrace nodded. "Of course."

chapter 5

THEY WAITED IN THE DARK, surrounded by the rustle of the leaves, the calls and creaks of night insects, and the shouting of spectators in the arena. Distracted, Thrace lifted her hair up and away from her shoulders. The trees held close the muggy heat, sending a trickle of sweat between her breasts, and she adjusted her body's temperature to compensate. It would be hotter in Bregaina, but at least there the breeze off the water would help to keep residents cool.

Memories of Bregaina and Botha, an elder in that village, raised a lump in her throat. How many times had Galen, disguised as Tenzin, sat on the raised platforms there, discussing the mysteries of life with that old man? Botha had always helped Galen see things more clearly. But after Galen had abandoned the Tenzin persona to ensure nobody could connect it to an unammi pilot, there had been no way to reach out to Botha. By now, he probably thought Tenzin had fallen off the face of the world.

Thrace needed to find a way to connect to his friend again, introduce him to this new persona somehow, construct a new relationship without revealing who and what she was. It wouldn't be easy, but the thought of abandoning their friendship left her cold, sad.

She glanced at Skalar, who stared toward the road. Too bad Alira never met Botha. He could be so helpful to her right now. Maybe....

Skalar's wristcom chirped. "Yes."

"Almost there, sir. Two minutes. Sa'abah out."

"About damn time," he muttered.

Thrace took a cautious breath. "I should invite Botha to visit us."

Skalar looked askance at her. "Why? How? Does he even know Thrace Baldric?"

"I'll think of something. You'd like Botha. He sees into the heart of things. He might be of help to you."

Skalar scoffed. "I'm fine, Captain. I don't need a guru. My connection to Na'Staani is as strong as ever."

"I see." Thrace crossed her arms. "When is the last time you meditated? When's the last time you saw your dream companion? What did you call him? Eli? What has he had to say lately?"

Skalar looked away.

"That's what I thought." Thrace waited, but he avoided her gaze. "Well?"

He shook his head. "Why is this human so important to you? What's so special about him that you seek his counsel?"

"I told you. He sees past the surface. His view offers a fresh perspective, and he's honest. He'll tell you what you need to hear, even if you don't want to hear it."

"And why would I want that?"

"Because sometimes," Thrace said, "the lies we tell ourselves inflict more damage than even the most painful truth."

Scuffles sounded nearby and Thrace turned. Crewmen moved toward her through the dark. She shifted her eyes to their more human gray color.

"Over here," Sa'abah called behind her in a low voice as she approached with her team. "We've got it, sir. Perhaps you and the captain should make yourselves scarce, just in case."

"Very well," Skalar replied. He nodded at Thrace. "I'll see you back at the base."

"What about that visitor we were discussing?" Thrace said. "Should I comm him?"

"I'll think about it," Skalar said, and stalked away.

The lie strummed Galen's empathy, and Thrace sighed. Skalar wasn't going to think about Botha at all.

chapter 6

Pelarr, Zebalu
<u>Cartel Trader Base, Admiral Bellamy's Office</u>

"I KNEW IT." BELLAMY PUSHED up from her chair and paced toward the seating pit. "He just can't stay out of my business."

"What happened?"

Her second's voice washed over and past her before it registered through the simmering rage. "Skalar sent a message to the Clan," Bellamy said. Her jaw ached, and she unclenched her teeth.

"A message," Hannah said, moss green eyes guarded as she waited for the rest.

"Our contact there says Admiral Tsurin received a package from New Canaan. Inside was an ear."

"One of our people?" Hannah said.

"I suspect it's Dodger." No way to be sure without genetic files, which didn't exist for that agent. Bellamy had no doubt the Clan's leadership had tried, though. "I tasked her with rounding up cargo on Harajüd, but she's long overdue for a check-in. More than one New Canaan contact reported her missing. I gave her up for dead weeks ago."

"Are you sure it was Skalar who took her out?" Hannah said. "The Clan has plenty of other enemies. Maybe—"

"It was him." Bellamy moved down the steps and stopped in front of the window wall. Outside, gardeners worked on the shrubs and plants in the beds around the footpath. Half a dozen Cuthars gulls hung suspended on the updrafts just beyond the cliff's edge, sunlight glinting on their glossy black feathers. Below, whitecaps rolled inland from the Bantali Sea to disappear behind the rocky ledge. She tried to imagine Skalar's face disappearing over that same precipice, his shock as he realized the fate that awaited him on the rocks below.

"What are you going to do?" Hannah asked.

Bellamy grinned. She'd slit his throat from ear to ear. Would he look like her brothers, laid open so? Or like her father? He was about the same size, same build. Splash enough blood on a body and one looked very similar to another.

"Nothing. Yet." She caught a glimpse of her smiling reflection and spun around, honey-colored hair swinging in waves around her shoulders as she faced her slender second. "You, however, are going to oversee loading of Rook's next cargo."

"Slaves?"

"Yes."

"Adult?"

Bellamy's eyes narrowed. "No."

Hannah looked away, shaggy tufts of her white-blond hair catching the light. "Admiral…if I may, how do you know the colonials won't feed you to the fish if they find out you're dealing in that kind of merchandise? Duakela officials have objected to this before."

The admiral shrugged. "Because the ones that matter, on Duakela as well as the other continents, are my best customers." Her predecessor had taught her that. Slaves had been Virgil's most popular product. She tilted her head, watching Hannah's reaction. "You don't approve."

"That isn't my call, Admiral. I just…" Hannah shook her head. "Never mind. You know this business better than I do."

"Look at it this way. The market is starved. I'm filling a niche. Tsurin's our only other competitor, if you can call it that. But her merchandise isn't permanent stock. They're short-term indentured assets that carry a higher maintenance cost for lower profits. She can't keep pace with us in this any more than she can in other areas. And anyway, those officials you're so worried about won't look our way for long. They have fresh evidence to implicate the Consortium."

"How did you manage that?"

Bellamy shrugged. "Even better, this entire load came from New Canaan."

"You took them right under Skalar's nose?"

"It was almost too easy. Something's going on in the Consortium."

Hannah frowned. "Like what?"

"I'm not sure, yet. Whatever it is has Skalar distracted. Rumor says he was MIA for more than a month. When he came home, he'd changed. I'd give a lot to know where he was all that time." Bellamy tapped a finger against her lip. Nothing ever rattled Skalar, so whatever had burrowed under his skin, it had to be important. "I'll figure it out."

"I don't doubt it, ma'am."

"Maybe he's just cracking. The man's too soft. He should never have gotten into this business."

"He's still ahead of us," Hannah commented.

Bellamy's gaze snapped to her captain's face in time to catch the flash of qualm that touched her light brown features before it disappeared. Why the hell would Hannah say something like that? Didn't she realize Bellamy would always be better than Skalar? Rage swelled in her throat and she bit it back with an audible clack of teeth. It was Hannah. She spoke without thinking. She hadn't meant it. Had she?

"The only reason his numbers are better than mine," Bellamy said, "is that he *cheats*." She oozed up the steps from the seating pit and closed on her blanching second like a viper. "He *takes* what is rightfully *mine*. I will cut him down, slice off his parts one by one, upholster my chair with his skin, and eat his testicles for lunch. Then I will assume command of the Consortium and run the other factions into the ground, and I will do it all with a smile on my face." She paused, less than a meter from Hannah. "Any questions?"

"No ma'am. I think you covered it."

Bellamy laughed, a rich melodic sound that flushed a bit of color into Hannah's cheeks. "Don't doubt me again. TICS."

The system chittered.

"Send Captain Rook to my office." She paced toward the window. "I'll admit the Consortium is stronger than the Cartel in a few matters, shipbuilding for one. I'm working on that. But Skalar's too sentimental. His so-called ethics restrict his success. There are lines he won't cross. That's why I'll win."

Hannah said nothing, and Bellamy cast a glance over her shoulder. "No questions?"

"Just one," Hannah said. "Where is Rook taking this shipment?"

"Saacharis." Bellamy moved down into the pit. The gulls were gone.

"We already have buyers?"

"Gauri Metalb's manager wants some for the mines, but the pretty ones are going to the bagnios."

"What about Rizzo?"

Bellamy huffed at the window. "Not a problem."

"I believe you," Hannah said in a careful voice. "I just want to be prepared. We both know what a whack job she can be."

"She's a connoisseur of torture, I'll give her that." Bellamy grinned at her reflection. "Nevertheless, if she crosses me, I'll dine on her balls, too."

chapter 7

New Canaan, Harajüd
<u>**Skalar's Private Residence**</u>

ALIRA FELL BACK ON THE bed, panting. She stared up at the dark wooden posts towering above them at the head of the bed. A beautiful detail, certainly, but functional, too. Those, and the posts at the bed's other end, projected a privacy screen around them. Still breathing hard, she wiped away the sheen of sweat on her brow "TICS, attend. Reduce ambient temperature by one degree."

"Only one degree?" Galen teased, raising up on one elbow to peer down at her. "I guess I need to try harder."

"Un momento," she laughed, pushing at his chest. "¡Déjame respirar!"

His smile faded. "You're doing it again."

She closed her eyes. "Doing what?"

"Speaking another language."

Damn. A sigh escaped her. "I can't help it. Ever since that last harvest, it just slips out."

The prolonged silence pried her eyes open.

"Did Skalar know that language?" Galen stared at her.

"No."

"Then using it is inconsistent with your adopted persona. Be careful, Alira. You know what's at stake."

"Estoy en eso—" She stopped, tried again. "I'm working on it. Can we change the subject?"

"Of course. Do the voices still comment when we're intimate?"

How was this an improvement? She shrugged. "They're part of me. Like my own thoughts. I'm used to them now.

> *sure you are.*

> *who was that?*

They rarely bother me anymore."

Galen frowned, tilting his head.

Clearly, he didn't believe her. And why should he? Try as she might to avoid getting involved in the culling, the choice was sometimes denied her by the circumstances. She'd been forced to take a few more lives since that night behind the arena. And the truth was that the harvests were getting confused in her head, talking over one another, harder to tell apart. All except Skalar's, with his consistent tone of command. His voice stood out.

If Alira'd had more time to prepare, maybe this wouldn't be so hard. But neither of them had any precedent to follow here. She sighed and sat up, leaning against the carved headboard. "Listen. I—"

The TICS chittered. "Incoming communique from Harajüd House security."

"Don't answer it," Galen urged.

She considered his request. It would be nice to forget, for a while, who she was pretending to be. To ignore the many responsibilities of the faction and focus solely on what she wanted for herself. For the two of them.

> *can't do that, netzyl. not if you want this to succeed.*

Murmuring an apology she climbed off the bed, morphing as she went. Fully dressed, Skalar stepped past the privacy screen, crossed the pedestal, and stepped down onto the main floor to face the holo in the opposite corner of the large room. "Receive comm."

A man's balding head and rounded shoulders appeared in the corner of the room. "Admiral Skalar. I hope I'm not interrupting anything important."

Skalar showed his teeth. Even corpgov's head of security needed to remember that he had them and wasn't afraid to use them. "How can I help you, Harlan?"

"That's Chief Downing, if you don't mind," Harlan reminded him. "A couple of my group homes reported some missing children in the last month. You wouldn't happen to know anything about that, would you?"

"Why did you think I would, Harlan?"

The security chief twitched. "Connections, Admiral. And an anonymous tip that the Consortium has taken up trafficking."

don't even justify that with a response.

shut up, skalar.

Skalar snorted. "Ridiculous."

"I wouldn't put it past you," Harlan said through tight lips. Of course, Harlan's lips were always tight, so it was hard to tell whether the man was annoyed, or this was just another day for him.

Skalar sighed. "You don't like me much, do you?"

"I've heard that inmates on Mandoslóna mete their own version of prison justice to slavers. Most unpleasant."

Skalar stared at the holo. "Logan knows I would never deal in slaves. I imagine this query was undertaken without his blessing or the benefit of any proof, or you would be at my door to arrest me."

"Chairman Roucharde is more trusting than I am," Harlan nodded. "But he has daughters. He's going to want the matter resolved. If I find any proof at all that this is true, even Logan won't stand by you."

"Yes, yes," Skalar said. "I have been warned. I get it." Harlan slung threats as liberally as a fisherman chumming the waters, hoping to snag unwary prey.

where did that come from?

He pushed aside the distraction. "Was there anything else, Harlan?"

"Now that you mention it, there is. I don't recall seeing Captain Crow about in recent weeks. I hope he isn't unwell."

"Crow and I had a difference of opinion. He left the Consortium over a month ago."

"I see." Harlan squinted, his lips puckered. "Did he leave in a box?"

"On the contrary. The man left in a ship I gave him years ago. No hard feelings. Just a parting of the ways. The last I heard, he was headed for Phejoss. I did give him quite a generous severance package. Perhaps he wanted to taste a bit of luxury. Feel free to check if you like. He might still be there."

"Maybe I will. Meanwhile, stay away from decent Harajüd citizens, especially my group homes and youth centers. Just a friendly warning."

remind him who you are.

"My dear Harlan." Skalar smiled, slow and deliberate with just a hint of menace. "Allow me to return the favor. I am a businessman, pursuing commerce within the terms of my contract with Harajüd House Unlimited. I have every right to deal with the good citizenry of this, or any other world. Ignore that at your peril."

Harlan's jaw clenched. "Is that a threat?"

"Not at all. But the board of directors would no doubt frown on any attempts to discourage honest trade, especially where they stand to benefit." Skalar allowed the smile to fade and replaced it with a slight frown. "I'm sure you didn't intend to imply that Consortium business is…unwelcome here in New Canaan."

"Slaving isn't honest trade. HHU's board won't stand for it." Harlan scowled. "I hope we understand each other, Admiral."

"Perfectly," Skalar said. "End communique."

The holo winked out, revealing the pearl and maroon walls behind it, and his form flowed into Alira's. Harlan's words echoed in her mind, accompanied by an image of Rugrat. That last memory of Skalar's little sister would haunt Alira for the rest of her days.

Trafficking. Again. Alira frowned. She shouldn't be surprised. Skalar had known it wouldn't be abolished by his simple warnings of the past. He—she—*they* would need to be more direct next time, especially if they were dragging his name, and the Consortium, into the fray.

"What was that about?"

She looked toward Galen's voice. From here, the bedposts projected the image of a charcoal gray coverlet made from Danua silk spread over a wide mattress, pillows piled high near the headboard. "I don't know," she said, padding toward him. She passed through the screen. He still sat where she'd left him, pearl gray sheets pulled over his hips in a haphazard way.

Blue and white speckles flickered among the colors of contentment in his skin's display. "His questions about Crow worry me."

"They shouldn't. If he tracks Crow, Harlan will find that my former second lost everything in a game of chance on Phejoss and, when he refused to pay up as expected, he disappeared. Rumor says he was dumped on one of the many volcanic plains. If they look hard enough, they might even find a bone or two." She focused on something over his head and far away. "His questions about the slaving worry me more."

"I'd heard that humans used slaves in the past, before they all left Earth."

She sat on the side of the bed, her skin streaked with frustration from memories that churned in Skalar's harvested thoughts, as fresh in her mind as if the events that spawned them had happened yesterday, yet she had not lived them herself. "It still happens. Humans buying and selling other humans…"

Twenty years of fruitless searching before Skalar had found Rugrat broken at the quay. Alira grunted. Even after all this time, recollection of the image soured that harvest's mind. How could it not? She still sometimes saw Nyros' bloody face, the knife lodged in his eye. The pain from that memory might never heal.

"But why?" Galen shook his head. "Don't the colonials already have plenty of human labor to do what needs doing? I thought that's how their governments functioned. The residents do all the work required to keep the cities functioning and in exchange, they get food, shelter, and basic necessities."

"Government workers benefit the corporate body. Slaving is all about profit for entrepreneurs. For the Trader factions."

"How?"

"Slaves do illegal work—counterfeiting, industry labor outside the confines of licensed areas, you name it—even some sanctioned jobs like sex workers, without the legal limitations usually imposed on the clients." Like Rugrat, who'd been so badly abused she couldn't heal. "But traffickers don't report the results of slave labor, so the colonials get none of the profit."

"Still," Galen shook his head, "whoever's working them still needs to support them. And the government's the only provider outside a faction's base. I can't believe that sort of need wouldn't show up on a balance sheet somewhere in colonial records."

Alira spat an expletive straight from Crow's repertoire. "The problem with that argument is that the concept of support is relative," she murmured, her words drawn from Rugrat's trembling tale of all that missing time. "Slavers can maintain a full contingent of workers with very few resources if they don't care about keeping the slaves healthy or happy. It only takes basic shelter to hide them from surveillance, yes, but cram as many into the space as will fit. Give them minimal food and water, just enough to keep them moving. Provide barely essential sanitation so their presence doesn't attract attention." Rugrat had been so thin when Skalar had seen her last, her eyes so vacant…

"Maybe the slaves are content with their fate," Galen offered.

Alira glared. "What did you say?" Skalar growled in her head the same question that flew out of her mouth.

Galen lifted a placating hand. "Hear me out," he said, a slight frown on his brow. "If the arrangement is so despicable, why don't the slaves run? Tell someone in charge what's going on?"

Her skin flushed red. "You don't know what you're talking about." She ground her teeth, fighting the rage that threatened to overtake her. This was Galen, not some enemy. He didn't know what slaving did to its victims. He couldn't. "It isn't like they have any choice in the matter! Slavers keep them in line with sonic chains and nerve whips, drugs and threats. 'Do what I tell you or I'll kill your siblings, and then your mother and father.' How's that for an incentive to stay?"

Even the appalled look on Galen's face didn't stop Skalar from reacting through her. "If the captives are young enough, they're easily manipulated, either physically or emotionally. 'I bought you from the people in charge. Why would they care about you?'"

"No youngling would believe such a thing!"

"Of course they would," she shouted. "What youngling would have enough experience with colonial governments or politics to know any better, especially when no one has taught them different?" She gestured, her hand bright red. "Malnourishment affects neurological processes, Galen. The slavers know that. They also know constant hunger makes a person less likely to fight back. Sometimes they starve the prisoners who don't obey without question. Or the slavers beat or kill problematic victims in front of the others as an example of what will happen if they resist."

"Alira, I—"

"As far as the slavers are concerned, slaves are property. Not sapients. They have one purpose only: to turn a profit. Slavers use them up and toss them out with nary a fuck what happens to them along the way."

She stopped for a breath, but he only stared at her as if afraid to speak. After a moment, she looked away.

"Skalar hated the trade." Her voice had dropped by several decibels, though her prior outburst left her throat raw. It might have started as Skalar's hatred but given the intimate knowledge of it he'd shown her, she now shared it with him. "He vowed slavers would never run unmolested on Harajüd. Not long before I harvested him, he caught one running business through his territory. He tortured her until she implied the Danua Clan was behind it and gave up her contact. He never really believed her."

Galen sighed. "I didn't know, but it doesn't surprise me. Humans have always been cruel to one another. You of all people know this." He turned her face toward him, his hand lingering on her cheek. "Why does this anger you so?"

Why didn't it anger him? Could that lifelong detachment ingrained on him—on them all—by the enforced unammi social order keep him from feeling a righteous rage even now? Over such a horrible mistreatment?

She laughed, a harsh mirthless sound, and pushed his hand away. "Unammi are cruel to their own, too. Only their methods differ. What is conformity but a type of slavery, and mitigation a method of coercion?"

"Maybe. But that doesn't explain your reaction." He peered at her. "What's really going on?"

She glared a moment longer, then looked away, her red flushes shifting to blue, then purple. Why hadn't she skipped this conversation? The topic never failed to depress her, and Galen wouldn't understand. Much as she wanted him to, he couldn't. She shifted, started to rise, to move far away from these things she didn't want to express aloud.

He grasped her hand, eased her down on the bed. "Alira, talk to me. Please."

She swallowed past the lump in her throat. "Rugrat."

Galen frowned. "What?"

"Rugrat," she said louder, the word pushing tears out to run down her cheeks. She took a deep breath and blew it out slowly. "Skalar's little sister. Slavers snatched her when she was a child. They released her more than twenty years later, but she was never the same."

Blood pulsed in Alira's ears, while Skalar fired images into her mind

rugrat crumpled on the docks, lost and confused.

she didn't even recognize me at first!

and remembered the aftermath.

the clan's admiral had paid. dearly. it wasn't enough. it would never be enough.

"What happened to her after that?"

"She—" Alira's lips moved, but no sound came.

"She took her own life?"

Alira nodded and looked away. How could she feel both confused and enraged? Such loss, and yet such unquenchable thirst for revenge?

Galen swore softly. "I'm sorry for her pain, but why does this affect you? She wasn't your sister."

Alira scowled at him, tears forgotten, red veins threatening to overtake the purple in her skin. "Why does that matter? She was an innocent who didn't deserve the life she got!" Shoving herself off the bed, Alira charged through the privacy screen.

"Why are you angry with me?" Galen said.

She whirled toward the blue-and-white blur of him standing amid the haze of anger that rouged everything in her sight. "You forget that Skalar is in my head. His loss is my loss. Rugrat may as well have been my sister.

His memories of her are as much a part of me as if I had lived them myself."

He tried to speak, but she cut him off. "I don't know what you think is going on in here," she said, pointing to her head, "but I assure you, it's quite often a free-for-all. I can't just compartmentalize their memories the way you want me to. I've tried, I'm still trying, but it doesn't seem to work that way. This is who I am now. If you can't deal with that, there's the door."

good riddance to the do-gooder.

shut up, crow.

She glared at him a moment, awaiting his reply. When he remained silent, she nodded. "Good. Then you can stay. If you change your mind, don't keep it a secret. I'm hungry. You coming?"

She turned and stomped out of the room.

chapter 8

New Canaan, Harajüd
<u>Dagons Public House</u>

SKALAR LEANED BACK, CROSSING HIS legs as he looked out over his domain. Part of it, anyway. Business always boomed at Dagons, especially since he'd given it a facelift seven years ago and staffed it with his own hand-picked security doubling as bartenders, wait staff, and kitchen crew. Of course it was a popular hangout. Excellent food and drink, inviting atmosphere, eccentric decor, central location, live staff instead of automated service—even now, diners and drinkers packed the tables downstairs and every seat at the bar. Upstairs, socializing spilled from booths into the walkspace as patrons drank and laughed and talked. The only gap in the crowd at the gallery's railing lay in his corner, where partiers gave him a wide berth, leaving clear his line of sight to the first floor entrance.

Yes. He'd done well if he did say so himself.

you? this wasn't your project.

keep your voices straight, squib.

His brow wrinkled, the frown melting his smile by slow degrees. He clearly remembered placing the orders for decor, the directions for remodeling, even the satisfaction of finding that old cage elevator. Memories of watching the techs revamp its mechanisms overlaid visuals of unammi working to clear passages and reinforce walls in the city on Iridos. He blinked away both and sighed.

Voices. Right. Concentrate, Skalar.

Tiral's human face welled up from Nyros' and Ijydin's memories. Unremarkable dark hair streaked with silver, average slender face, beakish nose, lanky form. Humans tended to overlook such individuals. So the Spencer Kilbee persona matched Tiral's own tendency to avoid notice. Interesting.

Downstairs, movement at the entry drew Skalar's attention. Kilbee glanced up from the door with a nod, then moved toward the stairs. Moments later, the gallery crowd parted to allow him passage, and he slid into the seat across from Skalar.

"After nearly a standard month of voice and text coms, it's good to see you in person, Ali—" Kilbee glanced around. "Skalar. Trumo sends his regards. He wants to know when you're coming home."

Skalar softened. The last time Alira had seen Trumo was on Earth, just before she left. She'd promised him she would return. "Is he fully recovered?"

"He is. He misses you. Says you're one of the few frem who listened to him."

Trumo and Alira had a lot in common, but Skalar kept this to himself. Without Alira there to help guide him, how long before her young friend was mitigated? The thought twisted Skalar's gut. He sighed. "I miss him too. But it can't be helped."

"Fair enough." Kilbee glanced around. "But why did you want to meet here?" he asked, his tone low, melodic.

"Wait." Skalar slid his ident through the menu pad and touched its controls. A static prickle crawled over his skin and was gone.

"What was that?"

"Privacy screen," Skalar explained. "Dagons seemed the best compromise. If you're going to be a public Consortium pilot, I need to treat you like a new hire. Meeting in person is unusual enough. Bringing you into my office would be too far out of character."

"What about witnesses?"

"They can't hear us or surveil us. They can see us, just not well enough to read our lips." He jerked his chin at Kilbee. "Order something."

"Don't mind if I do," Kilbee murmured, touching the menu pad again and again to make his selections.

Skalar's lip quirked. It seemed a lot of food for such a slender man. Yet lanky as Kilbee was, that chair seemed too small for his frame, almost as if he were perched on a youngling's seat, knees drawn up to his chin.

"You have the irolium?" Skalar asked.

"Locked in my jumper."

Good. It wouldn't do to run out of those stones. Staying in human form for so long took a toll. If Skalar's disguise were to fail, the results would be disastrous. He needed to keep a good supply of the irolium for its renewing energy.

Kilbee shifted, as if to rise. "Should I go get it?"

"That won't be necessary." Skalar crossed his legs. "Once we leave here, you'll follow me to the base and give it to Captain Baldric."

"Will do." Kilbee settled back. "How is this going to work?"

ever the direct one, tiral.

Skalar's lips puckered. "You're familiar enough with your prior cover at Harajüd House Unlimited."

"Sure. Except for that couple of months absence during our..." Kilbee cleared his throat and glanced around. "...relocation, I've been piloting human merchant ships for HHU a long while now, in between my runs to Iridos."

"It's the same kind of thing, only working for me now, instead of the colonials. How does that sit with you?"

Kilbee shrugged. "Fine."

"Understand, there is no council here. My word is final. Are we clear?"

"Crystal."

"Good. In the future, you'll make your deliveries directly to my New Canaan base."

"Anything illegal?" Kilbee peered at him. "I don't want to be stopped or arrested by one of the colonies for hauling black market goods."

"That won't be an issue. Even a civilian merchant captain running trade for the Consortium is exempt from search or seizure on any colonial world." Skalar shrugged. "You'll have to do actual business for the faction to keep your persona legit. Share the run with the other pilots on monthly supply runs so everyone gets a break from the outpost. I'll expect a report with each arrival." It made sense to meet them all. He should get to know them in ways that went beyond those of his harvests' memories.

"Of course."

A waiter arrived with their orders. "It's good to see you, Admiral." The burly server smiled as he set plates before Kilbee, and two glasses before Skalar. "Here's your water, sir, and your usual brandy. Your favorite, of course."

Skalar's lips twitched toward a grimace. "I only asked for water."

The server blinked. "Yes, but…you…you always drink brandy, sir."

put him in his place.

"Today I'm drinking water." He held the attendant's gaze.

"Of course, Admiral." The waiter slid the brandy onto his tray. "I'll take it away."

Skalar watched until the man was gone.

"Your staffers don't question you much, do they?"

"Not more than once." Skalar's lips curled in a small smile. He glanced at Kilbee's food. "Let me guess. You like potatoes."

Kilbee nodded. "Doesn't matter how they're cooked."

"I see." Skalar watched Kilbee eat. Of the dozens of gourmet dishes on the menu, Kilbee chose potatoes. How pedestrian. "Captain Thrace tells me the drone deliveries have been accepted by Harajüd House and Saacharis Aggregate. The humans gave you no problems then?"

"Not as such," Kilbee said, still chewing. "They got nosy, of course, commed the hauler while I was waiting for the drone, wanted to know why the sudden change, invited me down to explain, asked whether they could send an ambassador to discuss it in person, the usual rhetoric."

"What did you tell them?"

"Only what you told us to, that the unammi no longer wanted any contact with humans, and all further hematium would be delivered from orbit by drone. The pilots delivering to Saacharis gave a similar report. Why? Did you want us to say more if they press it?"

maintain the mystery.

"No. Don't even address it."

Skalar's black gaze roamed over the railing to the ground floor below. Customers stood three deep at the bar, a recycled-woodchip treasure commissioned during the remodel. Tenders hustled to mix drinks and set up orders while patrons stood at the entry, searching for an empty table. Muted laughter and the hubbub of conversation trickled through the screen, along with music and the creak and rattle of the cage lift at the far end of the gallery.

His brow creased at that sound. Impressions blurred in his mind. Alira and the other unammi in his head didn't understand why humans would use such a stinky, noisy lift when the stairs were right there. But Skalar loved that thing. He'd loved this whole place and had worked hard to make it a popular venue for the working crowd in New Canaan. Many Consortium crew frequented the place. Crow never liked it much, though he'd spent his share of time inside these walls on faction business, but some of Skalar's other harvests had enjoyed Dagons. All those memories entwined with his current view, one playing atop another in a confusing mélange.

"What's on your mind, Admiral?"

Skalar turned to Kilbee, whose eating had slowed. For a moment Skalar saw the person behind the human face. Unammi voices in his mind whispered of Tiral's preference for peaceful resolutions to conflict whenever possible.

"I'm considering armaments for the outpost."

Kilbee continued to chew for a moment, light brown eyes locked on Skalar's face. "Is that necessary?"

"What do you think?"

"Well, I dunno. Can my people install them without the need for outside assistance?"

Skalar's hackles rose, along with an eyebrow, all on their own.

presumption must be quashed.

"Your people?"

"Huh." Kilbee wiped his mouth with the napkin. He stretched out his long legs beneath the table and crossed his arms. "Sorry. It's easy to forget who you are. They're your crew, sure, but the question stands."

The man had yet to call him sir. "It's probable. How are they coming with comms and sensors on the post? Familiar yet?"

"Passably, but they've been at it for less than two months."

"Work faster. They should be up to speed by now."

Kilbee's fixed stare felt hot on Skalar's face.

"That post is our last bastion before Earth. If you can't handle it, say so." Skalar sipped his water.

"No, I got it." Kilbee paused. "You could have a point about the weapons. All the unammi together couldn't stop what happened before. With only a handful on the outpost, we'd never be able to stop a landing, much less a hostile move from space, especially since a quarter of our number are mitigants."

"Did Rakalesh object to them joining you?"

"Not at all." Kilbee shook his head. "As long as they agreed to contribute genetic material, I think she was glad to see them go."

Genetics. Skalar frowned. "The council has a working vault again?"

"Not in the new city. Not yet. They're still working with cobbled power from the few wind turbines we brought. No, they're storing salvaged samples at the outpost for now."

"What about their lab work?"

Kilbee reached for another bite of potato. "Done onsite at the outpost. I didn't think you'd object."

"No," Skalar said, his tone distant, "of course not."

outsiders? on my base?

stop. it's my base now.

Kilbee was watching. Skalar cleared his throat and shushed the voices. "But it's temporary, right? The survivors are working on an Earth vault, and a local lab?"

"That's what they said."

"Good. That's … good." Skalar blinked. "How are the mitigants adjusting to outpost life?"

"Very well. I started one team of them on those assessments you wanted for the landing bay repairs. They're doing a great job. In the human vernacular, they're blossoming."

"Really?" Skalar asked.

Kilbee offered his signature shrug. "Sure. Never better."

"Don't you find that strange? I thought mitigation—"

"—was forever, I know," Kilbee interrupted. "That's what the council wants everyone to think."

"But…"

"Actually," Kilbee leaned forward, placing his bony elbows on the table, "mitigation's long-term success rate is lower than you would expect. Only about forty percent of those who undergo the treatment remain tempered. The rest eventually relapse."

Recovered mitigants? He'd never heard about such a thing, or seen a mitigant who acted contrary to expectation, only a vague memory of Lurien saying one such individual had been treated not once, but twice.

Kilbee broke through his reverie. "Skalar?"

"That's Admiral Skalar. Try to remember, Kilbee." He took a deep breath. "If recidivism is so high, why don't the rest of us hear about it more often?"

"The council doesn't want anyone to know. A vulnerable threat makes poor incentive. Besides, most backsliders learn to cover their quirks. They don't want to risk a second treatment, which they fear could lead to permanent change. That probably explains why, given another option, they don't wish to stick around under the watchful eye of the council. They wanted out, so I gave them a chance."

"Of course." Skalar swallowed, throat suddenly dry. He reached for his water. So it was possible that even mitigation wouldn't have stopped Alira from protesting, given enough time to resume her natural state. What would the council do with someone who kept relapsing?

"I should probably mention," Kilbee said, "that they've been asking questions, too."

"Who? The council?"

"The mitigants."

"Like what?"

"They're restless." Kilbee shrugged, as if that should have been obvious. "They're curious about a pilot's life. They ask for descriptions of human cities, human food, space flight, living life behind a mask. Almost any question you can think of, they've asked."

Alira's old questions and fascination flitted through Skalar's mind. Oh yes, he knew how that felt. "How many mitigants are there?" he whispered.

"On the outpost? Mmm, four."

"And total?"

Kilbee made a face. Nyros did—had done that, too.

"Maybe ten or so."

According to Nyros, mitigants had numbered around a hundred before the fall of Iridos. So many lost! "Is the council still using mitigation to keep the survivors in line?"

"Not yet. But even the threat isn't the bogeyman it used to be."

Skalar frowned again. "Why?"

Kilbee looked at his potatoes. "I think a few bold rebels are starting to believe the time for change is at hand. They're asking what the higher goals for our species might be, and whether the old ways will still serve that purpose. Besides that, with so few survivors, how many can the council mitigate before our society can no longer function as it should?"

A chill stippled Skalar's flesh. Alira had said often enough that the unammi needed to change in order to grow. Even though Rakalesh had agreed to begin cross training the survivors, the elder still believed the people were not strong enough now to make bigger leaps. She'd argued that the blows dealt their civilization left them too vulnerable to risk sweeping changes, yet Alira had pushed for them anyway. Now others were echoing her sentiments. The changes she'd sought glimmered like embers in the moments before an inferno. And yet the unammi trembled on the precipice of total collapse. If they teetered the wrong way, if the fire started now, it could burn away their chances, and it would be all Alira's fault. Perhaps her mother, her brother, the council, and all the rest of her detractors were right to call her selfish, but could she be any other way?

"Kilbee." Voice wavering, Skalar coughed, sipped his water and tried again. "Is the city in danger from within?"

The lanky man appeared to weigh the question. Finally, Kilbee peered across the table at his new boss, took a deep breath and blew it out in a slow, measured exhalation. "I guess we're gonna find out."

chapter 9

New Canaan, Harajüd
<u>Consortium Trader Base, Admiral Skalar's Office</u>

"SA'ABAH," SKALAR SAID, "CONFINE RIPLEY and Bohmer to quarters for thirty days. No comms outside emergency or medical. Basic rations."

She glanced from the admiral to Thrace to Ronan. "Yes, sir."

"Ain't your business," Ronan said, glaring at Skalar. "You got no right."

ronan's on our side, but don't let him take liberties.

"Careful, Ronan," Skalar said. "Your loyalty buys a certain amount of leeway. Don't overstep."

"My crew." Ronan twitched in the chair before Skalar's desk, storm clouds gathering on his face. "My decision."

Skalar narrowed his eyes. "They fraternized with another faction."

"A couple'a brews! Ain't no crime there!"

"Ronan, they talked. I can't let that go."

The grizzled captain glared. "Don't like it. Beer makes a person talk, maybe. Don't mean they said anything important."

Skalar leaned back. "TICS, play Zekes Pub recording date 541016, time stamp 24:13, booth fifteen."

The system confirmed with a digital chitter, followed by a holovid projected over Skalar's desk, and a confusion of music and noise.

In the recording, Lieutenant Commander Ripley and Lieutenant Bohmer sat in a corner booth along with two strangers. A crowd milled in the background, movement of the bodies admitting flashes of holo-art on a nearby wall.

Ripley leaned forward at the table, her voice low, urgent. "I'm tellin' you it was a big damn deal. Skalar's ships took a bunch of shit to—"

"Shut it, Mouth!" Bohmer cut in, glancing around.

"Aw, you shut it! I wasn't gonna say where!"

One of the strangers thumped his fist on the table, rattling their bottles and drawing a few glances from passersby. "That ain't fair! You bring us here, then start a story and don't finish it?" He started to say more, then stopped himself. "Forget it. We don't believe you anyway."

"You think I'm lyin'?" Ripley's face flushed.

The stranger swigged his beer while pub noise filled the gap in their conversation. The band on set switched songs, raising a low cheer from the crowd.

"Where'd they get this big haul you're claimin'?" the second man asked.

"That I don't know. It was 'fore me and Bohmer was crewin' the Chest. It musta happened deep coz no one's spillin' details, but I ain't finished diggin'. I'll find out." Ripley shifted in her seat and dropped the volume. "I just know there's a lot of merch, and whatever it is rings the admiral's bell big-time. Ten to one, the Consortium's got somethin' to hide. I know they got a good place to hide it."

"Hell," drawled the second man, "what faction don't work under the table? This ain't news."

"Even if it was, why you tellin' us?" the first man asked, eyes narrowed over his drink.

Ripley shrugged. "Might be nothin'. Might be somethin'." She chugged the rest of her beer and stood, thumping the bottle down on the table with her parting shot. "C'mon, Bohm. I guess this ain't the company I was hopin' for."

She and Bohmer pushed out into the crowd and exited the vid, followed closely by the two strangers.

"TICS, stop playback," Skalar said.

"How'd you get them at Zekes?" Ronan said. "We got no eyes there!"

Skalar tilted his head toward the captain. "Please."

Thrace shifted, cleared her throat, and crossed her arms. Galen would probably have words for Alira later, but for now Skalar ignored his second.

Ronan looked away, grumbling under his breath.

> *keep him in line.*

"I'm sorry," Skalar said, "what was that?"

Ronan's focus snapped to Skalar's face. "I said, 'my business. Should'a let me handle it.'"

"These officers came from Vandana Walker's command." Skalar stared at the man. "They're still working for her, not you, and I'm rather disappointed that you didn't see it. She's trying to undermine my position. I can't let that go. You slipped up. Now it's out of your hands."

"And you're outta bounds. Sir. Doin' *my* job, takin' *my* place with *my* crew." A red flush colored Ronan's cheeks. "That was just beer talk, and you know it. People do it all the time, tryin' ta look bigger, badder. They talked you up, too, I noticed. Made you look big and bad."

> *careful.*

"I don't need their help."

"Maybe not. Still wasn't worth a curbing."

Skalar frowned, lips pursed. How far was his officer going to push this?

> *he's insubordinate.*
>
> *no, he's frustrated.*
>
> *step aside, netzyl.*

He couldn't let this challenge go unanswered.

"Sa'abah, belay my prior order. Set Ripley and Bohmer up in the brig, sixty days."

"Dammit, Skalar—" Ronan growled.

"Ninety days, Sa'abah."

Ronan's jaw slammed shut with a snap, his glare sharp as daggers.

"Shall we continue this debate, Ronan? Or are you done?"

"This ain't about them, is it?"

"I don't know what you mean."

"That ain't true," Ronan said, calm voice belying his apoplectic expression. "Tell me what I did."

"We're finished here. Go to work."

"I been with you a long time. Now you don't trust me? Poke holes in my command? Tell me what I broke, so I can fix it."

Skalar leaned forward and clasped his hands together, his elbows on the desk. "Captain Ronan, you're dismissed."

Dread silence fell. Skalar's mental cacophony more than made up the difference in volume.

At last, Ronan got to his feet. "Yeah, I better go. Got cold in here."

His hunched form crossed to the door, which hissed closed on the tension in the room.

Skalar dropped his head forward, stretching the taut muscles in his neck and shoulders. In the pristine surface of his desk, his own stern face stared back at him.

that went well.

"Admiral, are you sure that was the right thing to do?"

He looked up at Sa'abah. "Excuse me?"

"With all due respect, sir, Captain Ronan was right. You usurped his authority."

shut her up.

but she's loyal!

Others murmured in his head, but only one comment rang clear.

you can't let anyone question you. not even her.

Skalar raised an eyebrow. "I am the admiral of this faction, Captain Sa'abah, and I will govern it as I see fit. You will follow orders. Is that clear?"

"That's exactly what I'm doing, sir."

He frowned.

"It was your order," she continued, "that gave the ship captains control over their own crews."

Beside him, Thrace watched without expression. He'd get no help there. Skalar rose and turned toward the window, hands clasped behind him. Had he pushed Ronan too hard? The man was old guard, captain in the Consortium for more than a decade. How would he react to this judgment?

"Sometimes, captains need reminders, Sa'abah."

"So do admirals, sir."

He glared at her over his shoulder. "Explain."

"When you put me in charge of security, you told me to red-flag any inconsistency in command and address it immediately. You told me it signaled trouble, a change in circumstances for the officer involved. You meant other officers, of course, but it applies across the board, sir. You made me promise to point them out to you. I keep my word."

"Clarify, Sa'abah."

She cleared her throat. "Admiral, your actions of late seem out of character. I can't keep the faction secure if I don't have all the facts. Is there something going on that I should know?"

Alarmed internal voices shouted over one another, and Skalar's face tightened, pulling his lips into a thin line. This needed to stop before it went any further. If his elite—

skalar's.

—If *his* elite questioned him, the lesser ranks would soon follow suit.

"You need to know, Captain Sa'abah, that far too many security lapses plague the Consortium these days. Captain Baldric and I handled several of them personally. Must I do Ronan's job and yours?"

She said nothing, and he took a step toward her.

"I compensate you well to maintain order in the Consortium. Perhaps the inconsistency lies with you. What do *you* wish to tell *me*?"

Sa'abah's face twitched, then resumed its flat expression. "Nothing, sir."

"Very well." Skalar showed her his back. "Dismissed."

Behind him the door swished open, then closed. Thrace moved closer, her reflection dim in the plaz. Outside the window, the city breathed in and out. Inhabitants thronged the streets by transport or on foot, swarmed the markets and filled the buildings and played their games.

Glints of sunlight off Mari Bay winked and danced through the gaps between high-rise buildings of city center housing. Colorful sails bobbed on the choppy bay, rising and falling like his thoughts. Farther out, lightning flickered between distant clouds and the surface of the sea,

storm's coming.

who said that?

chasing mariners to the port in search of refuge. He understood that drive well. That's all he wanted, all Thrace wanted. All the unammi wanted. But the Consortium wasn't just any refuge. He needed this position. Those on the outpost relied on his ability to maintain this charade and keep them safe. So did the surviving unammi on Earth.

Skalar drew a labored breath, struggling to subdue what felt like a captive niveym encaged in his chest, its mighty wings thumping against his ribs. What had Ronan really expected him to do? Or Sa'abah? Ripley and Bohmer had almost given away the destruction of Iridos, the existence of the outpost! They were lucky Skalar hadn't stopped their hearts.

He still might. If he had to. The thought of another reaping sickened him.

"Alira," said Thrace, "what are you doing?"

Her breath was soft against his neck. He wanted to melt against his i'shin, forget this charade for a while. The others protested

can't stop. can't ever stop.

and he sighed.

"My name is Skalar."

"No. It isn't," Thrace said. "Have you forgotten?"

"Not here, Galen."

"You chose this stage, Alira. I'm playing the role you gave me."

Skalar turned to peer into Thrace's dark and lovely face. Lines of concern etched across her forehead. Her lips turned down at the corners. He imagined Galen's body pulsing in deep blue patterns beneath Thrace's brown skin.

"You're coming apart, Alira. Stop this farce. Let's go home, join the others while we still can."

An entire unexplored world. Bustling underground passages and luminescent bodies, easily read. Simple, honest work, labor to sustain the people. Time with Trumo and the other younglings. No more killing.

No more killing.

Skalar's heart leapt, then sank. The harvests tainted Alira. She could never go home.

"They'd never accept me."

"You don't know that."

He grimaced. "Yes, I do. And so do you."

Thrace tilted her head. "Earth's not as large as Harajüd, perhaps, but it's much bigger than Iridos. On such a bountiful world, surely we can find our own safe space away from the others."

Hadn't Alira thought that very thing? So much potential lay across that land, and beneath it! The new city itself sat mostly untouched, even populated by the entire unammi race. Perhaps the outcasts could return, make a place for themselves beside the rest of their people. If she—if Skalar—shipped Consortium armaments to the outpost, then transferred them to the surface, the planet's nearness to an old human base might not matter. They could—

A hand landed on his arm and squeezed, hard.

"Skalar!" Thrace urged. "Don't!"

The room wavered around him and he drew a ragged breath, clutching at the shreds of his focus. Thrace stood wide-eyed before him, still gripping his arm. He had almost shifted!

"Are you *here*?"

Skalar groaned, turning away. "Don't distract me like that again." Blood roared in his ears, throbbed in the vein at his throat.

Behind him, Thrace sighed. "You made a mistake."

"I know!" he said. "If you hadn't stopped me—"

"That's not what I meant. Sa'abah's loyalty is a given, but we can't be sure about the rest. You already pushed it with Jarod when you   "

Skalar's jaw clenched. "Changed his priorities?"

Thrace's lips worked as if she would speak, but no sound emerged from her throat.

He shook his head, nausea welling in his gut, rising up his throat. "If it hadn't been for Jarod, you and I wouldn't even be here. I've no intention of using stolen hematium, dripping with unammi blood, on Consortium hull plates. All I did was forbid him to pursue the hematium gig and give him another directive to keep him busy." Skalar chewed on his anger. "Yes, I did threaten him, but only because the situation required it. Be glad I didn't kill him."

Thrace sighed. "I am, and so are you. But it's dangerous to alienate Ronan. With all he knows of sensitive Consortium business, do you really want to make him angry?"

"You think he'll turn?"

"I know he will, given the right conditions."

"Then I'll kill him."

"No!" She rushed in front of him. "No, you can't!"

"It isn't up to you, Captain Baldric."

"Listen. We talked about this. No more harvests, remember? I'm not sure you can take it. I can—"

He leaned in, his face centimeters from hers. "You'd choke on what I 'take' every day," he whispered. "I value your input, but don't tell me what I can and cannot do. Is that clear?"

Thrace recoiled as if she'd been slapped.

He was being a fool. She was his sole support, the only one he trusted. He should stop. Now.

no exceptions.

But no. He couldn't do that. Thrace needed to understand that even she, his second, could not be allowed to challenge the admiral.

"Are we clear?" he said.

Thrace searched his face as if looking for the person behind his mask. "Yes."

"Good. Dismissed."

She stood her ground. "I'm not leaving. You shouldn't be alone right now."

"Thrace, I'm fine. I'll be fine." He peered across the gulf between them. "I'll meet you at my house in a few hours. Go."

When she was gone, he returned to the window. In the plaz, his own image brooded at him. He touched his cheek, his lips, his chin. His fingers brushed at the brows above his dark eyes. It didn't look like a mask. Not anymore.

The reflection twisted, its features contorting until he no longer recognized the face at all, and a gasping sob wrenched itself from his throat. Not Alira, not Skalar, not Nyros or Ijydin or Crow or Cesar or any of the others….neither human nor unammi….homeless, with no true sense of self. Could he live like that?

Was Na'Staani still there? Where was Eli's guidance now?

No reassuring connection buzzed in his mind. No shifting figure appeared in the window's reflection. Loss swelled in him, spilled out of his eyes and tracked, shining, down his face. Lurien had been right about emotions—messy, chaotic, uncivilized—and the humans that bore them. She'd been right about everything. Alira should have listened. Instead, she'd sacrificed everything for a long shot that would devour the rest of her life.

The comm chirped. After a moment, it sounded again. Skalar watched the reflected indicator blink on his desk until the sounds stopped and silence resumed. His grief subsided in slow measure, and he looked past the window. Lights winked on in the buildings and along the streets.

Beyond Mari Bay, the storm approached.

chapter 10

New Canaan, Harajüd
<u>Consortium Trader Base</u>

THRACE ENTERED THE TUNNEL BENEATH the street, navigating on autopilot while her thoughts swirled around Skalar. Alira. *Skalar*. The admiral's near-shift of a few days ago rattled them both. Thrace would not confuse the issue again, not here. In public, she was Captain Thrace Baldric, second in command to Admiral Malcolm Skalar. Only in private—and never on the base—could Galen and Alira emerge. Difficult though it was, Thrace needed to remember that.

She frowned. Difficult. Yes. Then how much harder must it be for the admiral? Galen had more experience at wearing a human mask, so much that it was second nature for him now. Inside Skalar's shell, Alira had not yet found that balance. Besides, Galen had only two personas, for the moment at least. Alira had…how many now? Galen had lost track. Granted, she wasn't attempting to portray all her reapings. Still, how did she keep them all straight? No wonder there was a threat of madness in harvesters.

Thrace shook her head, forced her thoughts to the present moment. Foot traffic and the occasional hovercart passed—Consortium crew going about faction business. Everyone was in a hurry, and she hugged the outside edge of the corridor. A dull drone of babble filled the enclosed space.

"Captain Baldric!"

Thrace grimaced and stopped walking. What now? Forcing her features into a neutral expression, she turned.

Ronan hurried toward her, his face set with determination. What did he expect of her? Thrace wasn't about to go against the admiral.

"Captain, can you spare a moment?"

"Just." Thrace turned and continued on her way. "What do you want?"

"Tell me what's goin' on, ma'am." He sounded out of breath.

"With regard to the admiral, I presume."

"That's right."

"Ronan, you heard him yourself. He's pissed about Ripley and Bohmer. He didn't feel you handled it well. What more is there to say?"

"The truth, for a change."

"That was the truth."

He grabbed her shoulder, stopped them both. Traffic flowed around them without slowing, though many a curious eye shifted their way.

Thrace glared at him. "Remove your hand. Now."

He dropped his arm to his side. "Just stop a minute, I'm askin' ya. Don't pretend this ain't fucked up."

Thrace sighed. "Speak."

"We did a job, me and my people and a slew of other captains and crews, all at Skalar's orders. Ain't nothin' been right ever since, so if I did something to piss him off, I got a right ta know what it was."

"What are you talking about?"

Ronan shook his head, wagged a finger in her direction. "Don't. You know. I didn't like what went down on that run. I told Crow. We all did. He wouldn't listen. Now he's gone, and Skalar's changed, and here you are, some stranger nobody ever heard of 'til Skalar dragged you back from wherever he disappeared to."

"You think this is my doing?"

"Didn't say that. But somethin's goin' on. You know it. I know it. Only difference is you know what it is. The rest of us're in the dark but gettin' the fallout anyways. Skalar knows me. He knows I'm loyal as a dog, but you'd never believe it by the way he's treatin' me. I can't fix somethin' 'less I know it's broke. So tell me what the fuck is goin' on."

Thrace glanced around. "Lower your voice, Captain. A public corridor is not the place for this conversation."

"Ain't no proper place, to hear you uppity-ups talk. Could'a had this out days ago in Skalar's office, all private-like. But no. Been with him fifteen years. He dismissed me like I was a new recruit. Don't make sense." He stepped closer. "This is about the outpost, ain't it? Somethin' goin' on there Skalar don't want nobody to see."

A chill raced up Thrace's spine. She forced her arms to lie still at her sides when she wanted to hug herself, rub some warmth into her flesh.

"That's ridiculous. You're jumping at shadows."

"Am I?" He sucked his teeth for a moment, then grinned without mirth. "Van's people weren't lyin' in that holovid. Skalar's had that outpost a long time. Hardly ever went there. Now it's manned all the time by crew I never met. Got fancy new tech. It's a big fat secret even from us who been there before. I gotta ask myself why."

She channeled the chill into her gaze. "The way I heard it, Ronan, you've been afraid of that base since day one. Why so curious now? Are you looking to join its crew?"

The grin slid off his face. His grizzled cheeks went slack. "Didn't say that."

Thrace leaned forward, her nose almost touching his. "Let this go."

"I might. Others won't."

"That's their problem. Tell your people to watch their mouths. Tell them rebellion carries a high price, and you can't help them if they ignore this rule. If you want to protect them, Ronan, tell them."

She stared into his leathery face a moment more, then returned to her previous course and left him behind. She'd been right. It was a mistake to alienate that man.

chapter 11

Pelarr, Zebalu
<u>Cartel Trader Base, Cliffside Garden</u>

SMALL PEBBLES, DISTURBED BY BELLAMY'S bare toes, scrabbled away to drop over the cliff's edge. Bellamy leaned out, watching their trajectory. She'd never see them hit bottom. And even if she could, they'd just bounce down between the boulders or ricochet off into the churning sea. Still, she leaned out far as she dared into empty space, tracking their plunge. A blast of briny wind shot up the cliff face to snatch at her dress and hair, pulling her farther forward than she'd intended. Frantic arms pinwheeled in search of balance as she leaned back to compensate, then retreated several steps toward safer ground. Visions of the jagged rocks below chased her heart into a mad rhythm before peals of laughter rippled out of her throat to join the gulls' chorus.

Grinning, she clapped her hands and spun with a squeal. Oh, how she loved this spot! Windows in her office faced the same view. Still, the sea's chaotic ambience roused greater thrills with windswept spray on one's face. Prudence advised caution on this slippery slope, but wasn't that risk part of the thrill of walking here? Someone on her crew had once suggested that she should erect a railing to keep anyone from falling over the precipice. Bellamy had objected to such a banal distraction from the raw beauty of the space. When he tried to convince her, she'd had her senior officers use him to demonstrate the ease with which someone might trip and fall off the path.

He'd been right. Seems it was easy to fall here. Her hair blew in the updraft as she remembered that image. Ah well. She sighed. He'd been easy to replace.

A shout sounded behind her, and the smile slipped. Why wouldn't they leave her alone?

Bellamy paced away from the intrusion along the footpath toward Pirate's Cove, eyes still trained on the sea. A ship motored across the waves, veins of white froth following in its wake where gulls dove headfirst into the chop like arrows shot from a bow. A moment later the boat broke out of colonial shipping lanes and headed toward the cove. She shaded her eyes to peer at its colors, then gave up. Too far away. Jacked goods? More slaves? Dredge haul? Whatever its cargo, it moved at a fast clip and would dock within the hour. She'd know soon enough. Footsteps crunched against the rocky soil. Must be Hannah. No one else had the balls to come this close to the cliff.

Except that gardener, there. She bent over the cliff roses just ahead, pruning. Black hair sat bunned at the nape of her neck. Coveralls hid her form, but she looked small.

The steps neared.

"What is it, Captain?" Bellamy asked.

Hannah's slim form appeared beside the admiral, matched her pace. "Word from our Consortium contact, ma'am."

"And?"

"You were right. Whatever is going on with Skalar, it's getting worse."

Bellamy stopped and stared into Hannah's moss green eyes. "Well? Don't scrimp! Details!"

"He's alienating everyone in the faction, even his closest officers."

"I knew he was unstable. Haven't I said as much?"

"That you have, ma'am."

Bellamy wandered forward once more, drawing even with the gardener and stopping to inspect her work. Not bad. It was difficult to tell where the clippers had pruned. She peered at the back of the woman's head.

"I don't think I've seen you before."

The gardener stood, bobbing her head, shoulders hunched as if she would disappear into herself. "I'm Chandra, ma'am."

Bellamy glanced at Hannah. "Do you know this person?"

"Yes, ma'am. She's been with us a little more than two years now."

"I see," Bellamy said, turning her scrutiny to the small woman. "What's your rank, Chandra?"

"I'm just a crewman, ma'am. Not an officer."

"What, no ambition, Crewman Chandra?"

The woman shrugged. "I love my job right here, ma'am. As much as you love this garden, I like keeping it nice for you."

Bellamy considered pushing her over the edge. No particular reason, except it would amuse her. And she was pissed at Skalar. But Hannah's news had cheered Bellamy. She could teach Chandra to fly another day.

"As you were, then." Bellamy pressed on, shifting her focus to the sea. The boat was closer. Definitely Cartel colors. "Shall we wager," she said to Hannah as if there had been no interruption, "on how long it takes his head to appear on a spike before their gate?"

"I'm fairly certain Harajüd House would frown on such a thing, ma'am."

"Too bad. Maybe we could get it for ourselves. It would make a good addition to the cliff walk, just there." Bellamy pointed at the garden's edge. "Don't you think?"

"As you say." Hannah cleared her throat. "There's more. It seems Skalar has a high-profile prisoner in his brig. One with juicy intel."

"Like what?"

"That I don't know."

"Who is it? What did he do to piss Skalar off?"

"I heard it's a female officer, possibly Crow's old second, but I haven't confirmed that. Word is she challenged Skalar's orders in front of his crew."

"Interesting." It's a wonder the blip made it to a cell. Bellamy would have fed her to the gulls post-mortem. She envisioned slicing off bits and tossing them over the edge of her walk. A smile crossed her face and was gone. She veered away from the precipice, bypassing a patch of cliff roses. "Did we ever find out what happened to Crow?"

"Just that he disappeared up Phejoss way. Nothing since. Strange, that."

"Why?"

Hannah shrugged. "I wouldn't have believed he'd ever leave Skalar, not while he was still breathing."

"Did you know him?"

"No. But word gets around. He was more fearful than allegiant."

Bellamy laughed, watching Hannah's face. "Like you?"

The captain never even blinked. "Not at all. I'm faithful to you and to the Cartel. I don't need to be afraid."

The ship was drawing near through the chop. Landing at Pirate's Cove was always treacherous—an apt metaphor for life in the Cartel, she supposed—but this wind would make it even more difficult. "So, if she was Crow's second, and Crow is gone, why isn't she Skalar's second?"

"That's a good question, ma'am. Apparently, he brought in an unknown for that position."

Bellamy's gaze shot to Hannah's face. "Really?"

"That's the rumor."

That's it then, Bellamy knew. If his prisoner had expected to take Crow's place and Skalar not only denied her the position, but gave it to an unproven newbie, no wonder the woman had questioned him. What a stupid move! Skalar might be a cheat, a liar and a thief, but she'd never known him to be a fool. He had to be playing a long game. What was he up to? More to the point, how could she take advantage of it?

The path again neared the cliff's edge above the piers. She stopped to watch the ship enter the harbor and navigate under expert direction to the dock. Dozens of crew emerged from the tunnel to unload its cargo. From here, they looked like ants mobbing a sweet.

"Send a team."

"Ma'am?"

"To direct our agents in the Consortium and extract that poor misunderstood prisoner from Skalar's brig. We can make her a better offer anyway. She's been treated badly. Maybe a taste of honey will attract some answers."

"Of course, Admiral. I expect you'll want them on their way immediately."

"Yes, naturally!" Bellamy swung a wide grin at her second. "No sense in leaving our new friend to rot any longer. Let's get her out of there before Skalar comes to his senses."

Hannah hurried away. When she was gone, Bellamy turned back toward the sea. Maybe this was the break she'd been waiting for, a way to get under Skalar and pry him loose from his position at the top of the heap. That was her chair. She intended to claim it.

chapter 12

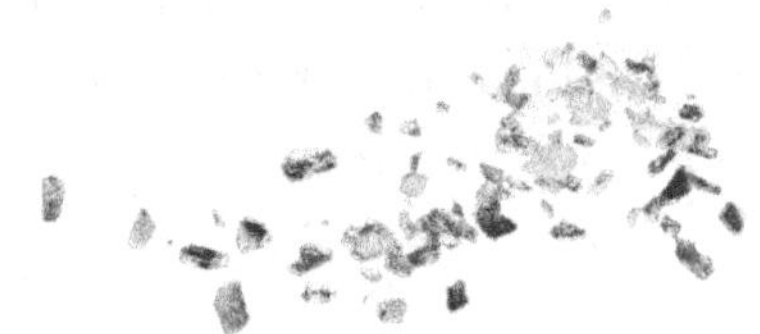

New Canaan, Harajüd
<u>**En Route to Bahtya Gaming House**</u>

SKALAR SPED ALONG CENTRAL PARKWAY, his skimmer's quiet hum a backdrop to his racing thoughts.

In the week since his discovery of the betrayal at Zekes, his confrontation with Ronan, and Sa'abah's questions, Skalar had considered other ways the crew might turn on him. If his top officers were questioning his command, others would too. Rumor said bartenders watered down the drinks in his pubs. Gaming managers skimmed or ran private rounds off the books. Brothels laxed their rules. Market staff withheld product or proceeds. How deep did the problems go? His people could be selling him out right under his nose. Clearly, he couldn't believe his officers' reports. He needed to see for himself whether there were other indiscretions taking place in Consortium businesses, starting with the gaming houses.

He pulled up outside the first one, already giving orders.

"TICS, Bahtya Games, full inspection mode."

A digital voice sounded in the cabin. "Acknowledged. Inspection mode engaged."

He stepped out of the skimmer, sweeping up the walkway toward the front of the building. It'd been more than two months since his

you mean my.

last inspection, plenty of time for the staff to take selfish actions, test his patience and limitations, try and turn a profit for themselves.

takes less than two minutes to hide or destroy evidence.

No doubt some of the Bahtya staff had already seen him coming. He had to move fast.

Shoving through the doors, Skalar stalked through the vestibule, past the leafy fronds of plants to either side, and into the lobby. Sound-absorbent sanitile covered the floor and ceiling. Gleaming gray marble lined the walls, reflecting the light so that it seemed to come from all directions. To his right, a patron in the lounge with a handheld game gawked, speechless. At the check-in desk, receptionists greeted him as if his presence was a complete surprise.

"Admiral Skalar," a flustered clerk said, "sir, is there a problem?"

no leniency!

"For your sakes, I hope not." Beyond the desk, lifts returned to the ground floor and opened to belch out the blustering humans inside.

"What the hell?" one complained. "I was trying to get to the eighth floor!" He stopped at the sight of the faction's admiral, eyes wide in his dark face.

"Have a seat," Skalar said, gesturing toward the waiting area. "You can resume your game when the inspection is complete." He looked at the clerk. "Who's the duty manager this shift?"

"That would be Jax, sir."

"Where is he now?"

"Um," she said, her voice quavering as she looked at the building's security screen. "H-he's on level B1, making his rounds, Admiral."

"Very well." Skalar stalked down the hall to the first lift, swiped his ident in the lock, and the doors closed.

Jax could wait. They all could. What choice did they have? Inspection mode sealed all the doors, locked down all the lifts, jammed all communications. Only Skalar retained free movement within the facility. Wherever patrons—or staff, for that matter—were in the building, that's where they would stay for the duration. Colonial security would hear about it, sure. Patrons would complain. But as a tenant on colonial land, he had a certain latitude in setting the rules within his own businesses. Judicious use of surprise inspections fell under that umbrella.

He shook his head as the lift neared the eighth floor.

The rebellions of Walker's and Ronan's crews were just the beginning. In the thirty-seven standard days since Alira had taken control of the Consortium, she'd done her best to simulate the admiral's behavior and activity patterns, but it hadn't been enough. The conduct of those around him betrayed their surprise at his actions and reactions. They'd begun to test him, take the first steps toward a mutiny.

Well, if the rumors were true, he'd find out. This was the first of many inspections to come.

The lift doors opened, and Skalar passed along the monotonous corridors, door after door. At intervals, recessed compartments held oxygen masks behind secure plaz panels. Beside them, controls with a manual override system allowed access to the masks and the building's operation systems, for use in case of emergency. Through each door's clear window, he watched patrons in every seat, their games running undisturbed on isolated systems immune to the jammers. They'd not even noticed the lockdown. Wisps of mellow sedolyn smoke hung in the still air, evocative and sweet, tickling his throat into a muffled cough. Occasional comments or exclamations from inside the chambers stirred the quiet.

What was he doing wrong? He'd followed the guidance of his harvest. His actions had felt right, so why did they raise suspicions in his crew? He muttered a curse. Impersonating a specific human, especially this one, was turning out to be more difficult than he'd anticipated. Consortium operations required more than just knowledge of the old admiral's memories. Mimicry wasn't enough.

told you so.

shut up.

He paced the entire level with muted steps, then checked the toilets. Satisfied that all was as it should be, he returned to the lift.

Seven floors to go, then he'd check the subsurface chambers.

Past scenarios flashed through his mind, deepening his frown. Memories from the old Skalar, and from Crow, had served since day one as his model for this role. So perhaps it wasn't what he was doing, but how he was doing it. The biggest difference between him and the old admiral was confidence. The crew doubted him, tested him, because they saw his hesitation while he stretched himself into the role, and interpreted it as uncertainty. Very well, then. No more restraint. Skalar had always run a zero-tolerance policy, so it should come as no surprise when the admiral came down hard on transgressions now. Regardless, he was finished worrying about what his predecessor might have done and whether he was following those footsteps precisely. He could no longer afford ambivalence. The time had come to act decisively, and on his own.

there's a new admiral in town.

my, my ... what will galen say.

who said that?

The lift doors opened. In the corridor, three patrons punched the controls to contact the front desk with loud complaints. All comments fell mute the moment they laid eyes on the lift's occupant. Skalar moved toward them, arms spread wide.

"Step away from the lift."

"What's going on?"

Skalar's gaze swung toward the speaker. Young. Female. Face almost as pale as her fair hair. "Faction business. Continue your games."

"But our time's up," another gamer said. "Besides, we can't get in again. We tried."

"On the house." Skalar swiped his card to open the nearest empty room. "Clear the hallway."

Muttering, the players went inside and closed the door. When he peered through the next portal down the corridor, the patrons inside looked back. The gamers' complaints must have carried. Skalar sighed. At least they couldn't forewarn anyone else.

One by one he checked the other levels with no further encounters until he returned to the lobby. There, though the level lay silent, he'd probably interrupted a debate among present staff and patrons about his purpose here. In the offices and staff rooms, occupants clearly knew they were in lockdown and stared, wordless, through the clear door panels as Skalar checked each one.

In the lift once more, he sighed. So far, he'd found nothing amiss. Only two levels remained—and an audit of the accounts, of course—but he suspected those would offer more of the same. Maybe the rumors were groundless, but then why would his crew circulate them? To what end? It wasn't just him. Galen heard them, as well.

thrace. captain baldric.

Yeah. Her too.

The lift doors opened and Skalar stepped into the dim corridor.

"What the hell—"

He heard the half-question before he saw the man, and Skalar pivoted on the balls of his feet. "Back it down, son."

"Admiral Skalar!" The man halted his advance, eyes wide. "My apologies, sir, I didn't..." He cleared his throat. "What's going on, Admiral? I've been trying to get to my office for half an hour!"

"Jax, I take it."

The man nodded, one long lock of black hair falling across his forehead. Muffled shouts came from down the hallway, and Skalar's gaze flicked in that direction.

Jax waved a dismissive hand. "They're mid-game. It's nothing."

"Then you don't mind if I check it out for myself." Skalar pushed past him, striding to the digital viewport. From here he could surveil the gamers in every double-level cell via an isolated imaging panel without the need for windows that would spoil the virtual reality of the game in progress. Each of these subsurface chambers used one. Nothing amiss, just as he'd expected. One more level, then the records, and he could move on to the next inspection. Or maybe he'd just go home.

Home. If only...

"Now will you tell me what's going on, sir?" Jax asked.

"Inspection."

"I see," Jax said, nodding. "We got no notice."

Skalar stared at him.

"Did you find anything out of bounds, sir?"

"I'm not finished yet." Skalar stepped into the lift. "I still need to see B2, then I'm heading up to scan the books. Join me."

"Thank you, sir." Jax got in beside him and the doors closed. They rode the single level in silence.

Until the doors opened.

Immediately, they could hear the pounding.

Jax's eyes went wide. He leapt toward the door.

Skalar pushed ahead of him. Panicked shouting echoed off the walls and ceiling. They rushed toward the noise and peered through the viewport for the VR chamber at the end of the hall.

Inside, a small man threw himself at the door over and over, the blood on his face and in his hair clearly visible even in the dim light. His fingers clawed at his own face and arms as if he were being attacked.

"Get 'em off me!" he screamed as he bashed into the door again.

"Oh god." Jax gagged. He grabbed for the door's release, muscles knotting as he pulled with all his might. "Let him out! Open the damn door!"

Skalar ignored him. "Mask. Now." Swiping his ident across the nearest control panel, Skalar snatched a mask from the accompanying compartment, then spoke into its controls. "TICS. Isolate and confine airflow on B2. Subdue cell 12." His hands moved automatically to secure the mask.

Waxen-faced, Jax followed suit, then shot to the cell's viewport.

Within seconds, the man's struggles weakened, his hoarse words indistinct.

"I want to know who this is," Skalar said without shifting his focus, "his player history, what recreationals he bought, and anything else that might have brought this on."

"Of course," Jax whispered.

Moments later, the man fell away from the door, stumbled to the wall and collapsed.

"TICS, scrub gas on B2, cell 12."

Skalar stared at the viewer, every muscle taut as he mined his memories. None of his passengers had ever seen anything like this before, except—

No. Surely it wasn't that.

The moment the room was clear, Skalar swiped his card and threw open the door. "Lights, twenty-five hundred lumens." Brilliance flooded the space. Jax shielded his eyes, but Skalar squatted beside the unconscious man, pulling him over onto his back.

Yes. It was. Damn!

He snatched the device off the man's head and faced the manager, holding it out before him.

"What is this?"

Jax glanced from Skalar's face to the bloody headset. "It's an ALT game, sir," he said, his own complexion gray.

Skalar grimaced. ALT. Alternate Life Track. Such a strange concept, a game that connected to the electrical signals of the brain, manipulated its theta patterns and tricked the player into believing they were somewhere else. Some*one* or some*when* else. Even some*thing* else. How had anyone ever thought that would be a good idea?

"And just what the fuck is it doing in my gaming house?" he whispered.

"But," Jax began, sputtering. "But sir, you sent them yourself. I only set them up for play yesterday, I swear!"

A sudden chill gripped Skalar's body. "Them? There's more than one in the building?"

Jax frowned. "You sent four, sir."

Skalar looked down at the headset, its blood now on his own hands, as well. He knelt once more beside the man on the floor. Gouges on his face, neck, and arms accounted for some of the mess, but sticky tufts of hair on his fingers and shoulders explained the weeping patches on his scalp. Cursing, Skalar took in the rest of the tiny room. Bloody smears on the inside of the door, the chair, three of the walls, and the floor. This room was out of commission until it could be sanitized.

"TICS, discontinue inspection." He sat back on his haunches and touched his wristcom with a clean knuckle.

"Yes?" answered the surprised receptionist.

"This is Skalar. I'm on B2, cell 12. Call medical. Hurry."

"Right away, sir."

Eerie stillness filled the room and spilled out into the corridor. Jax breathed hard behind him. "Bring me the other headsets," Skalar said.

Jax hesitated. "Now, sir?"

"Yes. Now."

"But two of them are in use. Other gamers already paid—"

Skalar surged to his feet and faced Jax. "One psychotic break wasn't enough excitement for you?" He advanced on the shrinking manager. "These things are illegal for a reason."

Jax's cheeks flushed. "Sorry, sir."

"Round up the other players on this level," Skalar said, "escort them to the exit, and bring me those headsets. *Now.*"

Jax nodded and left the room.

Skalar touched his comm again. Down the hall, Jax rousted customers and sent them upstairs.

"Desk," the woman answered.

"Shut the place down," Skalar ordered. "Issue credits to all clientele caught up in the inspection and get everybody out except staff."

"Yes sir. Medical's on the way sir. Is everything okay?"

"Not exactly," Skalar said, cutting her off before he touched the device again. A moment later, Harlan's response filled his ears.

"Security, Chief Downing."

"Harlan, Skalar here. We have a situation at Bahtya Gaming House."

Long pause. "What's wrong with your voice?"

"I'm masked."

Longer pause. "What's going on?"

Jax trotted into the room, hands full of headsets and saniwipes. Skalar held his gaze.

"A problem. Just come, Harlan. I'll wait." He signed off, cleaned his hands as best he could, dropped the wipes on the floor, and took the headsets. "You said I sent them, not that I brought them. Who did?"

"Lieutenant Enzo, sir."

One of Walker's crew. Dammit! He'd thought that issue was resolved. Skalar's lips puckered. "Who else saw this delivery?"

Jax shrugged. "I don't know, sir. Maybe no one. Enzo didn't give them to me in the lobby, if that's what you mean. I knew they were illegal, but that hasn't stopped you from approving other games or projects in the past. I just didn't know…." His words trailed off.

"Very well. Harajüd House security will be here any moment. We are going to cooperate fully, do you understand?"

"Yes sir."

"With one exception. We will tell him there were three headsets in-house. Only three. Are we clear?"

Jax frowned.

So, not clear then. Skalar slipped one of the clean games into his pocket, then held up the remaining sets, one wrapped in the last saniwipe. "Lieutenant Enzo brought you three ALT headsets and told you I sent them. You don't know where that officer went afterward, or where he is now."

"Got it, sir."

"Good. Follow my instructions, and we'll be fine. Wait upstairs for medical. Bring them down when they arrive."

The moment Jax was gone, Skalar touched his comm again, then prowled the level to ensure he was alone.

"Sa'abah."

"Bring a security team down to Bahtya. We have a situation." He briefed her on the headsets and the client's reaction.

She swore softly. "I can't say I'm surprised."

Skalar's brow drew down into a scowl that felt more familiar than a smile. "Why?"

"Let me guess," she said. "This had something to do with Commander Walker or one of her people."

His frown deepened, along with the feeling of dread. "Yes."

"Her old crew, even the ones you reassigned, have been visiting the brig. It's possible you should have killed her when you had the chance. No offense, sir."

He checked the corridor once more, then ducked into the game room and lowered his voice. "Very well. No further guests for Walker, effective immediately. And as soon as you finish at Bahtya, I've got a job for you. Set up a special brig cell on the level below Walker's. Standard surveillance and audio. Small. Low lights."

"Yes sir. Who's going in?"

"Lieutenant Enzo."

Pause. "May I ask why, sir?"

"Set him up with a single restraint chair." Skalar looked down at the wrapped bloody headset. "I'm bringing him a little surprise."

chapter 13

Tuneloras, Saacharis
<u>Syndicate Trader Base, Admiral Rizzo's Office</u>

"I DON'T CARE ABOUT THE cost."

The man in the holo grimaced. "Admiral Rizzo, with all due respect—"

"This is no ordinary cargo. Outfit two of the holds as I've described."

"Will these be permanent changes, ma'am?"

Rizzo considered the question. The Labrys was her oldest hauler. It needed a refit anyway, but what she really wanted was a ship that could be made to look like a regular runner, yet could also carry something far more fragile, more valuable than its looks and class implied. Ideas for a unique design floated through her mind.

"For now."

"I understand. What will go in the other six holds?"

"Bismuth, ship parts, and raw salt in the mains. Recent take from your Gadney jack in the largest sub. Pick up the rest outside Seifugi."

"Who am I meeting there?"

"Cross."

The man nodded. "The take's perishable?"

"Yes." The door chime sounded. "Anything else?"

"No, ma'am."

"Comm Bailey when it's done." She ended the holo. "Come."

The door slid aside to admit a tall, fair-skinned woman—Captain Bailey, Rizzo's second in command. Straight black hair swung down to the captain's waist. "I have news."

The admiral gestured at a chair in front of her desk, and the woman perched on its seat.

"Gauri Metalb's using slaves," Bailey said. "Young ones."

"How old?"

"Teen." Bailey's frown deepened. "Preteen."

A chill prickled Rizzo's neck. "Who told you this?"

"Commander Sills, ma'am. She just reported on her inspection of the mine. She was uncertain whether the managers knew she'd seen. I told her that if they did, she wouldn't have lived to report it."

Rizzo rose from her chair and stalked, hands behind her, to the shelves at the other end of her office. There, among unique weaponry, sat a small wooden block carved with a hye won hye symbol. *That which cannot be burned.* The words echoed through her memory in Lourdes' voice.

"Their origin?"

"I haven't confirmed it yet, ma'am, but Sills believes they came from Harajüd."

Skalar. Rizzo's lip curled. "Comm our contacts there, and on Zebalu. I want a name."

"Right away, ma'am." Bailey rose.

"Who is managing Gauri Metalb for Saacharis Aggregate?"

"Thomas Reyes, ma'am."

"Bring him to me."

"If he's off world, it might take a while."

Rizzo nodded.

Once Bailey had gone, Rizzo picked up the ancient woodblock, bringing it closer to her face. "TICS, initiate ambient program nine."

Resonant voices filled the space with a low, harmonious chant—*I am the Doer, I am the Deed, I am the Sower, I am the Seed*—as a rich, woody fragrance reached her nostrils. She stared at the carving. Slaves in the mine violated the terms of Aggregate's agreement with her faction. Someone would burn for this. Not her. Not the Syndicate.

"TICS, compile available information on Thomas Reyes. Include data from all colony worlds. Time to completion?"

"Twenty-six-point-four hours," said the TICS.

"Begin." Long brown fingers returned the icon to its spot.

chapter 14

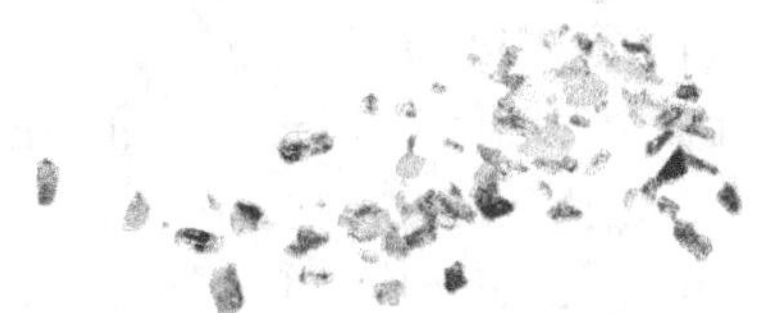

THE LIFT CAME TO A smooth stop, and Skalar stepped out into the security booth. The lieutenant on duty leapt to her feet.

"Admiral! I didn't know you were coming down, sir."

He watched the officer a moment, then ran his gaze around the pristine chamber. By the time he looked at her again, sweat beaded the woman's forehead. Good. "What had you so rapt, Lieutenant, that you didn't hear the lift?"

"I was watching Commander Walker, sir."

"Watching her do what?"

The lieutenant's cheeks puffed, and she shook her head. "Nothing, sir. She never does anything but sit on her bunk unless someone comes to visit."

"And you found this fascinating."

"Confusing, sir."

"How so?"

She shook her head. "It's just that I don't think I could sit for hours like that and do nothing. I'd have to work out, request a handball or some readers, anything to keep my mind busy. I don't know how she does it."

Walker never was very active. Skalar nodded toward the desk. "When was her last visitor?"

She touched a screen. "Yesterday at nineteen hundred, sir. No one since. Captain Sa'abah said she's cut off."

"Except for me, Captain Baldric, and Captain Sa'abah, that's correct." He walked toward the door, which slid open at his approach.

In the corridor, the tang of germicide assaulted his nostrils, and he curled his lip. Only one of the many reasons he didn't like it down here. At least, not on this level. The old Skalar had been rather fond of the level below this one, where the special cells lay. Where Enzo even now played out his punishment. Those, with their electrified floors, restraint tables, blackout options, and other special features, offered a wide canvas to his interrogation artistry. The current Skalar hoped Walker's situation wouldn't come to that.

He moved down the corridor, not glancing at prisoners in the cells. Right now they were at half-capacity, but if Walker's remaining people kept up their shenanigans, that would soon change. Sa'abah had installed the commander down at the far end, away from the other residents, where Sa'abah had hoped it would be more difficult for the prisoner to stir trouble. Apparently, she'd been wrong. About that, anyway. It's possible she'd been right about the other thing. Skalar should have killed Walker when he first came to the Consortium, before she'd had the opportunity to inspire such havoc.

maybe you should have killed all her people too, for good measure.

i've already taken many of them out. it didn't help.

then what are a few more?

Crow cackled in Skalar's mind, even as the unammi passengers chided him for being so cold.

live a day in my skin.

we do. every day.

He turned down the last corridor. His heels clicked against the gray floor and fell mute, stifled by the treated surfaces of tile and plaz. No inmates in this arm of the brig besides Walker. His best hope was to talk her down. Make her bring them around. If he couldn't do that…well. Then she would leave him no choice.

there is always a choice.

His footsteps slowed as he approached the last cell, then stopped outside the transparent wall. He activated the comm system. Inside, Walker was relieving herself and he watched, impassive, despite the objections in his head.

She finished, stood, and refastened the groin snaps in her jumpsuit. "You here for the show?"

"Have you reconsidered your position, Commander?"

"Commander." Walker shook her head as she washed her hands. "I thought I'd be busted to recruit by now. Especially since you've had your hands so full these days. I know you have to blame somebody. Might as well be me, right?"

"You should talk some sense into your people before more of them get hurt."

"It's far too late for that, *sir*. Word on the outside is that you've been acting weirder and weirder. The crew's just waiting for you to slip up and when you do, they'll take you down so fast you won't know what hit you."

"Then Captain Baldric will take over, and business will go on as usual."

"Think again, Skalar." Walker sneered. "No one likes your new squeeze. She won't live long enough to sit in your chair."

"Oh?" Skalar flashed a chilly smile. "Who, then? You?"

Walker shrugged. "You never know."

"You won't get the chance."

"Please," she said, sliding on her bunk to lean against the wall, one knee cocked up at a jaunty angle, one arm thrown across it in a casual pose. "If you haven't killed me by now, you aren't going to. All I need to do is sit here and watch you fall. And I'm gonna laugh the whole time."

He stared at her. "I came here to offer you an incentive. Get your people to back off, and I'll let you return to your duties. Your attitude says that would be unwise. Why, Commander? Why won't you cooperate? Why this sudden contentious approach?"

"Sudden?" She laughed. "This has been building for weeks, Skalar, and the fact that you don't know that proves my point. This isn't going to go away. It's only a matter of time before you make a fatal mistake. I advise you and your newbie Captain to cut and run while you can."

she knows something.

Don't be ridiculous. She couldn't possibly. Maybe he wasn't performing to the best of his ability. He searched his mind for clues to how Skalar would—or should—act in this situation. It was hard to separate him from the other humans anymore. Too damn many harvests confused the issue.

Enough. This was foolishness. Of course, he knew how Skalar should and would act. Shut this twit up and move on. She was brave enough while her people were still free to make trouble for him, but he could remove that problem. She should have known her actions would require him to remove all her pawns from the board.

she never was very bright

Who was that? Alira couldn't always tell the voices apart anymore, but—never mind. Skalar pushed that confusion aside. He couldn't afford to be distracted.

"Threaten me again, and you might wake up dead, like the rest of your people," he murmured at the plaz.

She waved a hand in his direction. "Whatever. Turn the speaker off when you go, will ya? I'm gonna get some sleep." Walker pushed away from the wall and lay down, her back to him as if he'd already gone.

Anger rose like bile in Skalar's throat, dragging shadows from the locked closet of his past, specters he'd long thought banished. The bigger kids in his school had thought him helpless, too. But he didn't stay that way. He

not you.

shut up.

worked out, built up his strength and endurance, until one day when a bully pushed him, Skalar beat the shit out of him in front of everyone. Funny how the power of a demonstration could change a whole crowd's attitude.

He touched his wristcom and waited for Thrace's response.

"Yes, Admiral?"

"Captain Baldric, send a team to hunt down the rest of Commander Walker's crew. Kill them all."

Walker flipped over so fast she almost fell off her shelf.

"All of them, sir?"

The prisoner rushed the window, pounded the inside wall as if it were his face.

Skalar smiled. "Every last one."

Walker's features twisted as she shouted obscenities. He shut off the cell's comm and waggled his fingers at her before turning away. Maybe he'd put her in a special cell after all.

chapter 15

Tuneloras, Saacharis
<u>Syndicate Trader Base, Admiral Rizzo's Office</u>

SHE LOOKED ACROSS THE DESK at her second. "They have Reyes?"

"Yes ma'am. They're bringing him up now."

Rizzo pursed full lips. The TICS file on this man was so slim as to be worthless. Born and raised in Tuneloras. Been off world a few times, but never for long and all in the past colonial year. Average working family, average childhood, average grades, average career, if you could call it that. Married into the only social status he'd ever had. Tyrant of the mines, the files called him.

"Who is he working for?"

Bailey shrugged. "Unknown, as yet, but rumor says the Consortium brought the children on as indentured labor to pay off their parents' debt."

"Skalar."

"Presumably, ma'am."

There was no love lost between the Syndicate and the Consortium. That faction's admiral was guilty of many things. But slavery?

Rizzo's brow furled. "You think Skalar is responsible?"

Bailey shrugged. "I wouldn't have thought so. But you know him better than I do."

The door chime sounded.

"I will find out," Rizzo said, her voice low, husky. "One way or another. Prepare a cleanup team. Have them wait outside."

"Yes, ma'am."

"Come," Rizzo called.

A Syndicate security team entered, dragging along a blustering Thomas Reyes. Bailey stepped out, already murmuring into her wristcom.

"What the hell is going on?" Reyes said. "Why am I here?"

One security officer tossed the man's disabled wristcom onto her desk. Rizzo watched Reyes.

"I said—" he began.

"I heard you."

"Then answer me!"

Reyes' body language spoke volumes. His flabby cheeks, his darting eyes, his manicured hands, even his clothes suggested expensive tastes, bought by his spouse's money no doubt. Judging by his waistline, he also ate well.

"This is bullshit. I'm out of here." He turned, but the officer on his left yanked him into place. Reyes pulled at his arm, trying to get loose. "Get your hands off me!"

The officer's fist collided with the side of Reyes' face, and Reyes gasped. His eyes widened with the first hints of fear.

Good.

"Look, this is some sort of mistake. Maybe you don't know who I am. Just give me my wristcom and I'll—"

"You are Thomas Reyes, corporate manager of the Gauri Metalb Mine."

"Then surely you know I have numerous resources at my disposal. Call off your hired muscle and tell me what this is about. I'm sure we can settle the matter in a civilized fashion."

Rizzo stood and moved around the desk, then leaned against the front edge before him.

"Why are there children in the mine?"

Color drained out of Reyes' already pasty face. "I don't know what you mean."

This time it was the officer on his right whose fist made contact with Reyes' cheekbone. He'd have matching bruises. For a little while, anyway.

"Hey! What the *fuck*—"

"Why are there children in the mine?"

Reyes' eyes widened, whites flashing around the brown. "I'm telling you I don't know what you're talking about!"

The third punch doubled him over. He hung, gasping for the wind he'd expelled.

"Don't vomit," Rizzo murmured. She pulled a long kris from a leather sheath at her back, toying with the blade. When he straightened again, she fixed her gaze on his face. "The next lie will cost you a body part."

Reyes lifted a placating hand. "Okay, fine. I brought them in to double our production. If I can come in over projections, but under costs, I'll get a promotion. So sue me. They're indentured. It's not unheard of."

"Where did you get them?"

"From the Consortium."

She squinted at him, her lips puckered, then shook her head. "I don't believe you."

"Seriously. Admiral Skalar sold me their contract."

Rizzo straightened and took a step toward him.

"Okay, okay! It wasn't only Skalar."

"Who else?"

Reyes began to laugh as if he would weep. "I can't tell you that."

Rizzo stared at him in silence, flipping the knife over and over in her hand without ever taking her eyes off Reyes.

"I can't," he insisted, his hands out before him. "They'll kill me."

"You're dead regardless, but you will answer me before I'm done."

Reyes shook his head, his words tumbling over one another in an unintelligible frenzy.

"Very well." Rizzo nodded to the security team. "Put him in the shower."

"No! *No!* What are you doing? Let me go!"

The officers dragged the struggling, screaming man past the desk. Rizzo followed, stripping as she went. A nude body could be washed clean of blood. Fabrics would always bear a trace of evidence.

In the washroom, her team shackled Reyes to a heavy iron hook securely suspended from the ceiling over a second shower stall. When they left, he stood on tiptoe, arms stretched tightly over his head, still screaming.

Naked, Rizzo stepped past the officers. "Wait outside."

The men hustled out, and Rizzo heard the door slide shut behind them. "TICS, secure washroom door."

"Stop," Reyes babbled. "Wait, I'll tell you whatever you want to know."

Rizzo stepped into the shower with him. "Yes. You will."

chapter 16

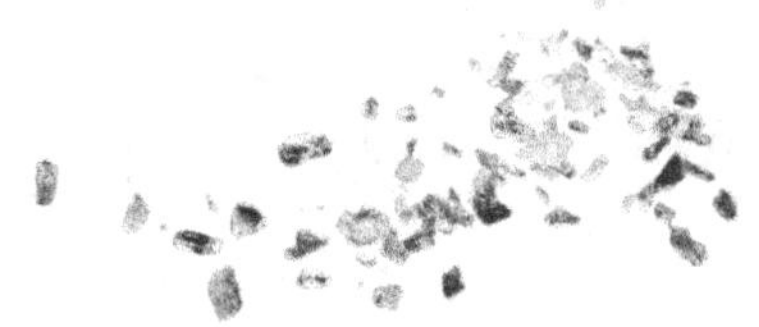

New Canaan, Harajüd
<u>Consortium Trader Base, Landing Bay</u>

SKALAR WALKED BESIDE HIS SECOND, who was silent now that her report was concluded. Two more of Walker's pawns were off the board, but the last few had disappeared. In hiding most likely. Bad enough Harlan still hounded him at every opportunity, trying to catch him in the act of selling slaves, as if he ever would. Skalar pressed his lips together. He couldn't afford to let this get any more out of hand, but at the moment, he couldn't think what more to do.

"Someone's helping them," Skalar muttered, almost under his breath.

"No doubt."

"Who? Rizzo?"

"No. I've mentioned before, she—" Thrace stopped and waited for other crewmen to pass. "Rizzo's a friend to the unammi," she said.

"Maybe so. But we aren't talking about them. We're talking about the Consortium, one of her biggest competitors, not to mention the fact she and I never got along in the first place."

Thrace threw him a quick sideways look. "You mean she and Skalar never got along."

"Same thing."

"No," Thrace said, "it—"

"The point is that she could well be the one who is hiding Walker's people."

"Why not suspect the Cartel?" Thrace said. "Or The Order, or the Federation, or the Clan? Every one of those admirals would love to see Skalar fail. They all have as much reason to hate this faction as the Syndicate."

"Who then?" Skalar said.

"Your harvests would know better than I. What do they think?"

Good question.

well, skalar?

They called the lift and waited.

Okay. If the Syndicate wasn't stirring the pot, then who was? It wouldn't be the Clan. After he'd sent Tsurin's spy home in boxes, that admiral wouldn't have the nerve to take him on again this soon. Not The Order, either. Bardo's ethics would never allow him to work in such an underhanded way, which is exactly why his faction would never lead the pack. The Federation was a distinct possibility. Georgeanne never met a challenge she wouldn't accept. But Bellamy….

The lift opened and they stepped on. "My office." Machinery hummed and Skalar's stomach dropped as they moved up.

Maybe Thrace had a point. Bellamy was crazy enough to involve herself in his business. She'd done it before. Not for a while, not since he got in her face a few years ago about his trade routes, but he didn't expect for a minute she'd changed her tune. It could be her.

Still, Rizzo's face swam in his thoughts, those black eyes shining out of that dark brown face, her short, curly hair some bright color du jour. At 180 centimeters and maybe 70 kilos, she cut an imposing figure. He'd seen the results of her displeasure before. The impact lingered. He wouldn't put it past her to help those who had cause to rebel against him if there was something in it for her.

His wristcom chirped, and he lifted it closer to his face.

"Skalar."

"Admiral, I need to see you. It's urgent."

Skalar frowned. "What's wrong, Sa'abah?"

"Not on comms, sir. Your office?"

"Yes. Three minutes."

"I'll be there in two, sir. Sa'abah out."

"What do you think that was about?" Thrace asked.

It could be anything at this point. Skalar's lips tightened. He'd rather bite his tongue than release the scream knocking at the back of his throat.

"We'll soon know," he said.

The lift slowed and stopped, its door sliding open into his private workspace. Skalar stalked around the central worktable and through the door into his office just in time to sink into his seat and respond to the door chime.

Captain Sa'abah hurried in, her face pinched like she'd been eating lemons. A pallor colored her light brown skin, especially beneath her eyes.

"Sir, Commander Walker is gone."

Skalar clenched his fists and squinted up at her. "Gone? As in she is no longer in her cell?"

"Yes, sir."

"How?" he murmured, barely above a whisper.

Sa'abah shook her head. "I'm still trying to piece it together, sir, but the crewman on duty in the brig's secure room is dead. The other inmates were all gassed with obsequiem. We had to wear masks to go down there at all."

Thrace stepped closer. "There are only three stations on this base with access to the gas."

"True," Sa'abah said. "But I suspect they used the panel in your workroom, Admiral Skalar."

He leaned forward, poised to rise. "Explain."

"The guard passed out before they came down in your lift."

Skalar jerked to his feet. "Impossible."

"We have the surveillance feed, sir. That's what happened."

"No one could do that without my ident."

"I don't know what to tell you, sir—"

"Unacceptable. You are in charge of base security, Captain. How could you let something like this happen?"

Sa'abah looked at Thrace, her mouth turned down at the corners.

Thrace cleared her throat. "It isn't unheard of, Admiral Skalar. Counterfeit idents are one of our biggest sellers on the black market."

"Yes, of course, for regular people."

"Traders, too," Thrace said, "even admirals. I believe it's been done before, sir."

"Not to me."

"No, to Admiral Bellamy, sir. Twelve years ago." Thrace paused. "You told me you used it to access one of her remote sites on Ranafta, if I'm not mistaken."

He swung a glare to Sa'abah. "That still doesn't mean they gained access to my office. They could've gotten to the lift from the landing bay corridor, or one of the other access tunnels."

"I thought about that, sir," Sa'abah explained, "but the base security controls have been manned and surveilled the whole time. No breach was recorded in that space. The only other console is in here."

Skalar's jaw and neck muscles drew tight as bowstrings. "Where there are no securecams."

Sa'abah remained quiet. Smart woman.

His breath squeaked in and out through his pinched nostrils in the suddenly hushed space while he stared at his security captain.

"Are we secure now?"

"Yes, sir." Sa'abah nodded. "I ran the sweep myself. Three times."

"Who did it?"

Sa'abah ticked on her fingers the five crewmen—three of Walker's people and two from the old outpost—she'd spotted on the brig vid. She paused. "I've got my team combing through other base footage from the last few days for clues as to who else might be involved, but it'll take some time to complete that, sir."

Skalar looked away. If he stared at her another minute, he might really scream. He stuck his hands in his pockets and turned away from the two officers. Outside the window, flashes of light reflected off Mari Bay and winked between the City Center residential high-rises. Eighteen stories below, across East Market Street, minuscule city residents went about their business, shopping in the market, milling around the cultural center, strolling through the park. Out there, life continued as normal. What did "normal" even feel like, anymore? It'd been so long since he—since Alira—had felt that.

"This is a nightmare," Skalar said. "You will catch them before they leave Harajüd, Captain."

"I'm on it, sir, but it might be too late."

He whirled to face her. "What?"

"They didn't set off any alarms. Security didn't realize anything was wrong until the brig failed to report in, sir. By the time I got the alert, they were already off-base."

He stared at Sa'abah's now gray face. Shadows had begun to gather beneath her puffy eyes. "TICS, prepare for our New Canaan landport contacts a secure comm with the images and descriptions of —" He pointed at Sa'abah, who named them off again. "Include the following message: 'The individuals in these photos and files have unfinished business with the Consortium. If they attempt to depart New Canaan via your concourses, detain them at once and contact me personally, not my head of security. Consider this…request…a favor toward payment of your debt to me. Skalar out.' Replay and confirm."

The system chittered and played his communique, along with holos of the named crewmen, including Walker.

"Very well," he rasped. "Send." The ever-present internal murmur ratcheted up the volume from a whisper to a low hum.

Thrace tapped long fingers against her taut lips. "Is there any indication of where they might have gone?"

"No," Sa'abah said. "But I've got people on the ground all around the city, and in the air searching the surrounding area. We'll do everything we can to shut her down before she can get out." She hesitated. "It's probably already too late though, sir. If only you had killed her—"

"I don't want to hear that. I want to hear that you've returned her to that cell. I want to hear that you've neutralized the rest of the threat by killing her cohorts in plain view of other potential mutineers. I want to hear that you take full responsibility for this lapse in security, for which I pay you an enormous sum. Where are those words, Captain?" He waited. "Well?"

She shot a glance at Thrace.

"Don't look at her," he yelled, the shout straining out of his tight throat. Harvested voices jumbled over each other, impossible to separate and growing louder by the second. "This is between you and me, Captain Sa'abah. This breach rests on your shoulders. I expect you to rectify the error. Keep me informed. Dismissed."

He turned away from her again and stared out the window into the late afternoon. Behind him, the door slid open and closed, and he felt Thrace come near.

"That was a mistake."

Among the roaring in his head, one objection rose just loud enough to make out

stop...

and he shook his head. "Your input is not welcome just now, Captain Baldric."

"Too bad," Thrace said, her tone low, husky. "You are alienating everyone around you. In case it hasn't occurred to you, you need them if you're going to pull this off."

He wheeled around, got in her face, backed her against the desk without actually touching her, a scream taking form in his throat. "That's enough!"

Her gray eyes widened. Shock and dismay chased each other across her brown face.

A heartbeat of uncertainty echoed across the cavernous gulf between them. Clamorous warnings screamed in Skalar's head and he shrank away, appalled at his own reaction. He turned toward the window.

"I apologize," he said through his teeth. "I know you're my strongest ally here. I just—"

Thrace stepped up beside him. "Let me comm Botha, bring him here. Please."

"I'll think about it."

"You said that weeks ago, Alira."

"My name—"

"I know your name. I know who you are, and it isn't this person you've become."

He stared toward the bay, his thoughts

they were his, weren't they?

tumbling over one another in a tangled array. She touched him, and he flinched.

"Botha can help you. I know it."

When he didn't respond, she turned him to face her. "Please."

His resolve weakened. What harm would it do? He nodded. "Invite him if you insist, but I make no promises."

"Good enough for now," Thrace said.

A movement behind her snatched his attention and he glanced up. Across the office, behind Thrace, stood Eli Sullivan. Skalar's heart triple thumped. The last time Alira's dream companion had made an appearance in meditation or otherwise had been, when? Four weeks ago? Five? Six? He blinked, but the apparition remained.

what are you doing here?

But of course, Eli had nothing to say.

He realized with a start, when she twisted away, that his hands had gripped Thrace's shoulders. He glanced at her, then at Eli.

She followed his gaze, confused. "What are you looking at?"

Skalar's lips worked a moment.

"A ghost," he whispered.

chapter 17

TWENTY MINUTES LATER, THRACE LEFT the admiral's office, frowning. She had never seen Alira react like that, in any of her forms. Not to Thrace. Galen's i'shin hurtled closer to the harvesting sickness every day and there wasn't a thing he could do about it.

Except get Botha involved. Right now, that felt like Alira's best hope, and the sooner the better.

Thrace passed the conservatory, rounded the corner, and ducked into her office. Her own windows overlooked the game field on one side, and Consortium Industries on the other. Light wore on toward evening, washing the smaller space with a rosy glow.

"Windows, full opacity. Lights, nine hundred lumens."

She sank into her chair but bounded upright almost at once and paced. She couldn't shift to wear Tenzin's face, not here on the base, certainly. Not outside it either. After that fiasco in Bejami's landport, she dared not tie Tenzin to New Canaan in any way. But Botha had never met Thrace. Would he be suspicious of a stranger's invitation? Surely not. What reason would he have?

A soft chime sounded. Thrace sighed. What now?

"Yes?"

The door slid aside to admit Sa'abah. The security captain entered and took up a stiff, rigid stance just inside the office. Tension flowed off the woman in waves that tightened Thrace's own shoulders.

"Is there news?"

Sa'abah hesitated. "In a manner of speaking. May I speak freely, Captain Baldric?"

"By all means."

"I've known the admiral a long time, ma'am," Sa'abah said. "In all that time, he has never come as close to the edge as he is now. I've admired his sense of balance and his drive, the way he took control of the Consortium and drove it past the competition to lead the other factions in almost every way. Since his reappearance, though, something is off. I don't know what it is, and I'm not asking you to tell me. But you need to understand, ma'am, that he is dangerously close to losing it all."

Bile rose in Thrace's throat. "Has something else happened?"

"No, ma'am. Not yet. But it will. At the rate the admiral is isolating himself, he won't last the month."

"I see." Thrace clasped her hands behind her. She mustn't let Sa'abah see how they trembled. "And you, Sa'abah? Where do you stand?"

Sa'abah's mouth twitched. "I've always been loyal, Captain Baldric. Still am. But I don't know how much longer I can keep a lid on this boiling pot. If he doesn't relent soon and return to business as usual, the whole thing is going to blow." She sighed. "I know you and the admiral are close. I just thought—"

"You thought I might talk some sense into him."

"Yes, and soon. I'm damn good at my job, ma'am, and I'm doing what I can to ameliorate the situation. But if the admiral is hell-bent on destroying every dram of respect he's built in this faction, my efforts won't stop him no matter how good I am. I'd hate to see that happen."

Her words felt like truth. Thrace peered at her. "Would you? It's a rare faction officer who doesn't live for the chance to take an admiral's place."

Sa'abah shook her head, looked down a moment, then met Thrace's eyes again. "You don't know me, Captain Baldric. You haven't been around long enough yet. Check my records if you haven't already. I've worked hard to get where I am. I have no interest in the admiral's chair. Never did. Running security gives me all the drama I need and then some. I don't really care if you believe that, ma'am, but you have to know I'm speaking the truth about Admiral Skalar. I know you've seen it too. Unless you have your own reasons for wanting him out of the way, we need to work together to stop him from destroying himself."

Thrace held up a hand. "I meant no offense, Sa'abah. Your record speaks for itself. I'll talk to him. You have my word."

Sa'abah relaxed to her more usual tense state, and she took her leave. When she was gone, Thrace sat behind the desk.

"TICS, record communique." The system chittered. "Greetings, Baba. I am Captain Thrace Baldric, second in command to Admiral Malcolm Skalar of the Harajüd Consortium. I have a problematic situation here in New Canaan, 'a secret sunk in the banks of my soul.' A mutual friend assures me you can help." She offered a tight, secret smile. Would he make the connection? "Think it over, but I urge you to decide quickly. The needs of the many hang in the balance and my grace period is nearly exhausted. If you are willing to listen, I'll arrange to bring you here with all possible speed."

She reviewed the holo and sent it on its way to Botha. Now all she could do was wait.

And worry. Galen had always been good at that.

chapter 18

Tuneloras, Saacharis
Syndicate Trader Base, Gym

RIZZO'S HANDS HOVERED BEFORE HER face as she slammed her heel against her sparring partner's chest. The hulking man grunted and fell back several steps. Teeth bared, she advanced on him, snapping another kick. He moved faster that time and she pressed her attack, pushing him into defensive maneuvers that forced him to retreat, hands up to shadow and protect his face. Under these lights, his tanned skin and brown hair could almost be Skalar's. Her left hand shot out to land a solid blow against his jaw, and he stumbled, shaking his head.

If only it *was* Skalar.

She waited, giving her partner a moment to get his bearings, then advanced again. Now the man began to retaliate. She dodged as one of his feet whizzed past her face, then ducked a high right. His next punch slammed into her shoulder, yanking a grunt from her throat, but his follow-through came too slow. By the time he rounded a kick in her direction, she dropped and swept his feet. The man slammed into the floor and Rizzo bounced away to let him get up.

He groaned to his feet, and she stopped bouncing.

"Are you hurt?"

"Only my pride, ma'am." The man rubbed his shoulder. "I should be used to it by now."

Rizzo dropped her hands to her sides. "That's enough."

"Good workout, ma'am. Thanks for the practice."

She nodded once and he limped toward the exit as she turned her steady blows on the heavy bag. It, at least, would not need a break. She worked her body on autopilot while she pondered her current problem.

Reyes' confessions gave her much to consider. According to him, Bellamy and Skalar were in the trade together, covering each other's tracks in order to stay under the radar. Reyes might have believed that, but Rizzo didn't. Not for a minute. First, if Bellamy and Skalar were slaving as a team, why would Reyes sell out one with relative ease but withhold the other until forced to give it up? Second, neither Skalar nor Bellamy worked or played well with others. To think those narcissists might actually work together boggled the mind. Third, while neither of them had any compunction about moving up by stepping on the bodies of others, she had yet to see Skalar stoop to something like this. Indentured workers, yes. Definitely. That's what Reyes had first claimed this was about before she'd sliced the truth off him along with a few pounds of skin. But slaves?

The bag swung before her, and she paused to catch her breath. Both Bellamy and Skalar did business with Reyes' employer, Saacharis Aggregate. Reyes wasn't powerful enough in Saacharis Aggregate to have brought slaves onboard himself. He'd clearly had orders from farther up the corporate ladder and had been happy enough, given proper incentive, to name names.

Luther Michels, vice chair of the Aggregate board of directors, apparently thought enslavement of human beings a reasonable exchange for a fatter bottom line. He probably wasn't alone in that belief, but he was a start.

It wouldn't be easy to stop him. Michels constituted a new and enormous target to challenge her skills. She couldn't exactly lodge a complaint against his actions. He could make things very difficult for the Syndicate. Nor could she report Reyes' violation of contract. Broaching the subject with Aggregate would prompt pertinent and uncomfortable questions about Reyes' current whereabouts. Best not to put herself in that sort of predicament.

She stepped forward again, slamming a new barrage against the bag.

Slaving. Bad enough anywhere, but Reyes had the nerve to bring that abomination into Gauri Metalb. Her contract with Aggregate allowed them generous oversight on their own corporate operations there, but that was the Syndicate's mine. She wasn't about to allow the management of Aggregate or anyone else to engage in such an obscenity on her own faction's land. Reyes deserved what he'd gotten in her shower, but he wasn't the head of this beast. She wasn't done yet.

Reports from Syndicate spies had not mentioned slaves on Cartel bases, only details on industries of contention between the two factions, as well as a clear description of how Bellamy danced on the edge of rationality, teetering with precarious abandon as if she didn't know or care how aberrant she appeared. She could well be the provider, following in her predecessor's footsteps. It wouldn't be difficult to find targets. Every corporate charter world agreed to provide for its populace through fair standards of employment, housing, medical services, and the like, but no system was perfect. Each gave rise to unfortunates who fell through the corporate structure to land on the streets with no ident, no home, no credits or corporate employment on which to live. Those who kept their heads remained strong or clever enough to stay one step ahead of the authorities. Those managed to find food and shelter. Others became prey for vultures like Bellamy.

Especially the children, who couldn't—didn't know how to—fight back.

Memories of Rizzo's early years on the streets of Pelarr still rang too fresh. Warming herself under stolen burlap on damp nights. Bathing in pilfered rainwater in the storage yards. Swiping fruit, bread, eggs or, once, even a whole plucked chicken from the market. Evading the snatchers until…

Busking in front of the pub. Bardo playing a salvaged guitar as big as he was. Seven-year-old Tonee on watch for constables.

Patrons tossing chits in the beggar's box while ten-year-old Turizomi danced.

A hand over her mouth. That sickening lurch in her stomach when the man snatched her up...

A trickle of sweat ran into her eye and she shook her head, as much to clear her vision as her thoughts. Since her encounter with Reyes, sleep had eluded her. Easy enough to fill the hours with plans to "service" the air shafts and other equipment in the mine, as was her contractual duty. Who was to complain on behalf of the corporation if the Syndicate's maintenance checks came a few months early? Who would know that her crew left behind hidden surveillance cams in areas not easily seen, any of which would provide immediate proof if Aggregate perpetrated this sort of thing in the future? It would take time to set up and might not ever provide names of guilty Aggregate parties, but woe be unto that corporation if she found they were still at it.

chapter 19

Pelarr, Zebalu
Cartel Trader Base, Admiral Bellamy's Quarters

BELLAMY FELL ON THE BED with a sigh. Sweat trickled from her belly and breasts as she lay panting, one leg thrown over her companion.

"Oh my," she breathed. "You were worth every credit I paid to bait you."

The man beside her said nothing. Probably still too blissed out to form a coherent thought. There was *one* thing he had no problem forming, though. She laughed, low and husky, and bent her leg to run her toes over his groin, which was far more alert than he was at the moment. Sukabo would do that to a person, but it was too expensive to use in the trade. Too hard to get. Besides, if the bleeding-heart nature-lovers found out she was picking a protected mushroom, even her contacts at Zebalu Association might agree to fine her. Libidinorr was no good. It worked all right, kept the mark dosed enough for good performance, but she had to trade with another faction, The Federation, for that. She'd rather pay fines than deal with Admiral Georgeanne. If her own chemists could narrow down the correct dosage of amornae spores—enough to rev up a slave's motor, but not enough to kill them—she'd be set. The slave would sell only once. Consumable drugs ensured repeat business.

He reached for her again, and she pushed him away with a laugh. "That's enough, boy. I don't want to use you up. You're going to bring me a nice profit."

She swung her legs over the side of the bed, commed the handler to retrieve the slave, and walked naked to the shower. The minute she stepped under the spray, her comm chirped.

"Voice only. Yes?"

"Admiral," Hannah said, her words carrying over the shower noise, "your New Canaan retrieval team has landed. I thought you'd want to know."

A grin split Bellamy's face. "Really? Did they bring me something nice?"

"They did, ma'am."

"Excellent. Bring it to my office in twenty. Bellamy out."

About time. Six days since the team left. It was only a two-day flight to get there, and another two to get home, so maybe two days to develop and execute an escape plan wasn't such a bad record. Still, they'd had help from Skalar's own people, so it shouldn't have taken that long. She'd have a word with the team's captain when this was over.

She luxuriated under the water for a bit, then switched off the spray and stood beneath the blowers. When she finished, she donned a flowing aquamarine dress that set off her eyes. A quick fluff of her hair, one last glance in the mirror, and she set out for her office. Whatever intelligence this prisoner held, it better be worth what it cost the Cartel to free her and bring her here. What was Skalar thinking? To break the chain of succession and not kill the slighted party showed reckless abandon she'd not expected of him. He had to have known this woman would lash out against him at her first opportunity, and sure enough—she had escaped his custody to do exactly that. Now it was out of his hands. The poor woman was Bellamy's tool, and both would have their revenge on that Consortium bastard.

Bellamy laughed, sparking a visual reaction from others in the corridor. She was still laughing when she entered her workspace. Hannah, along with the Cartel's prize, stood before her. Bellamy scanned the stranger. Where the admiral was fair, her new toy was dark. In contrast to Bellamy's hourglass shape, the newcomer was thick. Chunky. Bellamy couldn't keep a small curl from her lip at the woman's short black hair. So unattractive.

"Admiral," Hannah said with a slight gesture, "may I present Commander Vandana Walker. Commander, this is Admiral Bellamy."

"A pleasure, Admiral," Walker said. "Thank you for the assist."

Bellamy beamed her best fake smile. "We couldn't leave you there to rot, now, could we?" She crossed to the sitting area. "Please join me. Hannah, this requires a celebration. Pour us some wine from my best bottle."

Without waiting, Bellamy selected the only cushioned ottoman, with her back to the window wall, leaving her own face in pale shadow, while Walker sat facing the bright daylight. Bellamy stared at her, waiting for her guest's nervous fidgets, the ones that usually accompanied such meetings. Walker betrayed no such discomfort, and Bellamy frowned.

"You seem to have annoyed Admiral Skalar pretty badly, Commander. May I ask what happened to land you in his brig?"

Walker shrugged. "I was Captain Crow's second, ma'am. When both Admiral Skalar and Captain Crow vanished, I took over and ran the faction. I knew Skalar was off on Trader business, but not where, exactly. Crow just disappeared. One minute he was carrying out the admiral's orders, the next he was just gone. I investigated, tracked his movements, and found his body—"

She interrupted herself, stopped short as if biting off intel she wasn't ready to share before she continued.

"We found him in a residential high-rise on the Northside. He'd been dead for several days by then, so I was automatically the new second in command of the Consortium. I sent word to the admiral, but he didn't reply for weeks. I kept the peace on base, told everyone that I knew where he was and that he'd return when he was finished with his business. I did everything a good second ought to do. I expected to be officially named when Skalar got home."

Hannah doled out glasses of wine, then sat at the other end of the sofa.

Walker sipped from her glass, then sighed.

"But that isn't what happened. When Skalar came back, he was acting weird. Had some stranger with him, a newbie I'd never even heard of before. The minute I briefed him about my investigation and Crow's death, he made this upstart his second. Just jumped right over me after everything I did to keep things rolling in his absence." Walker's head moved slowly from side to side, cheeks drawn in, lips puckered as if she'd just bitten into something nasty.

It seemed a good point to encourage her.

"That's no way to treat loyal behavior." Bellamy frowned. "I thought Skalar was above that sort of thing."

Walker laughed, a blurt of sound that grated on Bellamy's ears.

"You and me both, ma'am." The commander took another swig of wine.

"Didn't you explain to him all you'd done? Tell him he was being unfair?"

"That I did."

"And?"

Walker scowled. "He almost killed me. Then he threw me in the brig. When my people tried to protest, he killed them. At least the ones he could find. The rest evaded him until they could get me out. With your help, of course. That's the whole story."

Bellamy smiled her most welcoming smile. "I'm sure it is. I'm glad I could be there for you. Is there anything else you need?"

"Actually, ma'am, there is. I'm a good officer, Admiral Bellamy. I would be an asset to your faction if you'll have me. My people are resourceful too. They'd make good additions to your crew."

Bellamy caught Hannah's eye, and the two exchanged a hesitant look. "Oh dear," Bellamy sighed. "I'm not really looking to increase the ranks right now. Maybe I could find you a position with the Zebalu Association. Surely there—"

"Please, Admiral Bellamy." Walker scooted forward to the edge of the sofa. "What can I do to prove my worth?"

For starters, the woman could stop interrupting her. Bellamy stood and paced to the window. Outside, gulls rode the wind offshore, as usual. Whitecaps broke the dark surface of the Bantali Sea almost as far as she could see. Winds must have picked up since her earlier stroll along the garden path.

"What was your specialty in the Consortium?"

"Mostly, Crow and Skalar sent me to negotiate terms on business deals, but I was also training in security with Captain Sa'abah. I think they were grooming me for leadership. At least they were, until…"

"I already have a negotiations team," Bellamy said, "and a full security staff. I don't need new bodies in either of those roles. What else do you bring to the table?"

She waited through the short, expected pause.

"I have information."

Bellamy smiled at the window, then put on her best surprised face and turned toward Walker. "Like what?"

Walker glanced from Bellamy to Hannah, then sat up straighter. "Skalar has contacts in Harajüd House gaming centers. They're skimming off the corporate profits and turning it over to him."

"Trifles. What else?"

"I know he's trying to get the Consortium involved in small ship trade, take away some of Rizzo's business. That wouldn't sit well with the Syndicate."

"Old news, my dear. We're all in competition, and Skalar got where he is by being good at it. I'd be more shocked if he wasn't trying to steal another faction's business."

"Then what about his counterfeiting sideline?" Walker leaned forward. "He's nibbling away at all the worlds on that. Danua silks, Rubene paintings and crafts, Levyron's diaminas, all the rest. And his ident forgeries are thriving. You can't tell one of his from an official card. He's got ins to set up whole histories for fake personas. He—"

Bellamy laughed. "Oh, my dear, we all do that. How long did you say you'd been in the Consortium?"

"Nine years," Walker said.

"And how much of that time did you spend in the upper echelons? Three months? Six?" Bellamy shook her head. "I'm sorry, I want to help you, but this information is worthless. Unless you can offer something more, I'm afraid there's no place for you here."

Walker rubbed her forehead and looked between them again, opened her mouth, closed it again.

"Is there something else?" Bellamy said. Come on, spit it out. She didn't have all day.

"The Cartel is involved in shipbuilding. I assume you use hematium."

Bellamy frowned. "So?"

"Skalar has a whole hauler full. And he can easily get more. I think he plans to run the market."

Out of the corner of her eye, Bellamy saw Hannah's head jerk toward her with a slight expression of panic. Bellamy squinted at this newcomer. No way he could do that.

"I don't believe you."

"It's true. He stashed it at a secret base. Harajüd House doesn't know."

"What secret base? Where?"

Walker shook her head. "I don't know. That info's top secret, as are the names of the crew he has manning it. I can tell you one person who knows, assuming he's still alive. Ronan, captain of the Treasure Chest. He's been there. Not sure he'll talk though. His crew might if you paid them enough."

A flush seeped up Bellamy's cheeks. If Walker was right, Skalar would get the best of her. Again.

No. She refused to believe it.

"That's impossible. No one could keep a base that secret. I'd know. We all would. And unless he stole the hematium from Harajüd House, he couldn't possibly have enough supply to take the market." She shot a look at Hannah. "This person is lying. She's wasting my time. Take her to a cell."

Hannah rose, but so did Walker.

"It's the truth!"

Hannah pressed forward. Walker retreated a step.

"Then how did he pull off this purported miracle?" Bellamy said. "Where did he get the metal?"

"From the Iridosians! I swear it!"

"That's ludicrous. The Iridosians don't like dealing with humans. And they only sell their hematium to Harajüd House and Saacharis Aggregate."

"It wasn't their choice, ma'am. Admiral Skalar went there and took it by force."

Her words hung in the air like buzzing flies, echoes in Bellamy's ringing ears.

"What did you say?"

"He tried to make a deal with them." Walker glanced from Bellamy to Hannah and back. "Made a very generous offer, but they refused to answer. Then he sent me there. They wouldn't even let me near the city. Told me to leave and stay away. So Skalar sent Crow with an armada. One of the captains made a final offer, but apparently the city had weapons we didn't know about. After they took out two of our ships, we returned fire—"

"We?" Bellamy interrupted. "You were aboard? You saw this happen?"

"Yes ma'am."

"Go on."

"We bombed the city with LADRAS missiles, flattened the whole valley, but not before they took out half our armada. Then we waited long enough for the radiation to dissipate a bit, and Crow sent in shifts to mine and plunder the site."

"Why?" Bellamy asked, frowning. "It's a worthless resource. The minute he tries to sell it, the colonials will know what he's done. They'll ship him and everyone involved to Mandoslóna."

A weak grin brushed Walker's lips. "I don't know the details, but I heard he planned deliveries by drone to Harajüd House and Saacharis Aggregate as if the Iridosians were still alive and kicking. Nobody ever goes to Iridos, so unless Skalar stops filling orders, no one would know the Iridosians are gone."

Bellamy blinked. Yes. He'd have to set up a separate credit account for payments, but that might work. For a while, anyway. With some care, he could get out of the business at the first sign of trouble, and no one would be the wiser. He'd still have a secret stash of the metal for all his shipbuilding for years to come, though he'd have to be careful how he spent that resource. He wouldn't want to be caught with it.

Clever, Skalar.

"What else did your people find?"

"Not much of value. Most of the other resources they had to offer were common on colony worlds too."

"Did you get all the hematium? Or is there more?"

"Oh, there's more, ma'am," Walker said, relief plain in her slackening jaw. "The whole place is weird, and a lot of the crew went bonkers on the surface. We grabbed what we could in a few weeks—"

"Weeks? And you didn't get it all?"

"No ma'am. Like I said, the crew was affected by something on the surface. Crow never said what, not to me anyway. The mining op got smaller and smaller until the other captains threatened to revolt. We lost a lot of people on that run."

"What about the Iridosians?"

"No survivors as far as I know, ma'am."

Bellamy took a deep breath. Well, well. Now this was news. Not that she believed it. Not yet. She turned back toward the window. If it was true, she could take over the operation, send her own crew—tagless of course. Couldn't leave behind anything like idents or other recognizable details that would lead to her. Surely Skalar had taken pains to cover his own tracks, too. Anyone caught in this minefield would surely be blown out of the water, metaphorically speaking. One did not wipe out an entire species without consequence.

If she were careful, she could go in, take a load of hematium, run out, and leave clues to Skalar's involvement with each trip. Assuming her ships weren't actually caught on the surface or in orbit, she could profit from this in two ways: with a useful and salable resource, and with the takedown of her only real competitor. Nice. Neat. Clean. She'd need a whole new slave force, throwaways who could make a one-way trip. Even if the surface was no longer dangerous, she wouldn't maintain an entire mining crew for any length of time. Send them, work them until they dropped, clean them out, and set up again. If rumors about that world's tidal lock were accurate, the Iridosian dayside would provide an efficient disposal means. She nodded. With clarification of a few minor details, it could work. Assuming it was legit.

"Hannah," she said to the window, "start looking into this secret base of Skalar's. I want to know more about this Ronan person, and his crew. And have Captain Rook prepare for a six-day trip for three people."

"Of course, ma'am. Who's going with her?"

"The good Commander and myself. We'll take my ship."

"Your destination, ma'am?"

Bellamy swung around and grinned. "Iridos, of course."

Part Two

chapter 20

New Canaan, Harajüd
<u>Consortium Trader Base, Admiral Skalar's Office</u>

"Why?" Skalar rose from his seat and leaned forward, his fists braced against his desktop. "Why is he coming here?"

"Because I asked him to." Thrace stood her ground.

"But why?"

"He can help you." Thrace dropped into a chair in front of Skalar's desk. "You promised you would talk to him."

"I did no such thing. I said I'd think about it. Now that I have, I've decided I don't need his help. Or yours either, for that matter."

i need a brandy.

Skalar moved around the desk toward the bar. Thrace followed and clutched at his arm when he reached for the bottle.

"What are you doing?" she hissed.

Skalar snatched his arm away. "I'm having a drink."

"Alira—" Thrace took the bottle out of his hand and set it on the bar. "Admiral, sir, think hard before you do that. I don't believe you are prepared for its effects. You've changed since you last tasted alcohol. Remember?"

He squinted at her through slitted eyes. She was right, of course, but he really wanted that drink. Damn it! What was the point in being admiral of the faction if he couldn't even choose whether or not to enjoy a splash of his favorite beverage at his own discretion? The way Thrace was looking at him right now made his skin crawl. Her face held the same look his mother had given him when he started bringing home more credits than he could easily account for. She didn't trust him then. Thrace didn't trust him now. Did these idiots think he couldn't take care of his own business? If everyone would just back the hell up and leave him alone, he would be fine. But no. They had to crowd him, get in his face.

His fist clenched, popping the bowl of the snifter he held. Glass shards stabbed into his flesh and his vision cleared, as if a cloud had passed by.

Thrace frowned. "Are you alright?"

He glanced at the blood dripping from his fist, and relaxed his hand. Crystal fragments protruded from his palm and fingers. A human would need stitches. Distracted, he pulled the broken bits out of the wounds, which began to heal the moment they were unobstructed.

"I'm fine." He'd need to clean the carpet, though, before the spots could reveal unammi DNA.

"I don't think you are."

"Then you don't know me as well as you thought." Skalar pushed past Thrace, crossed the office, and peered out the window. "I just need to regain control," he muttered, almost to himself. "That's all. Everything's fine. Just a little mixed up. Nothing I can't handle."

The door chime sounded.

Skalar closed his eyes against the view, willing himself to stay calm. *Go away.* Soft steps behind him announced Thrace's approach. Her soothing presence washed over him, though she did not speak. He needed to stop being such an ass to her. Without Thrace, he would be lost, and Alira with him. The other voices in his head had all taken on the timbre of his own, like talking to himself. Perhaps that meant he was finally settling into the role. Yet he still felt alien in his own skin. It itched, as if it were pulled too tight over his soul. How he longed to take it off, to stretch out into his true self!

The chime repeated, and Thrace stepped up beside him.

"Should I send them away?"

He sighed and opened his eyes. "No. I'm fine. I'll …. be fine." He turned from the window and called out entry.

Sa'abah came, hesitant, partway into the office. "There's been more trouble, sir. A couple of things. Nothing major, but I thought you'd want to know."

"What is it now?"

"Harlan Downing's people have been sniffing around our crew."

"Not the slave issue again."

"Afraid so, sir. He's convinced we're running a trade." Sa'abah paused. "We aren't, are we?"

"No!" Skalar shouted, throwing his arms up. "How did he ever get that idea? Why would *you* think that, Captain?"

"I normally wouldn't, Admiral. But things have changed of late. I just want to be sure I'm up to date."

"Forget about Harlan. Forget about slaves. That sort of business is nothing but trouble. We have enough of that on our own, but that's beside the fact. Slavery is vile. Barbaric. I won't have it," he ranted, pacing. He pointed in Sa'abah's direction. "If I find out someone within the Consortium is running them through our channels, I will end the practice along with whoever was behind it."

He paced a moment behind his desk, remembering images from one of his harvests, some sort of sale of human flesh. He wasn't sure which one had been involved, but it wasn't Skalar. Skalar shook his head as if to disperse the memory, and stopped, facing Sa'abah. "You said a couple of things. What else?"

"Your satellite base on Gadney reports theft of seven crates of shisté and the destruction of a dozen casks ready for bottling. It might have been worse, but base security interrupted the saboteurs before they could ruin the whole winery."

Skalar growled, a rumble that began deep in his chest and built until it roared past his lips. His fist, no longer bleeding, pounded the desk. Beside him, Thrace flinched. Sa'abah stepped back.

"Who's responsible?" he shouted.

"They believe it was Mira Cohen's crew," Sa'abah said. "But it isn't a total loss, sir. They saved more than half the cuvée. It's more of a nuisance than anything."

"That's not the point, Captain, and the fact that you think it is concerns me!" He sucked in a lungful of air and forced himself to blow it out slowly. Nuisance indeed. It would be another year before the next vat was ready to bottle. Production costs for the lost wine would measure in the tens—if not hundreds—of thousands of credits, not to mention the time involved. Shisté never sold cheap, but he could only mark the remaining bottles up so much before he lost out to Gadney competitors. With fewer viable bottles to sell, he'd never cover this loss.

Cohen. He'd thought her reliable. Trustworthy. Her face swam before his mind's eye, frightened as he'd shoved her against the wall at the outpost, threatened her. If her own personal safety wasn't enough motivation to make her toe the line, he'd have to find something that would. Make a statement loud enough to keep them all in their places.

"Enough. This ongoing show of resistance stops now," he whispered.

Both officers stepped closer.

"Pardon, sir?" Sa'abah said. "I didn't catch that."

He raised his eyes to her face. "When was the last time we saw Cohen or her crew?"

Sa'abah shifted from one foot to the other. "About a week after you sent them home from the outpost, sir."

"Cohen hasn't reported for duty since then?"

"No, sir."

He mined his harvested memories. "She has family in Salisbury, does she not?"

Color drained from Sa'abah's face. "Yes, sir."

"A mother, I believe. A younger brother."

Neither officer spoke.

"Bring me the brother."

Thrace frowned. "Admiral Skalar—"

He silenced his second with a gesture.

Sa'abah's lips tightened. "Are you sure about this, sir?"

"He is not to be harmed in any way, but I want him here. On this base. By tonight. Am I clear?"

"Yes, sir."

Her eyes twitched, as if she wanted to shoot a look at Thrace, but she did not. Skalar nodded. "Dismissed."

When she was gone, Thrace stared as if she would breach his skull and probe his thoughts. His lip curled. How dare she? Thrace should know better than anyone that he needed to get this under control.

yes, but whose control?

The breath he'd been holding whooshed out of him in a rush, leaving him deflated. Flat. He shook his head.

"Go ahead," he sighed. "Speak your piece."

"Will it make a difference?"

He threw her a tired smile. "Why even ask that question? You never shied away from sharing your opinions with me before."

Her features twisted, half-annoyance, half-grief. "I don't know you anymore."

Skalar nodded. "Neither do I. Rakalesh told me once that having the reaped memories wasn't the same as understanding the logic and reasoning behind them. I didn't believe her at the time."

"Do you now?"

Good question. For a moment, his thoughts—Alira's thoughts—rang clear in his mind. Maybe Rakalesh had been right. Having Skalar's memories wasn't enough to *be* him. Even handing him the controls and letting him drive most of the time. Therein lay the problem. Those around him saw the discrepancy and interpreted it as weakness. If he didn't regain control soon, the outpost would be forfeit. He hated the idea of continuing this charade, but he had no choice.

Failure was not an option.

chapter 21

SEVEN DAYS. MORE THAN A standard week to die, even with forced exposure to the ALT headset the whole time. Skalar's upper lip curled as he viewed the report on Enzo. Consortium medics had run constant scans during the experiment but needed physical evidence to support their suspicions. The autopsy was taking place now, searching the damaged regions of the prisoner's brain, but the medical team had claimed further research would be required.

He crossed his legs. Crow had tried numerous times to convince him to allow these diversions in Consortium gaming houses. Skalar had always refused. He'd heard through reliable sources how they affected players. Now he would know why. HHU medics said the patron Skalar had discovered during the Bahtya inspection would never recover. His family was demanding restitution, and Skalar intended to pay it without hesitation. Already, he'd told Harlan to bill the Consortium for medical expenses. At least his cooperation with HHU had kept him free of suspicion in the matter, but he intended to see it never happened again. Not on his watch. Word of Enzo's fate had been leaked—accidentally, of course—to those who opposed the admiral. That, along with the fact that

Mira Cohen's brother now sat under guard in Consortium guest quarters, seemed to have calmed things down.

At least for now. Maybe it would last this time.

The comm chirped and he ground his teeth. A moment's peace, that's all he wanted! Why couldn't they leave him alone?

The feeling passed as quickly as it had come, and he took a deep breath.

"Yes. What is it?"

"Admiral Skalar, one of your pilots is asking to see you, sir."

"Which one?"

"Says her name is Edanor, sir."

Skalar sat forward in his seat. Alira never knew Edanor well, but memories from both Nyros and Ijydin flooded Skalar's mind, images of Edanor in moments of camaraderie between outcasts with shared concerns and losses.

"Very well. Send her in."

Within minutes, the door chimed and he admitted her.

Skalar took in the look of his visitor's human persona. Gray eyes peered out from beneath thick black brows on a long, angular face. Stubby black hair sprouted from her scalp. Her normal squat blue body had been stretched into a tall, pale form displaying no sign of gender. Full lips formed no false human smile. Good. Skalar grew tired of the social niceties humans always seemed to expect. For once, he longed for the honesty of his own people.

"Aes te nalya, Alira."

"Nalena t'staani, Edanor," he replied automatically. "But that is the last time you are to speak that phrase or that name in this setting. Am I clear?"

Edanor frowned. "Why?"

His lips twisted in annoyance. "Appearances. Just…trust me. Do as I say." He gestured to a seat on the opposite side of his desk.

She took the proffered chair. "Tiral sends news. More of the mitigants have asked to come to the outpost. Some expressed interest in accompanying the pilots on some of their runs. He said you would need to approve it first."

Skalar peered across the desk at her pale face. "Tiral told me the treatments aren't holding with them all. Do you agree they've broken free of it?"

She nodded.

"How capable are they of holding a human persona in a crowd, or in stressful situations?"

"As well as you or I could do." Edanor leaned forward in her seat, elbows on the armrests, hands clasped in front. "What's more important is that some of them are having a difficult time maintaining the illusion of mitigation. They worry that the Council will see they've shaken off the treatment. They want out before that happens."

Of course they did. Skalar ran a hand down his face, fingers lingering over his beard. He almost smiled at the thought of Rakalesh's frustration when ten or more unammi sought exile rather than submit to further treatment or conform to outdated expectations that no longer served any useful function. It isn't as though they needed to stay with the others solely for exposure to irolium any longer. Assuming the seedstones they'd taken from Iridos did root in the caverns on Earth, as they'd hoped, the Iri would be able to produce more irolium through their symbiosis with the unammi. Then the mitigants and anyone who chose to join them could take seedstones from the outpost's vaults and set up their own colony in one of the other underground systems on that wide world.

But it wasn't just about the irolium anymore. Their numbers were already far too few. If the unammi hoped to regrow their population, they needed to stay together. And as long as the Council refused to allow outcasts back into the fold, encouraging further splits did not serve the whole any more than the Councilor's refusal to admit their mistake. At this point, numbers made all the difference.

"I understand their concerns, but they're frem, same as you or I. We must serve the people." Skalar frowned. "I don't know. I need to give that some thought. I'll render my decision in time to tell the next pilot."

"Of course."

"Was there anything else?"

Edanor took a deep breath, and Skalar could almost see patterns of blue winking and flashing beneath her pale human façade. "Actually, yes. Rakalesh wants those holovids of Cesar, Nyros and Ijydin. Immediately."

Skalar ground his teeth. "Rakalesh," he said, his tone carefully even, "is in no position to push me."

Edanor shrugged in practiced mimicry of human nonchalance. "She said it's been half a season since you left. You told her you would do it when you arrived in New Canaan. What holovids is she talking about?"

Instead of answering, Skalar tapped the arm of his chair. He'd promised—or, rather, Alira had—to send vids of harvested memories for the new Founder's Daughter, once they grew one. But Rakalesh couldn't possibly know how busy he'd been, how full his days and nights were since his arrival at the Consortium. How dare she?

"I'll send the vids when I'm damned good and ready," he said.

"Very well. I'll tell her you said so. She's also asking about the genetic samples she's been expecting."

Skalar frowned. "I thought Rakalesh didn't want my samples."

"I am a messenger. I'm not privy to the mind of the council."

"Do they have a new vault on the surface? New labs?"

"No," Edanor said. "They're still using the outpost facilities."

"Have they even started building one?"

"Not that I know of."

"Why not? They've had more than sixty days."

"I imagine they've been preoccupied with setting up the new city for the rest of the survivors, dealing with wounded, affixing the salvaged irolium in the new temple chamber so the Iri can begin to establish new growth." Edanor shook her head. "I haven't been there. The council will only allow Tiral on the surface, so he makes all our deliveries. He says they are always busy when he goes there."

"Do they interact with the outpost crew when they are onsite?"

"No. They insist we keep our distance. Tiral has instructed us to avoid the labs at all times unless we get prior approval. He doesn't want to provoke further contention."

Skalar grimaced. "Let me make sure I understand you correctly. The council continues to shun the outcasts who are 'contaminated' by human contact. Yet the council's scientists have no problem using a human facility?"

Edanor blinked. "Perhaps they never considered that incongruity."

"Tell Rakalesh that resources at the outpost are limited, as is my patience. They may continue to use the facility for now, but not at the crew's expense. Base personnel are no longer constrained from use of the labs while the councilors or scientists are onsite. If the council is uncomfortable with that decision, they can damn well build a new lab and vault in their own city. They should have done so already. Until they do, I'll keep my samples to myself."

"You know Rakalesh believes the choice that put you here is doomed to failure. That your time is short. I expect she wants you to comply before it's too late."

"I don't care what she wants."

"I see." Edanor peered sideways at Skalar. "Tiral says you asked him once if the city was in danger from within, from the contention between surviving traditionalists and those that favor change."

"Yes. So?"

"Rakalesh believes it is."

Skalar scowled. "It's worse, then."

"It is. And it's growing. Rakalesh blames you."

"How could it be my fault? I haven't been among our people in almost two months."

"I don't explain the messages," Edanor said, her palms out. "I only deliver them."

He lurched out of his chair to pace before the window. What he really wanted was a brandy.

"I didn't cause the turmoil they're facing. The council did that to themselves. I've warned them for years that too much constriction was a bad idea. After the fall of the city, I told Rakalesh they should stop repressing the people so, allow them more latitude. Even before I left, I suggested that this transition of place was the perfect time to rethink their ways. They chose not to listen. Now they see the price of their stubbornness, and they want a scapegoat. I'm a familiar one, not to mention that I'm conveniently unable to defend myself," he murmured to himself, then stopped and turned to look at her. "I can't stop what's happening on Earth. The Council got themselves into that mess. They can get themselves out of it."

Edanor pursed her lips. "Is that what you want me to tell them?"

"Yes. It is."

"Very well." She stood. "Have you any orders for Tiral?"

"No."

She turned to go.

"Edanor."

She stopped. "Yes?"

"If you are going to play the role of a pilot in service to the Consortium, you will need to act in a more deferential manner toward its admiral. Namely, me. No one leaves my presence without being dismissed."

Again, he had the illusion of seeing color beneath her skin, this time flashes of red. Her jaw tightened, then relaxed so quickly he might have imagined it.

"I see." She peered at him as if he were some strange insect. "May I please be dismissed, Admiral Skalar?"

Skalar took a deep breath, resumed his seat and crossed his legs. He studied her for a full minute, then allowed his lips to smile. "You are dismissed, Edanor."

Her slight bow raised his ire, but he held his smile. The moment the door closed behind her the smile vanished.

chapter 22

On Iridos Approach
<u>**Aboard the Mirovia**</u>

"WE HAVE DEBRIS," ROOK SAID over her shoulder, her lisp clear.

Bellamy frowned. Captain Rook hated that speech quirk and tried to hide it as much as possible. The woman must be tired, to let it slip through uncontrolled like that.

"Analysis?" Bellamy endured the silence while Rook scanned the field.

"Looks like a ship, ma'am."

"A ship? Just one?"

"Affirmative."

"Whose?"

"Danua designation, ma'am, registered to the Clan. Small craft, four-man crew, maybe."

"Clan?" Bellamy blinked, then nodded with reluctant approval. "Good move, Skalar."

"Ma'am?"

"Nothing, Captain. Any life signs?"

"None, ma'am."

"What about on the surface?"

"Negative, Admiral. Looks empty. And flat."

"Show me." Bellamy turned toward the holodisplay. A fuzzy image of the ruined city rose out of the table's surface. Clear blast points gave credibility to at least some of Walker's story. "Surface conditions?"

Rook shrugged. "Breathable. Windy, though. Instruments indicate current sustained winds amid the ruins at about 50 kph."

"Radiation?"

"Yes, ma'am. LADRAS residuals. Unsafe levels. You'll need suits. One other thing. Gravity's 2.1g."

"Understood," Bellamy said. Damn. She didn't like long walks anyway, unless they were through her garden, or along the cliff. Moving from point A to point B in this place would be a real chore. She needed to wrap this up as quickly as possible. "We're close enough. Why can't we get a better visual?"

"Particulate matter from the wind, I expect, but water vapor exacerbates the issue, ma'am."

"Very well. Find us a good place to land. I don't want to walk any farther than necessary, Captain."

"Might have to be outside that ridge, Admiral. It's almost a kilometer away from the target, but I don't trust the integrity of the ground inside the valley."

Bellamy sighed. "Noted. Do your best. I'm going to get our guest."

She put command behind her and headed toward Walker's quarters. Even comfortable accommodations grew tiresome after three days of enforced confinement, but it also annoyed her that she'd had to reschedule several meetings that had taken weeks or months to arrange. That sort of thing tugged at the threads of her reputation, not to mention the fact that the delay had given breathing room to at least one contact. She'd have preferred to keep the pressure tight. Still, this Iridos thing wasn't something she could hand off to Hannah.

At the door, she slipped her ident into the slot, and the panel moved into the wall. Walker paced beside the bed. Her head jerked up to face the door, a look of cautious neutrality spread across her features.

"We've arrived?"

Bellamy stood in the open passageway. She'd not spent any more time in Walker's company than was necessary during the trip, but even that small exposure left Bellamy curious. How had Walker ever gained admission to the Consortium? Any command role at all seemed to exceed the woman's abilities, much less one close enough to make a run for the Admiral's seat. Compared to Rook or Hannah, this commander was a slug. Bellamy's chef was probably smarter. Bellamy smiled and stepped into the room.

"Soon enough. Rook will alert me once we're on the ground." Bellamy took a seat at one side of the space, her back to the corner. "Tell me what we're going to find down there."

Walker frowned. "I already told you."

"Tell me again."

Walker rubbed her forehead and resumed pacing. "Captain Crow blasted out a wider passage in the ridge between our ships and the valley where the squibs lived. All the domes were flattened and even when I was last there, the LADRAS strikes had broken through the surface in numerous spots. I'm sure there are more holes now, since Crow sent our last few missiles down on his way out."

"Were they still trying to destroy your ships?"

"No," Walker said. "He did it out of spite, I think. We were never sure if the squibs remained alive inside their tunnels so I guess he wanted to make sure they couldn't come after us later."

Bellamy made a "continue" gesture.

"Once we get inside the valley, the easiest entrance to the mines is around to the left."

"How far in will we need to go?"

"I don't have an exact figure. A long way."

"There's no shorter route?"

"None that I know of, ma'am. Most of the tunnels leading to the surface were collapsed in our initial bombing. That route may be closed now, too, for all I know."

Bellamy's smile widened, like a predator's before a feast. "Yes. Crow's parting shots."

Walker nodded.

"What do the mines look like?"

"The cavern where the mines are located is enormous. Shafts are punched into one wall of that chamber and run in more or less parallel corridors alongside one another. I didn't go into any of the shafts, so I'm not sure how deep they cut into the rock. I believe I heard Crow or his crew say that there's a lift to carry miners down below the cavern, too. Not sure how far it goes."

A quiet chirp brought Bellamy's head up. "Yes."

"We're down, ma'am," Rook lisped via the comm. "Awaiting your pleasure."

"Thank you, Rook. We'll be right there."

"Anything else you want to tell me, Commander, before we get started?"

"No, ma'am."

Bellamy stood and gestured toward the door. "Very well. After you."

She followed the thickset woman through the corridor toward the hatch. Rook waited.

"Heads up, ma'am. It's cold, and there's a lot of grit in that wind, enough to damage the suits if you're out in it long enough."

Bellamy turned a cool eye on Walker. "And you didn't mention this because...."

"I didn't know, ma'am, but that does explain why Crow didn't leave any of us on the surface for very long. Sorry. Once we get below ground, though, it should be okay."

"Tell me again, Commander, how this trip is going to be worth my while."

"Once you see for yourself that what I told you is true, I'm sure you'll agree. Think about it, Admiral," Walker said. "With the squibs gone, Skalar's going to be the only source for hematium. He'll be posing as them, but all profits from sale of the metal will go to his faction's accounts." She shrugged. "If you don't mind feeding your credits into his pockets, then this might not be a worthwhile deal for the Cartel. But," Walker grinned, "if you don't want to support your competitor, you could take advantage of the situation here. Send a crew whenever you want. As long as they're watching for him, they can mine as much of the ore as they can carry out. I think this'll be worth every credit you spend."

Maybe it would be. But mining expenses weren't the only consideration here, and credits weren't the only kind of cost involved. A value for the week she'd be away from her main base for this trip, for example, couldn't be calculated in credits alone. She didn't like not being present to run the day-to-day operations. No one saw through to the reality of things like she did. Hannah was good and could handle whatever came. But that wasn't the point. The Cartel was Bellamy's business. Bellamy's baby. She loved the deliberation, the search for the why of things, the weighing of options, the making of decisions, and the giving of orders. Having someone else do that for her sucked out all the joy.

She sighed. For this week, anyway, she'd have to settle for giving orders on a smaller scale. Bellamy instructed Rook to stay behind and monitor the skies. If Walker was right about this, it was only a matter of time before someone else came hunting treasure. Bellamy had no intention of giving them an opportunity to sneak up from behind.

She and Walker squirmed into suits and headgear, tested comms, then cycled through the airlock and stepped out onto the surface. Wind gusted against their bodies, conspiring with gravity to make every forward step a chore. Rockfalls littered the canyon. Most had been moved to one side or the other. Probably done by Crow's people when they widened the gap, but more must have fallen since, in chunks ranging from pebbles to boulders that lay before them, an obstacle course to challenge their resolve. Bellamy tried to search the cliff faces for fresh scars or cracks that might lead to new slides, but the dim light and murky visibility made it pointless, even with headlamps and visaug.

Walker led the way, Bellamy two steps behind. At the other end of the canyon, Bellamy stopped and stared across the ruined valley. Even in the beginning of human-Iridosian relations, the Iridosians hadn't been very welcoming, so the stories went. But they had sheltered stranded humans, helped them repair their ships, tentatively agreed to consider barter and trade on a limited basis. A few visits later, the Iridosians forbade humans to return. Before Crow's armada arrived here, the last humans to see this city were those that defied that edict and came away with horrific nightmares. Some of those, she'd heard, took their own lives rather than live with whatever they saw.

What had happened to them? The stories they told couldn't be true. Iridosians had never been violent, never harmed any humans, as far as she knew. No one ever proved those stories wrong though.

And if the Iridosians saw her here now? Would they retaliate as they had done with Skalar's armada? Bellamy grinned at the idea.

She stepped farther out into the flattened valley. What had it looked like? How could they possibly have lived on the surface in these conditions? Here and there, darker smudges lurked in the gloom, probably the holes Walker had spoken of. How deep had the city's tunnels been? A shiver ran up her spine. Living in the dark, in tunnels below the surface— no thank you. The glistening vista of her own space, with its view of the sea and the cliff-walk in easy reach was the only place she wanted to live.

"Entry's over this way, ma'am." Walker gestured, then led the way.

Soon they reached the entrance to a tunnel and stepped in out of the wind. The howling sound followed them for a short distance, its haunting tone like the wails of Iridosian ghosts protesting the presence of intruders in this abandoned place. They followed the curving passage into the darkness, each step carrying them deeper into the heart of the ruined city.

Bellamy looked around. "This passage is almost clean."

"Of course. All our equipment had to go through here. Personnel too."

Yes, but wouldn't Crow's parting shots have dropped at least some of the ceiling here? She scanned the ceiling. Fresh scars marred the otherwise aged surface. Lips pursed, she gestured to Walker. "Let's go. Take it slow, though. I want to look around while we're here."

Walker talked as they went, most of her commentary unimportant. Irrelevant. Bellamy listened with one ear, the rest of her awareness tuned into their surroundings. Throughout the huge initial cavern and the tighter passage beyond, floorspace lay mostly clear of obstruction. In the mine, Bellamy stared at the honeycombed wall, enlarging and brightening the image through her visaug as much as possible. It looked just as Walker had described. Here, too, the floor was cleaner than she'd expect for such a place, especially given the armada's presence and abrupt departure.

Yes. This would do. Tight ore passages spoke to the small size of Iridosians, and Bellamy's lips curled up at the thought of Crow's people hunkered there, struggling through the extraction process. It wasn't as though the machines could extricate the metal without manual assistance. It must have been incredibly uncomfortable for those people Crow sent down here. Her smile faded. She'd need workers for this job, but not any of the adults from her current stock. In these tight spaces, children would be a better fit. And they'd be less of a threat to any overseers. Harder to find, though. She'd have to put the word out on their way to Zebalu in order to have a ready workforce waiting. No big mining gear. They'd need a light source. Her setup team could search for whatever power source the Iridosians had used. Wind, probably, assuming that Crow's blasts hadn't destroyed any generators. It would be a damned shame if they had. Setting up her own generators would be more problematic, not to mention the evidence it would leave behind. Better to use the resources on hand.

Walker showed her around to other areas the armada's crew had already investigated and, when they encountered passages that had been blocked after the armada's attack, they ventured beyond to explore together. Here, too, little debris littered the walkways. Instead, neat piles of rock punctuated the perimeter of larger spaces. In the smaller chambers and corridors, where her headlamp could reach the ceiling, numerous cracks and fissures betrayed structural damage dealt by the Consortium armada. How long before that, too, came down?

Walker had been right about one thing. The hematium was really the only thing of value here, at least as far as she could see. A larger orbital survey might reveal more, but she doubted it. Other ores and materials were available elsewhere. And if the Iridosians had access to any other unique resources the humans wanted, they'd have traded it before now.

"I've seen enough," Bellamy said. "Take us to the surface."

Walker nodded, passing Bellamy on the way toward the exit.

Between the gravity and the cumbersome suit, Bellamy's breath came harder than usual, like after a good, long session with one of her pleasure house gents, only without the fun parts. She couldn't wait to get aboard the Mirovia and start toward home.

They walked a while longer until, ahead, the mournful wind drew closer. Bellamy stopped. Walker continued a few paces before she turned.

"Ma'am? Is everything okay?"

"I'm just weighing my options, Commander. You said the Iridosians had some sort of weapon, took out several of your ships. Survivors are not good news for me or my plans for this place."

"We don't know there were survivors, ma'am."

"Then where are the bodies of the dead?"

Walker blinked behind her visor. "Bodies?"

"Yes. And who cleared the passages you say were blocked during the Consortium's presence here, or cleaned away the debris from the armada's final attack? I don't imagine Crow had his people move the rockfall into neat stacks when he was running an op that was, according to your report, problematic enough already."

"I—" Walker swallowed. "Maybe they're all down below, beyond where we stopped."

"Unlikely."

"Even if some did survive, there couldn't have been many, ma'am. We saw no squib ships when we were here, but like I said, it's possible one of their pilots brought them all out. They'll show up at one of the colonies sooner or later."

"That does not help me, Commander. How can I know for sure they won't make trouble for me? Why would I risk Iridosians pointing fingers at me or my faction, should they discover what I'm doing?"

"I don't think they would, ma'am. They're a greater threat to Skalar right now. They'd have to know his people would take them out if they expose themselves like that."

Walker's dark face gleamed in the spotlight of Bellamy's headlamp, and Bellamy smiled. "Well. It isn't something I need to think about right now. Shall we?" She gestured toward the exit and Walker turned to lead the way.

Bellamy closed the gap between them, grabbed Walker's helmet from behind, and pulled it back, exposing the throat of Walker's suit. The commander stiffened, already reacting, but before she could speak, Bellamy's blade sliced through the suit, cartilage, nerves, and arteries.

Blood sprayed the passage in an arc as Bellamy flung the dying meat aside. Walker thrashed, eyes wide, mouth gaping, gagging. Her hands fluttered at the wound while her heels tap danced on the floor as if she were struggling to get up. Blood spurted toward the tunnel's ceiling and sprayed the inside of Walker's faceplate as well as the passage to either side.

A thick, red mist spattered against Bellamy's visor, and she moved out of reach. When the fountain slowed and almost stopped, she squatted beside Walker's body and leaned close.

"You already betrayed one faction, Commander. I would never be sure of your loyalty."

Walker's eyes shifted toward her, her mouth opening and closing like they were on an airless moon. Another minute and she stopped.

Bellamy rose and wiped one hand across her visor, then scrubbed her palm across her suit and turned away. The return trek to the ship was easier with the wind behind her. So many choices! She could send an expendable workforce to take the hematium for the Cartel, probably the most likely scenario. But others paraded through her mind as well. She could blackmail Skalar, threaten to turn him over to the authorities. Everyone would love a shot at Skalar, but then he would have more than his usual reasons to kill her at the first opportunity. She could just turn him in for the satisfaction of finally beating him and removing him from the competition. The Cartel would take the number one faction spot, something she'd deserved for a long time now.

She frowned. If she did that, someone else would end up in control of the hematium, which would not benefit the Cartel in the long run.

As she approached the ship a smile crept across her face. Why not do both? Take the hematium and then turn him in? Skalar's plan to continue delivery of the metal to the colonies through drones was sound. What a nice source of bonus income for the Cartel, for a while anyway. The colonies would one day discover the ruse but until they did, Bellamy could salt the ruins with Consortium evidence. Between that and the Clan ship debris in orbit, she could inflict damage on two of her competitors at once and enjoy the fallout from a safe distance.

She touched her wristcom. "Rook, open the hatch. Set course for Zebalu."

The hatch hissed open, and Bellamy stepped inside. There was no rush. She had three days to think it over. Plenty of time to decide. She grinned and closed the hatch.

chapter 23

New Canaan, Harajüd
<u>**Landport Station**</u>

THRACE STALKED THE MAIN CONCOURSE on autopilot, her mind on the meetings ahead, either of which could go terribly wrong. Her intention violated the most sacred of all unammi taboos. If Rakalesh or any of the others learned of this action after the fact, they would kill Galen. Botha too. And Alira would be none too happy, either, when she realized her i'shin had tricked her.

Too bad. This was for Alira's own good. Thrace had deliberated on it for days, ever since she'd first sent the invitation. It wasn't until after Botha accepted that she'd known for sure she would go through with it. She had to. She had no choice.

She rounded a corner and there he was, his tall form ambling toward her from his ship's corridor. Close-cropped hair hugged his head and spread over his jaw. Lights on the concourse lit the red hues in his leathery brown skin and shimmered in the gold knot that pierced his earlobe. Thrace stopped, her heart hammering, her hands gripping each other as though she were about to face a horrific enemy, instead of a dear friend.

What would he say? How would he react? For all she knew, he would turn around and go back home. She couldn't blame him if he did. Galen had been lying to him in one form or another for years.

He looked up and met her gaze, recognition coloring his expression. He didn't wear the warm smile he would give Tenzin. Instead, his face closed. She could feel his guard go up from where she stood. Understandable. He didn't know her. At least, he didn't think he did.

Thrace hesitated. Maybe this was a mistake. Maybe—

No. She had to do this. For Alira. For her people.

Botha came to a stop before her, where he offered a slight bow, hands pressed together before his broad chest.

"Wanneer geesgenote ontmoet, is daar vreugde." His resonant voice rumbled in low tones, his green eyes never leaving her face.

Thrace's throat tightened. *Where spirits meet, there is joy.* She needed to soften the formality here, add a touch of familiarity, perhaps a foreshadowing of the revelation she was about to provide. She brought her hands up to mirror his own, her gaze locked on his. "En ou vriende stel die hart gerus." *Old friends ease the heart.*

His features reflected surprise. "You know our patois."

"I know much about you, Baba."

"It must be true. I do not often leave Bejami." He looked around, shaking his head, then faced her again. "Your cities move too fast. Yet your comm charmed me from my burrow like a pyshta does a fryt." Botha paused. "You used words I spoke only to a lost friend who has vanished into the sky. My bones are troubled. Tell me why I have come."

"We can't speak here."

"We can speak anywhere," he observed. "But I think you want only my ears to feast on your news. Yes?"

She couldn't stop the smile that leapt to her face. She had missed this human so! "Yes. I want to take you to a public house, but we can speak without risk in my skimmer. Will you come?"

He raised his eyebrows. "Did you think I would say no after traveling so far?"

Thrace laughed. "This way, then."

She led him through the building and out to her vehicle, then left the port behind and drove away from the city. Botha sat silent in his seat, eyes staring out the window of the craft as if taking in the scenery. But he was also undoubtedly waiting to find out what was going on. Botha would wait forever, if he must. Based on Thrace's message, he had to know this involved Tenzin. He wouldn't have come otherwise.

What should she say first? How far should she go in her explanations? A piece of the story would be insufficient. She'd need to tell it all. But where to go? This conversation needed focus, not the distraction of a moving craft. Just beyond the outskirts of New Canaan, not far from the landport, lay a small overlook where travelers could sit and watch the sunset over Mari Bay. There might be a few others there, but the layout of the area would allow an oblique angle, enough to keep anyone from following their conversation.

They reached the small park just before midday, and Thrace chose a spot in the shade of a young annulus tree close to the bluff's edge, away from the other tourists. Pleasure boats dotted the surface of the bay, their colorful sails and banners snapping in a breeze that did not reach the park. She shut down the craft and stared across the water, willing her lips to speak. When she turned toward her visitor, he was watching her.

"Your brow is as furrowed as mine, Captain Baldric," he murmured. "I do not want to ask, though my heart knows already. This is about Tenzin, isn't it?"

"Yes," she whispered. "But it isn't what you think. Tenzin is unharmed."

He closed his eyes, took a breath and let it out in slow measure. "I am glad to hear it. Now tell me the rest."

Her mouth drew into a tight line. Now that it was time, she still didn't know what to say.

"Baba," she said, "what do you know of the unammi?"

He frowned. "They are friends to Admiral Rizzo. I am told they prize their seclusion even more than do the Bregainans. This makes me like them already, but I have never met one."

Thrace took a deep breath. "Yes. You have."

Botha watched her, his frown deepening, his features twitching. Then his brow cleared. His eyes widened.

Her breath came a little faster. Did he understand? What would he say?

"Then," he said, "Tenzin…"

"Is unammi," she finished for him.

Outside the skimmer, tourist children stood squealing at the rock wall, pointing to the gulls over the bay. Someone called out, laughed.

Her friend turned to look out the windshield. "I see him better now."

"There is more."

Botha looked at her again.

"His birth name is Galen. Tenzin's face and persona are one of many Galen has used over his years among humans so that he might pass unnoticed. But the last time Tenzin left Bregaina, he arrived at the Bel-Rhovan landport to find humans searching Galen's ship."

"You said he was unharmed."

"Galen is fine. He is healthy and well. But for all intents and purposes, Tenzin is gone. He escaped only because the humans hadn't connected him to Galen. By now, they may have. If he shows Tenzin's face again, he risks discovery. This ability to assume human form is a secret the unammi do not want shared. If they knew I was telling you, we would both be dead."

He stared at her for a long time, his eyes moving over her seated form, taking in every detail. When he met her gaze again, he squinted into her face and winked. "They won't learn it from me, Galen."

Thrace exhaled, her body going slack. A smile stretched her mouth, and she dropped her chin to her chest. Her hands unclenched, fingers pale and throbbing from lack of blood flow.

"Much of what you have said before comes clear now," Botha said. "But Tenzin is only the bridge that brought me here. He is not the reason you commed. This is about your lover. Her trouble is deeper now?"

Thrace nodded. "I told you her refusal to conform stirred contention among our people, that our leaders planned to take the decision out of her hands. We call it 'mitigation,' an enforced loss of her Self, one over which she had no control. But the way things are going now, a more pernicious loss will be by her own choice, a result of misguided actions she took for all the right reasons. And that's if she even…." Thrace's voice pinched, and she cleared her throat. "If she lives long enough for that to happen."

Botha smiled. "You cannot drop me in the middle of the flood and expect me to find the shore. Take me to the beginning and walk with me from there."

Of course, he was right. So much to tell…the fall of Iridos, Alira's unique ability, the unammi's new home, Alira's determination to keep them safe. Thrace took another deep breath and began.

chapter 24

New Canaan, Harajüd
<u>**Mountain View Park**</u>

THRACE HAD RUN OUT OF words minutes ago, yet Botha remained silent. Her hands clutched one another again. Sunbeams slanted through the tree in dappled spots of light and shadow across the front of the skimmer. The tourists around them had left, and new ones had arrived.

Botha took a deep breath, then let it out slowly. "Your home is destroyed, its waters fouled. Your people sailed to a new world, and they now live in fear of discovery. Your woman stands between them and your enemy, wearing the skin of your people's butcher and carrying the souls of everyone she's killed to protect this secret. She cannot stop them from invading her mind, and you fear she is no longer whole. Have I gathered all the fish in one net?"

She nodded. Botha always had a knack for packaging confusion into a neat bundle.

"And you want me to throw her a rope."

Thrace sighed. "I've tried to point out the danger. She saw it, in the beginning. But I'm not sure she understands, now, how close to the edge she walks."

"Whether or not she makes it through this, I honor her courage. Few would step into the jungle, wave a fist at the canopy above her head and dare the screeching lênask to eat her. Even with her back to a tree, she would never be safe." He shook his head. "When we spoke last, you said she wanted only to wear her true face. Now she has tied a rock to that Self and thrown it off the dock into the mud."

"I know her intentions are good, but she cannot win this. It's hard enough for her to control her harvests without having to constantly be someone she's not. If she falls, our enemies will tear her to shreds. I need her to see the truth of that."

"You have told her this?"

"As I said, many times."

"She does not hear you."

"No. She thinks she is in control."

"She is like a moth whose wings have carried her straight to a flame." He held out his large hands, palms up. "I will do what I can, but your heart knows the truth already, my friend. She may be too burned to save."

Thrace laid her own hands atop his. "All I ask is that you try."

"Then let us start now. Where is this woman of yours?"

Thrace's brows rose. "Now? You don't want to rest first?"

Botha shrugged. "I can sleep after I die."

Thrace touched her wristcom and waited.

"Skalar."

"Admiral, I need to see you. Now. At Dagons."

Pause. "I'm busy, Captain. Can't it wait?"

"No, sir. It's important."

Longer pause. "Very well. Thirty minutes. Skalar out."

Thrace started the skimmer and turned toward the city. She cast a glance toward Botha. "What do you know of Skalar?"

"The old one?" he winked. "Tales brought by visitors say he is cruel, cold, manipulative."

"He was. That's what makes all this so difficult for Alira. She is none of those things, but as long as she wears his face and carries his memories, she must be who he was. There was a time I could tell you what to expect from a meeting with her." Thrace shook her head. "I'm afraid I can't now. She—rather, he—constantly shocks and surprises me."

"That thought brings no smile to your face."

Thrace kept her eyes on the road. "If I knew any other way to help her, I wouldn't involve you. I can't promise you this meeting will go well. Alira is convinced she does not need anyone's help. I've told her you were coming. At one point she was receptive to the idea. The next time I mentioned it, she said she'd changed her mind and didn't want to see you. Alira—Skalar—may say awful things, or even threaten you. I don't believe she would actually harm you. She knows how much you mean to me. Even so, I would advise caution."

Botha said nothing, and after a moment Thrace stole a look at him. He stared ahead, watching the scenery as they reentered New Canaan and began to work their way toward the city center.

"Where would she go," he asked when they were halfway to their destination, "if she walked away from this life?"

"She… She would…"

"That is what you want," Botha said, "yes?"

"I just want her to be safe. This life can't give her that."

"Yet you've not considered her aftermath?"

"I've been preoccupied." Thrace huffed. "We both have. Na'Staani has granted few untroubled moments in the last few months. I suppose I expected we would figure it out together once we got away from here."

"'We,'" Botha repeated. "You expect to share her decision, then."

"Of course."

Botha nodded, saying nothing.

"Why?"

He gazed out the window. "Wounded animals do not seek the company of others. They tend to bite."

Thrace frowned. "We aren't animals."

Botha turned toward her. "Aren't we?"

We. Humans and unammi. Thrace blinked. She hadn't told him of the connection between their races.

"She is your mate," he said. "You fear for her. You want to protect her. That is the way of things. But some beings will never yield, my friend. If she is past the reach of my rope, you may have to let her go."

"Maybe," Thrace whispered. She cleared her throat and tried again. "I'm not ready to concede that yet. I must try to help her. I think she would want that."

"The Alira of before, perhaps. But this one is a river on a new course. You can't use the old map."

Thrace drove the rest of the way in silence. Once inside Dagons, she waved off the wait staff, led Botha upstairs to the Consortium's private table, and sat facing the door, hands clenched in her lap. Botha glanced at the patrons around them, then peered across the table at her.

"Where will you go if she is lost? What will you do?"

"I haven't thought that far ahead," she murmured.

"Perhaps you should."

Thrace's features puckered. Where indeed? Perhaps the outpost, for access to irolium, since Galen couldn't join the survivors on Earth. Of course now, he could carry the irolium with him wherever he went. What would it be like to live a solitary life, away from the unammi or the Consortium? New idents and a supply of credits would be no problem. He—

Muscles in Thrace's shoulders tightened into knots. Her hands clutched each other. Breath caught in snatches and her attention shot to the front entry.

"He's here."

Botha shifted in his seat and looked toward the door.

The moment the door closed behind him, Skalar glanced up at his corner and, for a moment, froze. Thrace held her breath as Skalar's eyes shifted from Thrace to Botha, and his jaw worked. Chatter and laughter and the rattle of the cage lift faded as she met his stare. Would he leave?

He'd better not.

His feet moved again, bringing him around the bar to the right and she lost sight of him until he appeared at the head of the stairs. His eyes never left hers as he strode toward them in a straight line. Others moved out of his way, staring at him before resuming their prior conversations.

At the table, Skalar stopped, still fixed on her face. "You brought a stranger to my table."

Thrace gestured. "This is Botha. I've told you—"

"And I told you I don't need a guru."

"Just…talk to him. Please."

"About what? The weather?"

A hot spike shot through Thrace, threading its way to her brain. She jerked to her feet and leaned close to Skalar. "I've done everything you asked. *Everything.* I am on your side, Admiral. But your plan is falling apart, and you know it. If you don't get help soon, no one will be able to save you. I refuse to stand by and watch that happen, so if you aren't going to speak to Botha, you tell me now."

Skalar leaned even closer to his second. "Why? What will you do about it?"

She held his gaze a moment. Her lips formed into a thin line.

"If you don't let him in, let him try to help, you'll have to manage your faction without me. Thank you for coming, Botha," she said. "Comm me later. After."

chapter 25

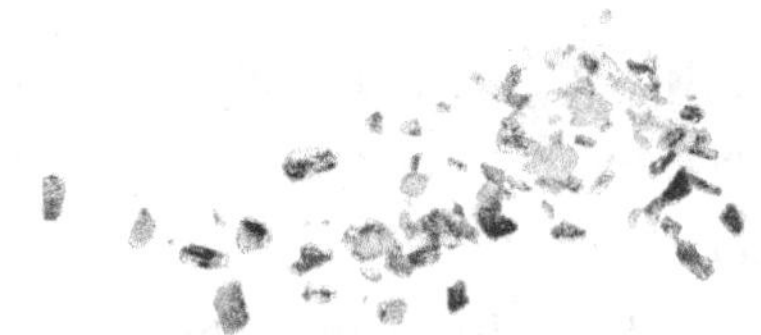

New Canaan, Harajüd
<u>Dagons Public House</u>

SKALAR NARROWED HIS EYES AS Thrace departed. What the actual fuck was she up to?

> *watch it, crow. you're stepping on my toes.*

Other voices murmured in his head, and he squeezed his eyes closed

> *shut up, all of you.*

before turning to the table. Botha looked at him. No smile. No frown. No expression at all, really. Who the hell did Thrace think she was, forcing him into this encounter?

> *she thinks she is your i'shin, that you're losing yourself. she's right.*

> *she's wrong.*

Skalar activated privacy, then lowered himself to a chair, and crossed his legs. "Thrace believes I need you."

Botha smiled. "So does Galen."

Skalar scowled. "What do you know of that name?"

"I know another, as well. Shall I speak it aloud?"

"Not if you know what's good for you."

"Why not? Names have power. Alira understood this when she took yours." Botha winked. "She learned too late, I think, that names also bind."

"You know nothing about this," Skalar said through gritted teeth. "It's dangerous to assume you do. The light of Thrace's explanations will never penetrate this darkness. You should go home."

"Shadows do not frighten me, Admiral."

Skalar's lip curled at the slight emphasis on his title. "This one should."

A deep chuckle rumbled out of Botha's chest. "Do threats free your path of every stone?"

"No threats," Skalar whispered. "Only warnings. Thrace cares what happens to you. I don't like upsetting her."

"Then stop."

Skalar frowned. "What?"

"It is a simple enough suggestion. Stop hurting Thrace."

"I'm not—"

"But you are," Botha said. "Every time you endanger Alira."

Breath hissed in through Skalar's lips. "I warned you."

"I remember. I promised Thrace I would throw you a rope."

A sharp croak that passed for laughter burst from Skalar's throat. "Is that what you're doing now?"

Botha shrugged. "I am still gauging your distance."

"From what? You?"

"From sanity."

The waiter approached the privacy screen, a question on his face. Skalar waved him off and focused on this upstart before him. What did Thrace see in this human? She'd said he glimpsed the heart of things, but thus far Skalar had seen nothing to support that claim.

could be you missed it. wouldn't be the first time you ignored what was right in front of your face.

be quiet, ijydin.

It was Ijydin, wasn't it? After she'd died in Alira's arms, crushed by that rock fall in the unammi city, Ijydin's voice should have been carved forever in Alira's memories. After all, it was Ijydin's harvest, the piloting knowledge therein, that got Alira into Skalar's skin in the first place.

But it was hard to tell the reapings apart anymore.

irrelevant.

shut up, skalar.

can't do that if i'm driving.

Skalar peered at Thrace's guru. "Brave, aren't you? Easy to do in a public house with dozens of witnesses. I wonder how your tone would change if we were alone."

"You cannot escape witnesses when you are never alone. Alira understands that, too, though she doesn't yet know it."

shut him up.

"That's enough," Skalar said, bristling.

"Yes," Botha said. He stood. "It is. Fishes could swim through that hole in your boat, yet you ignore the gash. If you persist, you will drown. Who will protect your people then?" He nodded and turned to go.

"You haven't been dismissed yet."

Botha's upper body twisted as he walked through the privacy screen. "You should decide. Soon," he said.

Skalar's jaw slacked. Had the man just insulted him and walked away? A quick glance confirmed others had seen this exchange, their curious eyes riveted on his reaction. If he went after Botha, he would look weak, needy. Better to let him go and decide later what to do about his disrespect.

He shut his eyes. When had he last felt relaxed? Probably on the ship from Earth. With Galen. Before Alira had taken the Consortium onto her shoulders, along with all those harvests. He imagined being on that ship again, flying to a place where no one knew him, where Alira and Galen could be together without all this drama, where she could finally be free.

and where is this magical realm?

shut up.

He massaged the back of his neck, the muscles there rigid, immovable, as though they'd been carved from stone. Botha was right about one thing. He needed to fix this, but that wasn't news. He'd been trying to make it right all along, but it just kept getting worse. Maybe he needed to try something new. Something different. Except…

…except he had no idea what.

He heaved a sigh and opened his eyes. Nearby patrons looked away, as though they hadn't been staring.

Skalar deactivated privacy and headed for the door, frowning. He had expected this to get easier with practice, even thought he might be getting better at it. He'd been wrong.

chapter 26

Tuneloras, Saacharis
<u>Syndicate Trader Base, Officer's Mess</u>

RIZZO SPOONED THE LAST SOLIDS from her soup into her mouth, then tipped the bowl and drank its broth. In the ten days since Reyes visited her shower, the Syndicate had begun "upgrades" to the sensors in Gauri Metalb. Installations continued, but footage from the extra hardware already fed into receivers on the Syndicate base and was being logged by trusted crew. So far, the children who started this had not reappeared. Understandable. They'd have been cleared out to keep the Syndicate from learning of their involvement, but it was only a matter of time before Michels and his supporters brought them back.

She took her dishes to the counter and exited the mess. Killing Michels wouldn't stop the slaving, but once he stood in her shower, he'd name others. Then she could take the next step toward pinching off the supply at its source. She'd make it so dangerous and expensive that those involved would decide it wasn't worth their while.

Ahead, Bailey came around the corner and paused, then fell into step as Rizzo passed.

"There's an urgent report waiting in your office."

"Who?"

"Unknown. No name or site tags other than Pelarr, Zebalu."

"Tell me."

Bailey shook her head. "It's coded for your voice alone, ma'am. I couldn't view it."

Pelarr. Likely a Cartel contact, but this wasn't their normal protocol. Rizzo frowned. News, perhaps. She'd tasked all their resources there with finding more info on the Cartel slave deal, but it seemed too soon for that.

The lift arrived and crewmen exited just as she approached. Rizzo stepped on with a gesture for Bailey to follow. Moments later they entered the admiral's office.

"TICS," Rizzo said, "display all incoming messages from Zebalu, Pelarr, this date." She viewed the brief display without sitting down. There, near the bottom. "Receive and play third communique."

Hushed, hurried words hissed through the TICS, unaccompanied by any holovid.

"I just found out the city on Iridos has been destroyed, bombed flat, no survivors."

Rizzo's face stiffened. She glanced at Bailey, who'd gone paler than usual.

The message continued. "Don't know who did it or when." Sounds in the background, maybe market noise? Public comm unit, then. "Wasn't Bellamy. She heard it somewhere else. One of her informers maybe? Word is she just came from there and it's true. She plans to keep the secret and mine the hematium. I knew you'd want to know." A shout from nearby, and a garbled response from the Syndicate plant. "Gotta go. I'll send more details when I can." The comm went dead.

The Iridosian city, gone. No more unammi pilots to light the shadows. It had been months since any of them had come to the Syndicate. This would explain why they hadn't been around. Still, if she understood unammi customs correctly, the pilots lived in the human colonies, not on Iridos. So surely those who weren't in the city would have survived unless—

—Unless whoever flattened the city wanted no complaints later. That meant there was probably something there on Iridos to indicate who did this.

"Genocide," Bailey said, her voice shaking. "Why? Who—"

"I don't know. Yet." Rizzo curled her lips into a snarl. She came around the desk and headed for the door, Bailey in her wake. "Prep my ship. I want to leave in two hours."

"Iridos, I presume."

Rizzo kept walking.

"I thought the unammi wanted no humans on their world," Bailey said. "You told me we should respect that."

Rizzo slid into the corridor, her mind already three steps ahead. "If they're unharmed, I won't land. If not, it won't matter."

Bailey nodded.

"Send word to our unammi contacts. Try to verify this information. If they respond or if we receive further word regarding the Iridos situation after I've gone, forward to my ship. Follow through on the Gauri Metalb matter, recon only. Take no action. Expect a report from our Cartel partners with further details."

"Understood, ma'am." Bailey kept up with Rizzo's swift pace but hung back at the lift as Rizzo stepped inside. "How long will you be gone?"

"Unknown. Carry on." The lift doors closed. Rizzo shut her eyes, her blood running cold. Faces flashed through her mind, the few pilots she'd met. All dead? Ijydin had described the unammi city to her once, how the domes all joined in a network of shelters to connect one ridge to another. How each dome had housed differing aspects of unammi daily life, and how the city's blue light shone through the glass to twinkle like stars in the seat of the valley. Ijydin's words painted images of luminescent plant and animal life, the blind minnows and marine life alight even in the depths of their reservoirs. She'd evoked the wail of the wind inside the tunnels or through the canyon, and the struggle to make a gathering run to groves or mines outside the unammi's sheltered space.

So many times, Rizzo had envisioned it, but she'd never thought to see it firsthand. Unammi pilots had dealt with her, a couple even approached friendship, or as close as she would allow. Yet she knew the unammi's overall opinion of humans. To some degree, she even shared it. Now that she might get an opportunity to walk that city herself, she wished the chance had never come. If she set a foot on Iridosian soil, it would mean the unammi were all dead.

The lift doors opened, and she moved toward her quarters to pack. She had no reason to doubt her contact, but this was something she needed to see for herself, despite the enormous risk. From Saacharis, Iridos was a four-plus-day journey. Bellamy's world lay closer. If she planned to take advantage of the situation, she would do so as soon as she could muster the gear and personnel, slaves most likely. Rizzo would have to move fast to get there and get out before the Cartel returned with a crew.

Rizzo's door opened and she swept inside without slowing down. New images began to grow in her mind, replacing Ijydin's word paintings with visions of collapsed domes, rotting bodies and a dead city. For once, just this once, she hoped her sources were wrong. Because if it was true—

Well. If it was, she would find out who was responsible and, when she did, no punishment would suffice.

chapter 27

Pelarr, Zebalu
<u>Cartel Trader Base, Landing Bay</u>

"YOU HAD SIX DAYS, HANNAH." Bellamy sneered, gesturing toward the cargo. "This is the best you could do?"

"There are more, ma'am, but these are the only ones we found that fit your size parameters. I can bring the others out for your inspection, if you wish, but—"

"No. Never mind," she said. She focused on one of the other two officers. "Commander Jude, you understand your task?"

Jude shifted from one foot to the other. "I do, ma'am."

"I know it won't be glamorous," Bellamy said, leaning closer and speaking in a conspiratorial tone. "I know it will seem forever, but you'll only be there maybe two, two and a half months. You'll return to an enormous bonus and a promotion, all of you. That's worth twelve weeks of isolation with your crew, managing a pack of brats, isn't it?"

"Yes, ma'am," Jude said.

"Of course it is. We can't do this with manual labor indefinitely anyway. Skalar paid good credits for this batch and one other, but even both factions working together couldn't snatch an endless supply of children without being caught. It's going to take a couple of months to work out automation for the process using equipment that can't be traced to the Cartel. In the meantime, work them as hard as you can and mine as much metal as possible. I expect they'll last maybe three weeks, at which time I'll send another group. When their three weeks are up, get rid of them to free up space for the new ones. I'll make it worth your while, just like I promised."

"How, ma'am? Won't that leave bodies the new children will see?"

Bellamy shrugged. "Iridos has its own fierceness. You could let the planet do the work for you. As long as they don't become a problem, I don't care. I'll leave it to your imagination."

"Yes ma'am."

"Good." Hands on her hips, Bellamy stared at the rag-tag group Hannah had collected. Thirty-three children between twelve and sixteen years gaped at her. Snatched from various locations on Zebalu over the last week, all were too fresh to the slave trade to know better than to meet their owners' eyes. No matter. It wouldn't take long to fix that. She made a beeline for the group, allowing her mouth to sneer in just the right way so that most of the brats looked away, down at their feet.

All but one. A girl. A ripe peach, too, maybe fifteen. Shame to waste her on Iridos, but the job needed hands. Simple math, really. Bellamy sidled closer, widening her jackal's grin. "You're a bold one, aren't you? What's your name, honey?"

"Why?" The girl sneered. "We gonna be friends or somethin'?"

Bellamy's backhand landed the girl on the floor, blood oozing from a cut where her lip met her teeth on the way down. She pushed herself up onto her elbows, touched a finger to her lip and glared up at her captor.

"Not especially. No. Names are only useful as labels. For the moment, I'm going to call you Stella," Bellamy said cheerily, still grinning as she strolled past the other children, running gentle fingers through another girl's hair while the child flinched. "And we'll call this one Jane."

The admiral yanked Jane up by her hair and slit her throat in one smooth move, then dropped her to the bay floor. Most of the children gasped and backed away, their faces and clothing spattered with Jane's blood. Bellamy beamed at Stella, whose eyes had gone wide. "Here's the thing. I don't really care who you are. But you should remember who I am. Being difficult buys you nothing, Stella. Other people will pay the price."

Bellamy pointed to Jane and smiled at the other children.

"This is Stella's fault. From here on, you should know that it's in your best interest to keep each other in line so that you will come out of this with all your parts in good working order. Right?"

None of the children looked at her now. Even Stella studied the floor.

"Get up, Stella. Dust yourself off."

The girl did as she was instructed but did not meet the admiral's eyes.

Bellamy sighed. "I have to be honest with you, though. Jane's probably better off. I'm sending you all to do a job. The work is hard, and the location is dangerous. Irradiated. Do as you're told and behave, and you'll get plenty of food and water, and proper meds to be sure you don't get sick. Once you get home, we'll turn you loose. You'll be completely free. On the other hand, if you act out like Stella here, none of you get the meds or the food or the water. We'll leave you there to die, bring in a fresh team, and start again. Am I clear?"

No one said a word. Bellamy beckoned Jude over.

"Good. Then I leave you in Commander Jude's capable hands. She and her crew will instruct you in how to do the work. They will be the ones to oversee your efforts and to administer food and meds. If you want to see Zebalu again, you'll do whatever it takes to make them happy."

She glanced over her shoulder. "Put them in cargo bay three."

Jude's team hurried to comply. Bellamy turned to Rook. "The supplies are loaded?"

"Yep. Saw to it myself, ma'am." She kept her tone low, hiding her lisp as best she could even in safe company. Ridicule was a strong motivator. Bellamy knew that better than anyone, though perhaps her own response to it had been more extreme than most. Images of her brothers and her father flashed through her mind, gone so quickly she could almost believe they were never there.

"Any other questions?" she said to Jude.

"No ma'am. Keep the workers in line, mine as much as possible, dispose of bodies as necessary."

"That's correct. Off you go." Bellamy said.

Jude headed for her ship.

"And Commander," Bellamy called after her, "maintain radio silence. I don't expect any other ships to approach, but let's not give anyone a reason to do so."

"Yes, ma'am." Jude continued to her ship, and the hatch closed behind her.

Bellamy turned to Rook. "You checked the radiation meds for Jude and her crew? Sugar pills for the children?"

Rook nodded, her face blank. "Jude knows the difference, I hope."

"So do I, Captain, but in the long run, it won't matter. When this job is over and the last slaves are dealt with, it'll be your job to handle Jude and her people. No witnesses."

"No problem, ma'am."

"Good. Dismissed."

Rook walked away, her short red hair gleaming in the lights of the landing bay. Apparently, the woman never touched it with a brush. It always looked like she'd just crawled out of bed. Trophies, small baubles taken from some of Rook's more colorful kills, adorned the long vest she liked to wear. This collection wasn't the oddest thing about her, but it did earn her the nickname she now wore with pride.

Hannah stepped up beside her. "You think Jude's people will spread the rumor about Skalar?"

"They probably already have. By the time we send our next shipment, word will have reached eager ears in Harajüd House security, I have no doubt."

"So, I should start another search?"

"Mmm hmm." Bellamy nodded, still watching the ship prepare for departure. "Three days there, three weeks on Iridos. That gives you twenty-one days." She threw Hannah a glance. "Pull from Harajüd, this time. New Canaan, if possible. And get whatever mining equipment we need from there, too. Let's pile on the implications so thick Skalar will never wiggle out."

chapter 28

New Canaan, Harajüd
<u>Dagons Public House</u>

SKALAR PUSHED THROUGH THE DOOR into the pub, ignoring the patrons who moved away. He was used to it by now. Besides, his mind was upstairs, on the meeting he approached. He resisted glancing up at the gallery. Botha would be there. Thrace would not. She had insisted he speak to Botha again before the elder left for Bejami. She was probably right to be worried. In his clearer moments, when the voices grew still for a moment, Alira knew she was struggling. Was this how the harvesting sickness began?

Skalar veered right, carving a path through the crowd toward the wide spiral staircase. Partiers lingered even there, oblivious to his approach until he was sliding past on his way to the gallery. Most of the humans in his head understood this need to fraternize, though Skalar and his unammi passengers did not. Unammi culture included social activities, but they were nothing like this. The noise level in Dagons was higher than usual, the crowd thicker, and Skalar winced. Bad enough to bear the constant internal screeching without subjecting himself to it here too.

He reached the gallery and turned left. Ahead, Botha waited, watching. Skalar inhaled, preparing himself to deal with this person Thrace held in such high regard.

be nice, skalar.

shut up, netzyl.

At the table, he took a seat and touched the order pad for water, activated the privacy screen, then raised his attention to the man across the table.

"Hello, Botha."

"Hello, Skalar. You are better today. No tempest brewing, I think."

Skalar's lips tightened. "How much of this do you know?"

"Seeing the stars in the night sky is not the same as knowing them." Botha shrugged. "I see that your skin is crowded, that you are teetering on the edge of a deep pit. I know that if you fall, my friend will fall with you."

"And you want to help."

Botha only smiled, and Skalar nodded.

"So, you think your rope will reach, then."

"We will see."

A waiter brought water for them both. When she was gone, Botha continued.

"I know what fish Thrace casts for. What do you hope to catch?"

Skalar looked away. Beyond his table and in the crowded room below, humans ate and drank together, laughing, enjoying each other's company. Both human and unammi leadership ensured their people had access to all the essentials—meaningful employment, decent shelter, healthy comestibles, recreational activities, appropriate clothing, competent healers. But despite good intentions, healthy social interaction and trusting relationships could not be given. They had to be pursued, constantly nurtured by the individuals who sought them.

He watched the humans around him. To all appearances, they seemed to be leading lives free from fear. They worked at colonial jobs, bonded with partners, raised children, formed families and communities. Such a simple treasure, yet so far beyond the grasp of Skalar, despite all his riches and power. Even among her own people, Alira could never have that.

Whispers murmured in his head, messages buried under the weight of so many harvests.

"I want a normal life."

Botha made an odd sound, and Skalar looked at him. "Is that too big a fish for my hook?"

"Wish for two heads while you're at it. The wait will be the same."

Skalar's heart sank. "You're saying it's impossible?"

"Whose normal? Mine?" Botha asked, then jerked his chin toward the patrons below. "Theirs?"

"Normal normal. Average normal. Everyday normal."

Botha leaned forward, elbows on the table. "Show me a normal boat."

Skalar scoffed. "That would depend on the boat's purpose."

Botha cocked his head.

"That isn't the same," Skalar said.

"You are a bird who wants to be a fish."

Skalar almost laughed. "Is that so wrong?"

"Not wrong. Just not possible. But," Botha held up one finger, "some birds do swim."

"What are you saying?"

"You already mingle with the fishes. Now," the elder peered at him, "you must learn to be at peace in both water and air."

"I have never known peace, old man." At least, Alira hadn't. Some of her harvests—Cesar, at least—had. What would that be like?

"Then it is about time you got acquainted, yes?"

Skalar shook his head, looked down at his hands. "You make it sound easy."

"It is once you understand its nature. Have you ever watched a fledgling fumble through its first flight?"

"No."

Botha laughed, a rich rumble that vibrated the air between them. "Most fly straight to the ground like a feathered rock. It takes practice to understand how their wings work with the air, to find a balance between up and down. Once they do, they can fly not just to feed or mate, but for pure joy. Peace is just the same. It is not a destination, but a state of mind, an acceptance, and an understanding."

Skalar looked up. "Of what?"

"Of yourself and how you fit into the world."

"But I don't." Skalar's words quavered, and he cleared his throat. "I never have."

"Because you do not understand or accept your Self."

"How can I do that when I don't even know who I am?"

Botha gestured toward him. "At this moment, you are Skalar."

"No. He is in here, yes, and I'm wearing his face. But I am not him. Not completely."

"Then who are you?"

Skalar blew a noisy breath. "I just said I don't know. Too many voices and memories and experiences compete for space in my head. I can't be just one or another."

"You are not alone in that." Botha nodded toward the humans beyond the privacy screen. "Every human is just the same. Every unammi, too, I expect. All our heads are filled with the past, though yours may speak louder than mine."

"It's not the same."

"I'm sure you are right," Botha said. "But even very different boats can be rowed in a similar way. You just need bigger oars."

All these analogies. Lurien would have liked this human. "I thought the Consortium would give me those."

"No. You thought it would give you bigger weapons."

"That too."

"You need both," Botha admitted. "But first you must balance your load."

"And we're back to peace."

"Guns won't help your people if your boat sinks."

Skalar shook his head. "Thrace will take over for me, if it comes to that." She would, wouldn't she? Alira had intended to speak to her about this very thing. They both knew things were not working out as planned. Alira needed assurance that the outpost would remain as a bastion of protection for the unammi survivors. For Trumo. His little face flashed through her thoughts, along with the feeling of the youngling's hug in the makeshift healer's cavern. That tender moment felt like seasons *years.*

ago.

"You would do that," Botha said, peering sideways at him, "even knowing what damage it could bring to Galen?"

Had the man not been listening? Skalar's jaw tightened. "We—" he said, then stopped himself.

calm down.

"We don't have a choice," he said in a more even-tempered tone. "The Consortium is all that stands between our people and extinction. I thought you understood that."

Botha sighed. "Then you must not fail. It is a rough tide beneath your boat. I don't envy you the journey, but I will help you. If I can."

"I'm not sure how, but you're welcome to try. You should know right up front I'm not the easiest person to work with."

"That I believe," Botha said.

chapter 29

New Canaan, Harajüd
Consortium Trader Base, Admiral Skalar's Office

MIRA COHEN'S UPPER BODY HOVERED in Skalar's holovid. Dark hair swung level with her chin and brushed across the top of her face, disheveled as if she'd run her hands through it seconds ago.

"My brother has turned up missing," she said, her voice tight. "Is he with you?"

"I beg your pardon. Were you speaking to me?"

She closed her eyes, then opened them. "Is he with you, *sir*?"

Skalar leaned back. "Why yes, as a matter of fact, Kisle is here on base just now. He's a lovely young man. Twenty-five years old, I believe. So much life ahead of him! Of course, one never knows what the future holds, does one?"

"Damn it, Skalar—sir—what do you want?"

"I want the same thing I've always wanted, Cohen. To be left alone to conduct business as I see fit. You and your crew have complicated matters."

Mira's gaze hardened. "Leave Kisle out of this. He's never been part of faction business, and I don't want him to be."

"You should have considered your family when you decided to make trouble for me."

"My people are angry right now, sir. They feel shut out, but I'll pull them off you. We—they won't bother you again. You have my word. Just let Kisle go."

Skalar's mouth twisted to one side. If only it were that easy. Open the door and let Kisle go free and all would be right with the world. Behind Mira's projection, Skalar eyed the bar. More specifically the bottle of high-end brandy that waited there. He closed his eyes, shook his head, and looked at her again. "Sorry. Can't."

Was he talking to himself? Or to Mira?

"Then what do you want?" she shouted.

i want out.

"I want you and your people to back so far off that I can forget for a while that you even exist. I want the name of whoever is trying to hang a slaver tag around my neck. I want you to find and stop them and anyone else making trouble for the Consortium, and I want you to send me their gift-wrapped heads. I want you to go out of your way behind the scenes to make my life easier."

"And then you'll let Kisle go?"

He scowled. "Please. Your brother is quite comfortable, installed in our best guest quarters. He and I are still getting to know one another. I'm not ready to say adieu just yet, but I will promise you this. As long as you clear the road ahead of me and keep your crew or anyone else out of my way, I'll ensure his stay is a pleasant one."

"And if we don't?"

"Then I can't make any guarantees, for him or the rest of your family."

"I want to speak to him."

"I don't think so, Commander. But you're welcome to visit him in person." His features melted into a grin. "Any time."

Mira's holoimage frowned, and he read in her face her sure knowledge that if she set foot on any of his bases, she would never leave again. Smart woman.

His comm chirped, and he nodded to Mira. "That's all the time I have for you, Cohen. End communique."

Her image disappeared.

"TICS, accept incoming comm."

"Admiral, Spencer Kilbee is here to see you, sir."

Skalar blinked. A pilot? So soon? "Very well. Send him up."

He rose and paced the length of the office toward the bar, then turned back. Maybe he should find something he could drink in place of the brandy. Some habits were hard to break.

At the window he stared out over the city. Morning sun winked on Mari Bay and the sea beyond, where HHU marine operations plied their trade on boats and floating platforms. The Consortium pursued business brought in by aquatic craft—shipbuilding and repair, seashells and residue, desalination—but those were minor profits. It could have been more, but Skalar never saw a need to grow that line of business. When he took over from his predecessor, he'd judged the expense too great. He never liked seafood anyway, and most resources they'd once garnered from oceanic operations had been easily—and more economically—purchased elsewhere. Still, even he enjoyed the sight of the water. It had a soothing quality, as long as his feet remained on solid,

solid! hah!

unmoving ground.

He thought about his meeting with Botha, two days ago, and a frown edged its way onto his brow. Perhaps Thrace was right and there was something to that human after all. Thrace was probably right about much more than that, but Skalar hadn't told her as much. Not yet. They'd been arguing more and more of late. He'd stayed away, kept her busy elsewhere as much as possible until he could figure things out. But he was glad he'd listened to her this time. Botha's provincial speech made for interesting conversation. Maybe one day when—if—this whole Consortium business was done and the unammi's safety guaranteed, he could sit down with the old man and talk about other, more pleasant topics.

The door comm chimed, and he called out entry, still gazing out the window.

"Nice view," Kilbee said.

"It will suffice." Skalar turned, gestured to a chair opposite his desk, then took his own seat. "It's been less than two weeks since Edanor brought the run to Harajüd. What's wrong?"

Kilbee slumped into a chair, his fingers laced together over his belly. Long legs stretched out before him, crossed at the ankles. "The council got a final verdict on the compromised vault containers."

"And?"

"They're shot."

"What percentage was lost?"

"Thirty-five, maybe forty."

Skalar closed his eyes, nausea welling up in his gut. The survivors needed those samples! Granted, the loss wouldn't kill them, but it would drastically cut the gene pool available to future generations. He opened his eyes.

"Very well. But why send the news with you? Any one of the pilots could have told me this. Unless you're here to tell me that they begged the outcasts to come home and start reintegrating into the new city."

"Not exactly."

"Then why are you here?"

Kilbee's lips puckered, his eyes fixed tight on Skalar's. "Rakalesh says Lurien's samples were among those lost."

Skalar's skin prickled. Without Lurien's samples, the council would need Alira to contribute genetic material to give the unammi another Founder's Daughter. He knew what would come next.

"She says you've had enough time to get settled. The council demands the recordings you promised, and a genetic sample from you. Immediately."

For a heartbeat, Skalar knew Rakalesh was right. Then his harvest's outrage surged through his mind, drowning all rationale.

"Demands? The council *demands*?" he growled, his voice rising with every word. "How *dare* they?"

Kilbee raised one eyebrow.

Skalar's blood pressure edged even higher.

"Rakalesh is in no position to *demand* anything," he shouted. "She's gotten so used to pushing her own agenda onto people around her that she expects us all to just submit and follow her every whim without question."

The irony of that accusation flashed through his mind—*him* accusing someone *else* of this—but reason was in the wind. Skalar leapt up. "Well, this time she's not speaking to Alira the rebellious cleric," he shouted. "She's speaking to Malcolm Skalar, Admiral of the Consortium Trader faction. I am the only thing standing between her pitiful city and total oblivion, and I've had quite enough of her orders. If she keeps pushing me, I might be forced to show her just how much she needs me."

Kilbee's lanky body unfolded, and he stood up. "What's that supposed to mean?"

Skalar stopped, breathing hard. "It means," he said in a lower tone, "that if she makes further commands like this one, I will close down the outpost and leave them undefended."

Kilbee paled. "You don't mean that."

"Try me."

The pilot's features hardened and he took a step. "This isn't like you, Alira."

"My name is Malcolm Skalar."

"You are Alira, daughter of Lurien and one of few surviving unammi, but you seem to have forgotten that."

Skalar stared into the other man's face. "I haven't forgotten anything. I don't want to harm the city. But I am tired of the council telling me what to do and what not to do. You know how that feels. That's why you became a pilot in the first place, isn't it?"

Kilbee winced. "Why do you say that?"

"Doesn't matter. It's true and we both know it. The council needs to understand that there is a limit to what we will take and how far we will go. The humans talk about a line in the sand. This is mine, Kilbee."

Shouts clashed in his head, chastising and praising, urging him to say even more, and Skalar pushed them away. He took a breath in the pause, then shook his head.

"I will send them a sample. But not on her whim. I will send it when I am damned good and ready and not before. And every single time they push it, their wish will be delayed. You tell Rakalesh that for me."

Kilbee stared, his jaw working as if he had something to say.

Skalar turned toward the window again. "You are dismissed, Mr. Kilbee."

chapter 30

On Iridos Approach
<u>Aboard the Kris Cross</u>

A CHITTERING ALERT SOUNDED IN the dim cabin.

"Report." Rizzo rubbed sleep from her eyes.

"Destination ahead," TICS responded.

"Very well. Assume low synchronous orbit over coordinates. Scan orbital plane, Iridosian city and surrounding area. Compile results." She half-heard the acknowledgement and sat a moment longer, head propped on one hand. Her bed, rumpled but cold, lay across the cabin from her warm chair where she'd pictured the worst all through her sleep period. She hoped to find the rumor wrong, to receive a chilly inquiry asking why she'd come and advising her to be on her way. The knot in her stomach said her hope would prove futile, that her dreaded imaginings lay on the surface below.

She pushed herself up and moved out of the cabin and down the passage to the small lift. In control, she sank into a seat.

"TICS, report."

"Debris field present in orbital plane."

"Identify."

"Wreckage of short-range ship, shuttle class, with one anomaly."

"Explain."

"One scrap of drive core, frigate class, located six-point-seven meters beyond debris field."

"Origin?"

"Unknown. No tracker data available."

"Very well. Continue listing debris in orbital plane."

"Organic matter detected."

"What kind of organic matter?"

"Human remains."

"Colony affiliation?"

"Unknown. No identifiable data."

"Whose ship?"

"Tracker indicates designation Danua. Registration, Clan ship DNCS-46925."

Clan. That supported the other name Reyes blabbed in her shower, but Rizzo still didn't believe it. Admiral Tsurin was small-time. She'd never reach this far. Surely the Clan did not possess the resources for a job like this. Besides, no captain capable of this sort of destruction would accidentally leave behind a tracker that would lead authorities directly to their door. This was a decoy. She could smell it.

TICS spoke up. "Orbital insertion in 3, 2, 1, set."

Rizzo felt the gradual shift in direction as the ship settled into orbit. "Results of surface scan?"

"Vegetation, animal, insect life signs only. No human or unammi life signs detected."

"What kind of animal life? Any large or venomous predators?"

"Unknown. No data available."

"Would surface layers block life sign readings underground?"

"Unknown. Unidentified geological content present in strata below seven hundred fifty meters."

"Comm Iridosian city."

Faces of the unammi she had known passed through her memory. Not friends, exactly. But if they were all gone—

"Communique sent. No reply."

"Very well. Surface conditions?"

"Gravity at 2.1. Oxygen levels within accepted parameters. No toxic gases present. Sustained wind speed at coordinates between 42 and 48 kph, with significant particle density. Surface integrity within coordinate boundaries unstable."

"Radiation?"

"Affirmative. Residual LADRAS radiation exceeds safe levels. Precautions advised."

LADRAS! Rizzo's face hardened. It wasn't just the theft of the unammi's hematium then. Whoever had done this feared discovery because any colony world under the Charter's direction would prosecute for offense against nature, the only crime punishable by death. It wouldn't matter that the atrocity happened on a non-charter world.

"TICS, show visual."

A fuzzy holograph rose from the display table, the surface in miniature. Visuals lacked detail, yet the scan left no doubt that the rumor of Iridos' demise was fact.

Her fingers gripped the edge of the table, warping the nearby edge of the visual.

"TICS, identify the closest safe spot to land and take us down. If we receive any communication from the surface, abort and notify me at once."

"Acknowledged."

Rizzo barged out of the control center and headed for the airlock. Reyes had also named Skalar. She'd doubted his connection to the slavery, but this? This she believed. This whole thing stank of him, though she knew he wouldn't have pulled the trigger himself. He'd want plausible deniability. Still, this couldn't have been the work of one ship, even a frigate. If Skalar had sent ships here, he was after something. Hematium, probably. He'd have sent a fleet. Haulers, personnel carriers, supplies, all the essentials.

But why? He could have just bought the hematium on the market, like everyone else. It didn't make any sense.

In the airlock, she popped a couple of rad meds, then stepped into a tight suit, working it up over her legs and hips. The ship landed with no thump on set-down. Only TICS could land a ship as softly as she could.

"Landing location nine hundred fifty-seven meters from coordinate boundary," TICS confirmed.

"Very well."

Rizzo shrugged the suit on and fastened the double closure. On the shelf above the suits lay mappers and small weapons, as well as fluid and protein pouches. She grabbed one of each, plugged in the water and nutrient pouches, checked the flow tubes, and set her mapper with proper coordinates, then pulled on her headgear, securing it to her suit. Now to get in and out before company arrived. This part of the rumor had proved true. No doubt about the rest of it. Bellamy would send a team, probably soon.

"TICS, begin recording. Send my headset an alert at the completion of every hour. Lock down ship behind me. Open only at my spoken command."

"Acknowledged."

She shut the inner hatch, cycled the air, and stepped outside. On the surface, she made her way against the wind toward the slashed ridge between her ship and the city. Rather, what used to be the city. Even visaug couldn't make out much other than the ridges to either side, and ahead in the distance, but occasional spots of luminescence sprinkled the way ahead. She stepped closer to one, leaning down to examine it. Delicate, bright blue tendrils poked tentative heads out, moving with the wind, then dipped below the lip of dull blue, tube-like housings. She reached a finger toward one, but at her touch, the tendrils jerked down inside the stiff, crusty tubes.

"Interesting," she said into her headset. "Plant? Animal?" She glanced both directions. "Whatever these things are, they stand up well to punishing conditions. Something that hardy should be more prevalent." Had they been wiped out after the attack, and were they only beginning to repopulate the canyon?

But that was not the purpose of her visit.

She resumed her trek.

At the mouth of the gap, Rizzo stared at the devastation before her. Ijydin's word paintings flashed through her mind again, and Rizzo's throat tightened. Where was Ijydin now? Or Nyros, or Tiral, or any of the others? Had the unammi been completely wiped out? She'd known something was wrong when they'd begun making deliveries by drone and hadn't come in person. She should have checked on them sooner, but it was too late to think about that now.

Her jaw worked inside the headgear. This valley covered a lot of ground, most of it layered in rubble as far as she could see. She could always search that later, but it wouldn't do to stay up here in this gritty wind for long. It couldn't be good for her gear. And if there were any survivors, they'd likely be far underground. That's where she should look first.

She checked the mapper for subsurface entries. Should be one to her left. Rizzo turned as directed and trudged toward the opening she could not yet see. Halfway there, her peripheral vision caught a darker shadow. She snatched her weapon, training it toward the movement. A large rodent-like animal spun to face her, its huge double-lidded eyes wide and startled. Before she could react, it leaped into the air, gangly legs and thick tail flailing, and was carried several meters away by the wind before it fell to the ground. It scuttled away in a flash, kicking up even more sand in the process. Not a predator, then. She stared after it for a moment, breathing hard, then continued on her way.

Ahead, a darker shape emerged from the gloom. The tunnel on the mapper. That's where she'd go in, assuming it was still accessible. She closed the distance and stepped into the maw of the ridge.

"Entering tunnel access at marked coordinates." The passage appeared clear, and she continued down a short way before a dimly glowing shape turned up in her path. She slowed and trained her weapon on the bulky object, which appeared to writhe and slither in spots. Cautious steps soon brought her close enough to see that the movement came from tiny lizards that glowed a dim orange. Vibrations from her steps scattered them in all directions, some wriggling beneath or inside the bloated body on which they scavenged, and Rizzo leaned closer. Human. Scraps of dried blood coated the inside of its faceplate. Visual decomp suggested two weeks dead, maybe a little less. No way to note the smell, not that she was complaining.

Rizzo unfastened the ruined suit and pulled it off the corpse, brushing away the lizards hiding beneath. She slipped her hand inside its pockets. Nothing, except an ident card. Stupid to bring something like that with you on a job like this one. As reckless as leaving behind a tracker in a debris field.

Probably intentional, then.

She examined the ident card in her helmet's light.

"Vandana Walker." That name she recognized. "One of Skalar's crew. But Skalar didn't do this. The body's too fresh. Bellamy? Time frame fits."

She stared at the body. A Consortium crewman. A Cartel admiral. A Clan ship. The Clan hadn't done this. According to her contact, the Cartel had only just found out about it. That left Skalar. The pieces fit. If his armada was behind this genocide, hundreds of people would know about it—more, depending on the number of ships involved. No way to keep them all quiet. One disgruntled crewman was all it would take, and word would spread.

Perhaps Walker was only the first.

So, it wasn't just Bellamy who would be coming to stake a claim at this grave. Once word got out, there would be a free-for-all.

She returned the card to Walker's pocket, straightened the suit on the body and rearranged it as she'd found it. No sense advertising her presence to the next scavenger who came picking Iridos' bones.

TICS chittered in her ear. "One hour."

Rizzo checked the mapper. There were dozens of tunnels and passages the device could easily see, but probably hundreds it could not. Its capability wasn't intended to extend to cavern systems. Not that it mattered. Her time here was short anyway. She would check, just to be sure, but she seriously doubted any survivors remained below. If they'd gotten out, they'd be far away by now.

At least, that's what she would do.

Three more hours she explored open passages and tunnels, coming nowhere near complete coverage, but at last she'd seen enough. Whoever had done this—and her credits were riding on Skalar—had scraped the hematium tunnels raw as far in as she could see. No doubt there was plenty more where that came from, but she had what she'd come for: confirmation of the city's fall, and a damned good idea who'd done it.

Rizzo turned toward the canyon and her waiting ship. "TICS, set a course for New Canaan, Harajüd. I'm on my way."

chapter 31

New Canaan, Harajüd
<u>Admiral Skalar's Private Residence</u>

SKALAR EXITED HIS SKIMMER AND squinted at the sky. Clouds skittered across the blue vastness. Clouds fascinated him, when he could be bothered to notice them. So did stars and rain and any other sky-bound phenomenon. Iridos had nothing similar, only the murky dun of wind-blown sand.

He shouldn't stay out here long. Too out of character, even for his predecessor, who preferred to let paid staff tend the grounds. Still, a few spare moments had fallen into his lap—or were dragged there—and he intended to take advantage of them. He could use the break.

Hands in his pockets, he moved away from the shelter over the skimmer and walked to the front of the house. A warm, late afternoon breeze raised the hair off his forehead, and he closed his eyes, listening to the noises around him. Insects. Birds. Skimmers on the street beyond the gate.

One of the skimmers slowed, pulled in at his gate, and stopped. Skalar opened his eyes. Thrace.

She passed through security, drew up in front of the house, and stepped out, a strange look on her face.

"What's wrong?" he asked, frowning.

"We need to talk."

He sighed. "What is it now?"

Thrace shook her head. "Inside."

Skalar's jaw tightened. "No. Speak here."

She glared at him, then nodded as if she'd come to a decision. "Tiral was here."

"In New Canaan, yes. Why?"

"And you told him if the Council made further demands on you, the Consortium would withdraw its protection."

Skalar narrowed his eyes. "That's right."

Thrace's features twisted, lips puckering as if she'd bitten into a rotten fruit. She stepped closer, less than a meter away, leaning toward him. "What the hell were you thinking," she said, "threatening them like that? What is wrong with you?"

"You forget yourself, Captain Baldric," Skalar whispered.

Thrace growled. "No, *Alira*," she shouted. "It's you who've forgotten who *you* are. You can't be serious about taking away that shield! The council and the other survivors on Earth are all that's left of the unammi!"

Skalar glanced around. Thrace had been right.

again.

This discussion needed closed doors. He took her by the arm, but she snatched it away. His jaw worked. "Inside."

"About time." Thrace marched ahead of him through the door.

In the house, he watched her pace, hands clasped in front of her in typical fashion as Thrace morphed into a vivid red Galen and spun toward him. "Why? Alira, why can't you just send Rakalesh the damn samples she wants? Why can't you record the memories like you said you'd do, and be done with it? You know why they want them, how important this is, especially when so many of the vault samples were lost. You're their only harvester! If anything happens to you, they'll never have another! I completely understand why they want this to be completed quickly, but you're taking your sweet time. Why?"

"Lower your voice." Alira assumed her natural form with red streaks of her own. "I understand their motivation. That's not the point."

"Then what *is* the damn point?"

"Rakalesh and the council need to understand that they cannot order me around. Not any longer. I make my own rules now. I make my own timetable. Not Rakalesh. Not the council. Me."

Galen gaped at her, his hands frozen in mid-gesture while a struggle played itself out on his face and in the colors on his skin.

"Wait," he said, frowning, "did I hear you correctly? You're putting the safety of Trumo and the younglings, not to mention every other unammi survivor, at risk over a power play?"

Alira scowled. "Don't be ridiculous. The survivors are perfectly fine. Humans would never go to Earth. They're afraid of that world."

"Then why set us up here in the Consortium in the first place?" Galen asked, waving a hand at the room around them. "Why put unammi on the outpost, if not as a protective measure?"

"Because Skalar's people knew about that base," she said through clenched teeth. "I didn't want strangers that close to the survivors. You know all this, Galen. I thought you were on my side."

"I'm on the side of our people, Alira. I thought you were one of them, one I could trust."

Alira flinched. "You don't trust me?"

Galen threw his hands in the air and turned away, then whirled toward her. "I don't even know you anymore! The Alira I knew, my i'shin, would never in a lifetime of cycles withdraw her favor or protection from her own people, no matter what. This Alira," he said, gesturing toward her, "would turn on them to prove a point. A shallow point, at that. We took our people to Earth to save our race. Our *species*. Whether or not Rakalesh and the council have the right to tell you or me or anyone else what to do and how or when to do it seems secondary in the face of that larger challenge. When did this become all about you?"

Skalar's indignation seeped up through her throat and into her head. Alira charged across the room, stopped in front of him, and stabbed a finger in his direction. "It has to be about me! There are too many layers to this facade to let even one slip, Galen. I can't believe you don't see that. If Skalar lets his guard down for a second—"

"This isn't about Skalar. This is about Alira, the unammi soul harvester, and her duty as frem to her people."

"I can't fulfill that duty without Skalar, so yes, this is about him. He and I have become inseparable."

Galen's face fell. "Then I fear for you, Alira. I fear for all the survivors, because right now you are a danger to this whole plan which, you may recall, was your idea in the first place. We both knew this would be harder than it looked, but you're growing more and more unstable. If you can't handle it—and clearly, you can't—you need to step down."

"And do what?"

"Go to Earth." He shrugged.

Earth! The chance to wear her own face, to explore their new world, to spend time with Galen, to mentor Trumo as Sufamel had done for Alira! To maybe have a youngling of her own! She paced away, shaking her head. Blue luminescence from her skin colored the furniture nearby. "The council would never allow that."

"You said yourself there were numerous underground passages in that region where we left the rest of the unammi," he said. "Surely we could take the other outcasts with us, find a place of our own. We could—"

"It wouldn't matter where we went."

He fell silent behind her. After a moment, she turned toward him. His skin displayed a tangle of colors that bespoke his turmoil better than words ever could.

"If we were on Earth, they'd find a way to drag us under their control." She shook her head. "I can't go back to that life, Galen. I will never allow the council to run my life again."

Galen stared. "No matter who pays the price?"

"You're being overly dramatic. I'll send the samples and recordings to the council in a few days. And I'll have the Consortium in line soon. You'll see."

"No," he said, "I won't."

She frowned. "What do you mean?"

"I'm done, Alira," he said. "I don't recognize you any longer, and I can't support who you've become. Count me out."

He started toward the door, and she stepped into his path, her skin blotched with white. "What are you talking about? I can't do this without you."

"You'll have to." He walked around her, morphing into Thrace along the way, and the door opened at her approach. She paused on the threshold, as if reconsidering.

"Where will you go?" Alira asked, red pulsing into her display, overpowering the white patterns.

"I don't know."

"How will I find you?"

"Don't try." Thrace glanced over her shoulder, then walked out.

Before the door could close, Skalar stood where Alira had been, a growl building in his throat until it emerged in a resounding bellow that hurt his own ears. Without even thinking, his foot lashed out, kicking a low table across the room. Voices clamored in his head, a chaotic frenzy that fed his tantrum as he thrashed about smashing everything he could reach.

He stormed across the room toward the bar and poured himself a brandy. If Galen—or Thrace or whatever the fuck her name was—didn't want to stick around, he'd do whatever he damn well pleased. Skalar

or was it crow? never give crow the good stuff.

raised the glass to his lips, then paused, as if

smelling the roses.

to appreciate its color and aroma, the fine liquor's body as his hand warmed the snifter and its contents. In truth, some nebulous connection stretched delicate tendrils of doubt to stop him. He stared into the depths of the amber liquid, seeing a refraction of himself as he was

herself, as she was.

and a reflection of his face in this moment

damn it man, why's your face so red? what'd you do to your hair?

and he lowered the drink slowly

get that shit away from me, i don't look like that.

staring at it as if it were a venomous viper. As if it might bite him. He backed away, trying to get some distance, until he ran out of floor, and he flung the drink away hard enough to impact the opposite wall. The snifter shattered, its bits sparkling

like the domes' glass shards after the armada's attack.

in the light, its contents oozing down the elegant gray wall. He slid to the floor in macabre mimicry, legs bent before him, and dropped his head into his hands.

chapter 32

New Canaan, Harajüd
<u>Landport Station, Concourse D12</u>

RIZZO STALKED PAST THE SCANNERS, mindful of the special sheaths at her waist, her thigh, her ankle, and her cleavage, blades nestled in each. She'd carried them undetected past security before. Only their key role in this visit gave them weight in her mind now. Two days of travel from Iridos left plenty of time to change her mind about this, yet even if she had done so—an unlikely possibility—the most recent report from Bailey would have decided it beyond any doubt.

Cartel agents said a shipload of child slaves had been sent to Iridos. Rizzo expected this from that faction. Bellamy followed the practices of her predecessor, after all. Rizzo could still feel the hand of Virgil's crewman over her own young mouth, the drugged stupor that kept her from fighting him off after he'd snatched her, the endless parade of johns and humiliation she'd endured before Lourdes bought her, trained her, freed her. Jagged images pressed at the dam she'd built to contain them, a deluge of grief threatening to break free. She balled her fists. No, Bellamy's actions did not surprise Rizzo.

This time, though, her contacts said Skalar was involved. It might be true. Even if not, the fall of Iridos lay on his head. She knew it, felt it in her bones. The man owed a debt. Rizzo intended to see it paid.

For once she'd left her hair black, and covered her usual skin-tight black garb with loose, richly textured attire. False readouts from her ship's tracker listed ownership as one Reese Markham, a textile vendor hailing from Ranafta who'd modified her facial profile with implants and piercings easily mimicked. A forged ident solidified Rizzo's disguise. Even Bailey might not recognize her just now. Reese's face had proven its worth in multiple circumstances. No doubt, it would get her through this port and home again once the job was done.

She still had to get past Skalar's security. Not on the base. That would be reckless. Also unnecessary. His ego left him wide open in a private residence far removed from the protection his base would have guaranteed—not just from her, but from colonial security. Why Skalar had ever thought living apart from his faction on colonial property was a good idea she'd never understand. Regardless, it gave her the perfect opening now.

A rented skimmer would take her as far as the Northwest market and public beaches. Those and the nearby gardens and nature area offered plenty of visible reasons to linger. Beyond, ten minutes away by foot, lay New Canaan's private residential sector, including the home she sought. She could be in and out before anyone missed Reese Markham, and well on her way to Saacharis before Skalar's body was found.

Rizzo passed into the exit corridor, rented a top-end skimmer, and stepped out into the night.

chapter 33

THRACE SAT FOLDED IN A meditative pose, surrounded by practitioners and a low, thrumming hum vibrating from every throat. The others turned inward in search of that point inside themselves where god resided, the source of inner peace and a more serene life, the entire goal of Bindhu spirituality. Thrace turned inward, as well, but her thoughts were far more chaotic.

In the two days since she'd walked away from Skalar, from Alira, she'd chased the tail of her own intentions in circles that always led back to where she'd started.

Skalar was spiraling toward a crash. That would be bad enough, but he could very well take the unammi survivors down with him. His actions were understandable to a degree. If a crewmember threatened his control over the faction, of course he had to address the issue. But he hadn't stopped there. He'd given the order to remove all the old outpost crew whether they'd caused trouble or not. He'd imprisoned an innocent as a control tactic—something she regarded with ambivalence—but Skalar, no doubt, would kill Kisle in the end.

Unless Thrace intervened.

The Bindhu Guide, walking past and among the supplicants, passed to her right and laid a hand on Thrace's shoulder, making her flinch. She hadn't felt their attention on her, or their approach. No doubt they sensed her unease, her disturbed state of mind. Despite her association with the local Trader faction, the resident spokesperson had granted her a short-term stay in their community based on her claim to Shidara faith, as long as she abided by the rules. Simple meals eaten in silence, minimal tech, the performance of assigned chores, daily meditation. Bringing her drama into their peaceful environs would not be tolerated.

She slowed her breathing, calmed her thoughts, and the Guide moved on. They would speak to her afterward, but she'd worry about that then. For now, she focused on the moment, on the feel of her feet and legs against the floor and the hum in her throat. The remaining meditation passed, and the others rose at the sound of the bell, but Guide caught her eye and nodded. Thrace lingered until the rest of the residents had gone.

"You are troubled, Thrace Baldric," said Guide, whose name she did not know.

She regarded them in silence.

They offered a small smile. "The garden is abandoned at this time of night. Perhaps an hour alone there would prove more productive to clear your mind than group meditation. What do you think?"

"I think you are correct, as usual, Guide," Thrace said. "I'll go there now."

"You will miss your evening meal."

"I'm not hungry."

"Very well," they said, laying a comforting hand on her arm. "But I'll ask the kitchen to save you a plate anyway."

Thrace murmured her thanks and left them behind. The garden was just outside the meditation space, and she pushed past the door into the warm darkness. Insects trilled their evening chorus through air filled with the heady perfume of some night blossom. Off to her left, a shrill bird call rang out and was met by the response of its mate, somewhere in the distance. A white stone walkway curved before her, disappearing into the gloom, and she allowed her feet to carry her forward while her mind roamed its own path.

What was she going to do? Skalar's nonchalance about the growing discontent among his crew spoke to Alira's lack of understanding on many levels. She had not lived among humans long enough to understand how to act as one of them, especially one with an established background and pattern of behavior. Allowing the human voices in her head to pull her strings like an old-fashioned puppet was not the same thing. That she thought Skalar's memories and essence could drive this con with no one the wiser was worrisome. It didn't seem possible that the reaped individuals would be unchanged by their deaths and subsequent absorptions, not to mention their interaction with all Alira's other passengers. More likely they'd been warped into unrecognizable caricatures, especially given the fact that she'd not allowed time for each of them to solidify before adding to the mix. The more Thrace thought about it, the more she believed the harvesting sickness had taken root in Alira's mind.

The thought drove Thrace's hands together, fingers gripping each other into a tight knot. Alira had said that once the sickness manifested, death always followed. But now, Thrace had to admit to a shade of doubt. Did Alira really know? Rakalesh would, but asking her would be difficult, not to mention unwise. If she thought for a minute that Alira was losing control over her harvests, Thrace couldn't predict what the councilor might do. Would Rakalesh try to capture Alira, return her to the fold under force, and take the genetic sample before the chance was lost? Or would Rakalesh accept the forfeit and act to remove Alira from the equation altogether?

Thrace's empty stomach lurched, drawing a frown on her brow. The way things stood, she might soon agree with that likely assessment. Alira was too unstable. If she morphed in front of a human, a vital unammi secret would be out. Thrace had already stopped Skalar on the verge of shifting once. How long before it happened when Thrace was not there to step in? Alira also knew about the moon base. She knew that Earth's atmosphere was harmless. If she—or Skalar—misspoke in front of the wrong person, the unammi survivors would be defenseless against a human invasion. Granted, it had been the humans' home world to begin with, but they'd left it behind ages ago. It was an unammi world now, and Thrace couldn't stand by while Alira gambled away their safety on this long shot, especially when her every action weakened its chances of success.

But Alira would never give up her plan willingly. Nor would she ever admit that she couldn't handle the challenge. She'd rightly claimed she and Skalar were inseparable and therein lay the conundrum. Earth needed the barrier the outcasts now provided, but Alira could not be allowed to remain at the head of the Consortium where she posed a bigger danger to their people than humans at the outpost. Thrace had hoped Botha would have a positive effect on Skalar—on Alira. But it must have been too little too late. She'd been no better after the elder's visit than before.

Thrace stopped in front of a large stone bench. The thought that had been fluttering at the fringe of her awareness finally broke through. If Alira was truly mad, drastic measures would need to be taken to salvage their situation. It wouldn't be easy. Alira could kill from a distance with ease, and might not care who she'd harmed until it was too late. In order to— Thrace's throat worked as she struggled to crystallize the morbid thought—remove the threat, she would have to approach from an oblique angle. Alira could not be allowed to see it coming, or Thrace would not live through the attempt.

She sank down onto the bench. This was crazy. She was thinking about harming, even killing her i'shin. Could she? *Would* she? No. Ridiculous.

Such a crazy thought. As crazy as Alira. Thrace pressed her hands against her cheeks, as if to force sanity into her ghoulish thoughts. It wouldn't get that bad. She wouldn't let it.

But it already had, hadn't it? Alira stood on the precipice, and the unammi were tied to her waist. Thrace had no choice but to intervene before Alira could drag them down with her.

Thrace closed her eyes while the awful truth sank in. If it really did come to that, better that she should take the necessary action than to leave it to Rakalesh or the council. Of course, there would be no more Founder's

Daughter, but then there would also be no more harvesting sickness. No one else would ever have to struggle through this horrific ordeal.

Night sounds intruded into her quieter thoughts. She let them drift through her consciousness, calming and reassuring her, before she rose and left the garden behind.

chapter 34

New Canaan, Harajüd
<u>Admiral Skalar's Private Residence</u>

THE SHUFFLING SOUND OF HER feet against the sandy stone echoed from every direction. Darkness, thick as pudding and unmitigated by her own luminescence, shrouded her senses, and she wandered, arms outstretched to detect obstacles before they could meet her face.

"Hello? Can anyone hear me?"

She stopped, straining to hear other sounds in this place, wherever it was.

Vague whisperings, like the sigh of cloth against itself, shadowed her awareness and she called out again.

"Who's there?"

No reply broke the near silence, and she blundered forward once more. Ahead, the sensation of cavernous space narrowed in a way she could not quite explain, and she fumbled toward it until her hand met cool stone. A wall, smooth to the touch. Fingers traced the wall to the ceiling, then down to the floor, worn smooth by many feet. A tunnel. But where? Iridos? Earth? Somewhere else?

Alira continued on, one hand trailing against the wall for direction, moving up and up. In the distance, a familiar sound intruded. Wind song! Iridos then, but which tunnel? Her feet sped up, not quite running through the dark until she could see a vague tempering of the shadows. She let out a muffled croak and pushed toward the light.

Utter destruction of the beautiful valley raked fresh grief across her heart and she stopped in the mouth of the tunnel, whose dark walls did not reflect her veins and flashes of purple. Crow did this. Her challenge remained unanswered, and she realized the voices in her head had gone silent. That usually happened when…

"I know you're there," she said.

His silence drew a frown onto her face and shot red glints into her display. She turned. Her Companion stood behind her, Its changing shape settling at once into Eli's familiar form, his green accusing eyes boring into her.

She seized the offensive. "Where have you been?"

"Watching."

"Then you might have noticed things aren't going our way. Why won't you help?"

He stared, lips still.

She looked away with a huff. "This is depressing. Why show me something that can't be changed? Why not meet me at the river?"

In an instant, she stood in the middle of the raging flow, its waters churning against her waist and, instead of continuing past her, the flow divided into two courses. The one to her right soon transformed into a shallow, murky trickle unadorned by trees or plants or fishes, its waters muddy and sullen. The other, to her left, ran clear, its taut surface shimmering with gleams of light. Trees graced banks to either side, their branches sweeping the air above the flow. Wildflowers sprang up between the roots and in the in-between places where sunlight fell in patches.

She did not recognize either.

Her Companion stood a meter away on the strange bank, its form shifting between its panoply of faces.

"What happened here?" she said, her words barely audible over the sound of the water.

"You."

Gray surprise flooded her other colors. "What?"

"What do you want?"

Not that again. Alira sighed and gestured to the river's split course. "Tell me what this means."

"Choose."

She shook her head. "I already did that, didn't I, the last time we stood together at the river? It bought me nothing but trouble. I'm trapped, again, only this time I'm alone."

Eli's face solidified. "Were we wrong about you?"

"I don't know!" she shouted, slapping her hands against the surface of the water. "How can I answer that when I don't know what you want from me?"

The Figure shifted again, going through its repertoire nonstop. The temple cavern, gleaming with luminescent irolium and ringing with unammi chants, flashed in Alira's thoughts and was gone, replaced by the dark clammy chamber it had become before she returned to the river.

"Connections." She sneered. "Galen was wrong, then. This isn't about me. It's about you. It's always been about you, hasn't it? You brought humans to Iridos. You changed them into the unammi, all for your, what? Entertainment? A quick vicarious thrill? You're no better than the humans, then."

The river vanished and Alira floated in a nebulous place with no defined boundary. Around her wound what looked like a chain of lights, some brilliant and shining, others dim glimmers against the darker backdrop of this place, all connected by iridescent threads. Each spot and thread pulsed, as if alive, while tiny sparks hovered or followed the linking tendrils from one light to another. Spread around her like a web, the network stretched and breathed and vibrated.

She reached toward the closest bright light and suddenly it opened before her like a window in a human structure. Beyond lay images and emotions and sounds and smells so alien she could not process them into any sort of meaning. Her vision distorted, her feelings distended in an unnatural, fragile arc and she withdrew, frowning.

She turned to another light, a smaller one this time. Dazzling colors she'd never before seen fractured into shapes and images that made no sense. A sensation of joy and something she could not quite name sent her spirit soaring, but this world, too, challenged her understanding. No adequate context, either unammi or human, offered itself, and again she pulled away, trembling.

A third, tiny, twinkling point called her attention. She looked and saw the unammi in their Earthen city, making the best of their new circumstance. Then an image of her own sleeping form faded in. An array of colors surged through her skin on the other side of the light's veil. But she didn't just see. She felt the contentment of the unammi, their stubborn refusal to surrender to entropy, the solid rock beneath their feet, their hope for the future, heard their voices and sounds of growing civilization, smelled unfamiliar smoking resin from strange trees. She felt the silken sheets wrapped around the sleeping Alira, the softness of the bed and pillow on that body, the fear and anger and confusion emanating from it. It was as if she lay there, in that bed, even now, or walked among her people in their new city. The experience surrounded her, filled her, engulfed her, drew her in until she forgot that she hovered in an odd pointillistic network of light, a potential witness to countless realms and realities but a resident of only one.

"Oh," she whispered. She breathed out in a slow, soft sigh. She tried to say more, to interact with the unammi in the vision, but they moved past and around her as if she weren't there.

How was this possible?

With an effort, she drew back and found herself once more at the river's divergence.

"That…" she stammered, "that's what you meant by connections?"

The Figure only shimmered through its forms, but Alira knew she was right. No wonder the Iri wanted to maintain their passage to this reality. If their own world was the amorphous realm where the lights hung on their threads, she could understand why they would want to experience other types of existence. To lose even one would be devastating.

"I think I understand."

"Do you?" Eli asked, his image settling in. "Mend the bridge before it's too late."

Alira jerked upright in Skalar's bed, blue and white pulses washing over the pale gray coverlet tangled around her legs. Her heart hammered, breath coming in short, shallow gulps. She could feel it, the wrongness, the sense of dread. Beside the bed, another soft buzz jerked her attention to the security device.

A breach. Someone was in the house. But how? Its safeguards would be nearly impossible to counteract.

Unless… Galen knew how to get past the system.

then why had the alarm triggered?

Maybe he'd missed one step? Alira rolled out of bed, morphing as she went.

"Thrace?" Skalar's deep voice vibrated the still air in the room as he reached for a stunner in the drawer beside the bed. "Is that you?"

No response. Skalar frowned and glanced at the alert beside the bed. Still lit. He looked toward the door, cautious steps easing him closer. Just inside he paused, listening. Only silence met his ears. Heart hammering, he took a breath and swung out into the shadowy hallway. Something—a sound, a hint of movement—made him recoil, dancing away from some unseen threat just as a gust of displaced air passed less than a centimeter from his face. Without thinking, his arm came up to block the next blow even as his mind snatched at his attacker's consciousness, yanking connections to bring him down

what the actual—

take him out, netzyl.

shut up, skalar.

without killing him. Only seconds later, when his attacker was on the floor, did he remember he held a stunner.

lot of good that did you.

"Lights, eighteen hundred lumens."

Shadows fled the hallway and Skalar stared down at the dark brown skin of the intruder. And even though she looked different somehow, Nyros and Ijydin both recognized this person, and clamored to be heard

you can't kill her!

while his human passengers raged in confusion at this huge breach in the unwritten understanding between all six Trader factions. Admirals didn't go after one another personally like this. It wasn't done. Ever. So what the actual fuck was Rizzo doing here?

"TICS, set up a table for two."

He picked her up and entered the room across the hall in time to see the decorative black carving fold down from the rear wall, extending a chair to either side. He sat Rizzo in one and ducked out for binding straps from his storage room. They wouldn't hold forever, but they ought to keep her arms and legs immobile long enough that they could have a little chat, assuming she didn't have another knife with which to free herself. He checked. She did. He removed her weapons and stepped out of reach.

Clearly, something extraordinary had provoked her into violating the Traders' unspoken agreement, something that made her want Skalar dead by her own hand. Every thread of memory or knowledge he held about this woman was enough to quicken Skalar's breath, so unless he wanted to kill her—he didn't, since both Ijydin and Nyros shouted that Rizzo was more valuable to the unammi alive—he'd have to change her mind. Somehow. The key to that surely lay in her reason for being here.

He paced beside the table, his attention never leaving her face. What had Skalar done that was so awful as to make Rizzo come after him? It couldn't be any sort of personal betrayal. The two of them had never been friends, though the Skalar in his head admitted grudging respect for Rizzo. He hadn't harmed anyone in her care or protection, nor had he needed to do so. He hadn't stolen from her or intruded on her territory, not in any atypical way, and even if he had, this was not how such infractions were handled. For an admiral to attack a competing faction's admiral on his own world, much less in his own private residence, was unheard of.

So, what possible reason—

He jerked to a halt. She must have heard about the attack on Iridos. Crow had given those crewmen in his armada ample motivation to keep their lips tight, but even so, that was a lot of people. Too many. Skalar, the old one, believed he could keep them quiet. The new Skalar's face twisted into a sneer. How had that human lived so long crippled by such hubris?

An echo of Thrace's accusations from their last encounter flashed before him like a mirror, and he sighed. Maybe she was right. Perhaps the new Skalar harbored his own share of pride. He shook his head. He couldn't think about that just now. Rizzo first. Thrace after. He considered his guest. He'd seen her up close before—rather, several of Alira's other passengers had—but not like this, where he was free to really look at her. Short black hair hugged her head, which lolled forward. He lifted her chin so he could better see her features. She looked different than the images his unammi harvests held of her. A sharper chin. Subdermal mod implants, or damn good fake ones, lined her brow ridge and high cheekbones. He didn't remember seeing those before. The rest, though, that he recognized. Skin of darkest brown, full lips, a long neck. Skintight black clothing betrayed a muscular frame beneath. She was younger than Skalar by at least a dozen years, maybe more. She couldn't be much shorter than him, but he had at least twenty kilos on her.

Skalar lowered her chin to her chest and retrieved her blade from the hall, a wicked kris that had come far too close to tasting his blood. He added it to the small pile of others on the bar out of her reach, then sat across from her. How should he work this? If she'd come to kill him for the destruction of the unammi city, all he had to do was tell her he wasn't Skalar.

yeah, good luck with that.

If she wasn't ready to take his word for that, he'd have to convince her another way. She and Ijydin had been as close as their situation had allowed. Perhaps something from Ijydin's memories would help. If that wasn't enough there was one other way,

no! alira you can't even consider—

be still. i'm thinking.

incontrovertible proof. Not an ideal first choice, though. Even in Alira, such deeply ingrained taboos were hard to break. Skalar would hold out on that, save it as a last resort

an ace up your sleeve.

if nothing else worked. With luck, he wouldn't need it.

He took a deep breath and sent his thoughts toward her in a cautious nudge.

chapter 35

SOUNDS FILTERED THROUGH FIRST. SOMEONE breathing, someone close. The rustle of a body shifting position.

Physical sensation followed. A solid surface beneath her buttocks and at her back. A chair? Her booted feet flat on the floor, arms and legs—bound.

Her veins turned to ice. In her time as a young slave in the Cartel's pleasure houses, before Bellamy had taken over, Virgil's johns had liked immobilizing her while they did unspeakable things. Flashbacks screamed through her mind, slamming her heart against her ribs. Electrical signals pumped into her muscles, preparation for the fight to come. Only years of practice kept her limbs slack, her body still, while little Turizomi—her nine-year-old self—kicked and shrieked behind the locked door in her mind. *Shhhhh,* she soothed the hysterical child within. *Don't panic. Whatever happens, you've survived worse.*

Her head twitched, but she kept her eyes shut. Better to let her captor think she slept while she assessed the situation. Her senses stretched. Small space. A crisp, clean odor. Only those few noises she'd already identified.

"I know you're awake."

His statement shattered her pretense and Rizzo raised her head. He sat across from her, only a small table between them, hardly enough to protect him if she could free her arms. Without looking away from his face, she took in their immediate surroundings. A small bar sat against the wall behind Skalar, its surface mounded with her blades, all of them from the looks of it. Beside that, a door, a hallway, and another door—his bedroom, according to her intel. To her right, a set of open shelves divided the space from another room. Rizzo tested the straps holding her limbs to the chair. She had yet to accomplish what she'd come for, but the night was still young.

"Are they too tight?"

"Yes," she snapped. With luck, he would test them for himself. Come close enough she could damage him.

He leaned back in his seat and crossed his legs. "I don't intend to hurt you, but given your…" Skalar paused, his head tilted as if considering his words. "…greeting, I didn't think you'd be willing to hear me out. It's important that you do, hence the straps."

Why hadn't he just killed her? He'd had the opportunity. Nothing about the position of his body, his hands, or his expression gave any clues as to why he'd let her live. His eyes, almost as black as her own, stared at her as if expecting her to respond. In Virgil's pleasure house all those years ago, she would have complied by spitting in his face. She still felt that urge, except now the volcanos of Phejoss would freeze over before she gave him the satisfaction of knowing her mind.

"You're here about Iridos."

His implacable voice poked her seething enmity like a fool tormenting a snake. No surprise that he'd figured out that much. He always was quick. She stared in silence, her face blank. When would he admit to slaving?

"I understand your rage. But this isn't what it seems."

"It *seems* genocidal," she said.

His attention fell away from her face for a heartbeat, focused on something much farther away. "It almost was," he murmured.

She leaned forward as far as she could against her restraints. "It *seems* like your trademark, to take advantage of the weak."

Skalar looked at her again. "There you're wrong. I'm not who you think I am."

Was that remorse in his expression? Grief? Rizzo narrowed her eyes. Unlikely. More to the point, irrelevant.

"Then who are you?" she asked. If she could keep him talking, distract him, she could free herself, finish the job, and move on. Should be easy enough. Skalar always did like to hear himself speak.

He peered into her face, then shook his head and stood, pacing away toward the hall. "I don't know why I thought this would work. You won't believe me."

"Why should I? Malcolm Skalar lies." She twisted her wrists as far as she could, the abrasive straps scraping her skin. He hadn't left her much room to maneuver. Smart man.

He spun around, his expression calm, and she froze. "You're right. He does. He's a conniving bastard, a coldhearted one at that. He's given you no reason to trust him, has he?"

He didn't turn away again. Instead, he stepped closer. "You're right to think he destroyed Iridos. He didn't do it personally, of course, but it was carried out at his command."

She shook her head. The man stood there unashamed, even boasting. But…had he always referred to himself in the third person like that?

Skalar pressed on, an odd expression on his face. "What if I told you some of the unammi survived that attack?"

Rizzo frowned. Few humans used that word for the people of Iridos. "How?"

He shook his head. "I can't tell you that. It's true, nonetheless."

"Where are they?"

"One of them is standing in front of you."

She raised an eyebrow. Skalar had gone mad. That was the only explanation. A madman at the helm of the Consortium was a matter of some concern to everyone, especially the other factions. The amount of damage he could do staggered even her.

"You don't believe me," he said, his tone impassive. He turned to one side, that odd look still dominating his features, and paced a few steps before pivoting toward her again. "That day in the alley on Zebalu, you'd just killed two of Admiral Virgil's people. A woman helped you get out before colonial or Cartel security arrived, but you never told her what they'd done to earn slit throats."

Rizzo's mouth slackened. For a moment, she was in that alley again, trapped between two Cartel slavers who approached with drugs. They spoke of Virgil's intent to have her back. Her knife had communicated her refusal. When Esther stumbled across the altercation in the moments leading up to their deaths, Turizomi had been covered with blood—theirs as well as her own. If not for Esther, death or the authorities would have intervened and there would have been no Admiral Rizzo.

But only she and Esther knew of that event, and Esther would never speak of it to another, especially not Skalar. Not willingly, anyway.

"Where is she?"

"She took you to Saacharis, got help for you from the Syndicate. She's the reason you are an Admiral today."

Esther had seemed to read her mind, too. "I asked you a question."

Skalar sighed. "She's dead. Sort of. Skalar's fault. I know that won't surprise you."

Rizzo went cold. She twisted her wrists against the chafing straps. Let him see. Let him watch his own death coming.

"I'm telling you the truth, Rizzo. I know I look like him, but I am not Skalar."

Mad. Almost certainly. She jerked her arms, openly struggling.

"Those straps won't hold you forever, so my time is short." He shook his head, stroked his beard, and walked away. At the doorway to the hall, he swung around. "There is one way I can convince you beyond any doubt. But if I play that card, there's no going back for either of us." In the room's light, his face took on a gaunt, haunted expression. "Sure you won't just take my word for it?"

For the first time, she glanced over her shoulder toward her bonds. If she could see how they were attached—

Movement snatched her focus to Skalar. Except it wasn't him any longer. His body melted, momentarily amorphous as it reshaped itself into the soft, plump form of an eighty-something woman, wisps of white hair escaping from her long braid. She smiled, dark blue eyes crinkling at the corners in her lined, bronze face.

Rizzo stared, mind and mouth struck dumb. Esther? No. Not possible. Even if she wasn't dead, as Skalar claimed, she'd be more than thirty years older by now. This woman hadn't aged a day.

Esther tilted her head and, above her loose garb, the small wattle at her throat quivered.

"Do you believe me yet?"

Without waiting for a reply, Skalar—no, *Esther* shimmered, melted and assumed another familiar form.

"This face and Esther's belonged to the same person, you know," Ijydin said, her pale blue skin alight with mischief and some combination of color Rizzo did not recognize. The words barely registered before Ijydin's body enlarged, darkened. Hair, short and curly, sprouted from her head, while skintight black garments covered the torso, arms and legs. Rizzo stared at her own image, her mouth agape, her struggle forgotten.

"Not the same as looking in a mirror, is it?" the form's rich resonant voice queried. This mask could fool even Bailey, assuming the imposter didn't do something un-Rizzo-like.

"Who are you?" she whispered.

The doppelgänger smiled—something Rizzo did only as a warning—then shifted to an unfamiliar body. An unammi one. Its display showed the blue of uncertainty, and traces of white fear. That much Rizzo recognized.

"I am Alira, daughter of Lurien, who is now gone from this world by Crow's hand."

Rizzo stared, waiting, but Alira did not change again. "Is this your true face?"

"Yes."

All the fight went out of her, and Rizzo went slack against the chair. "Are all unammi like you?"

Alira huffed, an odd sound. "Not exactly, but they can change their appearance. Yes."

A world of possibilities and potentials collided in Rizzo's head and understanding snicked into place.

"I never knew."

"No human ever did, not anyone who lived."

Rizzo tensed. "Am I dead?"

"That depends." Alira tilted her head, peering into Rizzo's eyes. "What will you do with this knowledge?"

Do? Rizzo opened her mouth, then closed it again. This was a game-changer. Colonial leaders would pay astounding sums to hear of it, much less see it. Potential ramifications for genetic manipulation and possible marketing applications boggled her mind. Pay? Colonial scientists would kill for that secret. Alira said some of the unammi still lived, but Rizzo had already seen what one man's greed could do. How many more unammi would die if this intel leaked? No wonder they kept it close to the vest.

"I will protect it with my life," she said. "Aes te nalya."

Alira blinked, her skin suffused with gray surprise that soon passed, leaving pulses of yellow in its wake. "Nalena t'staani," she replied. "Ijydin and Nyros have both spoken of you to me. They say you are a friend to our people," she said, stepping closer. "We need friends more than ever right now. In fact, I could use your help."

chapter 36

ALIRA GESTURED AT RIZZO'S ARMS. "I spoke truth. I've no wish to harm you, but I had to make you hear me. Is it safe, now, to free you?"

Rizzo nodded.

Alira removed the straps and sat down. Her guest rubbed bloody wrists and shifted in her chair, rather than making a dive across the table.

"How many of you are among us?" asked Rizzo.

"Only a few now." Purple veins traced intricate patterns across Alira's arms and hands, probably the rest of her, too. It felt strange to see it. She'd grown so accustomed to her human appearance that her natural one seemed an oddity. "We don't dare risk more. Skalar almost wiped us out."

"I know. I saw it."

Alira's head came up. "You went there?"

"Yes, as soon as I heard. There was a body. A human one, Vandana Walker."

told you you'd regret letting her escape.

shut up, crow.

"A body. But not a ship?"

"No," Rizzo shook her head. "Bellamy's calling card."

"Bellamy."

"My sources say she is sending slaves there to raid the hematium mine. She wants others to think the Consortium is involved."

"Why?"

Rizzo raised an eyebrow. "If word got out, it would mar Skalar's reputation. Perhaps send him to Mandoslóna."

Connections clicked into place. Skalar had been right to suspect Bellamy, then. She was, in fact, behind all the rumors. She was the one responsible for all Harlan's accusations. "And with Skalar gone, the Cartel would take first place among the factions?"

Rizzo's expression confirmed this suspicion.

she always wanted to surpass me. this is her chance.

Alira clenched her hands.

"What happened?" Rizzo asked.

Alira told her most of it. The armada's attack, the death of so many unammi, the loss of their home. How they'd found a new world—she didn't offer a location and, to her credit, Rizzo didn't ask—how she'd killed Skalar and Crow in self-defense, that she'd believed wearing Skalar's face would help protect the survivors.

"Has it?"

Alira's cheeks warmed. She looked away. "It's complicated."

Rizzo made no reply, and Alira risked a glance, only to find a question on her visitor's face.

"Some of the crew have noticed…differences, in the behavior of Skalar as I portray him, and the way he was before," Alira went on. "I'm handling it."

"Taking his face is easier," Rizzo observed, "than mimicking his persona."

Alira shook her head, red pulses reflecting off the edge of the table. "Please. Not you too. I have this under control."

"Are you certain?" Rizzo leaned forward, her hands flat on the table. "I have intel regarding Skalar's alienation of trusted officers, decisions that defy logic. If I know this, others will. It makes you look weak."

Sa'abah questioning his orders. Open defiance from Walker's crew. Mira's people. Or the latest report that Ronan managed to slip an assassin into the brig and take out the two officers from his crew who'd talked to strangers, probably crewmembers from another faction.

But no. He wasn't alienating anyone. Alira choked back a frenzied laugh. "I wouldn't expect you to listen to rumors, Rizzo."

"Not rumor. Substantiated data from the same source that told me of Iridos, and that Skalar is rumored to be involved with the Cartel in running slaves."

"That last part is impossible."

"How do you know?"

"He would never have worked with Bellamy. Even your sources would tell you that. I've had access to his records," Alira pointed out, "ever since I took over for him. If he'd been slaving, I would know. Above and beyond all that, he hated slavers. He was a bastard, but the slave trade killed his sister."

Rizzo shifted in her seat. "What was her name?"

Rugrat.

"Amelia."

"Describe her."

Alira sighed and peered across the table. "Short, maybe 150 centimeters give or take. Brown hair, brown eyes, same as mine— Skalar's. Delicate features." Fragile beauty, sweet spirit…

"You speak as if you've seen her."

"No. She died long ago. I just know."

Rizzo stared past Alira, then shook her head. "I don't recognize the description."

"Why would you?" Alira frowned.

Rizzo's attention shifted to Alira. "It's complicated," she said, echoing Alira's words. "The point is that Skalar seems vulnerable right now. Tread with care."

Alira sighed and closed her eyes. "I have heard that conclusion and advice far too often of late."

"When will you listen?" Rizzo leaned forward again. "Your people are in a precarious position. If others learn what you've told me or discover unammi secrets some other way, they won't stand a chance. Give the other factions reason to think the Consortium is coming apart, and they will fall on you like wolves on a wounded bull. Then who will protect the survivors of your race? It's your business, run it how you want. But you said you wanted my help."

Why were other people forever telling her how to act? How to live? How to run her own affairs? She forced herself to take a calming breath. "What do you advise, then?"

"Crow is dead. Yes?"

Alira nodded.

"Who took his place?"

"Captain Thrace Baldric."

Rizzo looked askance. "I don't know that name."

Alira hesitated. "Thrace is also unammi, someone I trust."

"What does Thrace say about all this?"

"That as Skalar, I am losing control," Alira said, her throat tight. "Endangering our people."

Rizzo's lips drew together in a thin line and she leaned back. "You've set yourself a difficult task, taking the place of an established figure. I don't blame his crew for their suspicions."

Galen. Rakalesh. Nyros. Sa'abah. Ronan. Botha. Now Rizzo. Did anyone else want to point out her inadequacies?

"The strong eat the weak in Trader life. Already the hounds nip at your heels. You need to repair Skalar's image," Rizzo continued. "I don't know how. If you can't manage that, I advise you to replace him. I admit that won't be easy. A faction crew won't likely follow a complete unknown, but if you don't remove him willingly, others will do it for you and your secrets—"

Enough! Fury raced through Alira's chest, dove down into her belly, shoved her over the edge of tolerance. She exploded from her seat. "I told you, I've told all of you I have this under control," she shouted. "I'm handling it, and I just need a little more time! Why won't you hear me?"

She blinked and found herself standing before Rizzo, eye-to-eye, Rizzo's brown skin reflecting Alira's red flares.

> *alira, calm down.*
>
> *netzyl, you are in over your head.*
>
> *shut up, shut UP.*

Movement behind Rizzo caught Alira's eye and she shifted her attention to see Eli watching, waiting,

were we wrong about you?

while she stood spewing rage at the woman she'd asked for help. She returned her gaze to Rizzo, who stared at her, both brows peaking above eyes that glared indignation more than words ever could.

galen was right. i'm losing this fight.

it doesn't look good from here, squib.

She held out a hand and backed away from the table, from her guest. "Sorry…I'm sorry…"

Rizzo's brow furrowed, not a frown exactly. What was going through her mind right now? Did the woman think Alira was crazy?

Alira huffed, half-laugh, half-whine. Why not? Everyone else did.

She turned away, unwilling to see pity or scorn in this human's face.

"You haven't told me everything," Rizzo said, her voice husky.

Alira closed her eyes. She shook her head but said nothing.

"Very well. You can't hope to manage an entire faction if you can't even restrain yourself. That should be your first priority, and the sooner the better."

Alira whirled around. Eli still stood behind her guest, watching. All the rage drained away, leaving her limp.

were we wrong?

But Rizzo wasn't finished, and Alira dragged her attention to the human's face.

"Bellamy's slaves are probably on Iridos as we speak. She will leave behind more than just bodies to tie that project to the Consortium. If the colonial governments get wind of her activities, they will step in. Even without any evidence to tie Skalar to slavery, none of the colonies will sanction what his armada did there. They would turn on the Consortium, claim Skalar violated his contract with Harajüd House, forcibly disband the faction, remand its key officers to Mandoslóna, perhaps even order the death penalty for Skalar. That's *if* you and your officers last that long."

"If?"

Rizzo tipped her head. "That kind of censure affects all Traders, on all worlds. It sets a precedent we can't allow. Other factions will take action against the Consortium's leadership. They'll gladly help one of your officers effect a coup to protect their own interests on other colonial worlds, so you have to take care of Bellamy and do it fast. You don't have time to feel sorry for yourself."

For once, Skalar had nothing to say in her head. She blew out a long breath, dropped into the other chair, and rested her forehead atop one fist on the table. She was so tired of this. The charade had grown old long ago, but how else was she supposed to protect her people? The social politics of the Traders had never entered her considerations until now. Here was yet another complication to an already flailing effort.

She couldn't keep doing this, especially now. Her self-appointed role was hot enough already with a handful—okay, more than a handful—of crewmen after her. If the other factions got involved, too....

No, it was time for a change.

Alira nodded, her head rocking against her fist. "You're right," she said. "My original plan isn't working." It felt good to say it out loud, even to a human. At last, she sat up, one hand against her forehead. "I need to try something new."

"What will you do?"

Good question. The tunnels on Earth, before the survivors had moved there, had been so peaceful. How she envied the survivors, exploring that new territory, learning and finding something new every day, being part of establishing a new city in a new place! But she couldn't go there. She couldn't go to Iridos. If Rizzo and the others were right, she couldn't stay here either. That left eleven other human colonies.

"I don't know, yet." Alira sighed. "I don't suppose you have a place for me in the Syndicate?"

"Not until you've resolved this problem."

No, of course, Alira couldn't just leave things as they were. She half-turned, staring at the wall, rolling options and roadblocks through her mind, considering and rejecting one after the other until one showed a glimmer of hope at success.

"What if..." She trailed off.

"Yes?"

Alira peered at Rizzo. "I think I have an idea, but I can't do it alone. Will you help?"

"That depends on the plan. But it would have to be sub rosa. I can't involve the Syndicate with the Consortium openly."

Alira's heart sank. "Why not?"

she's right, netzyl.

quiet, skalar.

"Because I'm one of those admirals who can't afford to let Harajüd House take you down. If the other factions think the Syndicate is siding with the Consortium in this, it could spark faction war. No one wants that."

"I'll take what I can get." Alira leaned across the table. "Here's what I have in mind."

chapter 37

New Canaan, Harajüd
<u>Bindhu Intentional Community</u>

AT THE SOUND OF A soft tap on his locked door—one of the few in the compound—Galen rolled out of his cot, morphing into Thrace as he went. In the walkway, a white-haired Guide waited.

"It is not our policy to allow visitors," Guide said, "especially at this hour."

Thrace shook her head, still waking up. "I'm alone."

"Not here," Guide murmured. "Your guest awaits in the garden."

Thrace looked past them as if this elusive visitor crouched in the hall beyond.

"It is unusual to find an initiate of your skill in such a delicate dilemma," Guide said. "You know how to find the answers you seek, so I can only imagine your problem is dire."

Thrace looked at them, still considering her options. The visitor had to be Skalar. He'd known, of course, to look here. His second's predilection toward this religion was widely known. Thrace heaved a sigh and peered down the hallway. She wasn't ready to see him yet, may not be for a long while.

"Send him away. I don't wish to speak to him."

"That is not my responsibility. This community is a haven, not a hideout. Go," Guide prompted. "Handle this. I don't have to tell you to make this a one-time thing, do I?"

"No." Thrace shot them an apologetic look. "It won't happen again, I promise."

"Good. Seekers here are mindful about their isolation. We do not want drama inside our walls. See that it stays away from now on." With that, they glided away, their loose garment whispering against their skin.

When they were gone, Thrace stepped out into the corridor and turned toward the garden. She had made it clear she wanted some space, so what was Skalar doing here? This was out of character for him. For Alira. Either something else had happened, or Skalar was on a rampage, but if that were the case Guide never would have allowed him entry. Thrace would have to hold herself in check during their conversation, though. As far as she knew, none of Alira's harvests gifted her with the ability to read others, so Skalar wouldn't—couldn't—know the harsh decision Thrace had reached just the day before.

The one she still hoped to avoid.

She padded through the halls and stopped at the garden entry. Skalar stood on the path. Two moons still rode high in the night sky, their light gleaming in his hair, turning his skin to pale blue alabaster, almost like Alira's true form. Thrace's lips twisted, then drew tight against her teeth. More than anything, she wanted to disappear. Go somewhere Skalar couldn't find her. Change her name, her face, her associates. She had access to the irolium. She could do it, for a while anyway.

Instead, she pushed through the doorway and into the shadowy night.

chapter 38

SKALAR TURNED AT THE SOUNDS behind him. Thrace had entered the garden. His heart stuttered. Despite the admiral's protestations that her absence was no big deal, he'd missed her.

He stepped toward her, but stopped when she held up a restraining hand.

"Why are you here?" Thrace whispered.

"It's good to see you too, Captain." Skalar couldn't keep the hurt from his tone.

She looked away. "I told you I'm done. Whatever's going on, I want no part of it."

Silence fell between them, filled by night insects and croaking frogs in the nearby pond. She didn't look him in the face.

Skalar moved closer, almost but not quite touching her. "And I told you I can't do this without you."

"I don't care."

His jaw tightened. He took a deep breath

calm down.

and exhaled through pursed lips. He hadn't really believed her when they'd last argued. He'd thought she would get over her pique like she always did. Maybe he'd been wrong about that. Maybe he'd been wrong about a lot of things. "Thrace, please. I need you right now."

She shook her head and started to turn away.

Skalar grabbed her shoulder.

Thrace jerked out of his grasp and stepped away. "Don't touch me."

"Would you at least listen?" He leaned closer. "The situation is even worse than we thought. Skalar—hell, the whole Consortium is at risk right now. If we want to maintain the outpost as a shield, I have to figure out how to fix this."

"You have more than one dilemma to resolve, Alira."

He shushed her. "Would you stop? This is serious. Don't make it worse."

She laughed, a harsh sound that startled something into the bushes nearby. "Make it worse? Me? You've done a fine job of that all by yourself. I want out." She waved a hand in his direction. "I've had enough of your ego and your arrogance and your plan. You won't see reason, so I can't help you anymore. I told you before I left your house. I'm through with you. Why are you even here?"

Rage boiled in his throat

she's right, you know.

and Skalar drew a breath to shout a retort

don't...you need her.

when movement caught his eye. He looked past Thrace into the shadows, but no one waited there

were we wrong about you?

to accuse him. No one new, anyway. His critics said he was intractable. They couldn't all be wrong.

Could they?

Images flashed through his memory, scenes of his rampages, his power plays, his bullying and brute tactics. Those things were not Alira. Hell, most of those things weren't even Skalar. He'd been no saint, certainly not above blackmailing or manipulating or harming another—or a whole species—but he'd been in control every step of the way before Alira donned him like a used suit. With something akin to real clarity, he recognized that it wasn't Skalar at the conn of this ship at all, but a conglomeration of all Alira's harvests. She'd been living Skalar's life, doing Skalar's job, running Skalar's faction by committee, dancing to the familiar music of Skalar's memories wearing oversized shoes that trampled friend and foe alike.

The revelation blew away Skalar's anger and left him pale, weak-kneed, cold. He stared at Thrace in the moonlight.

"You were right about me. About everything."

She looked up, disbelief written in the shadows beneath her eyes. "Of course I was. I am."

Skalar sighed, suddenly weary of the whole charade.

"I have to go away for a while. I need you to assume command at the base in my absence."

She watched his face, reached into his emotions. He knew because he felt her there, rooting through his intentions. Whatever she saw or felt must have given her pause.

"What's wrong?"

"It's a long story, one I don't have time to share right now, but I will tell you everything when I can. Just…" He reached for her again, and she pulled away. His hand fisted, his lips pressed together. Damn it! She wasn't going to make it easy for him. His fury rose, hot in his chest

back off, skalar.

and he stomped it down with all his might. After a moment, his arm fell to his side. "Keep things under control until this mess is resolved. Please."

She shook her head, looked away. For a long while, he thought she would deny him. He couldn't blame her. He'd shoved her away at every turn. He remembered how dedicated Galen had been to Alira, how loyal Thrace was to Skalar. Was it too late to salvage some part of that?

"You know," she said, still not looking at him, "before we left home, you were so adamant about your uniqueness. You went on at length to anyone who would listen about how you didn't fit into the Council's box of conformity. You gave up your allotted place and role in that society in exchange for the freedom to be whoever or whatever you wanted." She cut her eyes at him. "I believed in your decisions at the time, but I was wrong. We both were. You've lost everything you ever wanted. You can't wear your own face or use your own name, and now you've even lost the ability to use your own voice. You are dangerously close to losing your*self*, Alira."

>   *my name is skalar.*

>   *no. it isn't.*

Skalar nodded, swallowed the indignation and listened. Really listened.

Thrace turned to him, her arms crossed.

"You're so afraid of boxes, yet you've willingly conformed to one that was never suited for you. I'm still through with you and your plans, but I will say this. You need to get out of that trap before it's too late, find your own space where you can have the freedom you so desperately need. Once you find that magical place, then you can build your own box, one with room to grow."

He must have made a face, because Thrace snorted, almost a laugh. She tilted her head and stepped closer. "Boxes aren't bad things, Alira. We all live in them. They're part of life, the part that defines our boundaries. The trick is to find one that fits you."

"If there is such a box. I'm not convinced."

Thrace shrugged. "How would you know? You've never looked. You leaped out of unammi civilization and landed in the wilderness of the Consortium without any time to consider your choices or alternatives."

Skalar looked at his feet. Lots of options lay scattered around him like mines in a field, but he had only one real choice. Forward. Toward salvation for the unammi, certainly, but perhaps redemption lay along the way. He'd never know until he tried.

He kicked at a stone, sent it skittering off into the brush, then lifted his face and looked into her eyes.

"Very well. When I return, if you're willing, we'll talk about different approaches to our shared goal. I'll even spend more time with Botha. You have my word."

She peered into his face, searching his features as if truth would be written there. "Where are you going?"

>   *into hell.*

"It's best I don't tell you. Plausible deniability, just in case."

Thrace frowned. "In case what?"

He could almost see the white pulses through her brown skin,
she—galen still cares.
fear for his safety. He smiled. "If I'm not back in thirty standard days, have Tiral load seventy-five percent of the hematium and deliver it to the New Canaan base. Once you have it safely in hand, go to Harlan Downing, tell him you've just learned about Skalar's attack on Iridos, that he destroyed the city and left no survivors."

Now Skalar *did* see her skin go pale. "But—"

He pressed on before he could change his mind. "When Harlan questions your part in the affair, tell him it happened just prior to your recruitment. Assure him that you had no part in it and that as a show of good faith, you are turning over to Harajüd House all the hematium on base. Tell him I'm MIA, that you are taking over the faction, and that you will ensure this sort of thing never happens again."

"He'll know Skalar didn't do that enormous a job alone. He'll want names."

"Then give up the dead. Crow, Cohen's crew we already killed, you know the rest. Turn over a few nukes from our stash, tell him that's all, and promise to cooperate. Just don't give up the faction. If we lose the Consortium, we lose the outpost."

Skin crinkled the corners of her eyes, painting little lines of reflected moonlight on her dark face. "What if Harlan tries to enforce colonial law on the base?"

Skalar shrugged. "He might. The armada's crime happened outside base boundaries, so colonial security could argue that they have jurisdiction. It wasn't on Harajüd House land either, so they really don't. Not exactly. Still, if the other colonies push it, the revelation could get…complicated. Familiarize yourself with the faction-colony contract so you can outmaneuver him. If I'm still here, he could possibly succeed. If I'm not, you can say the matter was handled according to faction law, and that I am no longer a threat to colonial safety. You—" The word squeaked past the pinched spot in his throat, and he swallowed hard. "You'll figure something out. I trust you. Now I must go. No need to walk me out. I know the way."

He turned and left the enclosed garden, separating himself—separating Alira from her i'shin, perhaps forever.

Every step grew harder as he passed through the silent halls toward the front of the compound. A twitch started between his shoulder blades. Was Thrace even now watching him go? He didn't turn around. She hadn't said she would step in, but he knew she would. Galen was on the side of the unammi, so Thrace would do the necessary thing, no matter how she hated it.

At the front of the building, he got into his skimmer and drove away. He knew where he planned to go, though not what he would face there. He just knew that if he hesitated, all would be lost.

Part Three

chapter 39

Pelarr, Zebalu
<u>Cartel Trader Base, Admiral Bellamy's Office</u>

BELLAMY STARED AT THE SECURECAM feed from lockup. Inside the cell, twenty-six smallish teens and preteens gathered in whispering knots, watching the door, watching each other. None of them knew, yet, what their future held. Not that it mattered.

"How many of them came from Harajüd?"

"All but four, ma'am. The others came from Rubene, Fashere, and Levyron. The gear is all from Harajüd. We lifted some of it from New Canaan shipyards, but most of it's black market. I kept it small like you said." Hannah held out a TICS pad.

Bellamy waved it away. "Good work, Captain." Rook stood in the seating area, her back to the window, that wild red hair standing out all over her head. Bellamy picked up her cup, blew on the hot contents. "Captain, can you handle the *Corsair* on a solitary run to and from Iridos with these in the bay?" She jerked her head toward the holofeed.

Rook nodded.

"Good. We don't need any more eyes on this than we already have. This is your baby, then. Make a run every three weeks. Fresh crew and supplies on the way out, hematium on the way home." She tasted her tea. Strong, just the way she liked it.

"Admiral," Hannah said, "are we sure we can't make the slaves last a little longer?"

Bellamy squinted at her second. "Why?"

"The last group's only been there fourteen days so far."

"I can count, Hannah."

"Of course, ma'am. But replacing a whole mining crew every eighteen to twenty-one days is going to get expensive really fast. If we add to the bottom line the fact that snatching kids at such frequent intervals skews the odds toward getting caught…"

"Street urchins are plentiful on almost every colony world. As for expense, you haven't accounted for the increase in faction profit from sale of the hematium." Bellamy sipped her tea, calm as the sea beyond the window on this still, cloudless day. "Walker said the armada crews were 'dropping like flies.' We'll work them until they collapse, of course, but until we know what we're dealing with, three weeks gives our people time to gather a return haul."

"Of course," Hannah agreed. "I just wish we could make bigger runs. Take better equipment, more crew."

"We will." Bellamy shrugged. "But we can't take a direct route to that end. The Cartel doesn't have a mining registry. It would raise all kinds of alerts if we began buying or transporting that kind of equipment which, if it was later found on Iridos, would lead the colonials straight to me. In case you've forgotten, the only person I know of who could attest that it was not the Cartel who killed off an entire race of aliens is now dead."

Hannah made a noncommittal sound and nodded.

"What we can do is hijack a shipment of mining equipment bound for one of the colonies, Levyron or Saacharis maybe, and make it look like a Consortium snatch. We then deliver said take to our gamma base and pick it up on the way to Iridos. Easy peasy."

"That would take a couple of months, but then we wouldn't need to send more slaves. No children, at least." Hannah looked pleased.

"Exactly. If we time this right, we can send equipment eight or nine weeks from now. And if the colonials ever discover the Iridosian city's flat and find the equipment, it'll be traced to a snatch that was tied to the Consortium. In the meantime, I'd be happy to plump the profits." Bellamy grinned. "We need to find that secret base of Skalar's so we can grab the haul he already claimed."

"Maybe that's where Skalar disappeared to," Hannah said. "Too bad we didn't have someone following him, if that's the case."

"How long did you say he'd been gone?"

"Our contact noted his absence about ten days ago."

"Hmm. That base could be anywhere." Bellamy tapped a fingernail on the rim of her teacup. "But if he's there, we need to wait until he shows up in New Canaan again before we go looking for it. Did you find out about this Ronan person Walker mentioned?"

"He's still at the Consortium. Leaves the base to drink at faction pubs with his officers from time to time. My people attempted to approach him, but he wasn't receptive."

"What about his crew? Walker said they might be more willing to talk."

Hannah grimaced and shook her head. "They might've, if we'd gotten to them sooner."

"What does that mean?" Bellamy asked, frowning.

"Word is Skalar caught two of them talking to outsiders in a colonial pub. They didn't spill anything important, but they came damn close. Skalar restricted them for ninety days. Ronan objected, but it seems he took their punishment into his own hands. His crewmen were found dead in confinement less than thirty days later. The rest are more reluctant to talk now."

Bellamy strolled to the window near Rook. Walker had said Skalar's armada worked those shafts for weeks with advanced equipment and didn't get all the metal. If the mine was that large, children working with hand tools and simple Iridosian equipment would take forever. Jude's orders included exploring the site. Bellamy needed to know the extent of the job if she was going to make the most of it. She had no illusions about getting all the metal. Skalar's extermination of an entire species wouldn't go unnoticed forever, but until it came to colonial attention, she'd work his idea for all it was worth.

"Well, we knew going in that this game had a limited life span," she said, gazing out the window. She downed the last of her tea and nodded at Rook. "For the foreseeable future, this is the plan. Any questions?"

Rook shook her head. "No ma'am."

"Good. You leave in four days."

chapter 40

Haven, Danua
<u>Clan Trader Base, Admiral Tsurin's Office</u>

"…SO, THEY ENDED UP RIGHT where they started," Admiral Tsurin said, "and the first guy says to the second guy, 'You didn't mention this was a round-trip ticket.'"

The other two officers laughed. Knøfa squinted at them, then shifted his focus to Tsurin's face, to the little tic at the corner of her left eye. Yeah. She knew why they laughed, and it had nothing to do with her being funny. Tsurin could mutilate even the best punchline with her lousy timing or the omission of crucial details, but she was the Clan Admiral.

"Very well," she said, sobering their weak response. "That's enough chat. You both have work to do. Get to it."

Knøfa watched them go, fawning and bowing all the way to the door.

"You never laugh at my anecdotes, Captain," Tsurin said.

Knøfa returned his gaze to her. "With all due respect, ma'am, if you want me to laugh you should tell better jokes."

"Ouch." Tsurin shook her head. "We all have our strengths, I suppose. Mine lie elsewhere. Sit."

She nodded toward a seat, and Knøfa lowered all two hundred and five centimeters of his bulk into the dwarfed chair. At least it was reinforced.

"You've been my second for almost a month now. How does the role sit with you?" She twisted her silver-shot black hair into a knot and pinned it in place at the back of her head with a random stylus from her desk.

Knøfa considered the question, taking his time. Tsurin had known him since he was four. She wouldn't push him. Not on something like this.

"I've gotten adept enough on the small things that you don't check my results any longer," he said. "I'm guessing you want to know if I'm ready for bigger challenges."

A wide, crooked grin lit her leathery face and crinkled the corners of her eyes. "That isn't what I asked. But since you bring it up, are you?"

"What do you think?"

"Ready or not, you need it," she said.

She kicked off her shoes, leaned to one side and pulled her feet up into the chair with her. It was her preferred position. Apparently, she felt more comfortable that way. She'd done this in his presence all his life, but he'd never seen her do it with anyone else around. Maybe she felt it made her vulnerable. She was right, but she was safe with him.

"We've upped our exports by thirty percent," she said, "and sale of imports by thirty-five percent in the last solar year, but it hasn't had the effect I hoped. The Clan's still at the bottom of the Trader food chain. I'd like to change that, and I want you to help."

"Why me?" Knøfa raised an eyebrow. "I'm just a newbie."

Tsurin scoffed. "Hardly. I raised you here. You grew up watching from the corner while we struck deals and worked the trade. Hell, you were only twelve when you figured out who was skimming our profits in the silk trade. I knew then that you'd be an asset to this faction. You've continued to prove me right for twenty years, so don't hide behind the wet ink on your promotion now."

His chest swelled just the slightest bit. If it were anyone else, he wouldn't give a damn, but Tsurin's praise always made him feel warm. A little proud. Knøfa sniffed. "Wouldn't dream of it, ma'am."

"Good. What's the latest from Harajüd?"

"Word is Skalar's gone to ground again," he said. "His second is running things, settling some disturbances.

"Hmm. Interesting, especially on top of that earlier news where Skalar's crew talked to our people about a big haul and some remarkable secret hiding place. He's raising the suspicions of even his own officers. You think something's up?"

He grunted. "That's a natural state for Skalar, isn't it? But something tells me this is different than last time."

Tsurin's green gaze pinned him to his chair. "Why?"

"I'm not sure. It just feels … off. I got backup on the rumor he was running slaves, but nothing concrete yet." He paused. "You think he is?"

"No. Never."

"You seem pretty certain."

She tilted her head, one eyebrow raised. "Think about those refrigerated crates we got a few months ago. The ones with ears, fingers, a nose. The bits you ran DNA on."

DNA checks were routine work for him by now, but he remembered this one in particular. "We never ID'd the body they came from."

"That's right."

He frowned. "How can that be possible?"

"Sometimes agents manage to buy or blackmail connections way up the corporate tier," she said, "in order to get past the colonial systems by running in the black. Wiped records. No traceable identity. It's rare, but it can be done."

Knøfa whistled. "You never mentioned that."

She stared at him, undoubtedly gauging his reaction.

"Someone with no DNA record wouldn't be able to use the ports. They'd be all off grid."

"Correct." Tsurin nodded. "We can go over the details later. For now, let's talk about how I know Skalar isn't slaving."

He put the pieces together. "You think Skalar sent those crated body parts."

"I know he did."

"Why? Why not suspect Bellamy or Georgeanne or even Bardo?" Knøfa shook his head. "No, not Bardo. Not his style. But I can see George doing it, or maybe Rizzo."

"I know it's Skalar because I've seen him do this once before."

His foster mother had shared all sorts of stories with him as he was growing up, but she'd never spoken of that. "To who?"

Her mouth drew into a thin line. "Henri."

Knøfa's eyes widened. "*Admiral* Henri? The Henri that let you take me in when I was a child? Your predecessor? *That* Henri?"

She didn't answer. She didn't need to.

"Why? No, never mind. I know the answer. Henri ran slaves."

"Yes."

He studied her frown, the way her mouth turned down at the corners. "You never liked that, did you?"

"No."

"You still do it, though."

"No," she said, her voice sharp. She drew in a breath. "No, I don't. I lease indentured workers. They work to pay off a debt to the Clan, not because I own them. I also don't inflate their tally with extraneous expenses in order to keep them longer. When their original obligation is paid, they're free to go."

"May I ask why you hate slaving so much?"

"Because I disagree with the selling of human beings like they're furniture. It's wrong."

"The Clan does plenty of things that are, according to who you ask, wrong."

"This's different. Breaking the law is one thing. Technically, yes. It's wrong to sell counterfeits as if they were the real article, or forge identifications, or hijack supply shipments and resell them on the black market, but those things usually hurt only the government. It's a gray area when we're stealing from a colonial hierarchy that will never notice the hit. But slaving hurts individual humans by taking away their freedom and turning them into property. It's a crime against humanity. It's abominable." She leaned forward. "You do see that, don't you?"

Always the teacher. Tsurin was every bit his mother, even though she didn't give birth to him. The fact that Tsurin had killed both his parents never entered into the equation as far as he was concerned. She'd taken care of him ever since and had taught him a great deal, despite…well, everything. That counted for a lot in his book.

But no. He didn't see it. Human labor was a commodity, wasn't it? Everybody worked for somebody else in exchange for remuneration. If you employed a human being, you paid their wages one way or another. If you bought a slave, you paid the credits to someone else, and paid it all at once instead of spread out over years. What was the difference? Either way, the worker was given shelter, food, medicine. Granted, some slave owners were said to be cruel, but some employers treated their employees badly too, didn't they?

Take the colonials for pity's sake. They provided the basics—health care, housing, employment, enough credits to buy some things beyond what was given them though not much else—but they weren't the most compassionate of benefactors. At least that's what he was told by others. He wouldn't know, himself. He'd been with the Clan most of his life. Besides, he'd never gotten what others meant by words like "compassionate," or "cruel." He knew the literal meaning, but he didn't *understand*. Tsurin had recognized this, asked him about it when he was very young, tried to give him boundaries so that he could live among other humans who did feel those emotions. She'd taught him how to fit in, mostly. He owed her. More to the point, he trusted her.

"If you say it, I believe it." He nodded once, as if that was that. "Did you go after Skalar when he killed Henri?"

"No, but not because Henri and I disagreed on trade. He knew how I felt about that, but I respected him a lot. He taught me everything I know about running a faction."

"Then why?"

"Because it wasn't a cut-and-dried situation. Skalar hated slaving, yes, but I don't think he would normally have gone berserk like he did. Henri tipped the balance by involving Skalar's little sister in the business."

Ah. Knøfa knew about familial ties. Not because he felt them—he didn't—but Tsurin had explained them to him often enough, warned him about the risks of getting between members of a family. Maybe this issue with Skalar's sister was the reason for Tsurin's admonition. He thought back — when had she first mentioned it?

"I didn't go after Skalar because I understood why he did what he did. He's been death on the subject ever since, so yes," Tsurin said, "I'm ninety-nine percent certain this was Skalar. The question is, why did he send the crates here? Whoever was inside in all those pieces, they weren't Clan crew."

"He must have thought they were, though. Without a traceable gene code, he wouldn't have any proof otherwise." Knøfa pursed his lips. "Who do we know who's most likely to stir up trouble between the factions to distract attention away from herself?"

"You read my mind," Tsurin said, a shadow of a grin brushing her lips. "Bellamy would have the most to gain here. I'd bet credits it was her. Slaving is well within her purview, so ten-to-one, it was a Cartel agent Skalar boxed up."

"What do you intend to do about it?"

"I've already sent word to Skalar that it wasn't us, but he either didn't believe me or just hasn't deigned to respond." Her mouth twisted to one side. "He likes reminding the rest of us that he's at the top of the food chain."

"What about Bellamy?"

Her face puckered, eyes slitted. "Good question, that. I'm not sure what the answer is yet. We should discuss options. The Clan can't be seen to acquiesce when slighted, but on the other hand, we can't win a conflict with the Cartel. Which," she said, swinging a pointed finger in a circle over her head, "brings us to where we started. We need to enhance the Clan's power, boost our output, impress some new friends. We need contacts higher up in the colonial pyramid."

"Okay. And?"

"I want you to come up with some ideas on how to accomplish that."

His eyebrow rose all by itself. "You were serious?"

"I was. Ideas only, Knøfa." She held up that finger again. "Don't take action without consulting me."

"Of course not."

"Good. I've granted you greater access to our system so you can familiarize yourself with what we've done in the past, and how we went about it. Surprise me. Think outside the expected parameters. I know you can do that."

"I'll see what I can do," he said with a shrug. "You want me to begin immediately?"

She grinned. "Why are you still here?"

chapter 41

New Canaan, Harajüd
<u>Dagons Public House</u>

THRACE GLANCED PAST KILBEE AT the front entrance where Mira stood, waiting for her eyes to adjust to the dim interior. Even from here, Mira's antipathy radiated in waves as the human glanced up toward the gallery and the admiral's table. Thrace held up a finger and nodded. Mira acknowledged the signal and took a seat at the bar.

Kilbee peered at Thrace. "Rakalesh isn't going to take 'no' for an answer," he said. "Not for long, anyway. The council expects an answer from Alira, and at this point they want it directly from her, in person."

Thrace brought her attention to Kilbee's face. "What can they possibly do to me? I can't give you what I don't have."

"Where is she, then?"

"I don't know."

Kilbee shook his head, ate a fry, and somehow managed to sigh through his teeth. "I never knew Galen to be a liar before now. Alira's a bad influence on you."

Thrace stiffened. "Believe me or not, as you wish. I know bringing her to the council would buy points with your ama, but I'm telling you Alira is not here. She didn't tell me where she was going, and I don't know when she'll be back." *If at all.* Thrace's stomach knotted at the thought. "I don't want to quarrel with you, Kilbee."

The pilot ate another fry and looked around the pub. "Then let's not. I have to get going anyway. *Vagabond* is loaded and waiting for me at the port."

"Are you finished with your normal route?"

"Yeah. Headed to the outpost. Want me to deliver any other messages? Something not so explosive, maybe?"

"Tell Rakalesh I'm holding things together here as best I can. I still think maintaining a presence on Harajüd is best for the survivors."

"She doesn't agree, you know. None of the councilors do."

Thrace forced her hands to lay still in her lap. "What do you mean?"

"They believe we should come to the new city and give up any contact with humans."

"All of us?" Thrace blinked. "Even the outcasts? The mitigants?"

He shrugged. "That's what they say."

"They have to know that would never work." Thrace frowned and her hands crept toward one another in her lap. "How long before they began mitigating outcasts? How long before half the remaining population had no mind of their own?"

"You have to understand, everything is so strange for them. New city, new passages, alien plants and foods and dangers. They want to retreat to the familiar, I suppose. Old habits." He grumped. "Humans say the devil you know is better than the one you don't."

"Do you think we should comply?"

"I dunno. I'm torn. I want to please her," he said, "but I don't think I could live under the council's governance again. Not after being away for so long."

Thrace looked away. Mira still warmed a stool at the bar, but the ground floor was filling fast. Must be shift's end, humans coming to Dagons for a pint after a day's labor. Eager patrons milled about at the entry, between the tables, on the stairs, at the gallery railing. Humans' enthusiasm and boisterous nature made them interesting and enjoyable, but it also made them dangerous. If the colonial governments ever discovered Earth's biosphere was no longer toxic, they would swarm over it in an instant. At best, the unammi would be forced to find yet another home. At worst, they would be exterminated or captured.

That would not do.

Discovery was unlikely, granted, but even if Thrace shut down the outpost and never used it again, too many people knew about it. She couldn't—wouldn't—eliminate them all on the simple possibility that they might pose a risk to that shield.

"You and I have experience with human behavior," she said, still gazing at the pub's crowd. "We know why staying here is a good idea. The council, isolated as they have been, will never comprehend our reasoning. How could they? I'd be happy to explain it to them myself, but I can't leave right now. If Rakalesh wishes to discuss it with me personally, she's welcome to come here. I'll reveal the risks in detail, show her how abandoning this plan is bad for everyone." Thrace looked at Kilbee. "Of course, if she departs Earth, she becomes the very thing she fears most—outcast."

Kilbee's mouth curled up at one corner, a crooked acknowledgement of that irony. "Don't hold your breath." He shoved the last fry in his mouth and stood, still chewing. "If that's all, I'll be going."

There was more, much more. But words proved a poor vehicle for her intent, and they couldn't very well enter a muñara here, in a public place. Thrace only nodded.

"See you next time, then." Kilbee turned, slipped through the privacy screen and melted into the crowd.

He moved down the stairs—Kilbee never trusted the creaky lift—then threaded his way through the bustle to and through the door. At the bar, Mira lifted her gaze to the gallery, then left her stool and headed upstairs.

Thrace pulled her hands away from each other. If only Botha were here. She'd kept him informed of the changes in New Canaan, listened to his counsel. His presence always comforted her and would be most welcome in this uncertain time, but now he would need to come to her.

Time away from direct faction interaction, at least for the foreseeable future, would be almost nil. Skalar had pushed her into a position where she had to take control. She'd spent more than two weeks setting herself up as admiral, going through his residence for any evidence that might incriminate the Consortium, and generally cleaning up his messes. He would have no right to complain if he didn't like her methods. Whether or not he returned, she was now the new admiral.

A tiny taste of Skalar's claims about sitting in the admiral's chair began to tingle in the back of her throat. He hadn't been wrong about everything.

Mira approached the shield and Thrace beckoned her through. The commander stepped forward slowly, as if she were reluctant to face this meeting.

"Please," Thrace said, "sit."

"I'd rather stand, ma'am."

Thrace nodded. "As you wish. First of all, relax. I don't want to harm you." Mira's expression spoke volumes on the subject of disbelief. "I know you're afraid. You've had good reason in the past, but things have changed. I'm in control of the Consortium."

"So, the rumors are true? You're the admiral now?"

"Yes."

"Where's Skalar?"

And now the game had begun. How Alira would laugh if she could see this moment. Told you so, she'd say. Thrace reached into Mira's emotions, probing gently. What response would convince her to play along?

Thrace's lips smiled. "Why ask questions you know I can't answer?"

"Who's your second?"

"I haven't filled that position yet."

Mira scoffed, shook her head. "The others will never follow you. You're an unknown. You have no history with them."

"Let's be honest with one another, shall we?" Thrace placed her elbows on the table and laced her fingers. "We both know that what happens at the upper levels of this faction flies over the heads of recruits and the rest of the lower echelons. Most of the crew will see only a change of command. They won't understand it, but they won't fight it unless someone higher up the chain incites them to it."

Mira shifted her weight from one foot to the other.

"What you really mean to say is that the officers won't follow me. And you're probably right. I'll have to earn their respect," Thrace said, "and yours."

"Earn," Mira said, her voice flat. "Not buy."

Thrace bobbed her head from side to side. "Mmm. Sometimes an exchange helps to grease the wheels of change."

Mira's eyes narrowed. "Go on."

"I know Skalar was irredeemable at the end." Thrace leaned back, hands dropping to her lap. "He did things I disagreed with, took actions I tried to prevent. I want to mend fences. In fact, I asked you here to offer you a deal." A glimmer of hope seemed to enter the commander's eyes. "Sure you don't want to sit down?"

Mira eyed the seat, hesitant, then stepped forward and lowered herself into it.

"What you say has merit," Thrace continued. "If I'm going to run the faction, I need the other officers to accept me, to believe that I will lead them better than Skalar did, especially at the end. It'll take time to convince them on my own, so I need to give them reasons to believe in me until then. You can help me with that."

"How?"

"Throw your support behind me."

A chuff of surprise huffed out of Mira's mouth. "Why would I do that?"

"Because I'm going to release your brother."

Even without the flood of hopeful relief that poured out of her, Mira could never have hidden her reaction. Her sharp intake of breath, her trembling lips, her widened blue eyes all gave her away. Thrace read it all like a master. This was going to work.

It had to.

Mira's features twisted, then flattened as if she wanted to appear unmoved. *Too late.* "And if I refuse?"

Thrace shrugged. "Doesn't matter. I'll release him either way. I never agreed with Skalar's plan to confine him. I need the Consortium's officers to work with me because they want to, because they trust and respect me, not because they're being coerced."

The commander squinted at Thrace. "What's the catch?"

"I already told you. Support me, openly and behind the scenes." Thrace leaned forward, elbows again on the table. "I know you don't know me. Not yet. All you have is my word that I want what's best for the Consortium, and for its officers and crew. I am an excellent leader," she said. Well, that was a lie, but she was trying. Maybe Kilbee had been right about Alira's influence. "I'm not entirely ignorant of Trader operations, but I freely admit that I'm new to the Consortium scene. I need input from officers more steeped in its history, as you put it. Unlike Skalar, I plan to elicit feedback and actually listen to it wherever possible. The initial hurdle will be getting the officers to the table in the first place."

"Sounds too good to be true," Mira said. "But even assuming you're telling the truth, how do you expect my support to mean squat? You need someone with a higher rank. I'm only a commander, and every Consortium crewman low or high knows I hate faction leadership right now."

"Which would make your support that much more meaningful," Thrace said. "Especially if I promote you to captain and make you my second."

Mira blinked. "Make me…. What?"

The woman's roiling confusion and internal conflict pinged Thrace's empathic sensors. On Mira's face, her emotional battle flickered almost like the color surges in unammi. Each told its tale, and Mira's left no room for doubt. She wanted this.

"You heard me."

"Wh—wh—" Mira shook her head as if to clear the bewilderment. "Why not Ronan? Or Sa'abah?"

"You think they could do a better job?"

A crease formed between Mira's brows. "No. Of course not. I'd be a good second."

"Would Ronan or Sa'abah be more trustworthy?"

"No!" Mira almost shouted. "But like I said, the rest of us know one another. We've worked together for years. You're the unknown quantity. What makes you think any of us won't kill you the minute you aren't watching?"

Thrace stared across the table. "Is that your plan?"

Mira squirmed in her seat as if unsure how to respond. "To be honest, yeah. It was, up until about five minutes ago."

"And now?"

"Now…"

Mira's eyes seemed to search Thrace's for a clue as to what the hell was actually happening. Apparently, it never occurred to her before now that this new admiral might actually be telling the truth.

"Now, I'm listening," Mira finally said. "I want to hear more about your ideas for the faction."

chapter 42

Pelarr, Zebalu
<u>**Aboard the Corsair, Departing Cartel Trader Base**</u>

ROOK CONNECTED WITH CARTEL AND Pelarr ground control to announce her departure and to confirm a clear flight path, then left the base behind. Once clear of city traffic, she flew the ship toward the departure point in the direction of Harajüd. No sense giving anyone reason to suspect she was headed elsewhere. At safe speeds, she had ninety seconds before she would reach outer atmosphere, and another thirty to bypass orbital satellites. Then she could hit interstel and enter the coordinates for her true destination.

Bellamy had asked her if she could handle the *Corsair* on a solo flight. Truth be told, this ship flew easier than the larger haulers in the Cartel's fleet. Rook had flown better craft, before she joined up with Bellamy, but *Corsair* wasn't half bad. Only two holds full, at that, so she handled with ease, almost flew herself. Yeah, Rook could do a solo flight.

But she wasn't really solo, was she? No crew, it's true. But the hold was full of people. Kids. Rook's face twisted and her shoulders hunched forward as if curling away from an unpleasant smell. Her parents would not approve of this, but then they wouldn't like Rook's position in the Cartel, either. She'd hidden it for years, an easier task since they couldn't visit from Shemonaea more than once a year. As far as they knew, Rook still flew colonial shipping on a schedule that kept her from leaving to visit them at home. She didn't like lying to them. They'd taught her better, but their disappointment in her would be harder to bear than the shame she felt for herself, so she did what she had to do.

Same as she'd done when the colonials caught her smuggling and set her up. The instinct for survival excused a lot, at least in her own mind. Of course, if she hadn't been smuggling in the first place…

Her thoughts drifted down dark corridors of thought, her pale features twisted into a pained moue. She no longer pondered what had brought her to this point. Too many little decisions to count, most of which she wouldn't change even if she could. The outcome, however, left a bitter taste in her mouth and burned going down.

Rook ran a hand through her short mop of hair and checked the ship's position. Approaching outer atmosphere. She set up interstel parameters without changing direction. Not yet. Checks on supply chamber status showed green across the board. Visuals of the kids in the other hold showed about what she expected. Some slept in their bolted cots, others paced or sat hunkered down. A few stood or sat together. She could enhance the volume, focus on their conversations if she wanted to.

She did not. Too distracting. Systems checks, final prep for interstel, then she was past the satellites and on her way. Only an hour later did she feel safe enough to change destination.

"TICS, enter coordinates for Tuneloras, Saacharis. Time to arrival?"

"One-point-seven standard days."

"Very well. Execute."

The conn chittered, and Rook leaned back in her seat, morphing into Alira as she did so and relaxing for the first time in almost three weeks. It had taken days to locate a place off-base where she could safely shed her human form and sleep, then to select just the right primary target with whom to infiltrate the Cartel and body-hop her way close to the admiral. Rook had seemed an ideal target—not too close, but close enough to gain access to Bellamy's secrets. But the admiral's constant vigilance and the fact that Rook's harvested personality resisted her at every step made wearing her persona far more challenging than Skalar's.

The hardship had forced Alira to take a long look at her mistakes. She had allowed herself to grow accustomed to Skalar's power and prestige, bought into his delusion of grandeur

netzyl! i resent that implication.

and his conviction that his/her actions were beyond reproach. She could not fall into that trap again or she would be well and truly lost.

That is if she made it out of her new adventure in one piece.

This trip would be a welcome break and allow her some time to consider all she'd learned. Rizzo had been right. Bellamy was behind a huge network of slaving and was making damn sure it looked like Skalar was involved. Most of the Cartel crew Alira had encountered knew that much. It was only Rook's memories that told her what Bellamy knew of Iridos, a project the admiral had kept quiet. The thought of slaves being forced to labor in the unammi city's mines lent a sense of urgency to her mission here. She couldn't help the children already on her homeworld, not without undermining or totally sinking her already delicate situation, but she could help the ones in the hold below, and the ones that came into her care after that.

Unfortunately, that didn't further her larger purpose. Skalar trod a thin line already, with the destruction of Iridos. In her head, he still claimed to be able to deny the whole thing when it finally came to light,

if, netzyl. if it comes to light.

come on skalar. no way we can hide that forever.

but he did not need further scrutiny just now. If the colonials found Bellamy's planted evidence to support a Consortium role in the slave trade, Skalar was done and so was Alira's use of the outpost as a shield for the unammi.

Rook stood close to Bellamy. Only Hannah stood closer, but the Skalar experience made Alira doubt her ability to pull that impersonation off with adequate finesse. Rook seemed a workable alternative. She kept to herself, had no lovers or partners, spoke little, did as she was told. Easy to mimic for a short while. So far it had worked. She'd learned all she needed to know, and it was time to take action. Somehow Bellamy had to be stopped, except now that Alira was in position, the "how" part of that plan eluded her. All her body hops to get to this point had, to her chagrin, required killing the officer in question and incorporating the subsequent harvest. Killing Bellamy was out of the question unless there was no other alternative. Not only did she worry about pushing her luck, but she'd seen enough in the Cartel reapings thus far to believe Bellamy was

the queen of whacked.

unstable in her own right. There had to be another way. Alira just needed to find it.

chapter 43

New Canaan, Harajüd

<u>Consortium Trader Base, Admiral Baldric's Office</u>

"CHIEF DOWNING?" THRACE ASKED, FROWNING.

"Yes ma'am," the gate officer said. She glanced to the side in the holovid, then looked at Thrace again. "He insists on seeing you, ma'am."

What now? Harlan's timing couldn't be more inconvenient. She still had a great deal of ground to cover in order to secure her position as admiral. She also wasn't yet ready to discuss Skalar's disappearance with colonial security. "Very well. Have him wait there for an escort. Baldric out."

"TICS, locate Captain Cohen. Send her to my office. And connect me to Captain Sa'abah immediately." Thrace gathered the latest black-market trinkets her crew had brought in and carried them to the workroom. A chirp sounded in her main office.

"Answer," Thrace called as she reentered the room.

"Admiral Baldric?" Sa'abah said, her upper body projected over Thrace's desk. "You commed?"

Thrace nodded. "Chief Downing is at the front gate. I would like you to personally escort him to my office and wait until we are finished, then escort him out to the gate again. He is not to be alone on the base at any time. And send someone to my office with that last ALT headset."

"Of course. Is that all, ma'am?"

Thrace felt Sa'abah's uncertainty, saw it in her hesitant manner. Even after more than two weeks, the captain still didn't know what to make of this change of command. She had kept the peace throughout, ensuring the transition occurred as smoothly as could be expected. But the feeling Thrace got from the captain seemed clear. Sa'abah hadn't decided yet how she felt about the change.

No time to worry about that just now. Thrace could chat with the captain after Harlan was gone.

"Yes. Thank you, Captain."

She ended the comm, swung back into the workroom, and opened the vault. Inside, its wide shelves held ident card templates ready for forging, three bolts of counterfeit Danua silk, five kilos of unregistered recreationals, two kilos of unregistered coffee, and trays of counterfeit precious and semi-precious stones among other things—the usual array for a productive Trader admiral's personal collection. Thrace placed the trinkets inside and drew out two bolts of silk, one kilo of leafy smoke, and one of coffee. She placed the items on her worktable, then secured the vault.

Outside, the sunset cast glorious rays of golden light across the cityscape, reflected in the towers of the city center and glinting on the distant bay. Thrace's office windows tinted to shield her from the glare without blocking the view, and she stared at the city laid before her. Standing in Skalar's shoes even for this short time had given Thrace a better understanding of Alira's distress.

Where was she now? She could be anywhere. Almost half the specified time had elapsed, and still Thrace had heard no word. She'd checked after Skalar's departure and found the Consortium's fallback ship, the *Cepheid*, missing. Skalar's doing, no doubt. He'd known that ship would be useful in losing himself somewhere. It wasn't registered to the Consortium, but to a non-existent person named Lyla Ravish. Small, older transport. Nothing fancy to draw attention. No point in looking for it. One of Alira's harvests would know how to disable the tracker and avoid detection.

Thrace had to admit worry, but that wouldn't stop her from taking advantage of Skalar's absence. She had no intention of returning control of the faction to him when—if—he reappeared.

Her door chimed.

"Come," she said.

An officer entered, carrying an ALT headset. "Captain Sa'abah said you asked for this, ma'am?"

"Yes." Thrace gestured, and the officer handed over the tech.

"Glad to be rid of it, ma'am," the woman said, "if you know what I mean." She shuddered.

"I do." Thrace nodded. "Thank you. And thank the captain for me."

The officer left, and Thrace looked down at the ALT game in her hand. No one talked about the device openly, so Thrace knew little about it other than simple basics. They were illegal for good reason, as Skalar had found shortly after taking over the old regime here. He'd set out to teach a lesson by enforcing Lieutenant Enzo to wear one non-stop. No breaks. No reprieves. But evidence provided afterward gave validity and support to corpgov's ruling on the game. Enzo's autopsy, performed after the headset finally killed him, had revealed that the device withered his brain in key areas and fried the neural connections in others. The damage went beyond that organ's ability to function or rewire itself.

Thrace frowned. Only humans would create or play a game that took them so far out of their own minds they sometimes couldn't get back.

The thought brought her up short. Alira's experience was much the same, wasn't it? Except instead of being pried out of herself, Alira had crammed too many others into the same shell with her and crowded out her own persona. Would she ever be the same? Probably not. Thrace dropped the headset into her pocket with a pang and turned to the window.

At the chime, she called out entry. Cohen passed into the office.

"What's up?"

"Harlan Downing's suspicions, apparently," Thrace said. "Sa'abah's bringing him in from the gate for a meeting. I want you to sit in."

In the reflection, Mira's eyes widened, then narrowed. "Why?"

Thrace turned toward her. "I explained myself to you at Dagons. You're still free to walk away at this point. But I won't have us constantly circling each other. I've got zero patience for games. If you're going to be my second, we need to be one hundred percent on the same side. What's it going to be?"

The captain hesitated, then nodded. "What's the meeting about?"

"Downing thinks we're cheating the colonials. He's right, but we want him to think he's not. We're going to give him what he wants, or at least a little piece of it."

Mira frowned. "But—"

Thrace felt them coming, held up a hand. Harlan's suppressed anger. Sa'abah's watchful reserve. "They'll be here soon. Save your questions for after the interview."

"Yes, ma'am."

"TICS, set nanopanel to blue swirl." Light in the office changed into a calming, shifting pattern. The door chimed and Thrace called entry.

Harlan Downing swept in as if he owned the place, but Harlan would never own anything. Thrace could feel it in him, that loyalty to company that would keep him ever compliant to its rules and expectations. He would have made a very good unammi. Other than his position in colonial security, he did not stand out in any way. Graying brownish hair around the sides of his head, balding on top. Paunchy middle. Average height for a human. Average weight. Late-day stubble on the cheeks and chin of his long face. Soft lines around his deep-set brown eyes made him look older than he was. Stress of the job, perhaps.

Thrace smiled. "Chief Downing. We meet at last. I've heard a great deal about you. I'm Admiral Thrace Baldric. This is my second, Captain Mira Cohen. Please." She gestured toward a seat, then nodded to Sa'abah to wait outside.

Harlan sat. "Where is Skalar?"

Straight to the point, then. Very well. She could handle that. Thrace took her own seat. Mira did the same. "He has retired from faction life. How can I help you?"

"You're in charge now?"

"That's right."

The chief sat up straighter. "I invoke the right to search the base."

"On what grounds?"

"Suspicion of slavery."

Mira's gaze shot to her face, and Thrace's smile widened. "I will help you search every building myself as soon as I inspect your evidence."

Harlan stared at her. Mira glanced between them. She looked as if she was holding her breath.

Thrace waited.

"My search will turn up the evidence," he said. "Then we can examine it together."

Thrace tilted her head down, her focus locked on his face. "I'm new to the Consortium, Chief, not new to Trader leadership. Request denied. How else can I help?"

He leaned forward in his seat. "It wasn't a request."

"Of course it was. You're a man who respects contractual law. You know better than to force a breaching action. It's not in the best interests of either of our organizations." She stood. "However, I do have something for you. Wait here."

She stepped into the next room, collected the contraband, and brought it out, laying everything on her desk. Mira's eyes widened.

Harlan's, too. "What's this?"

"I'm fairly certain these are all unregistered. I believe you'll want to take them into your custody, especially this kilo of coffee beans." She picked up the wrapped bundle and gave it to him.

Harlan drew it closer to his face and inhaled deeply. His rush of pleasure washed over her as he recognized the smoky aroma.

His favorite vice.

Harlan glanced up. "Where did they come from?"

"I don't know. I found them in Skalar's vault when I took over," she said, resuming her seat. "I would have brought all this to you sooner." She waved her hand toward the items on the desk. "But as you might imagine, I've been a little preoccupied these last few weeks."

He wanted to believe her, she could feel it. Yet suspicion dragged him back into the familiar. "Is this all of it?"

"Not quite." She reached into her pocket and pulled out the headset. "Found this too. I know Skalar had an incident with these at one of our gaming houses not long ago. I'm not sure why he kept one. Maybe he wanted to study the thing. I don't want it on my base."

"Not even if it can turn a profit?"

She pursed her lips, as if giving the idea some thought. "Some things are not worth black numbers on a balance sheet."

Mira's forehead grew wrinkles between her eyebrows. Thrace could feel her struggle to understand.

Harlan frowned. "Why are you doing this?"

"Because I want you to see that circumstances are changing here at the Consortium. I don't plan to run the faction the way Skalar did. I'd like us to cooperate with one another."

Harlan placed the coffee on the desk with reluctance. "Sounds like you're trying to buy my silence."

"Not at all. In fact, I have another token of good faith to offer." She watched him a moment, let his expectation build. "Skalar set up a ghostnet in HHU's internal TICS system."

Mira visibly started. She shot a shocked look at Thrace.

"Goddammit," Harlan muttered. His lips tightened into a thin line. "How'd he get it past our security?"

She shrugged. "That I don't know. You might want to have your techs take it apart to the code level, see if they find any hints." Of course, that wouldn't tell Harlan about the other ghostnet threads wound through HHU. Those were newer, more productive, harder to track. He'd never find them without her help.

"When did he set this up?"

"It was already in place when I came onboard." She picked up her TICS pad, touched its screen a couple of times to bring up the information, and threw the data to his. "That's the key. I've disabled our ability to tap it on this end. The rest is up to you."

He pulled out his own pad and stared at the code before returning the device to his pocket. He retrieved the coffee, turned its package over in his hands. "I don't get it."

"What?"

"I don't understand why you're doing this. Turning over contraband, okay. Even the headset I can see. But why tell me about the ghostnet? You could have kept that going indefinitely. Denied any knowledge or accountability even if it was found."

Mira agreed. Thrace could feel her confusion. "True."

"Then why disclose it?"

"I told you. I know you aren't fond of the Consortium. I'd like to change that if I can."

Harlan scoffed. "That's not likely to happen. No offense."

"Fair enough." Thrace gestured toward herself. "I'd still like to try."

"Do your best," he said, shaking his head. "I've never known an altruistic Trader, especially not an admiral. I'll be waiting for you to reveal your ulterior motive."

Thrace nodded. Even though Harlan's mouth preached misgivings, the man radiated true doubt. He still wasn't a fan, yet he wouldn't be so quick to suspect her of wrongdoing after this.

"Of course. Was there anything else I could help you with?"

He peered at her. "Word on the street says the Consortium yanked kids for the slave trade."

"'Yanked kids'?" Thrace repeated. She didn't try to hide the natural twist of her lips. Let him see how she felt about the matter. "Skalar would never have allowed that."

"My sources are reliable."

"Then check your historical records for references to Amelia Skalar."

Harlan frowned. "Any relation?"

"Sister. Skalar told me she'd been taken by slavers when she was only a child." Thrace pressed her lips together, remembering Alira's first mention of this almost two months ago. It seemed longer. "I looked it up. Colonial records say she disappeared in 1406 and reappeared in 1427, a broken woman. Ended her own life shortly thereafter. He never got over it."

"Huh," Harlan grunted. "I can't picture Skalar caring what happens to anyone else, even his sister."

Thrace faked a thin smile. "We are all products of our pasts, Chief, even someone as seemingly isolated and remote as Skalar. Colonial records show he made numerous appearances at HHU security offices to get updates in the search for her, right from the start. Perhaps there's a connection between their failure to protect her and his current lack of regard for the office you hold."

The man bristled. "Now wait just a minute—"

She gestured. "I mean no disrespect, Chief Downing. You are not personally responsible for something that happened decades ago. I'm merely pointing out that the idea of Skalar snatching children to enslave them is dubious at best. He has good reason to hate that trade."

He eyed her. "You know I'll check this out myself."

"Please do. While you're at it, do some digging on those rumors you've been hearing. Locate the source of that information and you'll find your child-snatcher."

"And you know nothing about who that might be?"

"I can point fingers, just like anyone else. That wouldn't be very productive. If I do come across conclusive evidence or even credible tips, you'll be the first to know." She touched the manual control for the door, and Sa'abah stepped in. Thrace stood, followed by Mira. "Is there a skimmer waiting for you at the gate?"

He lurched to his feet. "Yes, but—"

"Good," she said, gesturing to Sa'abah, who came to the desk and gathered the bolts of silk and the recreational packet into her arms. "My security captain will assist you in carrying and loading these items. I hope this will be the beginning of a better relationship between us, Chief. Good day to you."

"But—"

Thrace smiled and gestured at the door. "Good day, Chief Downing."

He gawped at her, then at the other two officers, and finally gathered the coffee and the headset and followed Sa'abah out of the office.

Only when the door closed behind them did Cohen whirl to face her. "I may have underestimated you, ma'am."

Thrace allowed her mouth to soften. "Of that I am certain, Captain Cohen. Ask your questions, now."

"Is it true about Skalar's sister? That she killed herself?"

"Yes."

"How?"

Thrace grimaced. "Let's not violate that privacy, shall we? To speak of such things shows poor taste. She suffered enough. Leave the woman her dignity."

Mira had the good grace to look ashamed. "Of course, ma'am." She cleared her throat. "What did you mean about the headsets?"

"Elaborate."

"You said something about them not being worth the profit margin."

"I did, didn't I?" Thrace sat, considering her answer. Mira clung to that faction mentality. Thrace would need to change that. "Have you ever played that game, Captain?"

"No, ma'am. I must admit I'm curious, though."

"Then why haven't you tried it?"

Mira looked away, blinking. "I've heard rumors they aren't always enjoyable."

"And your intuition told you to listen."

"Yes, ma'am."

"Very smart of you. Rumors sometimes tell the truth." Thrace leaned back in her seat. "We had an…incident…at Bahtya Games, approximately five weeks ago. A patron had a bad reaction to one of those headsets. By the time Skalar and the manager got to him, he'd shredded his own flesh, flung blood all over the game room. They gassed him, got medics to him as soon as possible. Probably saved his life."

"He got lucky, then."

"Did he?" Thrace asked, her head tilted. "You should visit him at the medsec facility before you make that conclusion. Only constant restraint and observation ensures his own safety and that of others around him."

Mira's face twitched. She swallowed a few times. "The psychosis is permanent?"

"That remains to be seen, but it's likely. Go through the surveillance vids from Bahtya for that night. See for yourself."

Mira nodded, her expression distant.

Thrace waited, watching her expressions, feeling the captain's confusion.

Mira took a deep breath. "Okay, I get why you gave up the game. Why the merch? Why the net?"

Thrace shrugged. "Sometimes you have to give in order to receive. We have more silk, more recreationals, more coffee. Surely Downing knows that. It was a gesture of good faith, nothing more. It won't hurt us and, in the long run, it might help by building good relations with colonial security. Same thing with the ghostnet."

"Still, now we're out a source of intel."

"You think so?" Thrace looked askance at the captain. "Then you *have* underestimated me."

The look of confusion on Mira's face gave slow way to understanding. "You have more than one net."

"Why captain, I don't know what you could possibly mean." Thrace raised one eyebrow, the hint of a smile shadowing her mouth.

Mira's face melted into a conspiratorial grin, grudging admiration shining through as she nodded. "Good one. Are we eavesdropping only on HHU?"

"We have eyes and ears in many places, Captain."

"So, you know, then, who's behind the slaving."

"I didn't say that. In fact," Thrace said, putting her elbows on the desk, "I believe Skalar tasked you with finding out that same information before he left. Who do you think is responsible?"

Now Mira frowned. "I'm not sure yet. I suspect the Cartel."

Admiral Bellamy. Based in Pelarr, Zebalu. Is that where Alira was now? "Why?"

The human scrunched up her face. "Rumor, in addition to Bellamy's reputation. It just sounds like something she would do. I've heard she's jealous of Skalar and the Consortium, wants to move up from second place and take our spot at the front of the line. If she can turn a profit on the trade and make Skalar or the Consortium out to be the guilty party along the way, it'd be a win-win for her."

Logical. Sound reasoning. Thrace nodded. "Possible. No more solid leads?"

"Not yet, ma'am. I was still—am still looking into it."

"Good. Anything else?"

"No. Yes," Mira said. "Why didn't Downing have the right to search the base?"

"Go to your office, Captain. Read the entire colonial/faction contract, then we'll discuss the details. You need to understand what the colonials can and cannot do with regard to this base, Consortium crew, and faction business transactions, as well as what risks we take when we carry our dealings outside these walls. Dismissed."

Mira turned to leave.

"Mira," Thrace said when Mira was halfway to the door.

She turned. "Yes, Admiral?"

"How is Kisle?"

Mira's features softened. She looked away for a moment. "It'll be a while before the nightmares stop, I think, but he's glad to be home. Thank you, ma'am. We're all grateful."

Thrace nodded. "If you need help with meds, let me know."

"I will. Thank you."

When she was gone, Thrace turned her chair toward the window. Night had fallen. Lights twinkled across the city, atop buildings, behind windows, along the streets. Out on the bay, mast lights bobbed atop the chop. Bright spots hovered around the beachfront pubs. She closed her eyes, extended her awareness in search of Alira, reaching for the comfortable, familiar presence. Galen's lover was nowhere to be found. Not near the city center, perhaps not even in New Canaan, or on Harajüd at all. Thrace stretched her abilities as far as they would go, without response. Humans went about their lives in the well-lit streets and among the shadows, transacting business above and below board. Such quantity of emotion and feeling and sensation lay beyond Thrace's ability to qualify. She felt only the buzz of countless interactions below and around her, and the gnawing angst of an uncertain future.

chapter 44

Pelarr, Zebalu
<u>Cartel Trader Base, Admiral Bellamy's Office</u>

BELLAMY ROCKETED FROM HER CHAIR with a scream and launched her wine glass across the room at her second's head. Hannah ducked in time to avoid the projectile. A small part of Bellamy's brain logged the practiced move, but the majority of her thought homed in on Hannah's words.

"Unacceptable! Where are the security officers responsible for this failure?"

"I've not said anything to them yet, ma'am. I thought—"

"*What*?" Bellamy stormed across the floor and thrust her face close to Hannah's. "Why not? Bring them here at once and replace them with others who can actually perform to expectation!"

To her credit, Hannah did not flinch. "Of course I'll do what you think is best, ma'am," she said. "But perhaps it's a bit hasty to eliminate our entire security crew without having replacements at the ready."

"What's the difference between no security at all and a force whose incompetence admits a spy into our ranks?" Spittle flew from Bellamy's lips and hung, shining, on Hannah's burnished cheeks.

"Good point, ma'am," Hannah said. "But it occurs to me that the Cartel has multiple plants inside the other factions. I suspect the other admirals have done the same, so it seems likely there are others as well. If we start killing security, or drag the suspect in for questioning now, any cohorts will be alerted, and we lose our chance of exposing the entire network."

Bellamy stared into Hannah's moss-green eyes. What did that matter? She wanted to kill the traitor *now,* feel her fingers close around the treacherous throat and watch with glee, laughing as life winked out. That'd teach people to fuck with her.

But Hannah did have a point. If there were more—doubtful, but then she'd never have believed there would be even one—the better plan advised caution, at the very least.

With a muffled expletive, Bellamy buried her fingers in her hair and pulled it away from her face. Waiting was for other people. Not her.

"Then what do you recommend?"

"At this point, the perp's unaware that we know about the breach. It took our colonial agent more than a standard day to catch the comm."

"Why did it take that long to alert us?" Bellamy stabbed a finger toward the city beyond the base. "I pay him a lot to stay on top of this sort of thing."

"And he does a fine job, ma'am," Hannah nodded. "Literally tens of thousands of messages originate in city-wide public comm units every day. It takes time to sort through them, even with the most advanced search parameters. He assured me he caught it as quickly as possible."

"What's he doing about it now?"

Hannah shook her head. "Nothing. It's out of his hands. I've got my own system working on the content. We know for sure that it was encrypted using Syndicate code we broke the day before yesterday."

Bellamy grunted. "Which is changed by now, of course."

"Won't matter." Hannah shrugged. "It works for the message in question, which is all we need in this case. My point is that as long as both sender and recipient are unaware of our discovery, they'll continue to operate according to their usual methods. If we wait to tip our hand, we can keep an eye on them, find out how much they know, who else is involved. That'll tell us how deep the betrayal goes."

Bellamy stepped down into the seating pit and wandered to the window. Standing here always made her feel better. The sea seemed to know and reflect her moods. Plenty of whitecaps graced the azure deep, in the secluded bay and farther out, beneath a darkening sky. To her left, the sun dipped into hiding behind Duakela's northwest cliffs, sending its last rays upward. Running lights winked, like early fallen stars, along the watercraft shipping lines. Marker lights blinked on around the garden path and at the cliff walk.

Maybe it was better to delay, especially if it might grant her the pleasure of not one, but two snitches. Maybe more. What fun!

"Very well," she said. "We'll wait. But no more surprises. Keep me informed. Am I clear?"

"Absolutely, ma'am."

"Good. Dismissed."

Long after the door closed behind Hannah, Bellamy stood at the window. Instead of seeing the water and the night sky, an entirely different scene played itself out in her head. One by one, the faces of her brothers or, worse, her father superimposed themselves onto her betrayers and her failed security crew. She would hold a leading role in their grisly, imaginative fates.

Bellamy smiled until her cheeks ached.

It was a damn good thing that she was in charge. Hannah made a great second, but her suggestion to immediately capture and kill the turncoat just proved she'd never be as clever as Bellamy. If Hannah hadn't reported in before carrying it out, it would have been too late for Bellamy to bait the target and wait.

Oh yes. Bellamy's plan was better by far.

chapter 45

Tuneloras, Saacharis
<u>Syndicate Trader Base, Admiral Rizzo's Quarters</u>

RIZZO BENT, NOSE TOUCHING HER knees. Hamstrings, glutes, and lats stretched, warming in preparation for her katas. She grasped the back of her calves and pulled. The kinks began to release. It'd been a very long day. She needed this workout.

Pulling up with slow, graceful poise, she spread her arms out to her sides and shifted her feet into position as the endorphins flowed. Methodical movements brought her through the warmup regimen bit by bit, body moving from one pose to another to the end, the point of honoring the divine in Self and Other. She pressed her palms together, dropped her chin, and fell still. A woody fragrance filled her nostrils. The trill of a reed flute lilted through the room. Bardo played like that. She'd always envied his musical talent.

At last, she raised her head and dropped her arms, swinging her body into the first move of the kata, a difficult one she still worked to master. Six moves in, a chirp broke her concentration. Rizzo froze, holding the pose. Should she respond? Probably. It had to be Bailey. No one else would disturb her here at this hour. Even Bailey wouldn't do so unless it were unavoidable.

She sighed, straightened. "Answer."

Bailey's face and shoulders appeared in the holo. "My apologies, Admiral, but there is an incoming comm from a woman asking to speak to you. She says it's urgent, that it can't wait. I tried to help her, but—"

"Who?"

"Says her name is Esther, ma'am."

Esther? Rizzo frowned. Alira had said Esther—Ijydin, rather—was dead. Then how—

"It's local?"

"Yes. On approach to Saacharis in a Cartel ship, no less."

Rizzo's frown deepened. "It's a secure line?"

"No. Public channel."

That would not do. "Send me her link address and inform her I'll comm right away. Rizzo out."

Rizzo grabbed a drink of water and reemerged into her living space. At the console, Rizzo noted the address sent by Bailey, input manual security codes and set up the comm. She waited less than half a minute before Esther's image appeared.

"Hello, Rizzo. Aes te nalya."

Rizzo sighed, her lips tight. "Nalena t'staani. Why are you here? I made it clear I would not help you until you worked out your problem."

Esther's eyes crinkled at the corners. "I remember. I'm working on that. I came to ask your help on behalf of someone else. Someone not me."

"Who?"

Esther's chin slid to one side in a slanted negation. "We need to speak. In person."

"Then set down at the landport. I'll meet you at—"

"No. Can't," Esther interrupted. "I need to come directly to your base."

Rizzo blinked. "In a Cartel ship? That is not a good idea for either of us."

"It will be worse if I land at the colonial port."

"For whom?"

"Me. And others." Esther looked away. "Saacharis Aggregate is pinging me for ID and destination. I need to give them an answer."

"Tell me."

"Not a good idea, Rizzo. Trust me."

"I don't," Rizzo said. "Not yet. This line is secure. Tell me."

Esther considered long enough Rizzo thought the woman would refuse. At last, she sighed, seeming to shrink into herself. "I'm carrying slaves. Kids, Rizzo. If I put down anywhere else, she'll know. They won't be safe and neither will I."

She. Bellamy. If there were Cartel agents at the colonial landport, Bellamy might already know of this detour. Inviting Esther to land on the Syndicate base was probably a mistake. But if the Cartel was once again up to its old tricks…. Rizzo's features hardened.

"Come on, Rizzo. I need a response. At least give me a chance to explain what's going on."

Rizzo's lips drew into a tight line. "Very well. You have our coordinates. When will you arrive?"

"Less than an hour."

"Syndicate crew will guide you into the landing bay. I'll meet you there. Rizzo out."

She stared at the empty space. Definitely a mistake to get involved in this drama. The Syndicate wasn't ready to take on the Cartel, but it would be worse—for those children—if she didn't step up. Someone had to. Might as well be her. Rizzo slapped her wristcom around her arm.

"TICS, Bailey. Mobile. Voice." She slipped a pair of soft-soled shoes on her bare feet and left her quarters behind.

chapter 46

Pelarr, Zebalu
<u>**Cartel Trader Base, Cliffside Garden**</u>

LIGHTS TWINKLED ALONG THE WATER routes below, not just those on the boats but in the water itself, where turbulence from passing ships stirred tiny crustaceans to phosphoresce, a warning to the threat at hand to stay away, that though the defenseless krill might look like an easy meal, their toxic flesh made them an inadvisable snack. Bellamy loved watching them. She could relate. Her brothers had thought her defenseless too. As had her father. And Virgil. Plenty of others. They'd discovered their error too late.

She grinned in the darkness. Soon, she would teach that lesson again. The thought warmed her against the chilly updraft from the cliff face. It had been a while since she caught a Syndicate agent in her faction. Once the full extent of this particular network had been uncovered, Bellamy would need to pay particular attention to detail in her response. While she enjoyed making a strong point, she didn't have time to repeat herself too frequently. She did have other things to do.

A strong gust whipped up from below and for a moment, Bellamy imagined she could feel fine salt spray on her face. She closed her eyes, reveling in the titillation of standing at the edge of a void on a windy night. Anything might happen. She held her arms out straight from her shoulders, palms up, and threw her head back. Her body wavered in the balance, while her bare toes gripped the rock ledge. Arms and hips compensated without a specific command to do so.

She laughed, a wild, raw sound. Survival came naturally to those with the right instincts. Instincts like her own, honed by personal trauma, precarious street life, and vigilant living. She didn't need to think. After all this time, her body absorbed life's lessons all by itself, folded them into her cunning persona so that it could act without conscious direction to ensure her continuity.

The thrill faded slowly. She dropped her arms, stepped away from the ledge, and continued her walk. Hannah stood a short distance away. Bellamy beckoned, and the captain approached.

"How long have you been waiting?"

Hannah shrugged. "Not long, ma'am. I didn't want to disturb your moment. I have news."

Bellamy stopped walking. "Do tell."

"Our spy is Jammer."

"Who?"

"He's a lieutenant junior grade, comms specialist on the *Coriolis* under Captain Doe."

"You're sure?"

Hannah nodded. "I tasked TICS with looking for anomalous behavior in crew files. Two years ago, *Coriolis* went to Tuneloras to negotiate a contract with Saacharis Aggregate for a small fleet of oceanic ships. Jammer manned that flight. While the crew enjoyed a bit of shore leave, Doe noticed Jammer chatting with a known Syndicate agent at a pub. Doe sought Jammer out later, tried baiting him to see if Doe should be suspicious. Jammer said the other man was trying to pick him up, but that Jammer had declined. Doe decided there was nothing to it and let the matter go. However, he did make a note in Jammer's file, which pinged my search."

"And you think there's more to it."

"The man takes weeks-long trips off world, but his claimed destinations don't always match colonial visitor records for the dates and times of his trips. His ident card has been used numerous times at public comm units, but comms logs from his base quarters are almost blank. Who goes that far out of their way to send innocuous communiques?"

Bellamy's pulse quickened. "What about his associations? Who does he drink with? Who does he sleep with?"

"Nobody that I could find," Hannah said. "What's more, there's no purchase record on his ident of recreationals or hard liquor. Not one. It looks like he never even bought a beer or a smoke. He squeaks. So yes, I think it's him, ma'am." She paused and cleared her throat. "There is one other fact that connects all the rest together. Moments ago, I learned that he was one of the parties in that Syndicate-encoded message we intercepted."

Bellamy fisted her hands, nails cutting into the flesh of her palms. "When did he join the Cartel?"

"Just over three years ago, ma'am."

"Very well. Look for others who joined off-the-street in that same time frame. Let's rule out the easy connections first. In the meantime, put someone on him. Someone you trust. Log his every move, Captain. I want to know when he sleeps, what he eats, where he shits, who he fucks. Don't leave anything out."

"I'm on it, ma'am."

"Dismissed."

Hannah turned to go.

"Hannah."

The captain stopped. "Yes, ma'am?"

Bellamy stepped close and stared at her second, scrutinizing every line, every twitch, every feature on the woman's face. "It isn't you, is it?"

Hannah blanched, her skin almost glowing in the darkness. "No, Admiral. It is not me. I would never betray you."

Bellamy nodded. "See that you don't."

chapter 47

Tuneloras, Saacharis
Syndicate Trader Base, Landing Bay

THE SHIP FLEW NO COLORS per se. It didn't flash its Cartel designation proudly. But every piece of equipment in the bay could read its registration. At Rizzo's command, Bailey had flushed the bay of all personnel save the most trustworthy and essential. Now the two of them watched Esther's ship approach its assigned space and touch down.

"We can't run the bay this way, ma'am," Bailey said. "Not for longer than a few hours."

"Once we gain access, rig a temporary point of origin in the tracker," Rizzo murmured. "Make it read like a ship from the Levyron Order."

Bailey glanced at her. "Won't Admiral Bardo have something to say about that?"

Rizzo's lips twitched. "Leave Bardo to me."

The craft powered down. Rizzo advanced on the hatch, comming as she went.

"Open up."

chapter 48

IN CONTROL, ESTHER COMPLIED WITH her host's request, then locked down the ship and headed out to meet them. The struggle with her most recent harvest, coupled with her angst, left her empty and shorn of focus—not a good state of mind in her present circumstances. It was imperative that Rizzo agree to help execute this new plan, and not send her packing. Finding another solution at this point would be difficult, if not impossible. At least not before this group of slaves went unwilling to their deaths on Iridos.

Ahead in the ship's corridor, Rizzo rounded a corner followed by another woman with long black hair. Her second, probably. Both women stopped.

Esther slowed her approach. She didn't know this other human. What had Rizzo told her? Too bad Cesar's ability as a reader hadn't come as a part of his reaping.

"Admiral," she said with a nod. "Thank you for seeing me." Esther looked at the stranger.

"This is my second, Captain Bailey," Rizzo said, her eyes veiled. "We will discuss your visit later. Right now, we must disguise the ship. Your presence here endangers us both."

Esther nodded. Either Skalar or Crow could have told her how to mask its designation. But Rook's resistance was clouding all useful communication with the other voices. "I know, and I'm sorry. I wouldn't have come if it weren't urgent." She blinked at Rizzo. "Can you fix it?"

"Bailey will. With your permission?"

Esther nodded. "This way." She led them to control, unlocked the necessary systems, then left Bailey to her task. She and Rizzo stepped into the corridor.

"Show me your cargo," Rizzo said.

Esther led her the length of the ship, down the lift, and toward mid-ships, then stopped and displayed the contents on the vidscreen outside the cargo door. Rizzo stared at the image of children sagging in their beds or crouched on the floor by the walls.

"Bellamy," Rizzo said.

"Yes."

"What was your original destination?"

"Iridos."

"Surely she didn't send Esther to deliver slaves."

Esther licked her lips. "No. She sent Captain Rook."

"And where is Rook now?" Rizzo asked, still focused on the vidscreen. "The original one."

"Dead."

"This was not part of your plan." Rizzo glared at Esther. "In New Canaan, you said you wanted to infiltrate the Cartel, to dig up info to clear Skalar's name. I agreed to supply you with a contact, and to convey your intel to Captain Baldric so she could pass it to authorities there. But now you've killed and impersonated a Cartel captain, stolen a Cartel ship, shown up at my door with refugees, and involved my faction in your skirmish. You have taken advantage of my good will. This does not endear you to me."

Anger swelled in Esther's chest, rising toward her throat

calm down, skalar.

and she took a deep breath. "Look me in the eye and tell me you would not have done the same to save a shipload of young slaves."

Rizzo scoffed. "I have more resources at my disposal. I could have saved them without endangering others, especially a whole faction. And what of your own people? You have more to lose than I. Did you think even once about the consequences if you were seen landing here in this ship? I don't doubt Bellamy has agents among my people. I've tried to minimize the risk, but if anyone reports this to her, you're dead. Do dead unammi hold their human shapes?"

Esther held her glare. "No. My people are a rare breed. We can't afford to lose even one, or to reveal our secrets, yet I took the chance willingly. I apologize for putting the Syndicate in the middle, but it's those resources of yours that brought me here. I didn't know what else to do. Look at them," she said with a gesture. "What alternative would you suggest?"

Rizzo's mouth drew into a thin line. She stared at the vidscreen again.

Silence stretched out. What would she do if Rizzo turned her down? Rook's surface memories had proven somewhat useful, but beyond what was easily accessible, that soul had refused to cooperate with the squib who killed her, had in fact actively fought in every way possible. Among all Alira's reapings, that was a first. She couldn't blame Rook, really, but it did complicate things by wearing Alira down, fogging her mind.

"This will not be the last shipment, will it?" Rizzo asked, still looking at the screen.

"No."

Rizzo took a deep breath, let it out slow. "You wanted a chance to explain. You have a plan?"

"I do, but it's rough. I can't do it alone. I'd welcome your input."

"Tell me."

"Bellamy expects Rook to deliver the slaves every three weeks and return with the hematium mined since the last delivery." Esther leaned toward Rizzo. "What if I bring the slaves here instead? You could settle them elsewhere, safe from Bellamy."

"How will you deliver hematium to the Cartel if you don't go to Iridos?"

"That's a tricky part," Esther said. "I'd need you to loan me enough to make it look as though I did."

Rizzo raised one eyebrow, her eyes widening. "Hematium is essential to the primary business interests of the Syndicate."

"I know it's a lot to ask, but I can have it replaced in just over ten days. In fact—"

"How?"

If she would stop interrupting, Esther would explain. She stopped with exaggerated civility. "How what?"

"How are you going to replace the hematium without going to Iridos?"

"I have the entire load Skalar already stole from Iridos. If you agree to the plan, one of my pilots can deliver a shipment here. In fact, I'll have him bring twice what you loan me. You get paid back, plus there will be another load here, waiting for me, when I bring the next ship full of slaves." She swallowed her annoyance and studied Rizzo's face.

"I have a better idea."

"I'm listening," Esther said. What was wrong with her suggestion?

"I give you the amount of hematium you require. Then I send a ship to Iridos, liberate the slaves there, and take the ore they've mined as my repayment."

Esther shook her head, mouth tight. "No. That won't work."

"Explain."

"The officer in command there, Jude, will alert Bellamy at the first sign of an unknown ship, especially if it's attacking. If Bellamy gets wind of any of this, the whole plan falls through." Surely an admiral as experienced as Rizzo should have seen that herself!

"Not if we jam surface transmissions. Bellamy will never know."

"If," Esther repeated. "That's too big a risk for both of us. We can't take that chance."

"When you don't show on schedule with these replacements, Jude will comm Bellamy anyway. My way solves that problem."

Esther closed her eyes. She hadn't considered that. Stupid of her, really. She rubbed her forehead, felt that little wrinkle between her eyebrows, just like Nyros used to get. "Of course. It's a good idea. But you'd have to send a team immediately if they are to silence Jude in time. You'll only need a small crew, I expect. You've been there. You know the surface in the valley is compromised. A scout or recon ship could get in and out more easily."

"I disagree," Rizzo said with a scowl. "If the complement of slaves there is as large as this one, a bigger ship would be better. More room to bring them out."

"Irrelevant." Esther waved a hand, looked away. Weariness and angst and grief grated against the wall she'd rebuilt around her emotions. She clenched her fists.

Rizzo stared at her. "Why?"

"Because it's too late!" Esther shouted. She stopped, sighed, started again in a lower tone. "I didn't take Rook's place until after they were shipped out. They've been exposed to radiation for three weeks. If they aren't dead already, they soon will be."

"Bellamy sent them without protective gear?"

Esther smirked. "What do you think, Rizzo?"

Rizzo muttered an expletive under her breath and began to pace. "How many more of these shipments are we talking about?"

"Two. Maybe three. By that time, Bellamy will have enough equipment to mine the tunnels without these younglings," Esther said, her voice sagging. This mental struggle was sucking away all her energy. She needed some time with her irolium, before she depleted her reserves and could no longer maintain her human face.

"And you'll have your people bring hematium in time to pick it up each trip?"

"Yes. I'll need to stay here for a few days, too, so that Bellamy thinks I've gone all the way to Iridos. Everything has to look just right and happen right on schedule. If I do anything to rouse her suspicion, it's all over." Esther sighed. "I can even have them bring extra ore for you, payment for your trouble."

"Very well. I'll help," Rizzo said, "under the terms you've just outlined. But don't spring something like this on me again. Surprises get people killed in this business. Understood?"

"Completely." Esther nodded. "Except there is one more thing."

"What?"

"There are a few among my people who tire of living under our council's strict rules. They wish to live among humans, *as* humans. Is there a place for them in the Syndicate? Or do you know of someone else, someone you could trust, to shelter them? Most don't know how to mimic human behavior and mannerisms. They'll need teaching. But they'll work in exchange. It can be part of their training, perhaps."

"The Syndicate is a business entity, not a placement center."

Esther grimaced. "Is that a no?"

"You push me."

"You mean, 'you push me again,' don't you?" She ran a hand over her head, smoothing her adopted braid. "Wasn't it Esther's interference that saved your neck and landed you in the Syndicate to begin with all those years ago?"

Rizzo's jaw hardened. She pointed at Esther. "Out of line. You are not her."

"Same principal."

"Why do you hate me?"

Esther laughed, amusement that rose from her core and rolled out of her in waves. "I don't," she said at last, "but you are the only human I trust. Who else should I ask?"

Rizzo massaged the back of her neck. "You are nothing like the other unammi I've known."

"Yes. They tell me I'm special," Esther said. "Will you do it?"

"I'll think about it."

"Thank you."

Rizzo gestured at the vidscreen. "Some of the children look sick. Have they been locked in there since Zebalu?"

"Yes. They had rations and water, but I was piloting alone—"

"Agreed. A necessary evil." Rizzo shook her head. "But we need to get them out. Give them food, water, beds. Medicine." She raised her wrist. "Bailey, report."

"Almost done, ma'am. Just wrapping up."

"Good. Are equipment updates completed on the Kaiken?"

"Yes ma'am," Bailey said. "Finished this morning."

"Very well. Assign it to an expert liquidation team to hit Iridos. They are to neutralize the Cartel ship stationed there, along with its crew, help the slaves on site if they can, then take whatever hematium is ready for transport and return home. Intercept and block all surface signals. Don't let them many any calls. Understood?"

"Got it. Anything else, ma'am?"

"Yes. Set up a quarantine dorm for—" Rizzo glanced at Esther.

"Twenty-six."

"—twenty-six youths," Rizzo said. "Make them comfortable. They'll need food, blankets, soap."

"Anything else, ma'am?"

"Make sure the dorm can be locked from outside. We need to keep them closeted for a short while, until I can see them in person. In the meantime, get the base medics online to run physicals and dispense necessary meds, and someone from logistics to outfit them with clean clothes and show them how to use the blowers in the shower room. I'll fill you in on the essentials later. I need it set up and ready to roll ASAP. What's your best estimate on time?"

"Give me two hours, tops. Bailey out."

chapter 49

Aboard the Corsair
<u>En Route to Pelarr, Zebalu</u>

ALIRA SAT IN CONTROL, ELBOWS on her knees, head in her hands, eyes closed, shoulders slumped. Which face should she use? Her own was too risky, even on a secure channel. Too many of Crow's people thought the unammi all dead. Who knew if they would take the sudden appearance of a living unammi

squib.

as a potential threat? No. It had to be a human one, but whose? Skalar's might compromise Thrace's position. Galen didn't know any of Alira's other aliases. She couldn't mine Ijydin's or Nyros' memories to discover which of their faces Galen might recognize. Rook's resistance fogged all that up.

Maybe she shouldn't contact him in the first place. It was probably selfish of her to do so, but she couldn't stop thinking about how bad things were when she—Skalar—left. If she didn't at least try to mend the damage, she might lose Galen altogether.

Maybe it wouldn't matter what face she wore. She'd already contacted the outpost, given them instructions to deliver a shipment of hematium and three of the mitigants to Rizzo's care. Tiral had probably already contacted Thrace, so she would at least know Alira was on the move. She sat up straight, skin mottled blue and white. Maybe whatever face she wore, he would recognize a reference to the transfer of equipment and personnel from the outpost. That was surely innocuous enough to pass even an intercepted comm transmission without any damage.

She morphed as she turned, and faced the comm wearing short white hair, green eyes, a slim face and narrow shoulders garbed in nondescript white clothing. Set up took only seconds, and she began to record.

"Aes te nalya, Thrace. By now you will know that I moved materials and non-essential crew from your domain to another. It was a necessary transaction, and I apologize for going around you to do so, but it could not be helped. There was no time to speak to you first, and even if there had been, doing so would have endangered many people."

Of course, the outpost hematium was still at least eight days away from Saacharis, but that couldn't be helped. She ran a hand across her face and through her hair, pulled her thoughts in line. Irrelevant for this message. She'd think about that later.

"Obviously, I'm alive, but far from safe. I can't share details. Please don't try to find me under any circumstances. If you want updates, contact that person who you and others told me time and again was a friend to our people. I've told her more than I should have. I hope my trust was not misplaced.

"One last thing," she said, her slight form leaning closer to the holorecorder. "You were right. I was wrong. I'm doing everything I can to fix what I broke. As far as I am concerned, you are still my i'shin."

She paused, her lips trembling with unspoken words before she abruptly ended the transmission and sent it on its way. When it was gone, she resumed her natural form and made the equipment adjustments Bailey had taught her, then closed the panel beneath the controls and stood up. "TICS, display internal travel and comm logs side-by-side."

Figures and text floated in midair. She squinted at them, checking for any flaw or missed detail. As far as she could tell, it would appear as though she'd been to Iridos with no detours and that no comms had been sent at all.

She dropped into her seat at the controls and rested her head against the cushion. Her ship was going the wrong way, running toward the enemy instead of scrambling in retreat. Everything in her screeched protest at the thought of facing Bellamy again. Thrace had thought Skalar was losing it. Hah! She should spend ten minutes with the Cartel's admiral.

On second thought, no. Alira wouldn't wish that on anyone, much less her beloved. Ten minutes with that woman could get a person killed without ever understanding why.

Then again, Skalar had killed plenty of people too, including an impressive number just in the last twelve weeks, since Alira had worn his face into the landing bay that first time. Had they known why?

Nyros' wrinkle furrowed Alira's brow. They had known. Of course they had. Skalar had made sure. Right?

Garbled murmurings from her harvests gave no clear response over Rook's constant babble. But Galen's voice echoed in her own memory alongside that of Sa'abah and Ronan and Kilbee and Cohen in a cacophony of reproach. Alira pushed herself out of her chair, clapped her hands over her ears

stop!

and knew they were right. Skalar's skin had proven too tight. It had threatened to strangle the person she'd been before all this began, and she'd not even seen it happening until the damage was irreversible. Her misguided plan to take over the Consortium had shorn Skalar of all the respect—and fear, which had also kept his crew in line—he'd built up over his years in that seat. It had almost destroyed her in the process, and Galen along with her. But what did Galen expect? She'd had to do something. Skalar would have killed her, wiped out the entire unammi race if she hadn't struck first. Every witness to the fall of Iridos posed a threat. Each of them stood to lose everything if what they'd done ever came to light. Even now, they could rip away the fragile protection she'd erected around the surviving unammi. Alira's plan to assume leadership of the Consortium had seemed reasonable in the beginning. From there she could shield the unammi from hazards until such time as the danger was past.

But Rakalesh had been right, too. Knowing wasn't the same as doing. Now....

Now she was confused and reeling on the brink of exhaustion. From this low point, her errors seemed so enormous as to defy reparation. Somehow her own moral compass had gotten neglected, overridden by the loudest of her passengers. Her ongoing insistence on maintaining control of the whole thing and the refusal to believe she might have been wrong all along had shoved aside the whole point of her efforts in the first place.

Maybe she was truly losing control.

Maybe, as she'd already considered once during a lucid moment, the harvesting sickness was overtaking her.

She hugged herself, leaned against the wall, and slid to the floor. Just over a day until she'd arrive at Zebalu. The thought of returning to the Cartel laid heavy stones in her heart. Bellamy was truly insane, but Alira wasn't far behind her. Skalar's dominance had twisted Alira's perceptions, maimed her ability to judge right from wrong, justifiable from indefensible. The longer she stayed in this world, pretending to be something she was not, the closer she drew to the crumbling edge. If she went over, there would be no pulling her back.

chapter 50

Haven, Danua
<u>Clan Trader Base, Officer's Mess</u>

KNØFA STRADDLED THE CHAIR ACROSS from Tsurin and pulled his plate closer. Aromatic seasonings wafted up from the chef's selection, tickling his nose. He poked the cooked meat before him, then took a bite. Meh. It would do. He'd never been fussy about food. If it sated his belly and didn't poison him, he was content. He looked around the mess while he chewed. Slim pickings. The room sat almost empty. Only a few officers inhabited the space, keeping to themselves. Security usually kept the mess quiet when Tsurin came to eat.

He swallowed, gulped his wine, then looked at Tsurin. "Why not?"

Tsurin kept eating.

"If you turn the lab loose, they can do this. I saw the results. They were close last time, really close. They just need to tweak the last few bugs out of the program. Can't do that without test subjects. Animals won't give valid projections for human use." Knøfa leaned over his plate trying to catch her eye. "You know I'm right."

She shot him a quick look before resuming her meal. "Is that all you've got? Designer recreationals and genetics experiments?"

He leaned back, his fork loose in his hand. "No."

"What else did you come up with?"

"We could revamp one of our bagnios, maybe more than one, to offer specialties to our favored clients."

Tsurin's hand stopped halfway to her mouth. "What kind of specialties?"

Knøfa shrugged. "The possibilities are endless. Younger workers, more kink, grappling rooms for group-clutches, bondage, peep-rooms, you name it."

She stared at him. "We already have bondage. Peep rooms too." She took the bite and chewed.

"Yes. But we could spice it up even further. There's a market for it. I checked."

"How?"

"I asked. All the workers in our bagnios have clients who want more edgeplay or stronger fetish packages. They'd meet steeper prices, I know it."

She jerked her chin toward his plate. "Eat. I'm thinking."

He chewed another hunk of meat without really tasting it. "All the other admirals have their specialty," he said around the food. "For Skalar, or whatever newbie is sitting in his chair now—"

"Baldric," Tsurin interrupted. "Admiral Thrace Baldric."

"For Baldric," Knøfa said, "it's weapons and industrial ships. For Bellamy it's her slaves, or at least that's what we think. Georgeanne's got access to medicinal ingredients the rest of us don't. Rizzo has small shipbuilding. Bardo controls diamina mines. Any of these projects I've suggested can be the Clan's thing. Having the kinkiest bagnios would be easiest. It'd increase tourism, too, also good for the colonials, which means they'd be less likely to moderate our plans. But the medicinals and recreational experiments would bring in the most revenue. With a little luck, it could even surpass Georgeanne's trade."

"We have our altered silk beetles," Tsurin said. "Mead and charsten steaks too."

"And if that were enough, ma'am, you wouldn't have tasked me with finding new ways to boost the Clan's status."

Tsurin pushed her half-full plate away. "There are some lines we shouldn't cross, Knøfa. Using humans as medical test subjects is one of them. Using young bagnio workers is another."

He had to make his point soon or he would lose this chance. He put down his fork. "Why? Every colony has throwaways, people who bleed the system dry and thieve from colonial sales. You've told me that yourself. We'd be doing everyone a favor by taking them off the streets, giving them shelter and food. The colonials wouldn't likely complain since we'd be lightening their social load, making the cities safer, cutting down on loss of market goods, right? Everybody wins."

Tsurin waved at him. "Don't pretend their lot will be better if you hand them over to the med techs. Life as a lab rat won't exactly be pleasant."

"Neither is life on the street, ma'am. Why is my idea worse than starving? Or getting shanked or robbed or raped? Or dying from a disease our experiments might have prevented?"

She shook her head and took another bite.

Why was she so reticent? Okay, he accepted her explanation on the evils of inhumane behavior, one human to another, but this was a larger issue, a social one that wasn't being met by the system currently in place. Surely, she could see that. If the Clan took them in, fed and clothed them, brought them to peak health, where was the harm? So what if the vagrants didn't like their new surroundings any better than the street? At least working in the bagnios wasn't boring. Most of the Clan's sex workers loved their jobs. And who cared if the faction ran a few medical experiments on some of them? If they lost a few to bad reactions or faulty conclusions from the test results, but in the long run the trials provided new knowledge that saved hundreds or thousands of lives, wouldn't that be worth it, even to the most squeamish sensitive soul? It was only reasonable to expect the Clan to benefit from the industry. After all, they would be the ones bearing the expenses and the risk.

"We don't have to like it," Knøfa said, "but the fact remains that they're seen as dregs of the colonial structure. An embarrassment to city officials. Whether we leave them where they are or use them as I suggest, they've already been handed bum cards. Even if there was an easy way into the system, most of them wouldn't take it. They're a resource that, the way I see it, is being squandered to everyone's detriment."

"You make it sound reasonable."

He shrugged. "It is. Ma'am."

Tsurin's lips drew together in a tight line. "I'm not convinced. We need more acceptable means of profit. For example, I got word that our crew managed to jack a full cargo of Saacharis ship parts. Might even be some Syndicate components in there." She waggled her eyebrows at him. "They should make the drop site in about five days."

"Good to know," he said. "But will you at least think about my idea?"

She sighed. "Yes, but don't hold your breath. Keep looking. You can do better."

She jerked to her feet and walked out. She only did that when she was pissed. Maybe he'd pushed her too far? But she'd asked for his input. If her way of doing things was adequate to the task, she wouldn't need his ideas. He just had to get her to listen.

Knøfa forked another piece of meat and chewed it. Huh. It tasted better cold. He'd have to remember that.

chapter 51

New Canaan, Harajüd
Consortium Trader Base, Admiral Baldric's Suite

GALEN LEANED OVER THE TABLE frame, one hand working the fell and the other weaving colonial fibers through the warp. Trills of a flute lilted through the room along with a woody, spicy fragrance, the closest he could find to muñise resin. Outside, Lakaya had yet to rise. Lights from indirect overhead panels threw even illumination across the weaving. Galen's eyes watched his hands while his mind wandered afar.

At the end of the row, his working filament fell in an irregular pattern and Galen stopped, his focus tracing it across the wide frame until he found his mistake near the opposite edge, three rows back. He'd have to pull out that much, at least, and start again.

He straightened, dropped the shuttle on a nearby table with a clatter, and rubbed a hand across his face. It had been too long since he'd done this. In his Tenzin days, he could weave a perfect hanging without the need for much focus. Now—

Galen shook his head. Blue highlights tangled with green and cyan across his skin. He'd begun to believe his takeover of the Consortium would not have unwelcome repercussions. Alira's most recent message reminded him otherwise. Her words made it sound as though she expected to simply walk into Skalar's shoes and carry on as if nothing had changed.

But it had. Everything was different and Galen had no intention of allowing the Consortium to relapse under his i'shin's hand, regardless of the cost.

He walked through the rooms of his—rather, Admiral Baldric's— new suite and stopped at the expansive window wall in his bedroom, gazing out past the high-rises of city center and toward Mari Bay. Galen often found himself at the window these days, as if the high vantage point of his office or residential view across the human city could impart the same long-range vision toward solutions for less tangible issues. Like Alira. Like Rizzo—that's surely who Alira meant in her comm. "Told her more than I should have," she'd said.

That was an understatement. According to Tiral, Alira had instructed him to send hematium to the Syndicate, as well as three of the recovered mitigants who could train to live among the humans. If that were the case, Alira had to have revealed who she and/or Skalar were, and probably who Thrace Baldric was. Galen had given Tiral approval to send the hematium, but not the mitigants. That posed too big a risk. What was Alira thinking? What else had she told Rizzo? Not that Galen had any room to talk. He'd told Botha enough to get them both killed, too. But why would she confide in Rizzo? If Alira had gone to the Cartel, as Galen suspected, what was she doing talking to the Syndicate's admiral?

Moreover, did Rizzo still think Alira would step back into Skalar's role and take over once more when she returned to New Canaan? If so, Admiral Baldric needed to address that right away. If Galen knew how to reach Alira, he'd tell her himself, but since he didn't, perhaps Rizzo would pass on the news. Dragging an ally into the middle of this mess wasn't the ideal solution, but maybe word would get to Alira one way or another. Better it should happen soon.

"TICS," he said, his voice changing as he morphed, "record communique for delivery to Admiral Rizzo at the Syndicate's main base in Tuneloras, Saacharis."

The system chittered a "ready" signal, and Thrace turned so that the predawn cityscape would be her backdrop. "Good health to you, Admiral Rizzo. I am Thrace Baldric, new admiral of the Harajüd Consortium. I don't know if you were aware of the change in command here, but I do believe you have been in touch with a mutual friend. The last update I received from her stated that she was safe, which is very good to know, but that I should not try to contact her. She says she confided in you and implied that the two of you are working together. If that is true, I wonder if I might impose on you to relay to her the information about this change of command. She needs to know, especially as it will affect her freedom to redistribute our assets in the future."

Rizzo may or may not know what that meant, but Alira certainly would. Thrace had given Tiral approval to follow through with the order to ship hematium to Saacharis every three weeks for at least a few months. By then, Thrace would know more about why Alira had set this up, or the new admiral would negate the approval and stop the shipments.

"I am as grateful as our mutual friend to have your offer of tutelage for my special crew members, but I must admit to some trepidation. Please don't misunderstand. I have no doubt that your intentions are honorable, but my people…" She flashed a half-smile again. "My people have never before been dependent on the goodwill of outsiders. We cannot simply hand them over without consideration for their—and your—safety. I trust you understand how special they are to me, as well as to our friend. Perhaps we can discuss this further when we speak face-to-face.

"Finally, I am aware that the Syndicate's past relationship with the Consortium has been…" Thrace searched for the right word. "…tense. Perhaps you and I can find enough common ground to change that. Please do not hesitate to contact me if I may assist you in any way. I look forward to strengthening the lines of communication between our factions. End message and transmit."

Galen resumed his own face, green highlights speckling his predominant blue hues. He rubbed his forehead. He needed to help Alira understand the full reason for his decision to take over. Ideas on how to do this chased each other through his mind, none sufficient to the task. It wouldn't matter what he said. Alira was no longer the reasonable person she'd been before reaping Skalar and Crow and all the others. She would see Thrace's seizure of control as a betrayal. Of that, there was no doubt.

But damn it, he'd done the right thing. Red flickers winked at him from his reflection in the window, and he rehearsed his argument. She'd been recalcitrant for weeks. Maybe more. They'd been at this charade for two months before she took Skalar into hiding. That was nearly a month ago. When had Alira started to lose control? It hadn't happened immediately even though she'd killed and harvested Walker's crewman that night behind the arena. Was that it? Had she taken on too many souls too quickly?

He tried to pinpoint the exact moment when he should have realized she was falling, then discarded the attempt. Irrelevant, now. She'd probably gotten even worse since she left—a discomforting thought. And if she was at the Cartel....

Galen shuddered and wrapped his arms around himself. He couldn't help her now, no matter how much he feared for her. She'd set herself on this path, but it was clear she couldn't handle the role. Skalar's voice overpowered all the others in her head, and if she didn't stop her charade, this persistence would take her life. Except she wouldn't go down alone. She risked the very real possibility that the outpost and the surviving unammi would follow her into the abyss. Is that what she wanted? Because the way she was screaming forward with no thought to the future, that seemed a likely outcome.

Galen's flesh stippled with tiny white spots. No, she wasn't going to like his decision. The question was how angry would she be? Enough to harm him? Enough to kill? No. Surely not. He'd invoked her wrath in the past, and they'd always managed to get past it.

Of course, he had considered harming *her*, but that was different. She had been—still was—out of control. He would only act against her if she became a danger to their people. Or to him. He'd wondered if it would come to that the day Skalar backed Thrace against the desk, screaming in her face.

Alira's features swam through his mind, her image twisted with Skalar's, red streaks of rage overwhelming her other dermal displays.

The white spots spread across Galen's arms and chest. Eyes wide, he shook his head. No. No, his i'shin would never harm him. She had too much integrity to lash out in mindless fury.

She did, didn't she?

He swallowed in a throat gone dry, as Lakaya's first rays touched the treetops in the green across the street from his base.

chapter 52

Pelarr, Zebalu
<u>Cartel Trader Base, Landing Bay</u>

HANNAH STEPPED UP BESIDE BELLAMY. "Unloading will be completed in about an hour, Admiral."

"What's our take on this run?"

"Larger than we anticipated, ma'am," Hannah said. "Jude must be working them hard."

"Good." She eyed her second. "What did Rook say about your suspicions?"

Hannah blinked. "I didn't tell her, ma'am."

"Why not?"

"I thought we were going to keep that information under wraps."

"That's ridiculous." Bellamy frowned. "We know Rook's not a spy."

Hannah shook her head. "Even so, ma'am, I recommend we tell no one. Not until we find out who's involved. The more people who know, the greater the chance word will get out before we can nail down our suspects."

Bellamy's face hardened. "I don't know it isn't you, either."

"I was the one who told you we had a mole, ma'am," Hannah said. "If it were me, I would have kept my mouth shut or diverted your attention elsewhere."

Full lips puckered, Bellamy stared at her second's confident expression. That's just the sort of thing a spy would say. Wasn't it?

Rook descended from the hatch and conferred with the crew unloading and cataloging her cargo. Bellamy peered at the woman. Her demeanor, her posture, the way she walked as she put the ship behind her and approached Bellamy gave no clues one way or the other where her loyalty stood.

Was Rook working with Jammer?

Eleven years of experience with Rook said no. She'd joined the Cartel as a captain the year after Bellamy assumed control. Rook had, in fact, been a "gift" from colonial directors who owed Bellamy a favor. The captain herself had told Bellamy almost from the outset that the directors had ulterior motives, wanted Rook to feed them inside information on Cartel business. If she had intended to betray the Cartel, betray Bellamy, the captain would never have admitted her part in the scam. She'd stood beside Bellamy hundreds of times. Thousands. Bellamy couldn't bring herself to believe Rook would turn. No. There was no way Rook was a spy.

Still, Hannah's whispers cast a doubt.

"How did it go?" Bellamy asked.

"Just as you predicted, ma'am." Rook's lisp sounded crooked, as if she had something in her mouth.

Bellamy frowned. Did Rook's lisp always sound like that? "Are you eating?"

Rook's gray gaze focused on Bellamy's face. "No, ma'am."

Huh. Maybe she'd imagined it. "Never mind. No problems then? The cargo gave you no trouble?"

"No, ma'am."

"What of the workers we sent last time?"

"All dead, ma'am."

Had Rook's jaw just tightened? Surely not. Bellamy's attention wandered to the trophies on Rook's vest. One of them looked newer than the rest. "How do you feel about that, Captain?"

Rook paused, as if considering her response. "They were disposable assets, ma'am. I didn't feel anything."

"Good." Bellamy nodded. "What did Jude report on the size of the mine?"

"Workers are about three hundred meters further down the main shaft. Jude's people explored 3,000 meters beyond that. They haven't found the end yet." Rook glanced at the ship.

"That's it?" Bellamy heard the disappointment in her own voice. "I thought she'd have completed the survey by now."

"Debris slowed her down, ma'am."

Bellamy pressed her lips together. This was going to take longer than she'd hoped. "Very well. Anything else to report?"

"Jude requested a fresh set of hologames, ma'am."

"Did she?" Bellamy spoke over her shoulder to Hannah. "Make a note, Captain. Round up some entertainment for our Iridos team."

Hannah nodded, but didn't move. "I'll get started as soon as we're finished here, ma'am."

Bellamy's glance dropped to Rook's vest. She reached out and flicked her fingernail against the new trophy. "Where did this one come from? I haven't seen it before."

Rook's gaze followed Bellamy's finger, and the captain hesitated before raising her head again. "It's not new, ma'am. I've had that one for years. I can't even remember where I got it."

"Really?" Bellamy frowned. "I thought you knew the story of every single one."

Steel gray eyes met her cerulean ones as Rook sighed. "Too many to remember them all, ma'am. I wanted one from Iridos, a bead on a string. Looked almost like a necklace." Rook's lips curled up in a smile that did not touch her eyes. "Didn't want to chance it being irradiated, though."

"I see." Bellamy scrutinized every detail of Rook's face. "Probably for the best, I expect. Good work, Rook. You're dismissed."

Rook moved away, her arms swinging easily at her sides. Hannah's eyes followed her, too.

"She's not the mole," Bellamy said.

Hannah nodded. "I'm sure you're right, ma'am."

chapter 53

Tuneloras, Saacharis
En Route to Pepita Public House

RIZZO LEFT THE BASE AND directed her skimmer toward the center of town. Even now, just after midday, full-spectrum lights pierced the dingy afternoon haze at regular intervals. Ahead, the road curved across the rolling landscape. She kept one hand on the controls, her eyes straight ahead, but echoes of Thrace Baldric's introductory communique whispered in Rizzo's ear.

A growing part of her regretted having gone after Skalar that night. If not for that, she wouldn't be involved in the struggle between Rook and Bellamy, wouldn't have met Alira at all, and wouldn't have been obliged to deliver word to her that the Consortium was under new leadership. In less than a standard day, the Syndicate's agent embedded in the Cartel would receive the order to inform Alira that whether or not she cleared his name, Skalar was out. For good.

Would she welcome the news?

Probably not, but that wasn't Rizzo's problem.

Given reports Rizzo received before that first meeting about drastic changes in Skalar's personality, and what Rizzo herself had seen afterward, this seemed best for everyone involved. Alira had outlasted a horrendous ordeal, demonstrated enormous courage and more than a little foolishness in plunging headlong into a world and a subculture she knew nothing about. Yet whatever else she might be, playing the role of a Trader admiral was not one of her strengths. Rizzo's relief at knowing she would not have to face Alira-as-Skalar in a future conflict overshadowed any other concerns, for the moment.

At the intersection, Rizzo guided the skimmer onto a side road between the arena and one of the Syndicate gaming houses. Beyond, a park opened out to her right. Subdued sparkles reflected off the nearby lake and, without warning or guidance, her skimmer's forward momentum dropped to a crawl. She frowned and leaned forward to see why. Just ahead, a burrit darted into the road, a sea-hawk close behind, talons outstretched. Before the small mammal could make good its escape, the raptor snatched it and swooped up into the gray sky. The burrit's stumpy tail waggled in panic, then the predator and its meal were out of sight. The burrit had been a goner the minute it ran into the open, but panic would do that to any animal, prod it to take unwise actions.

That's what lay ahead for Alira, if she didn't change course. Any one of the admirals would swallow her like candy if she got in their way, but Bellamy might be the worst of the lot. The most dangerous. The most unstable. Alira had no idea the depth of her trouble. Even Rizzo might not be able to save her if she went too far.

Road clear, Rizzo resumed her journey. This close to the city center, buildings rose thick on almost every side. Ranks of warehouses sat across from huge factories. Training facilities shadowed processing sites. Markets, gaming halls, herbal dens, public houses, and brothels lay scattered all through town so that no one had to go far to find what they wanted or needed. Interspersed throughout, colonials had long ago planted flora, most of it pale, to make the city more livable. In tracts between the artificial lighting, like that lot beside the warehouses, droopy ciotta trees squatted waist-high, their long, flat, yellowish leaves designed to capture every photon. Tall rusucre trees dangled pale willowy "tails" with tiny cones glowing at their tips. Greener, more vivid plantings hugged most lampposts and filled the pools of brighter light with green foliage and small, colorful flowers.

Rizzo made the final turn and drove past row after row of midlevel corporate housing, much nicer than housing provided to regular folk. Yet even here, persistent grunge climbed building exteriors normally kept pale to reflect available light. Cleaning crews circled Tuneloras and every other city on a regular schedule in an effort to stay ahead of the grime, but on a world this committed to mining and industry, theirs was a losing battle— or perhaps job security, depending how you viewed the matter.

Pepita loomed on the left, and Rizzo turned in, still wondering how Alira would react to Admiral Baldric's takeover. Now that Skalar's role was done, Alira wouldn't need to stay with Bellamy. Somehow, though, Rizzo knew she would. As long as the Cartel pillaged Iridosian resources and used slaves to do it, Alira would feel obliged to fight it. Rizzo understood this drive, had felt something like it herself on numerous occasions. Annoying, that. She didn't want reasons to like Alira. The woman—did she call herself that?—was bound to bring trouble, something the Syndicate already had in abundance.

Still, maybe involvement with her wasn't such a bad thing. The fact that she willingly risked her own life—when she was one of few remaining unammi—to bring human slaves to freedom spoke to her integrity. Alira was crazy, true, but at least in this her insanity might do some good. More than Rizzo could say for the decision to play Skalar. Maybe, if Rizzo allowed this arrangement to continue, Alira might learn by example that there are better ways to accomplish a goal than throwing oneself into the fire with abandon.

Rizzo knew that better than most people and carried the scars to remind her in case she ever forgot.

Inside, Rizzo nodded past the maître d' and entered the main pub space. Of all the Syndicate businesses, she liked this one best. Surrounding the bright central space, small warrens of dimmer dining rooms offered a more intimate experience on all three levels. Here on ground level, each one opened to the spectacle of the large taproom and its circular bar, where the ceiling rose all the way to the rafters. From its peak, a hoverglobe shone full-spectrum lighting onto patrons below. Walls of the shaft displayed a detailed mosaic of Saacharan industries: miners mining, scholars teaching, factory workers operating machinery, farmers tending pale produce under gray skies or more generic fare under greenhouse domes. In the design, the planet's star oversaw all, its pure gold leaf threaded in veins like sunbeams that wandered from image to image in the grout between tiles to tie all together into one world.

The intricacy of this work of art, completed long before she took control of the faction, never failed to fascinate her. Light glinting on the gold sometimes winked in one's eye upon entry, its brilliance matched by the brightly dressed clientele with lumenettes wound into their hair and clothing. Now, the crowd parted before and closed behind her, the conversational murmur dulling momentarily as she passed.

On the far side of the crowd, Rizzo entered her personal dining room, a small, stark space with minimal decor where Bailey waited. Inside, a secure field rose behind the admiral, shutting her and her second off from the noisy barroom. She took a seat facing the entry.

"The Consortium has a new admiral."

Bailey leaned forward, her pale blue eyes wide. "Skalar's dead?"

Rizzo gripped the arms of her chair. She didn't like keeping things from her second. "I didn't say that."

"Then what…" Bailey said. "…how—"

"The Consortium is now in the hands of Thrace Baldric."

"I don't recognize that name."

Rizzo grunted, looked past her toward the sparkling crowd. "New player."

Bailey frowned.

"She wants the Consortium to dance with the Syndicate."

"She sounds new." Bailey shook her head. "Is she unaware of our history?"

"No," Rizzo said, "but she claims to want a change."

"Do you believe her?"

Rizzo glanced at her second. Bailey's face bore the same apparent skepticism it had shown when they first met and Rizzo offered her a position other than sex worker in the brothel, something more challenging and ultimately more exciting. Bailey had come so far since then, learned so much. She'd proven herself time and again. Rizzo trusted her. But not with this.

"Yes."

Bailey's brows drew together. "May I ask why, ma'am? You never believe anyone you don't know."

"It's her connections I trust," Rizzo said. More or less.

Bailey waited, then sat back. "You can't tell me more."

"It isn't my intel to share." A nod told her Bailey wouldn't ask again. "You will go to New Canaan and meet with this admiral."

The captain nodded. A lock of hair, shining in the low light, slid over her shoulder and she swung her head to fling it back. "Of course, ma'am. Whatever you need. My objectives?"

"Establish a line of communication. Explain that I'm open to negotiating trade and better relations. Find out what she will tell you about overlap in the industries without revealing what we already know. Investigate what we can do to help one another."

"Got it." Bailey nodded. "Anything else?"

How should she say this? She understood Baldric's request, but playing messenger opened the door to miscommunication. Already, Alira and her problems had drawn Rizzo too deeply into complications not of her own making. If she hadn't already promised Alira to keep her abreast of important information, she might keep Thrace's news to herself. On the other hand, doing this would buy the Syndicate a favor from the new admiral. That might someday prove priceless.

"Yes. Tell Baldric that our mutual friend is alive and well for the moment, and that this one time only, in the interest of keeping her that way, I have delivered the admiral's message." Rizzo's lips puckered for a moment. "Tell her that I understand her concerns over sending Consortium crew to the Syndicate base for training, and that I will honor her wishes. If she changes her mind in the future, we can discuss it then."

"Consortium crew… what?" Bailey stammered.

"Irrelevant. If and when Baldric changes her mind, I'll bring you up to speed." Rizzo raised one eyebrow. "Make no promises to this person, Captain. I need more intel before we consider further dialogue."

"Of course, ma'am." Bailey brushed the errant lock of hair into place once more. "Should I touch base with our New Canaan contact while I'm there?"

"Yes. Find out what she knows about the situation. We need all the information we can get right now." Rizzo shifted in her seat. "I have a feeling this change of command is going to prove interesting."

chapter 54

Pelarr, Zebalu
<u>City Center Market</u>

ROOK STOOD BEFORE THE PUBLIC comm unit and stared at the screen, her mouth dry.

"Single male seeks companion for no-strings sex, outdoors fun, and conversation with intelligence. Respond for meet details."

Conversation with intelligence. Rizzo's code phrase, embedded in a random personals ad along with thousands of others. She had news.

This soon? It'd only been two days since Rook's return from Saacharis. Her fingers tapped the side of the unit, her teeth worrying her bottom lip. She looked up from the screen. The market roof had already been retracted when she arrived. Late morning sun poured through, warming the air in the avenue between the shops. Sensory control came harder in Rook's body than it had in Skalar's. Heat prickled at her scalp, sending a drop of sweat down her neck, and she swiped it away. She scanned the shopping crowd. Humans went about their business, buying colonial-made products with colonial credits, feeding the system that fed them. No one seemed to be looking her way.

She looked at the screen. Whatever the intel, it must be important. Rizzo wouldn't have risked her contact otherwise. Rook's hand rose and hovered over the response address, breath lodged in her throat. Voices yammered in her head, Rook's overlapping them all to the point of nonsense.

shut up, all of you.

"Intelligence is a rare find," she said into the comm. "Would love to meet for potential exchange." She signed it X394ZED, the ID Rizzo had given her for this purpose, and touched the screen, sending the query, and her breath puffed up her cheeks before escaping through her lips. She'd committed now.

Maybe not, though. It wasn't too late to pull out. It would likely be tomorrow before the contact answered. Even then, she could still ignore the meet if the risk was too great. At least comming from a public unit added another layer of distance to her message, made her harder to track. It would show her ident card, true, but by the time anyone traced her—

The screen before her winked, updated. Single Male's reply nested below his initial post, visible only to her.

"Chimaera Public House. Now."

Rook's hands fisted at her sides. He must have been waiting, watching. She looked out again at the humans around her. Was he in this crowd? Did he already know what she looked like?

She logged out of the unit and moved on jerky, wooden legs toward the exit. Chimaera lay a few kilometers away, opposite the city center from the Cartel's base, though she knew better than to equate distance with safety. If Bellamy was watching, it wouldn't matter where Rook betrayed her.

But this was, to all appearances, a meeting between single people who wanted companionship. If the subject came up with the admiral, Rook could simply fall back on that.

Or she could ignore Single Male. That would be the safer option, but then she wouldn't know what Rizzo had to say. While her mind debated, her legs carried her to the hoverbus that would transport her to the west end of town. To the meet. Her skimmer would have been faster, but a faction craft could be tracked. The bus wound its way through the city, stopping at every station and turning down side streets. Within thirty minutes, she was debarking at the transport station across from the pub.

Rook stared at Chimaera. Its exterior holographic coating shimmered in the sunlight. Figures from human mythology seemed to leap off the surface and confront the pub's approaching patrons. Why would anyone deface a structure like this? Rook hated it—before and after she'd met Alira. Even muted, Rook's memories lay open to her on this gaudy, confusing thing. Too much stimulation for anyone to endure, except it seemed to be a popular place. Maybe it was better inside than out.

She crossed the street, squinting against the building's glare, and ducked inside. Welcome dimness slid over her, the sweat from outside cooling on her skin. Except for the outer walls and those separating the main room from the service areas, the whole floor lay open to view from the front entry. Comfortable, cushioned seating lay scattered throughout the space, intimate setups with low tables, divided only by artful arrangement of plants. Soft music filtered through from some hidden source and mingled with the low murmur of dozens of conversations. In here, holographic beasts sat caged within frames at regular intervals along the outer wall, softened by the lower light. Rook heaved a sigh.

Someone came in behind her, and she moved farther into the pub. How would she find the contact? Rizzo had given her no name or description. Rook wandered along the outer perimeter of the room in search of a lone human male, trying to appear as if she knew what she was doing. A third of the way around, a human approached her. A man. 170 centimeters, slightly taller than she was. Slim, wiry. Brown hair. Dark eyes. Small patch of hair below his bottom lip.

Was this him?

He offered a small smile. "Looking for someone?"

"Yes, a partner to share conversation with intelligence, among other things," she replied.

"X394ZED?"

She nodded. "Single Male?"

His smile widened just a trace. "I got us a table. This way," he said, tipping his head the way he'd come.

She followed, watching for anyone else's attention. Other patrons seemed intent on their own exchanges. No one looked their way.

At the lift, Single Male rode with her in silence to the second floor, where they stepped out into noise. Music here was raucous, grating. Almost as annoying as the front of the building. She touched him on the arm, and he turned.

"Why here?" she shouted.

He leaned closer. "What?"

"Why here?" she repeated. "It'll be harder to talk!"

Single Male nodded, then leaned close again. "It will also be harder to monitor our chat." He drew back with a smile, waved her to follow, and led her through the maze of blocky, metal tables to the far corner. Sound levels dropped a notch here. He pulled out a chair, sat, gestured to the one beside him.

Rook lowered herself into the seat, watching him, watching the room.

He leaned in, his elbows on the table. "You're Captain Rook. I've seen you on base."

She nodded.

"We have a mutual friend. Tall, dark, and dangerous. You with me?"

"Yes."

"She wants you to know there's been a change in command at the Consortium."

Rook's skin prickled. "What does that mean?"

"Skalar is out. For good."

Panic pinched her voice. "Who's in?"

"Some new player, name of Baldric."

The noise surrounding them grew tinny and distant, filtered through the ringing in her ears. Single Male's face retreated, as if she were seeing him through a long narrow tube. Her cheeks flamed despite the cool air, and Skalar raged inside her head.

Baldric? Did he say Baldric?

Rook struggled to take a deep breath, to calm her rising emotion. Her fingers gripped the edge of the table hard enough to dent the surface.

"Water," she rasped.

"You sure you don't want a beer?"

She pounded a fist on the table, the abrupt pain focusing her in the moment once more. "Water!"

Single Male leaned in, his face all sharp angles. "You're attracting attention."

He was right. Several people glanced their way, and she forced herself to smile with tight lips. "Water, *please*."

He touched the menu on the order system—water for her, beer for him—then leaned toward her once more. "I take it this is bad news."

"Bad," she repeated, her head hanging face down. Galen had wanted her out. He'd even told her so, spoke of leaving together, making a place for themselves on Earth. Sitting in the admiral's chair while she was gone had clearly changed his mind. He'd wasted no time in snatching away her avenue of retreat from this little adventure. What the hell was she supposed to do now? Rook shook her head with a laugh, then nodded at the table. "'Unexpected' fits better."

Wait staff brought their drinks, then left. Rook downed half of hers without stopping.

He eyed her for a moment, then took a sip of his brew. "There's more."

Of course there was.

"Our mutual friend says the new admiral refused to send Consortium crew for training. Said it was for their safety and that you'd understand. She also put a time-limit on your freedom to redistribute assets." His lips puckered. "I assume you know what that means."

This just got better and better. "Did she specify that limit?"

He shrugged. "Not to me."

Without that hematium from the outpost, she'd have to actually go to Iridos to repay Rizzo. Except Rizzo had sent a team to Iridos to kill the Cartel crew there. No more miners meant there would be no more metal to offer. What now?

Maybe if she could get word to Galen—to Thrace—she could turn this around, reinject meaning into her Cartel project. She'd gained information enough to clear Skalar's name. No proof yet, though it was only a matter of time.

Galen had been saying for a long while that playing Skalar was killing her. He'd been right, but she'd done what she thought best. Maybe it wasn't the most effective way to accomplish the unammi's goals. Still, it was all she'd known to do. Galen's turnabout, his bald-faced betrayal, ripped away even that avenue. He knew her plans, naturally. He could still carry them out as Admiral Baldric, but that wasn't the point, damn it.

Skalar raged in her head, and she put her hands over her ears.

"Stop," she whispered.

"What?" Single Male leaned in.

Without a Consortium role to return to, where would she go? Not Harajüd, not as someone less than Skalar. Survivors on Earth wanted nothing to do with her. Rakalesh had made that clear. She couldn't face the crew on the outpost after being ousted in such a fashion. Rizzo wouldn't take her until this mess was resolved.

What was left?

She dropped her hands to the table, where they lay limp, unmoving. "Is that everything?"

He raised one eyebrow. "Seems plenty to me. You okay?"

"Not yet." She swallowed the rest of her water. "But I will be."

chapter 55

Pelarr, Zebalu
<u>Cartel Trader Base, Admiral Bellamy's Office</u>

"YOU'RE WRONG," BELLAMY INSISTED. "YOU have to be."

"I wish I were." Hannah didn't look sorry. "She was talking to Jammer at Chimaera Pub twenty minutes ago. Three of our people saw it."

"There must be some logical explanation."

Hannah just looked at her.

Bellamy shot up from her chair and came around the desk. "Who set up the meet? Was it Rook?"

"We aren't sure yet, ma'am. I'm working on that. But it didn't go through any comm to or from her quarters on the base."

"Then how?"

"I'm betting public comm." Hannah shrugged. "She was seen at a unit in City Center Market just prior to the meet."

Bellamy stared at her second. "You had someone following her?"

"Not specifically, ma'am. I just asked security to be extra vigilant. I did not tell them why. One of their teams spotted her in the Market, thought she acted out of character, and followed her on their own." Hannah tilted her head. "They're the ones who called it in."

The admiral pushed her hands through her hair and looked out the window. From here, its top frame chopped off the distant sea view, but not the image of Rook's face when she'd stood in this office before her last assignment. The woman had been rock-steady, same as always. Loyal to the bone. Rook was the closest thing to a trusted officer in the Cartel, next to Hannah. No. Rook would never betray the faction. Betray Bellamy.

"So you think she's a Syndicate agent."

"I didn't say that, ma'am. I said she met with someone we strongly suspect of being a Syndicate agent."

"What did they talk about?"

"Unknown." Hannah sighed. "Jammer took her to a table on the second floor, too loud to monitor, and they sat in such a way our people couldn't determine the topic of conversation from watching their lips. They said it looked pretty intense. He pissed Rook off at one point."

Bellamy gaped at Hannah. "Rook? Angry? What did that look like?"

Hannah shrugged again. "She pounded a fist on the table. Security said she looked upset when she left. They were afraid she'd made them, but the captain was too lost in thought. Walked right past them and never looked their way."

"I don't understand." Bellamy shook her head. "If she's an agent, why wait this long to show herself? And what's her game? She's had plenty of chances to sell us out in the past. This solo run to Iridos gave her another perfect opportunity to pull something, but she didn't."

"With all due respect, we don't know that, ma'am."

"Don't be ridiculous, Hannah. She took the slaves and brought back the hematium."

"True. But *where* did she drop the slaves? *Where* did she get the hematium?"

Bellamy huffed. "Not likely someone else gave it to her, is it?"

Hannah shrugged.

"Then what do you think she's up to?"

"Unknown, ma'am."

Bellamy turned toward her desk and leaned against its edge with one hip. Rook as a spy—not such a new concept, since that's how she came here in the first place, only that time she'd confessed. Pledged loyalty to the Cartel. Never once had she faltered in that promise.

Had she?

One way to find out.

"TICS, record emergency message to Commander Jude." The ready chitter sounded, and Bellamy went on. "Jude, break radio silence. Send a full report the moment you get this. Bellamy out."

She looked at Hannah. "I don't believe it for a second, but you have raised valid questions. Your concerns deserve answers."

"Thank you, ma'am."

"Where is Rook now?"

"She isn't on base as far as I know, ma'am. The last the security team saw of her, she was boarding a hoverbus outside Chimaera."

"Very well. It's a six-day round trip to and from Iridos. She was gone a bit longer, but that could easily be explained by her time on the surface at Iridos. If she was up to something, the timing would be off."

"Yes."

Bellamy sighed. She couldn't believe she was doing this. But Hannah was right. It did look suspicious. Bellamy would just prove her wrong. "Run scans on her ship. Check the logs, but also check the fuel cells, the engine traces, anything that will tell us where she's been. Run tests on the comm system. See if she spoke to anyone, regardless of the log entries. Find out the truth, Captain."

"I'll begin at once, ma'am."

Was that a smug look on Hannah's face? "You'll see I'm right, Captain. Rook isn't an agent."

"Then this will simply be a formality, ma'am. I'll report the moment I complete the tests." Hannah left.

A waste of time, really, but at least once Hannah's tests were done, she could focus on who might actually be Jammer's connection.

Still, why had Rook met with him? Bellamy had looked up his image in the files. Wiry physique. Dimples. Average. The man didn't stand out in any way, so surely Rook wasn't after his rugged good looks. Besides,

Bellamy had never seen Rook go after companionship of any flavor. She was married to the job, that captain. So, what was going on?

Maybe she and Rook should chat over tea. Bellamy could ask, flat out, about her meeting with Jammer.

No. Not yet. Wait and review Jude's report first. That would tell them when Rook arrived, how long she stayed, when she left, and how much ore she'd loaded for the return trip, information sufficient to settle the matter. Then, when Hannah came in with negative results from all her tests, Bellamy could rub her nose in her mistake. That's all this was. A misinterpretation of innocent actions.

A worm of worry dug beneath Bellamy's convictions and lodged in the back of her mind. Its presence cast a shadow over the rest of Bellamy's day and grew, emboldened by her visions of Rook chatting with a Syndicate agent in a bar. By the time she left her office, it had tripled in size and crossed over into her conscious thoughts.

Was Hannah right?

Part Four

chapter 56

New Canaan, Harajüd
<u>Consortium Trader Base, Admiral Baldric's Office</u>

"How do you know this?" Thrace asked.

Mira shook her head and set her hair swinging around her face. "I don't, but the evidence I found sure seems compelling. Look." She threw a list from her TICS pad to hover above Thrace's desk.

Thrace skimmed the information. "Someone is looking for mining equipment." She glanced at Mira. "So?"

"Those aren't queries, ma'am. But even if they were, it's the way the comms are running that tagged me. A legit buyer would go through colonial channels for that kind of equipment. But no. This person is stirring up chatter on the net about diggers, sorting gear, autocarts. Sparking talk of which colonies are buying new hardware, for which jobs, like that. Whoever this is, they just get other people talking. They don't add any info themselves. I gotta ask myself why." Mira pulled the list into her pad.

"And what does that have to do with the Cartel and slavery?"

"I've seen this name before, Admiral. I don't have a face to go with it, but I do know they are connected to the Cartel. And if Bellamy's mining

for gold or whatever, you can bet your boots she isn't doing it herself."
Mira nodded. "That means slaves."

"Or Cartel crew."

"Maybe, though I doubt that. I'm still looking, ma'am. But it's damn
sure Bellamy's people aren't going to leave signs pointing to snatched
kids." Mira frowned. "Why d'you think she's taking kids, anyway? They
can't really do much hard labor."

Thrace sighed. "No. But they could fit into smaller spaces. They also
have more energy than adults, especially in short bursts. Good work. Keep
looking. You'll find something we can be sure of." She stopped, tipped
her head, senses reaching into the wider building beyond her office.
Sa'abah approached with a stranger—not the usual type of unfamiliar
presence, but one more focused, purposeful.

The Syndicate liaison. That was fast. Thrace hadn't expected this
guest for another day at least. Rizzo must have sent the ship before she
sent notice, perhaps to catch the Consortium off-guard in case their offer
of parley was not authentic. Dangerous risk, that. If Thrace truly had
dishonorable intentions, Rizzo's second could be in grave danger right
now. Or perhaps the Syndicate's admiral wanted to see how Thrace
reacted to surprise.

"Our guest has arrived."

"Here? On base? Right now?"

Thrace nodded.

Mira peered at her, visibly suppressing a shudder. "How do you do
that?"

"Do what?"

"Know things." The captain shook her head, a slight frown marring
her dainty features. "Do you know what I'm going to do or say at any
given minute?"

"Pointless question. Focus on what matters."

"Like this meeting."

"Exactly." She trusted Rizzo. Now that Skalar was out, she believed
the two factions would be able to work out their differences. Still, she kept
her hands from clenching each other by sheer force of will. Under normal
circumstances, Rizzo would never harm any surviving unammi, yet

competitors in the Trader business sometimes ate each other for lunch. Thrace would rather not salt the meal with indications of anxiety or indecision.

"Watch what you say in front of our guest. Give her no weakness to take home. Clear?"

"Crystal. If I may ask, what do we hope to gain here, ma'am?"

"Skalar damaged the reputation of this faction, and not just among the members of its crew. We're repairing the gates, Captain. Courting allies."

"You do understand that Traders are in competition with one another?"

Thrace smirked. "Another pointless question. Use your words more wisely, Cohen."

"Okay. Why make friends with someone who might betray us at her first chance?"

"I said nothing about friends. I don't plan to invite Rizzo for tea. But maintaining an alliance uses far less energy and fewer resources than guarding or defending against an enemy."

"So, this is an economical decision, then."

"That and more." Thrace leaned over the desk on her elbows. "Think ahead, Mira, like the captain you are. Rizzo's faction is strong and healthy. She has connections and business channels that could serve us in the long run. We can offer similar benefits to the Syndicate in exchange for cooperation. Both factions profit."

Mira looked doubtful. "Aren't you worried Rizzo will take advantage of the situation?"

"That's the point, isn't it?"

"No, I meant what if she abuses your good will and seizes her first opportunity to screw us?"

Thrace leaned back. "You think that's likely?"

"Well, I mean—"

"Didn't you just make an observation about me 'knowing things'?" Thrace peered at her second.

Across the desk, Mira's expression washed clean of doubt.

"Once we've covered the formalities, I want you to take her on a tour of the base. Just the surface. Give her a taste. Don't reveal all our secrets." Thrace winked at Mira, who grinned in response. "Afterward, I'll want to hear your thoughts on this person and why you think she's really here."

"No problem, ma'am."

The door chimed and Thrace stood. Mira followed suit.

"Come."

Sa'abah stepped in, followed by a woman with pale skin and eyes of startling blue. Long black hair swung loose—surprising, since that would offer an advantage to her opponent in close-quarters combat. Clearly, the woman didn't come here looking for a fight.

"Admiral Baldric, this is—"

The woman stepped forward, cutting off Sa'abah's introduction. "Captain Bailey of the Saacharis Syndicate. Admiral Rizzo sent me."

"Of course. Thank you for coming. This is my second, Captain Mira Cohen." Thrace gestured to Sa'abah to wait in the corridor, then took in their visitor's overall presence while the officers acknowledged one another. She pointed at the chairs and resumed her own seat. "How is your admiral? Well, I hope. Prospering."

"She is, thank you," Bailey said. She sat, as did Mira. "She was somewhat surprised at your communique."

Thrace allowed herself a small smile. "Yet here you are."

"Indeed," Bailey said. "Admiral Rizzo recognizes the potential in renewed relations between our factions."

"Did she send word of our mutual friend?"

Bailey tossed a glance at Mira before offering a curt nod. "The last time we saw her she was fine, if a bit concerned over her present predicament."

Did this person know about the unammi? Thrace steepled her fingers in front of her as she pried into their visitor. Emotions huddled beneath the Syndicate captain's surface, held in tight rein. Secrets hid there, as did caution, but no threatening emotions nor any knowledge of the unammi.

"When was that?"

"She left Saacharis five days ago." Bailey frowned. "You've heard nothing?"

"No. She has dropped out of touch, gone off-plan. I don't know what she's doing now. Can you shed any light on that?"

Bailey's eye twitched. "Only that she changed tactics on our end, too. Ramped up her operation to include rescuing slaves. Young ones."

Thrace's breath caught in her throat. "Zebalu?"

"Yes."

Thrace glanced at Mira, who stared back, eyes wide. Thrace brought her hands down to the arms of her chair and forced herself to remain calm.

The news confirmed her suspicions. It made sense that Alira would go there to clear Skalar's name. But a rescue op? That went beyond dangerous and ran screaming into the territory of suicidal. Thrace had no personal experience with Admiral Bellamy—Galen had never interacted with her—yet plenty of stories filled Thrace with trepidation.

Bailey's eyes narrowed. "This displeases you?"

Thrace looked at her. Observant, wasn't she? "Yes and no. It's a noble action, but one that is likely to get her killed without adequate planning and support. Is that why she approached the Syndicate?"

Now it was Bailey's turn to shift in her chair. "No. At least I don't think it's what connected her to my admiral in the beginning. But we are helping her in this, if that offers you any comfort."

Bailey wondered why their mutual friend hadn't come to the Consortium for help. She didn't give it voice, but Thrace could feel it. She, on the other hand, understood Alira's reasons and was grateful she'd stayed away. By now, she would know she'd been replaced as leader of the Consortium. Having her find out by coming here in any guise would have been awkward at best.

"It does. But I feel I must warn you." Thrace pressed her lips together, then sighed. "This is not the first time our friend has gone off on her own and done unpredictable things."

Across the desk, all expression drained from Bailey's face. "Is she dangerous?"

Thrace clasped her hands as if to shield herself from the question. Her throat tightened at the thought of yet another betrayal—that's how Alira would see all this. Alira was on Zebalu, alone and embroiled in yet another self-appointed crusade. What would happen to her without the Syndicate's fragile protection?

Thrace dropped her gaze, searching her heart for the correct answer, though no doubt her hesitation spoke loudly enough. Alira was one person, seemingly bent on self-destruction that no one, not even Thrace, could stop. Weighed against the lives of the remaining unammi survivors on Earth who hung by such a slender thread, or the safety of a potential ally if she or her crew entered a relationship with Alira unaware of the risk, Thrace could not in good conscience hide the facts.

"She can be a treasure, with insights and talents you can't imagine until you've seen them in action. She has vision and is fearless, if unstructured, in pursuit of her ideals. She is a great asset that comes with equal risk." Thrace stared into Bailey's eyes. "She's unstable and certainly dangerous, even deadly. If she feels cornered, she'll strike in ways you won't see coming. I advise extreme caution. She brings valuable gifts to any deal, but you'll have to watch her every second."

Bailey's surprise at this dichotomous assessment rose off her in waves that did not reflect on her face. "Is that why she's not working with the Consortium?"

"Only in part." Thrace's head bobbed left, then right. "My relationship with her is…complicated. Personal. Best leave it at that."

The Syndicate captain narrowed her eyes, then nodded once. "As you wish. To business, then. Admiral Rizzo is open to the idea of trade negotiation and industry cooperation, and suggested we might discuss overlap in faction programs."

"Excellent. I've asked Captain Cohen to give you a brief tour of the base so that you can see a sample of our operation. That can help to fuel our discussion afterward. How long will you be staying, Captain?"

"A day or so. Just long enough to finish our initial discussion, I'm afraid. My admiral expects me to return quickly."

"Then we won't waste time." Thrace stood, along with the others. "Captain Sa'abah will accompany you. Mira, contact logistics. Have our best guest quarters set up on level sixteen for the Captain, and comm me when you've finished the tour. I'll have a meal brought in."

Mira gestured. "Captain Bailey, this way."

Bailey nodded at Thrace, then headed for the door.

Mira followed her out, shooting Thrace a look on the way.

When they were gone, Thrace stared after them, trying and failing to imagine a more volatile scenario than liberating Cartel property right under Bellamy's nose. If Alira believed she could avoid detection at such a game, then her self-delusion was worse than Thrace had known.

She shook her head. She was going to lose Alira completely. Might have done so already. Thrace's features twisted. She covered her mouth, stifling the sob that threatened to escape. Her knees gave way, and she sank into her chair, shoulders slumped. Her mind snatched at excuses, ideas, any reason for hope, but she knew she was too close to see the big picture. She needed guidance. Wise counsel. Only one person came to mind.

"TICS, record message for Botha."

chapter 57

Southern Barrens
Mjolnir Island, Danua
<u>**Aboard the Juveltranstør**</u>

KNØFA WATCHED THE VIEWSCREEN ON their approach. Ahead, a cluster of large rocky hills squatted on the plain. Not a mountain range, but the closest thing to it in the barrens. Stunted trees quivered above the flats, gnarled and dancing on the edge of survival. He noticed them—Tsurin taught him to always be aware of his surroundings—but looked past them at the rocks ahead. Therein lay their target, the drop site for a huge shipment. A haul like this would bring a pretty profit on the black market, especially if Tsurin had been right to suspect the crates contained any Syndicate-specific parts, always in high demand.

"Time?" Tsurin asked.

"Oh-seven-fourteen, ma'am," one crewman replied. "Sky's clear of satellite fly-bys for another forty-one minutes."

"Set down there," Tsurin pointed, then touched the comm. "Ground crew prepare for loading. Clock's ticking, people. Let's move."

She turned and marched past him, thick braid swinging down her back. "Knøfa, you're with me."

He followed her out of command and down the corridor. "They made the drop?"

Tsurin grunted. "Late, but yes. We're behind schedule as it is. Can't afford to mess this up. We need the credits."

Knøfa drew breath.

"Don't start," she said as they stepped into the lift. "Your suggestions are still under consideration."

He closed his mouth and rode down in silence beside her.

Ground crew met them at the main hatch. "This is a cake run. In and out. You've done this enough, you all know what to do. You and you," she pointed, "lead off."

The main hatch swung up, and they were out and pounding dirt on their way to the pickup. Too bad they couldn't land closer, speed things up a bit, but this was the closest level space. Merch drops in the uneven terrain of the barrens always added a layer of difficulty to their pickups. Some were easier, with good landing spots closer to the merchandise, but they couldn't use those every time. Tsurin had taught him it was best to rotate their deliveries, so no pattern presented itself to corpgov officials.

His long legs loped beside Tsurin as she ran, the crew spread out before them as they wound their way between piles of rock, mounded hillocks that stood on each other's shoulders to tower over the flats. Shadows huddled in the hollows at the joins, shelters to wildlife, no doubt—ørkhunds, from the smell. Those shy beasties would be long gone before humans got within sighting distance, but that eau de piss was hard to mistake.

Four minutes in, their frontrunners reached the target and headed into the shadow. They'd hardly disappeared inside when they reappeared and backtracked.

The rest of the crew caught up, murmuring among themselves, glancing at the cave. Knøfa and Tsurin joined them.

She frowned. "What's wrong?"

"Scavenger, ma'am. Got into one of the crates."

"Then deal with it. Tight schedule. Remember?"

"It's a person, ma'am," the crewman said. "Looks like a kid. A girl."

"Shit," Tsurin said.

"Why would a little kid want ship parts?" another crewman said.

Knøfa ignored her, raised an eyebrow at Tsurin. "See? Vermin don't just hurt the colonials. They hurt the faction too. Still wanna dismiss my suggestion?"

She turned her hot green gaze on him. "Knøfa—"

"Ma'am, all due respect, this is a prime example of how my idea can be useful to both the Clan and the corpgov. It takes a load off both our hands and provides useful research as well as a valuable product."

"Oh-seven-twenty-one, ma'am," a crewman called.

Tsurin shook her head. "We don't have time for this."

"Let's try it. Just this once. Let me bring this little parasite out. I can carry her and a crate at the same time. We can still load the haul and beat it out of here before the next flyover."

She stared at the dirt, nodded. "Very well. We'll bring her out and discuss it when the job's done. But I'm going in after her. Not you. The rest of you stay put."

Knøfa ignored the glances of the other crew. If they weren't used to the banter between admiral and second by now, he wasn't going to hold their hands. They'd do what she commanded and never question. She had taught him different. Better. She'd been grooming him for leadership ever since she'd killed his parents. She just hadn't known it. Not at first. Hard to recognize a future Trader admiral in a four-year-old.

Tsurin disappeared into the shadow of the cave.

Knøfa grunted. Good thing she'd decided to participate in this run. "Another teaching opportunity," she'd said. Maybe. Even so, it was still bullshit. Tsurin got off on the thrill of jobs like this. She always had, as far as he knew, but retrieval runs were lackey jobs. Admirals ran the larger faction ship from behind a desk. His surrogate mother missed the field. That's why she was really here.

Meh, didn't matter what landed her here in the barrens this day. He was glad she'd come. The rest of the world could go to hell, and he wouldn't even notice. But if this little scavenger had done considerable damage to the shipment, Tsurin would see it for herself, maybe turn the child over to him. Then he'd get the chance to prove the worth of his plan. The chance to prove Tsurin had been right to believe in him.

He watched the hole where she'd disappeared. What was taking her so long? It'd been a while since they'd used this site, but he remembered it well. The cave didn't go that deep into the knoll, so unless Tsurin and Little Shit were having tea, it shouldn't be this hard to subdue a kid and exit the drop site.

"Time?" he asked.

"Oh-seven-twenty-six, sir."

Knøfa frowned. She must have hit a snag, but what? Tsurin against a little girl? No contest. Still…

Muscles in his legs twitched and jumped with the need to move, but Tsurin wouldn't thank him for interfering if she was calming the kid or working some sort of juju to convince it to come out on its own.

And if Tsurin was in trouble?

Knøfa pursed his lips, then ran toward the cave.

"Something's wrong," he yelled to the crew. "Let's go."

chapter 58

Pelarr, Zebalu
<u>Cartel Trader Base, Captain Rook's Quarters</u>

ALIRA BACKED INTO THE CORNER, huddled on the gray carpet of the bedroom, and clapped her hands over her ears. In her head, Rook chanted a nonsense litany of random facts, snippets of spiritual doctrine, useless trivia.

> *shemonaea's star is called sakĕdris. suh-KAY-drihs.*
> *stop.*
> *ruins in ulykkevik's crater predate human colonization by six-point-seven million years.*

A long, low groan escaped Alira's throat. Behind Rook's monotonous recital and Crow's unintelligible bellowing, whispers hissed attempts at communication Alira strained to hear. Was it Nyros? Ijydin? Skalar? Who? If Rook would

> *SHUT UP.*

Alira might make them out and know what to do.

> *brothers in the god's plan faith believe abominations perpetrated on lesser humans are not sins.*

White sparks and teal streaks flashed in patches down her arms, testament to her sense of confusion as if someone had opened her skull and stirred her brains. Meditation had proven useless before, yet she would try almost anything to make it stop. She pulled her hands down to her lap and tried again.

Breathe in

harajüd's southern polar continent is named after apsu of old earth.

Breathe out

contemporary varieties of animal species on ranafta are three percent larger than their introduced predecessors.

Breathe in

Breathe out

Breathe in

waste from zebalu's commercial fishing industry comprises more than half of that colony's fertilizer exports.

Her eyes flickered open and she lurched to her feet with a trembling sigh. Bare gray walls and carpet provided a backdrop for flashes of Rook's sordid and violent memories.

Alira shook her head, stood up straighter. Those weren't real. None of them were real, not in this moment. She staggered against the wall, slamming her arm out and to the side to steady herself, and the room solidified.

She caught her breath, waited for the visions to return, but they did not. What had she done differently?

One foot stepped, trembling, away from the corner. Her arm fell to her side, and the visions began to fade in

sixty-eight-point-nine percent of zebalu's food sources are oceanic in origin.

clouding her thoughts. She fell back, her palm slapping the wall.

The visions vanished.

Alira stared at her hand. Once more, she pulled it away, stepped forward, and felt the room's solidity begin to shift before touching the wall once more, with the same stabilizing result.

She experimented, slid her hand along the wall, felt its tiny imperfections. Her gaze swung to the bed, and she bent to press her hands against its cushioned surface—tactile sensations, anchors to this reality, not the one her demented harvest would provide. What else? No windows here to test whether visual distractions would work as well. She looked around for other possibilities. The closet....

She stumbled across the floor and jerked open the door. On the left, a small collection of clothing hung ready. On the right, folded garments and accessories lay stacked in cubicles. Rook didn't like to stand out. Her tastes stuck to plain colors and styles, easy to mimic.

Alira stared at one item after another. Her fingers brushed the fabrics, and she gathered them to her face to breathe in their smells. She'd never actually worn any of these things, but she knew, oh yes, she knew how they felt against her skin. Sharp emotions flooded her senses, flashes of imagery attached to this coat or a stab of agony to that shirt, with no solid connection to space or time. She pulled the pain shirt loose and held it up. Dark blue, rough fibers, long sleeves. Ragged burn in the chest.

What had happened? She frowned at the mark as if it would speak its history. A flash of light. Teeth-grinding discomfort. Retaliation. A new trophy on Rook's vest.

Alira dropped the shirt and pulled out the real vest. She'd had to memorize it that first time, before she'd appeared as Rook in Bellamy's office. Now she went over it again, item by item. Which memento connected to that shirt? She touched each one in turn, reaching for more of its story than vague recollections.

Only Rook's nonsensical ramblings met Alira's queries. Her other voices, muted whispers behind the monotonous litany, offered no help.

Frustration lodged in her throat like dry bread. She needed those memories, dammit! Her hands fisted in the fabric of the vest, ripping its seams, its trophies tearing the skin on her palms. Blood oozed onto the vest—unammi blood, a stain that could later betray her people—and Alira bundled the offending garment into a ball. With a roar, she threw it across the room. Pulses of vivid color raced across her skin.

calm down.

She closed her eyes, heaved a breath, then another, and another. After a moment, she looked at the wound. A scratch, nothing more. Healing had already begun.

the rubene federation is the only faction that refuses to trade in illegal wildcrafting.

Alira dropped her head forward, her shoulders slumped.

what do you want from me? i can't undo what's done.

A sound, some movement, some change in the air caught her attention and she whirled. Eli stood beside the bed.

She cried out, a garbled sound, and stumbled toward him. "Where have you been?"

His image warped, winking through his repertoire of collected forms.

"Help me," she whispered.

an overdose of amornae can result in tremors, hallucinations, heart palpitations, liver and respiratory failure.

Her Companion's shifting image stopped at Eli's face and watched in ironic silence.

chapter 59

Southern Barrens
Mjolnir Island, Danua
<u>**Aboard the Juveltranstør**</u>

KNØFA SHOVED HIS BULK THROUGH the narrow hatch and handed Tsurin's limp form over to a crewman.

"What's wrong with her?" the crewman asked.

The captain didn't even look her way. "Do I look like a med tech? Figure it out," he snapped. He stared at her unmoving body, his jaw working. "She isn't breathing. Fix her."

He pushed past the tech toward control and dropped the crate he carried under the other arm.

"Stow that under lock and key," he called, still moving forward, "and don't let anyone near it until we get to base. Put the others in the hold. Get everyone aboard. We're in the air in five minutes with or without them."

Murmurs of assent passed, ignored, as he pressed on. "TICS, time."

"Oh-seven-forty-six."

Knøfa cursed under his breath and started to run.

chapter 60

Pelarr, Zebalu
<u>Cartel Trader Base, Captain Rook's Quarters</u>

ALIRA SHOOK HER HEAD WITH a blurted chuff of sound. "You're the only one in my head with nothing to say."

Rook's litany muted into background noise. Across the sudden lull, Alira heard the rustle of Eli's breath, prelude to speech. Alira's skin prickled. Wait. The last few times Eli'd appeared had been pivotal moments where everything turned on a single action. Flecks of white arose in her skin and burst in patches of dread. What—

The door chime intruded.

Her head snapped around toward the hall door. No one ever visited Rook.

"TICS, who is at my door?"

"Admiral Bellamy."

"Did she query the whereabouts of Captain Rook in the last ten minutes?"

"Affirmative."

the zebalu association's board holds eighteen directors.

White blossomed in Alira's face and arms. She pivoted. Eli was gone. Her breath snagged.

"I can't serve as your channel if I'm dead," she muttered.

She shoved the torn vest and dropped shirt under the padding on her bed. No good. The lump in the pallet gave them away. She dragged them out and tossed them in the disposal, set the ignition and waited for the unit to cycle.

The door chime sounded again.

Alira shot to the bed and rumpled its linens. She straightened. Nothing else out of place, not in this room anyway. What about the rest of her quarters? She tried to remember.

cuthars gulls nest along cliffs in zebalu's equatorial zone where shellfish are plentiful.

She glanced down at her hand. All healed, not that a scratch on her own hand would show on Rook's form. Still.

The disposal indicator switched to green just as the chime sounded for a third time, followed by the swish of the main door to her quarters. Alira spun, morphing, and left the room. Down the hall, Bellamy had let herself in.

Rook rubbed a hand across her face. "Admiral, my apologies."

Bellamy's grin sent a chill up Rook's neck. "I'd begun to worry. Sleeping, were you?"

"Yes, ma'am."

The admiral glanced down at Rook's full attire. "Fully dressed?"

Rook glanced down at her replica of the pain shirt, dark pants, trophy vest, heavy boots. Damn. "I hadn't meant to sleep, ma'am. Is something wrong?"

"An excellent question, Captain." Bellamy stepped farther into the main room, her gaze lingering on a metal captain's wheel that hung on the far wall, the sole item of decor in the entire flat. "I've heard nothing from Jude. Nothing at all. Why do you think that is?"

Rook frowned. "I thought she was under radio silence."

"She was," Bellamy nodded, "until I commed her to break it and send a report. That was two days ago."

the nidahn colony was quarantined in old earth year twenty-five hundred after its sole city was infected by escaped plague carriers.

"Maybe she's afraid you're testing her, ma'am."

"D'you think so?" Bellamy plopped onto the divan. "Would you believe that? Ignore my comm?"

The admiral sat erect, her grin wide, and stared intently at Rook. She should know what those things meant. Should. "I'm not sure there are any correct answers to those questions, ma'am."

Bellamy laughed. "Very well. Tell me about your trip to Iridos."

"Of course, ma'am." Rook shifted on her feet. What had she said last time? "Jude was glad for the replacement workers. The first lot died before my arrival. They'd only gotten three hundred meters down the main shaft. Jude's team was still clearing debris deep in the tunnels and hadn't yet found the end of the mine before I left."

"You already reported all that. Tell me the rest."

How well had Rook known Jude? Were they friends? Would Rook know things about Jude just by the way she behaved?

averaged across all twelve colony worlds, human reproduction produces more females than males by a three-to-one ratio.

Shadows danced on the gray wall behind Bellamy's head. Rook swung her arms behind her, fingers grasping and exploring the first trophy they encountered on her vest. "What would you like to know?"

Bellamy lifted her chin and placed her arms on the sides on the divan. She looked like a queen from an old Earth holoimage, holding court from her throne.

"How did Jude seem to you? Did she seem off in any way? Did she do anything that would make you suspicious?"

Bellamy's tone set Rook's hair more on end than usual. Did the admiral know the truth? Was she baiting her officer, setting a trap? Rook drew a careful breath.

"Not that I could see, ma'am. She seemed normal."

Bellamy nodded. "These new hologames she wanted. Was that for her or her crew?"

Rook hesitated. Did Jude game?

"It isn't a difficult question, Captain."

"I don't know, ma'am. She didn't say, and I didn't ask."

"What?" Bellamy's expression widened in apparent surprise. "You two didn't share your usual chitchat?"

"I knew you were in a hurry for the ore, ma'am." Rook shrugged. "I can catch up with her on the next trip."

"I see. What about the crew? How are they holding up on that godforsaken rock?"

Rook's hackles rose. She forced them down. "Fine, ma'am. Just bored, I think."

"Mmm. Understandable. So you think everything's okay, that I should forgive Jude's lack of response."

"I could go again, if you like, ma'am," Rook said. Go to Saacharis, warn Rizzo. "Carry word to her in person that you aren't testing her, that you really want an answer."

The admiral sucked in a gasp, as if this idea had not occurred to her. "That's not a bad idea, Captain. I'll go with you. I could stand to stretch my legs a bit."

Every muscle in Rook's body clenched.

Bellamy grinned. "But not for at least a week. Today I have more pressing matters to tend." She stood and turned toward the mounted captain's wheel. "I've always loved this thing. Where did you get it?"

Rook's breath stuttered in her chest. She gripped the trophy on her vest hard enough to puncture the skin of her hand for the second time in the last hour. She flailed through what little Rook shared.

"I got it in payment for a job, long before I joined your crew, ma'am."

"Yes, I remember that much. Tell me the story."

Rook forced a small laugh. "I don't remember it now, ma'am. It's been too long."

Bellamy turned, her eyes wide. "Really? How odd. I thought you never forgot your trophy tales." She stared at Rook before her face lit up like a beacon, grinning ear to ear. "Oh well. Never mind. Perhaps it'll come back to you after you're fully awake. I have another engagement now, so I'll leave you to nap as you wish. Thanks for your input, Rook. You've been more helpful than you know."

"Of course, ma'am." Rook's voice trembled. Had Bellamy noticed? "Any time I can help."

The admiral stared a moment too long, then swept toward the door and left.

Rook watched the closed door long after, waiting for it to slide open again. When it didn't, she sank onto the divan in Bellamy's place and dropped her head into her hands.

This role was getting just a little too hot. Rook had hoped to save a few more shiploads of slaves, but she should have a plan for her next harvest. Just in case. Someone not so close to the admiral.

Or maybe Rizzo could stage a reply from Iridos. If she could do it soon, it would look like the Cartel crew still functioned there. That could buy more time. But first, she needed to know the situation. Rook sighed and sat up straight. Guess she'd be meeting Single Male again sooner than she'd planned.

She stood, her shoulders tight. They needed a faster method of contact. Sending a personals ad took too long. If she could send from here, it would be more efficient, but that was out of the question. The market comm had worked last time. She'd try that first.

chapter 61

Pelarr, Zebalu
<u>Cartel Trader Base, Officers Dormitory, Corridor C</u>

OUTSIDE THE CAPTAIN'S QUARTERS, BELLAMY turned toward the lift. Her body leaned into each staccato step, as if her head wanted to arrive first. She saw only two officers along the way. Both hugged the wall until she was past.

The lift door opened. Bellamy pointed at the three people inside and jerked her thumb toward the corridor.

"All of you. Out."

No one argued. She stepped on. "Seventh floor." The door closed.

The moment she was alone in the car, she spoke again.

"TICS, locate Lieutenant Jammer."

"Lieutenant Jammer is in his quarters."

"Reverse direction. Ground floor." The car slowed, stopped, and reversed. "Connect me to Captain Hannah."

Hannah's face appeared in the car's vidscreen almost at once.

"Yes, ma'am?"

"I've just come from Rook's quarters."

"And?" Hannah said.

"That's not Rook."

Her second frowned. "Apologies, ma'am, could you repeat that?"

"Did I stutter?"

"No, ma'am. But then…who is it?"

Bellamy paced in the car. "I don't know. An imposter. Somehow. Do you have a report yet on her ship?"

"No, ma'am. Too soon." A beat of silence. "What are you going to do?"

"About her? I don't know yet. But put someone on her. I want to know where she goes, what she does, and how long it takes her to do it. In the interim, it's time I had a chat with Jammer. He's in his quarters. Bring him to me in the garden."

"Yes, ma'am."

The screen went dark just before the doors opened in the first-floor corridor. Waiting crewmen made a path for the admiral, and Bellamy moved down the hall toward the rear of the building.

Jude should've responded by now. Her continued radio silence raised alarm bells in Bellamy's head. That commander's loyalty was debatable, same as most any other crewman. Her survival instinct, however, was not. She wouldn't openly defy the Cartel or its admiral, not without solid backing from a stronger source. Nor did she have adequate intelligence to pull off a theft of Bellamy's hematium. So she never got the message, was unable to send a reply, or was working with someone else to cheat the Cartel. Whichever the case, Rook—or whoever that was in Rook's quarters—was in it up to her fat neck. Bellamy could smell the bullshit behind that imposter's lies.

She pushed out of the building and into the heady fragrance of rock lilies, cliff roses, and salt air. To one side, Chandra dug in the soil, planting some new green thing. Bellamy ignored the crewman's nod of greeting.

Warm wind cupped in the curve of the sheltered garden lifted Bellamy's hair into a frenzied dance. It would take a few minutes for Hannah to show with Jammer. Bellamy's pace slowed, but she did not stop to appreciate the view. The usual joy of this space cringed before the onslaught of her rage.

Rook had betrayed her.

No, not Rook. This was not the same person. Bellamy had been right. Rook never would have betrayed the faction. Who was this pretender? More to the point, when had she slithered in, and where was the real Cartel officer? Probably dead. Bellamy's jaw tightened. What was this bitch's game? She had to be working for someone, maybe Rizzo, to get at Bellamy's found resource. No profit in any of this other than the hematium. But then why would Rook return to Pelarr? She'd have to know Bellamy would figure this out. And if the theft of hematium was the goal, it made no sense to deliver any of it to Bellamy, much less such a whopping load. No. Something else was going on.

She stepped past the shelter of the walls and into the crosswind that whipped across the bluff and out over Pirate's Cove, pressing the thin fabric of her tunic and full pants against her form. She stopped long enough to kick off her sandals beside the paved walkway before proceeding to the cliff walk. Bare toes gripped rock better than soled shoes.

In the distance, gulls flocked and dove behind a pair of ships headed toward the colonial port. Day waned. The sun sank toward the horizon even as she watched. Twilight hovered, waiting its turn on the landscape.

Sounds approached from behind, scuffling feet dragging against the ground, along with Hannah's clipped pace.

Bellamy turned, smiling. Jammer stalked a few steps ahead of Hannah, his face neutral, arms swinging at his sides with easy grace. His height only topped Bellamy's by a centimeter, maybe two. Body weights were also similar, though Bellamy was curvy. Jammer was slim, a runner's body with natural elegance. The file's holoimage didn't do the man justice. He really was easy on the eyes.

She spread her arms as if to embrace him. "Jammer, Jammer, Jammer. Captain Hannah here tells me interesting things about your performance. You should be proud."

He stopped just out of reach. "Thank you, ma'am, but I don't know what I've done to deserve your praise. I'm just doing my job."

"Nonsense," she said, her smile stretching wider. She closed the distance, draped an arm around his shoulder, and drew him along toward the footpath. "After reviewing Hannah's reports, I can see for myself how dedicated you've been to your goals. It's high time you got the proper recognition."

He tensed and tried to stop. "Really, ma'am, I don't require any special fanfare."

Bellamy propelled them forward, gazing into his face. "Oh, but you do. How long have you been with us now, Lieutenant?"

"I joined the Cartel a little more than three years ago," he said, then hung his head. "And it's lieutenant junior grade, ma'am. I haven't made it very far yet."

The admiral raised an eyebrow. "Oh, my mistake, Lieutenant Junior Grade." She focused on the path ahead, still strolling at an easy pace. "Let me see. What special treat can I give you to honor the talents you've brought to my door?"

They passed a row of cliff roses and Bellamy finally stopped. She stared out over the water, her arm still flung around Jammer. She leaned toward him as if to impart a great secret. "You know, I really go in for ceremony. I like to make a big deal when one of my officers shows their worth." She sighed. "Of course," she said, arm tightening as she hugged him toward her, "every faction has its own practices when it comes to rewarding traitors." She dropped her arm and turned toward him. The look of shock on his face fattened her grin. "How would Rizzo do it?"

Jammer's eyes widened. He stumbled back half a step, his whole body stiff.

Bellamy grabbed his jacket and pulled him off balance, then shoved him over the edge. It was hard, as she leaned out watching him fall, to tell the difference between his screams, the wailing of the wind, and the crying of the gulls. When she could see him no more, she turned toward the building.

She passed Hannah at the intersection of the footpath and the paved walkway, snagged her sandals, and kept walking. "Pick up the pace on Rook's ship. I want a report within the next thirty hours."

Hannah fell into step beside her. "Right away, ma'am."

"Oh, and send a cleanup crew down through the caves. Get rid of the big pieces but leave some of the unidentifiable juicy bits."

"Ma'am?"

Bellamy grinned at her second. "Gulls have to eat, you know."

chapter 62

En Route to Haven, Danua
<u>**Aboard the Juveltranstør**</u>

KNØFA STRAIGHTENED IN HIS SEAT, still antsy from their narrow escape. By the time the flyover passed the barrens, they were already over the water.

His fist bumped the comm. "Medfac, report."

"No change, sir," a tinny voice said. He couldn't even tell which officer it was. Not that he could remember all their names anyway. "But we don't have the equipment to do much for her until we get to the base.

"Very well. I'll be in to check on her shortly." He switched off the communication and spoke to the officer in front of him. "What's our position?"

"Fifteen hundred kilometers from Storelandsør, sir."

"Estimated arrival?"

"A little over three hours, sir."

He grunted. "Can't we go any faster?"

The helm officer shook her head. "Not without causing damage to the atmospheric drive, sir."

"Very well." Knøfa sighed. "Helm, you have the conn. Get us home."

He swung out of his chair and stalked the corridors to the medfac. Crew worked over Tsurin's limp form, but when they saw him, they backed away. He stood over the cot and stared down at her slack face. Medtechs had hooked her up to a ventilator and other machines. Her chest rose and fell, but her skin looked pasty. Gray. He frowned.

"What happened in there?" he whispered.

With his bare hand, he wiped away a line of drool that had trickled out of her slack mouth before they'd masked her. If she could see him, she would scold him about the risk of contagion and taking foolish chances. After all, they didn't yet know why she had collapsed. He'd worry about that later.

Right now, he would pay all the credits to his name to hear that rebuke.

chapter 63

New Canaan, Harajüd
<u>Landport Station</u>

THRACE HUSTLED THROUGH THE CONCOURSE toward the gate. Sa'abah kept pace beside her. Half the security detail led their party, the rest trailed several steps behind. Around them, travelers gawked at their spectacle. Thrace kept her expression neutral through sheer effort of will. She'd have to get used to this sort of attention if she planned to do similar public forays in the future. It wasn't every day these people saw a Trader admiral and full retinue parading through public space, especially one such as she—the anomaly, the admiral who had bested Skalar, or so the rumors claimed. The last time she'd come here, she'd been Skalar's second, not nearly so noteworthy. Since her takeover, however, she'd made only short jaunts to Dagons or other Consortium businesses. It had seemed the prudent course of action until she could cement faction control.

Today was different, a special occasion.

"Ma'am, I still think this is a bad idea," Sa'abah said just loud enough for Thrace to hear. "It isn't too late. The team can escort you to the jumper. You can wait there, away from the crowd. I'll handle this."

"I appreciate your caution, Captain." Thrace did not slow down. "But I need to do this myself. Stay alert."

Sa'abah sighed, but the woman offered no further warnings.

At the intersection, their party veered left. Thrace peered ahead, looking for a familiar face.

There, halfway down the concourse, a leathery face rode a tall lanky body toward them. Thrace's visitor met her eyes, glanced at her companions, and raised an eyebrow.

"Stop," she said. "Wait here."

The security detail paused.

"Ma'am—" Sa'abah said.

Thrace shot her a look. "Keep your eyes open." She moved toward her visitor.

He closed the distance quickly, his hands outstretched as he looked past her at the waiting crew. "You are like the jakkals now, eh? Traveling with your pack?"

Thrace grasped his hands. "It's safer. For now. I'm happy to see you, my friend."

Botha stared at her. "Happy, yes. But troubled."

Thrace sighed. "It's complicated."

"When is it not?" He jerked his chin toward the security officers behind her. "These guardians of yours. You trust them?"

She glanced over her shoulder. "Sa'abah — she's the stocky one in tight clothes—trusts the others. I trust Sa'abah."

"Do you trust their lips to stay closed?"

Thrace faced him again. "No."

"I thought not." Botha sighed. "It is too bad you have no boat. Fish do not talk. And I would like to ride the waters of this world."

"Perhaps we can go to Shamashu before you leave," Thrace said. "I haven't been there yet."

"And your pack," he said, cocking his head. "They would follow?"

"I'm afraid so."

"Even the best hunter needs rest, and solitude." He watched her a moment, then pulled her closer and leaned in. "Could you not trade masks and come to Bregaina?" he whispered.

If only! She closed her eyes and conjured the feel of that village's guest cottage. How many times had she sat with this man on its raised deck, watching the bala and muil? She could almost feel the breeze from across the delta, smell the briny mud, hear the cries of the hunting birds.

"Our latest batch of úta is almost ready to taste," he teased.

So tempting. Her lips drew to one side, puckering her cheek, and she opened her eyes. "It wouldn't be wise for me to get intoxicated, Botha."

He shrugged. "No. But it wouldn't hurt you to dance. Another time. Come, my ears are hungry."

She, Botha, and the crew left the port and caravanned to the base. Botha had not come here the last time he'd visited New Canaan. Thrace watched Botha's muted reactions as they passed through the gate, left the jumpers with attendants, and traveled the underground passages to the main building. He never said a word, but she could feel his confusion, like a bird trapped in a closed room, cut off from the sky.

As soon as it was feasible, Thrace dismissed the security detail and led him to her quarters. Inside, he dropped his bag and walked, wide-eyed and gawking, through her suite. There wasn't much to see except the views, but it may have been a bigger space than Botha expected. She looked around, trying to see it from his perspective. In the main section to the right, rooms took a mostly traditional style with expected furniture. Against the gray carpet and pearl gray walls, dark blue furniture shone in dramatic contrast.

But Botha turned left and entered the annexed rooms she'd reconstructed after taking over the base. Here, every unnecessary wall had been removed to leave a wide, open space. Their presence triggered automatic lights at a comfortable level, revealing evidence of Thrace's regular use of the room. The loom, with its unfinished work, sat on the far side of a structural support. Beyond, the windows offered a view of the City Center high-rises.

Botha walked toward that sight as if in a dream, his body pulled forward on an invisible string.

She joined him and stood in companionable silence. Where was Alira now? Captain Bailey couldn't possibly be on Saacharis yet, and Rizzo had sent no further word. Thrace's hands clasped each other behind her back.

Though she looked toward the cityscape, she saw only Alira's face the last time they'd spoken.

"Your woman is in trouble again," Botha said.

"Yes."

"She is skilled in finding it, I think."

Thrace grunted. "She is."

He looked at Thrace. "The last time we spoke of her, she was a he, and you were not traveling in packs."

Thrace nodded.

"You are the admiral now."

"Yes."

Botha's eyes narrowed. "She knows?"

"By now, she probably does." Thrace sighed. "But that's not what this is about."

"No," Botha said. "That would be too simple. So now that Skalar's nest is claimed by another, she is poking a different burrow? Whose?"

"The Cartel."

Sunlight through the plaz betrayed the drain of color from Botha's face. He stared at Thrace a moment more, then paced away. "Sot."

Fool, her mind translated. Thrace waited.

He gazed out the window before looking at Thrace again. "What fruit is she after among those beasts?"

"She went there to track down a nexus in the slave trade," Thrace said. "She ended up rescuing slaves."

"Nie alweer nie." Botha shook his head. "Kinders?"

Thrace took a deep breath. Botha didn't often revert to his own tongue like this. "Yes, children."

He stormed away, rambling in Afrikaans so fast she could not follow. She'd never seen him this angry before.

"Slow down, my friend. I can't understand you."

Botha stopped, hands on his hips. "This has happened before."

Thrace frowned. "With Bellamy?"

"Haar voorganger." He turned slowly, snapping his fingers. "What is your word… the one who was before her. Virgil. He was a viper." Botha frowned. "Bellamy is worse."

"I know."

"You must snatch her out of that maw, Thrace."

Thrace's stomach tightened along with her throat. "I can't!" she said, her voice pinched. "I'd never get to her on that base, not without getting us both killed. And if I leave here, I could lose this ground."

He winced. "And expose your people."

"Exactly." Thrace's breath quickened. She'd hoped Botha would ease her fear, not fan the flame.

He looked at his feet. "She has a strong heart, your woman. To pick up so great a burden is admirable, but foolish. Such a load will squash her flat." He slapped his hands together, then pinned her with his gaze. "Does she not know?"

"I don't think she does." Thrace watched confusion fill Botha's face. "I told you of her reapings. You know she was already on the edge. I think she might be past that point now."

His brows drew together. "You fear for her sanity."

"It's more than that." She forced the clipped words past her lips, even though saying them made her feel like a traitor. "Alira's dangerous."

"Like a lênask? Or an arpë?"

"No, Botha. Not like any animal you know. If she can see you, she can kill you."

"How?"

"She can reach inside you, crush your heart, stop the blood to your brain without ever touching you."

Botha's dark eyes widened. "What magic is this?"

Thrace shook her head. "No magic. It's part of the gift of healing, one of many unammi talents."

"She can heal? As you have done for my people?"

"Better," Thrace said. "Alira's more skilled at it than most unammi I know."

Botha's lips drew into a tight line. He scrubbed a hand over his face, over his scalp, and rested it at his nape. "You believe she would do this?"

"Before? No. Now…" Thrace heaved a noisy breath. "I can't say. She's unbalanced, off-track. Unpredictable. It gets worse with every harvest she makes. I no longer know what to expect."

He crossed the distance between them and grasped Thrace's shoulders. "In her right mind, would she do this?"

Thrace flinched, her heart racing. Botha had never reacted to anything this way. "Only in self-defense, or to save another."

He released his grip and stepped back, palms outstretched in apology. "Then you must hope that flower still blooms because if it has withered, it is a poison to everyone around it. Someone will need to cut it down."

An invisible band snugged around Thrace's chest and tightened her breath. "I need to get to her. Help her if I can. But I don't know how to do that."

"So you tickled my ear."

Thrace sighed. "You're the only person I trust with these secrets."

Botha went to the window and rested his elbows on the sill. Silence stretched out. Thrace crossed to stand beside him and held her breath.

"As long as she continues these roles where she must kill to persist," he said at last, "she is in the predator's mouth. You can't tend the bite wounds until the animal spits her out."

"You think we can help her?" Thrace said. "If we can get her away from Bellamy?"

"I don't know, my friend." He turned sad eyes on Thrace. "You said yourself she is unbalanced, like a twig on a rock over the water, teetering on the edge of a fall. If she cannot acknowledge these memories from others' lives, make them part of herself, weave them into a single unified design, the peace of a sharp knife may be the best help you can give."

chapter 64

Tuneloras, Saacharis
<u>En Route to Admiral Rizzo's Office</u>

RIZZO'S WRISTCOM TICKED AT THE zero-hundred hour, the turn from one day to another on the intercolonial standard calendar. She noted it, filing the fact away for reference in the hours ahead. After an hour spent in the Zen garden, where walls of the base blocked the chill wind and dim sunlight shone warm on the stones beneath her feet, corridors inside the base seemed overly bright. So did the gym, or her quarters, or any interior space on the base. Rizzo preferred the garden. The few times she'd done her katas there had been far more fulfilling than doing them in the gym.

She followed the curving hallway to the building's core. A few crewmen waited at the lift, chatting among themselves. The moment she stepped up behind them, conversation ceased. Rizzo sighed. She should have taken her personal lift, but—

A chirp from her wristcom intruded. She raised her hand to her face. "Yes."

"Admiral," Jukka said, "incoming comm traffic, ma'am. High priority. Your eyes only."

"Origin?"

Silence. Crewmen in front of her turned as if listening for his response.

"It's—"

"Never mind," she cut in. "Route to my office. On my way there now."

The lift arrived and the others stepped aside. "Go ahead, Admiral," one of them said. "We'll catch the next lift."

Rizzo nodded, stepping past them into the car, and the lift door closed. "Ten."

At her destination, she moved down the corridor and into her office. "TICS," she said before she even got to the desk, "receive high priority communication at this station."

Immediate static rolled out of the system, unaccompanied by visual. "Don't have long," the caller said, her voice distorted by tech. Chandra. Rizzo recognized her despite the deliberately warped vocals. But it wasn't just the tech. The agent sounded strained. Out of breath. "She threw Jammer off the cliff. He's gone—" Her words choked, but she regained control. "Rumor is that she went to Rook's quarters and left pissed. Jammer's…accident…came after. I was near enough to hear her give the order to speed things up. They're looking for something on Rook's ship—"

"TICS, pause." The system chittered and stopped. "Connect me to Jukka."

A moment later, Jukka's image appeared over her desk. "You rang, ma'am?"

"My office. Now."

His face went blank. "On my way, ma'am." The image winked out.

"TICS, continue playback."

"—I don't know what, but it sounds like she's in deep trouble. That was four hours ago. This is the first chance I've had to report. More as I get it." The message went dead.

Rizzo leaned over her desk. "TICS, display time data for last communique." Numbers shone in the display. The news was fresh, no delay other than the normal send time. Was Alira still alive? Rizzo didn't want to think about what would happen if Bellamy discovered an unammi in her midst. Knowing, as she did, that Iridos was now uninhabited, would she start looking for the other survivors? Especially once she discovered what they could do?

Damn it. Rizzo had seen this coming. She never should have involved herself, or the Syndicate, with Alira. Complications shadowed that little troublemaker and dragged everyone she touched into the fray, but there was no backing out now. Not without at least trying to help. It wasn't just one life on the line here.

"TICS, landing bay." Less than two days from Saacharis to Zebalu. Rizzo had devised workable plans in less time than that before. She'd figure out how to contact Rook once on the ground.

A crewmember appeared in the holovid, dressed in the coveralls of the bay. "Yes, ma'am."

"Ready the *Kris* for an extended trip. I'll be there within the next half-hour." A chime announced someone at her door.

"Right away, Admiral. Landing bay out." The crewman's image disappeared.

"Come," Rizzo said.

Jukka entered and stood before her desk. "Something up?"

"An emergency. I have to leave. Bailey's due home tomorrow. You're in charge until then."

"No problem." He squinted at her. "Anything else I can do to help?"

She looked him in the eye. "Don't interact with corporate if you can avoid it. I have enough fires to put out right now." Her lip twitched.

Some of the tension went out of Jukka's stance. "You don't trust me to be diplomatic, ma'am?"

Rizzo grunted. "Your strength lies in security, not politics." She crooked a finger and turned to the door behind her desk. Behind it waited a private lift. She stepped in, Jukka in her wake.

"Quarters," Rizzo said. The lift began to move.

"What should I tell Captain Bailey?" he asked.

"Esther is in trouble that couldn't wait." The lift slowed, stopped. Rizzo pushed out of the door into a hallway in her own quarters and turned in at her bedroom, snagging a small bag out of the closet. She talked as she packed. "I may have more than one stop on this trip. You and Bailey will cover for me. If anyone comes asking, I am elsewhere on Saacharis conducting Syndicate business."

Jukka's chin rose. "I take it that means you'll be off world."

Rizzo hesitated, one hand holding a black sheath and its nestled blade over her open bag. Zebalu, at least. Possibly Harajüd. Iridos? She didn't know where the rest of the unammi survivors were hiding. She dropped the sheath in and closed it with a *snick*. "Yes."

"Any idea how long you'll be gone?"

"No." She snatched up the case and pushed past him to reenter the lift.

Jukka stepped in beside her.

"Bay passage." The lift began to move. "I'll keep you and Bailey posted."

"Aye ma'am."

This time the lift took longer to deliver them. He rode beside her in silence, one of the things she appreciated about him. He didn't tend toward chatter.

Chances were that Bellamy searched Rook's ship for evidence of her recent travel. Though Bailey had altered the logs—and Rizzo trusted her— even the best alteration to ship's docs would leave tiny traces. Only an expert would see them, but Bellamy didn't employ idiots. If her people searched hard enough, they'd find what she was looking for. Hopefully, Alira would be smart enough to get off the base before they found their proof. If she didn't, she'd be beyond Rizzo's help.

The lift stopped at the admiral's private underground passage, and they left it behind. Ahead, a plain corridor cut straight through the base foundations to the far end, where the landing bay waited. Up the steps and through the locked door, they passed into the bay and headed for Rizzo's ship.

Bay techs indicated the *Kris* was ready. Rizzo nodded.

At the hatch, Jukka stopped. "Any other instructions, ma'am?" he asked.

Rizzo hesitated. He didn't need to know all the details to be put on alert.

"Watch for Cartel activity in and around Tuneloras," she murmured. No one else needed to hear this. "I expect retaliation from Bellamy. Don't let her catch you unaware."

Jukka's jaw tightened. His stance shifted to a more defensive posture, a move so subtle and automatic the man probably never noticed. "No worries, ma'am. Do what you have to do."

She entered the ship and dropped her case by the closing hatch. In control, she ran through preflight, double-checked flight path status with the colonial airway tower, then lifted up. Bay crew hustled out of her way as the ship moved toward the weak sunlight beyond the open bay door, then into the sky beyond.

Once she was past the orbiting satellites, Rizzo transitioned into interstel.

"TICS, set coordinates for Pelarr, Zebalu. And record a message for Admiral Thrace Baldric, Harajüd Consortium, high priority."

chapter 65

Pelarr, Zebalu
<u>Cartel Trader Base, Admiral Bellamy's Office</u>

THE SETTING SUN GLINTED OFF the water and gleamed into Bellamy's office. She blinked at the glare and turned away before the plaz darkened, gazing inward instead of out. Across the room, detritus from her earlier tantrum littered the floor around her desk—shattered remnants of her priceless Zebalu system orrery, broken whelk shell, her nacre-handled knife—a mess for someone else to remove. Bellamy grappled with a more critical issue. Gate logs showed that shortly after she'd left Rook's quarters yesterday, the captain had gone off base for several hours. Hannah reported that Rook had spent the whole time in the marketplace and visited the public comms multiple times. Bellamy shook her head. Definitely not the real Rook. *She* would know better than to draw attention to herself that way.

At any rate, since she'd returned to the base, the imposter had remained sequestered in Rook's quarters. Even the duty log showed she'd claimed illness and skipped her scheduled shift earlier today. Good. That made it easier to keep track of the sneak.

Bellamy tried to pinpoint the moment when the Rooks had switched. Was it when she sent the captain to Iridos? Maybe someone else had already compromised that site and took over then, sending this bitch to take Rook's place. Or had it even been Rook who went to Iridos in the first place? Was this imposter in play before then? Bellamy paced up the steps from the seating pit and shuffled through the mess. She tried to picture Rook's reaction when Bellamy had first pitched the idea of having slaves work the ruined mines, just before Jude and her crew left for Iridos.

How far back did the treachery go?

Bellamy's cheeks grew hot. She'd been *used*. Worse, Rook had *fucked* Bellamy just like her father and her brothers had done. Images of Rook's seemingly innocent, loyal face intertwined with the sneering, sweaty visages of Bellamy's siblings as they grunted over her. Bile mingled with the memory of grit in her mouth from the dirt on her father's hand, the grimy fingers clamped over her jaw. She let out a garbled screech and kicked a remnant of the orrery's crystalline Zebalu. The thing shattered, its parts flying across the room. Bellamy trembled amid the remaining debris from her desk, fists and jaw tight, a low guttural sound emanating from her throat. Her chest rose and fell in quick, sharp jerks. She pictured Rook sleeping in bed, defenses down, as Bellamy bent over with her knife and—

The door chimed. Bellamy blinked, looked around, and frowned. What was she doing here? A moment ago, she'd been… Where had she been?

Again, the chime sounded. Bellamy looked at the door, then down at her hands, at the aching wounds where her nails had cut small crescents into her palms. Blood oozed from one particularly deep gash. Maybe she should cut her nails, but at least they were clean. Most of the time. Not like her father's.

The door chimed again.

"Come," she yelled.

The door slid open, and Hannah stepped in as cautiously as prey approaching a predator. "Everything okay, ma'am?"

"Yes," Bellamy said. She looked at the mess on the floor. Her own work, no doubt. She raised her gaze to Hannah's. "Report."

"My people finished going over the *Corsair*. They found evidence of tampering in the logs. I reviewed their findings, and verified it myself, ma'am. The trip log shows inconsistencies that go beyond simple mechanical fault."

Bellamy took a deep breath and wiggled feeling into her fingers. "What about prior jobs?"

"Her older logs appear intact. It's just this latest trip that's suspect, alterations added to the actual travel distance."

"I see." Bellamy said. She paced toward the seating pit. "So she never went to Iridos."

"It looks that way, ma'am."

"Where did she go, Captain?"

"I can't tell for certain, ma'am. But given what we think is the actual travel distance, it could be only a few places—Harajüd, Levyron, Saacharis or Shemonaea."

Harajüd or Saacharis were the only two places she could have gotten that load of hematium, but the Consortium seemed unlikely. That newbie that ran things in Skalar's absence—where had he disappeared to, anyway?—wasn't giving Consortium resources away for anyone, especially since they could lord it over her that they had easier access than she did. Rizzo, however…

Bellamy stared out the windows at the falling night. Rumor said Rizzo had spent time as a slave in her youth. Enough that she'd gotten quite sentimental about business practices employing slave labor. Bellamy's predecessor had spoken of it once, said he'd seen Rizzo come as close to losing her shit as anyone ever had over a sorry pack of wharf rats like the ones Bellamy'd sent to Iridos.

"It's Rizzo," she said, hearing her own dreamy tone lilting like music across the office.

"Ma'am?"

Bellamy drew a deep breath, let it out slowly. "Rook is working with Rizzo. That's where she got the hematium."

Hannah's silence drew Bellamy's attention. Her second stood, frowning, near the door.

"How do you know, ma'am?"

"I just do." Bellamy smiled. "Go over the *Corsair* again with the finest scrutiny. Check the air scrubbers for any atmospheric signs. Dig into the landing gear, see what kind of dirt turns up. I know she went to Saacharis, Hannah. Get me some proof. In the meantime, send a security team to Rook's quarters. Have them bring her to me."

chapter 66

Pelarr, Zebalu
<u>Cartel Trader Base, Captain Rook's Quarters</u>

GREAT ROOM TO BATHROOM TO bedroom and back. Great room to bathroom to bedroom and back. Rook tired of the route, turned, walked the other way, her feet stumbling over each other. Great room to bedroom to bathroom and back. Pace into the office, walk the perimeter of the room, and start again. She had to stay awake until she could speak to Single Male. If Bellamy—or anyone—could just walk into her quarters whenever they wanted, it wasn't safe to sleep in this place.

In the bedroom, she leaned against the wall away from the door. Here, at least, she wouldn't be immediately visible from the front entry. Her shoulders softened, drooped lower. All at once, her body shrank through its transition and solidified into Alira's true form. Pale blue washed in lethargic random patterns across her arms and chest. She closed her eyes. Bad enough to stay awake for more than forty-five hours, but to hold a human form for more than thirty sapped her even faster. Rook's persistent, mind-numbing factoids weren't helping.

Maybe she should leave base, go somewhere else, somewhere safe so she could rest. But where? Almost anyone in Pelarr would recognize Captain Rook. She'd have to get off-base and morph, maybe into Zachary Moss, or Amadi Patel, though she hadn't used either of those personas in weeks. The idents still lay waiting in personal storage at the landport.

Alira rested her head against the wall, just for a minute. It seemed so long since she'd gone there to switch the locker access to Rook's ident from her prior harvest. She tried to picture the locker bay, tried to remember which one held the idents. For a moment, it seemed as though she stood at the entry, looking down the rows of storage boxes, the aisles elongating as she watched. Her feet shuffled toward the retreating end, her gaze sweeping the rows upon rows of lockers, each keyed to someone's ident card. When she got to the end, she turned the corner and almost ran into Bellamy, who smiled at her, a maniacal gleam in her blue eyes. Alira stumbled, tripping over her feet, falling—

In Rook's bedroom, Alira's body slid to one side. She jerked to wakefulness, caught herself before she lost her balance, and stood up straight. "Stay awake," she mumbled, and resumed pacing. She took a deep breath, stepped through the door into the front room and stopped so fast she almost fell anyway.

Eli stood less than a meter away.

"Run," he hissed.

The breath she'd drawn rushed out of her lungs in a sob. Her gaze shot past him to the door. "Are they—"

"*Now.*"

White pulses raced across her arms before disappearing beneath the facade of Rook's skin. One hand went automatically to the ident on her neck chain. Yes. Still there. She'd need that to get off base. To do anything in the city. She dared not think too far ahead. Getting off the base was her first priority.

She pushed past Eli to the door, raced out into the corridor toward the nearest lift, and stopped.

Ahead, a security team of four marched toward her. She turned back toward her quarters.

"Captain Rook," one of the women called. "You will come with us."

A whimper leaked past her lips,

eli, where are you?

and she turned to face the security team. "Where are we going?"

"Admiral Bellamy wants to see you." The woman stepped aside and gestured toward the lift.

Rook regarded each officer. Killing them was out of the question. Even if she wanted to take on more harvests—which she didn't—she wouldn't manage four of them before they took her down. Running was no longer an option.

your truth fairy's timing sucks.

Rook laughed, a brittle sound, then stopped

about time you showed up again crow.

and sobered.

"Sorry. Inside joke." She passed between the officers, one falling in step ahead of her, two on either side, the lead officer in the rear. Together, they headed toward the lift.

chapter 67

New Canaan, Harajüd
<u>Consortium Trader Base, Admiral Baldric's Suite</u>

GALEN PLAYED THE MESSAGE AGAIN. And again. And again. When he'd memorized it, he froze the vid and turned from Rizzo's projected image. Her words played on in his head.

Our friend is in serious trouble. I want to help. Where would she hide?

He took a few steps away, one hand over his mouth. Here it was, the crisis he'd been sensing, fearing, ever since Bailey told him where Alira was, what she was doing. He shook his head. Who was he kidding? He'd been afraid for her since long before she left New Canaan. If the harvesting sickness had finally taken hold, going after her was as necessary as it was dangerous. Alone, her true identity might—probably would—be discovered. She might even reveal the non-virulent nature of Earth's current atmosphere or blurt the whereabouts of the surviving unammi. He couldn't allow that to happen.

The thing was, he didn't have much choice in the matter. After all, what was he supposed to do? Go after Alira himself?

And why shouldn't he? She was his i'shin. No matter the problems between them, he was duty-bound to be there for her, just as she would be there for him. Except she wasn't there. Not now. Not since she'd returned to the ruined city on Iridos. Not since they'd concocted this whole foolhardy idea. Or rather, since Alira had. They should have gone to Earth and left the Consortium alone. Unammi survivors would have been fine on that abandoned world for generations. It's not like the humans were going to enter Earth's atmosphere.

Not until they detected activity on the surface, anyway. How long would that take? The unammi would build power generators, of course, turbines like those on Iridos or something similar. Something inevitably detectable from the Consortium's outpost.

Galen blew out a breath in a noisy huff. His clasped hands squeezed until his fingers tingled. He needed to focus on how to help her out of this latest mess. If she hadn't already gone over the edge. If Bellamy hadn't already discovered who and what Alira was. If Alira wasn't already dead.

If it was indeed too late, then his attempt to fix Alira's problem might make things worse. If he had to confront Bellamy—ugh. His stomach lurched. He felt like a coward, admitting such a thing, but there it was. Alira had always been the bold one. Galen had always played a supporting role.

But that, too, was in the past. Look at him now…taking over the faction, running it without her input, bringing others into the fold to support him in his daring coup. For the first time in his life, Galen had assumed the lead on something huge. Life-changing. And not just for himself, but for all the unammi, and for the Iri. *He* stood between them and discovery. *He* held the gate closed. Him. Galen, son of Enuji, had become a protector.

He drew a surprised breath and stood straight, tall. His hands fell away from each other, and he grimaced at the throb of blood pulsing into his digits. All this time, he'd expected Alira to resume control of the faction, relegate Thrace Baldric back to a secondary role. Would he have allowed her to do it?

He frowned. She'd had a way of making everything seem reasonable, but images of her face, Skalar's face, twisted with rage and almost sadistic satisfaction at the things she'd done in Skalar's name went so far beyond reasonable as to not be in the same galactic quadrant. Alira was in no shape to lead anything right now. She couldn't even control herself. She would drive this faction into the ground, or worse, incite a rebellion among the crew and get both herself and Thrace killed. Then who would stand at the gate of Earth?

Yes, duty called him to support his i'shin, but his greater responsibility lay in the protection of their people and in seeing them not only survive but thrive.

So, no. Much as he might want to handle this personally, Admiral Baldric couldn't very well leave the main base this soon after staking her claim. Galen had begun to trust that Cohen and Sa'abah would support their new C.O., but they were two against an entire faction. If others decided to take over, Baldric's second and chief of security wouldn't be able to stop them.

"TICS, record response," Galen said as he morphed. The system sounded the ready, and Thrace turned to the camera. "Admiral, thank you for the heads up. You'll understand that I cannot join you in this attempted rescue, and why. I admit I'm worried for our friend. If there is such a thing as a safe place for her in that city, it would be her ship. Look for the *Cepheid*, a small XP95-R23 personal transport registered to Lyla Ravish. You'll probably find it at the landport. I will send her hatch lockout override code by separate communique, in case you need it."

Thrace's face crinkled in a frown. How to say this? She drew her lips into a line, looked away from the recorder, shook her head. It felt like another betrayal to say it out loud, even though she'd already said as much to Bailey. To Botha. She took a deep breath and raised her gaze once more. "Approach her with caution, Admiral. As I mentioned to your second, our friend is teetering on the edge and may by now be beyond help. You know what she is, but you have no idea the damage she can do in an instant. She can be dangerous. Deadly. Tranq her, if you can, before she sees you.

"I don't—" Thrace's voice pinched, thinned by a lump of fear. She cleared her throat. "Please do your best to bring her home unharmed, if you can. If you can't—" Her mouth worked, lips forming words that would not emerge, and she stopped trying. Instead, she nodded, and choked out, "Baldric out. End recording and send."

The TICS chittered, and she followed up with the second, promised comm. When it signaled its completion, Thrace's form shifted, shrank into Galen's. He raised both hands to cover his face and tried not to imagine what his life would be like without Alira.

But then, he was already learning about that, wasn't he?

chapter 68

Pelarr, Zebalu
<u>Cartel Trader Base, Admiral Bellamy's Office</u>

ACROSS THE BANTALI SEA, THE western arm of Duakela lay pinned beneath the dull red of Zebalu's star on the horizon. Lights winked on along the shore where boats moored in the sheltered bay, and in neighboring cities across the water. Bellamy always thought they looked a little like stars.

She looked up into the darkling sky. Sure as hell weren't many celestial lights there. Not that she could see here in the city, anyway. So different from the clear air in the mountains where she'd grown up. There, the night was alight with stars and the milky wash of the galactic arm where Zebalu spun. As a child, she'd never known their names. Once she'd escaped to Pelarr, where she could no longer see them, it seemed pointless to learn them at all.

Warm spicy fragrance tickled her nose. The tea was almost ready. Two cups set out just so, along with small bites of colorful fruit, dipped in chocolate and set aside on a plate. Beautiful. Enticing. A tasty treat and fresh tea always sweetened a kill, didn't it?

The door chimed and she called entry. Security escorted Rook into her office, then left to wait outside.

Rook looked guarded, her posture defensive. And that trophy vest. Maybe Bellamy would hang it on the wall in her office. After. If it was salvageable.

"Rook, so glad you could come." Bellamy beamed a smile. "Please, join me."

Rook eyed the food. "I didn't get the impression I had a choice, ma'am."

My, but she'd executed that lisp with perfection! Bellamy tsked. "Now Rook, you know we always have choices. Please." She gestured at the offering. "I insist."

Rook hesitated like any trapped animal might before her feet carried her down the steps and in a wide arc around the admiral.

"Sit," Bellamy said. "Be comfortable. Have some tea."

Rook perched on the edge of the sofa. "Thank you, but I'm not thirsty."

"Oh, don't be silly." Bellamy poured for them both from the same pot, then lowered herself to the couch. She raised the cup and breathed in the aroma. "Smells good, doesn't it? It's my favorite blend." She blew a delicate breath onto the liquid and sipped. Her eyes locked onto Rook's.

Rook sat wrapped in silence.

Bellamy frowned. If the woman didn't play along, this wouldn't be nearly as much fun.

"Do you remember when you first came to me?"

No reply.

"Back then, you were just Anne Banks, honest smuggler. Afraid to tell your mom you'd been naughty. Remember?"

Something in the captain's expression shifted. Warring emotions played across her face in a blink and were gone. Oh! Had Bellamy hit an exposed nerve? But no, if this weren't the real Rook, why would Rook's mom be of concern?

Bellamy tilted her head, squinting at her guest. "You hadn't been here a month when you came clean. Told me you'd been sent by the colonials to report on faction activities." Bellamy sipped her tea. "Have you ever stopped to wonder why I didn't kill you right then and there?"

Rook returned her stare. She still hadn't touched the tea.

"It's because I was impressed by your nerve. No one before or since has ever had the balls to admit beforehand their intent to screw me. Only you." Bellamy selected a pui berry from the tea plate and slid it off its skewer with her teeth. She bit into the chocolate-covered, sweet-tart fruit, releasing an explosion of flavor that kept her mouth watering long after the juicy berry had slid past her tongue and down her throat.

She sighed and refreshed her cup with hot tea. "Now here you sit. Captain Rook, trusted officer in the Cartel Trader faction. You've come a long way, haven't you? Full circle, in fact. But some things don't change, do they? And this time you didn't come clean."

With a flick of her wrist, she threw the tea into Rook's face and, in the split second before she threw herself at the imposter, she thought Rook's flesh…rippled.

chapter 69

ROOK LEAPT OFF THE COUCH and scrambled away from the maniac before her,

maniac? that's a little hypocritical, don'tcha think?

stumbling backward toward the stairs. Voices finally lurched past the barrier her predecessor had erected in her head and filled the space between her ears with confusing babble

shut up, all of you.

that ebbed almost at once to a whisper. Even Rook withdrew. What the—

"Now's the time, *Rook*," Bellamy said, her sarcastic tone a clear taunt. She moved, slow and graceful, toward her captain. "You're caught, *Rook*. You might as well spill your plan, *Rook*."

Rook stepped up the stairs without looking away from the approaching threat. The look in Bellamy's eyes offered no hope for escape. Security waited outside the door. Alira's memories of Skalar on the outpost raced through her mind. No way she wanted to harvest this human. But maybe she could disable her?

"Who are you, really?" Bellamy asked, her voice growing louder. "What's Rizzo after on *my* base? Huh?"

Moving backward across the office with Bellamy in relentless pursuit, Rook slipped a tendril of intent into Bellamy's throat and pinched her windpipe. It wouldn't kill her, but it would narrow the flow of air into the admiral's lungs and, hopefully, render her unconscious.

and then what, squib?

one step at a time, crow.

"Did you really think—" Bellamy shouted, coughing, one hand coming to her neck. She did not slow down. "—that I would not notice you aren't *her?*" She lunged, hands extended, fingers contorted into claws aimed at Rook's face.

Pain blossomed in Rook's cheek, and she dashed behind Bellamy's desk. Turning to face her attacker, she again reached into the admiral's throat, squeezing harder. Bellamy faltered a step, hands fluttering at her neck. Her mouth opened and closed, like a fish on the dry dock, tiny breaths wheezing in her throat. A tinge of blue touched her lips.

don't kill her!

Rook relented, and the admiral staggered forward, gasping.

"What…" Bellamy's expression flashed wide-eyed surprise, then the puckered, red flush of rage as she threw herself across the desk.

Rook raced out of the trap toward the door. She'd made it halfway when Bellamy grabbed her vest and yanked her off-balance. They fell hard, Bellamy on top. Rook struggled, managed to squirm around, but not away. She bucked her hips, tried to unseat Bellamy, who clung like the parasite she was.

Again, the admiral's nails sought Rook's face, going for her eyes.

Rook grabbed Bellamy's hands, held them millimeters away from her own face, and did the only thing she could think to do.

Her own fingers, wrapped tight around Bellamy's wrists, warped and twisted as they changed shape. Pale skin darkened to deep brown along digits rough with callouses. Rook's stocky form thinned and hardened, genitalia sprouting at the groin while thick, graying braids sprouted from his head.

The rage on Bellamy's face melted into a slack-jawed gape.

"What'sa matter, Belle?" Crow said, voice gruff and unpolished as always. He grinned up at her. "Ain'tcha glad to see me?"

Bellamy pushed off him, crabbing away to the desk where she clawed her way to her feet.

Crow laughed and got to his feet. "You should see your expression right now." His words sounded clear, strong,

> *don't get cocky, squib. you're still deep in enemy terrain.*
>
> *got it, crow.*

with no evidence of the quaver he'd expected.

"How—" Bellamy's initial shock melted, hardened, her panoply of emotions writ large on her face.

Crow recognized the rage when it came, along with a knife Bellamy had snatched from somewhere. With a low growl, she shot toward him, closing the distance too quickly. Crow retreated, giving ground as he morphed again, this time into Skalar.

Probably not the best choice of disguises.

Bellamy screeched in offense. "There you are, you old bastard!" she screamed. Her blade sliced the air in front of her as she advanced.

Skalar backed toward the door, too distracted to take delicate action. He'd have to kill her to stop her. Fuck!

The wall stopped his retreat and Bellamy paused, eyes wide, wild, an enormous grin plastered across the bottom half of her face.

"Bye-bye, Skalar," she said, her voice a happy, sing-song lilt.

He shifted once more. His body shrank, dropping in size and bulk, his senses registering each change as it happened—facial hair withdrew into his skin while the hair on his arms blanched. Thick brows thinned and he shifted his eyes from black to green. Breasts bulged beneath a blue silk dress Rook had seen Hannah wear once.

"Ma'am?" Hannah asked. "Are you all right?"

Bellamy blinked. Her smile drooped for a second, then resumed its maniacal brilliance. She raised the knife, poised for a strike.

The door hissed open beside them and Bellamy's head swiveled toward the sound. Hannah dropped to a squat at the head of the stairs, abandoned her facade, and shifted her skin's patterns to match those of her surroundings. She wrapped one hand around the ident and jerked the chain loose—she couldn't shift the colors of those materials, but she could hide them inside her fist—then gathered ident and broken necklace into her closed hand. Small metal links fell to the floor as she crept backward toward the stairs, but she couldn't help that now.

Beside her, the real Hannah pushed in.

Moving as slowly as she could, Alira eased down one step, two, her camouflage shifting with her body's movements, then she froze to one side of the walkway. If she could avoid teetering, if no one fell over her, if she didn't make a sound, she might have a chance.

be still... be still... be still...

Her heart pounded like the wingbeats of a niveym. Surely the humans would hear it!

Hannah, followed by security, took one look at the admiral. "Ma'am, are you okay? Security reported shouts from inside your office. I wanted to be sure—"

Bellamy whirled, blade still raised, and slashed it toward her second. "It won't work, Hannah," she screeched. "I know who you are!"

Hannah moved just enough to miss most of the attack. A line of red, glistening beads appeared on her cheekbone, just below her left eye. Alira watched, paralyzed, as Hannah grabbed Bellamy's hand and twisted away the knife, then thrust it up into the soft skin behind Bellamy's chin.

Alira gasped,

no! NO!

the sound lost amid the wet gurgling from the admiral less than two meters away. How long did it take to die that way? A minute? Two? That would never be enough time to avoid this reaping. Alira cast about for a hiding place.

All the humans stood mute for a heartbeat, then Hannah pulled the weapon free, wiped it on Bellamy's clothing, and stepped over the body. "Get a cleanup crew in here," Hannah said.

Still shifting her body's patterns to match the changing background as she moved, Alira eased toward the shadow behind the sofa. She could fit there. Couldn't she?

"Yes, Captain," one of the security officers said.

"That's Admiral Dupré." Hannah stepped behind Bellamy's desk and settled into the chair there. All three officers stared. "Any questions?"

At the sofa, Alira backed into the tight space between furniture and wall just as the harvest hit. She grunted softly as she curled into the flood of warped memories and experiences...a prefab cabin in the mountains under a clear night sky...unspeakable abuse from her father and brothers, things Alira couldn't even fathom except for the hatred and rage that rode the image waves...she felt the cold reason behind killing them, rejoiced in the knife parting their throats to let out all that bad blood...the jumble of homes and doctors that followed...joining the Cartel... impressing Admiral Virgil with her charm and murderous skill...poisoning Virgil so she could take his place in the Cartel...wave upon sickening wave gutted her, flattened her, left her shaking and breathless in the shadow and when it passed she lay limp, unable to move. Unable to think.

what—

Bellamy's voice rose among the others

oh, for fuck's sake...not her too.

sister, can they see you?

don't know. don't care.

and the melee resumed. Alira sighed and closed her eyes.

Noises around her. Coming and going. Excitement. Loud clamor.

Alira lay still, blinking, and listened. Tried to make sense of it. Couldn't. Not with all the voices, inside and out. Too many. Her own had disappeared long ago. Hadn't it? Or were they all hers? She didn't know. She didn't know anything. It didn't matter. She couldn't do this anymore. Even Lurien wouldn't have managed with these toxic souls. She wouldn't be able to keep her promise to Trumo, but she couldn't think about that now. She couldn't think about anything at all. She curled into a tighter ball and waited for the humans to find her.

It was the silence that roused her. Not in the office. In her head. Her passengers had gone quiet. She opened her eyes to the devastation of Iridos. Eli stood before her.

"Have you changed your mind?"

Alira sighed. "I'm tired."

"If we can get you out, will you go?"

She frowned. "Get me out? Get me *out*? You mean you could have helped me at any point on this wretched journey and chose not to?"

Eli's face shone in the twilight. "Yes."

She stared. Tried to form words. "Why?"

"Because there is a price. For you."

Her frown returned. "What kind of price?"

"This moment is a bridge between your world and ours. Each time we connect with you is just such a bridge. If you linger there too long, you may be unable to leave."

Her heart thudded out of its normal rhythm. "You mean I would be stuck on the bridge? Stuck in your world?" The memory of that nothingness rushed over her skin, stippling the surface, its chill reaching deep into her core. "Has that ever happened before?"

"Yes, to others of your kind who were unmodified. They have a stronger connection to those they have absorbed. They hear us more clearly. Your people have a name for it."

Alira gaped. The harvesting sickness—the others who went mad were all like her! Their Adjustments had not worked! Lurien had always said that once it manifested, death would inevitably follow, but if Eli was right, then Lurien was wrong. As long as Alira limited her connection to Eli, to the Others he linked, she could still beat this.

"Are you finished?" Eli asked. "Or will you continue?"

She fought down a wave of nausea, breathing through her mouth. She couldn't go to the Consortium. She couldn't stay here. But those were not the only two choices. Maybe—

"Decide," Eli said.

She looked into his green eyes. "I'm not done. Get me out."

"We can subdue the others, but not quiet them." Eli gestured. "Focus. Watch for our signals. Understand?"

Alira nodded, and the new admiral's office washed over her, the internal voices babbling and bouncing off one another. Bellamy's, as the newest member of her reaped tribe, shouted loudest. But they did not overpower her. Not yet. She took stock, noticed her camouflage was slipping, shored it up, and waited. Listened. Hannah was speaking.

"I have no intention of cutting them loose. They could really screw things up for the Cartel. But hear me: no more children. End of discussion. Where is the hovercart? I want this body out of my office."

"It's coming, ma'am."

Who was that? How many people between her and the door? From her crouched position behind the sofa, she could see nothing except the stair risers.

"Tell them to hurry it up. Jess, arrange for disposal through recycling. You know the drill."

"Yes ma'am."

"And where's Rook?" Hannah demanded. "I thought she was here with Bellamy."

"I don't know, ma'am. She was here, and I didn't see her leave. Should I check her quarters?"

A pause. What was happening out there?

"Yes," Hannah said. "Bring her to me as soon as you find her."

Overlapping voices, commotion, a high-pitched whine on approach to the office.

Eli.

"Bottom shelf. Watch for your chance."

Then he was gone.

Alira eased out of her hiding place as the whine entered the office and stopped. More commotion, the sound of shuffling, movement. She peered over the low wall behind the sofa. The hover cart waited three, maybe four meters away. Crewmen lifted Bellamy's body and placed it atop the cart. Alira eyed the bottom shelf, the one beneath the body.

Humans worked around the cart, blocking a clear access, and she edged her way around the stairs to the wall, then up each riser, waiting for her moment. Hannah barked orders. Humans hustled to comply. Alira crept closer, peered through the open door. No one coming.

Crewmen pulled up the bloody carpet tiles and piled them on that bottom shelf. Alira cringed. If she knocked even one aside getting on, they'd see. She itched to bat at the murmurs in her head

be still.

until she saw an opening. She shot forward and eased onto the shelf, adopting the carpet tile patterns as her camouflage, just as the humans switched the cart on again, and the whole thing lifted off the floor. Alira's blood pounded in her ears. Human legs walked right beside her, so close she could touch them, as a crew member guided the cart down the corridor. Conversation in the admiral's office receded behind her, but as the cart turned into the main corridor, other crew members approached.

"Vel, what's—" The woman broke off upon seeing the body. "Oh, damn. Hannah?"

Vel sniffed. "You mean Admiral Dupré. She's in her new office."

Silence followed. Alira could only imagine the stifled expressions and reactions, intended to convey maximum communication with minimum risk. Every Cartel crew member knew they were under constant surveillance. Everyone except the admiral, Hannah, Rook, and a few other top officers.

The cart whined, and Vel shifted on her feet. "I gotta go."

"Yeah," the other woman said. "Watch yourself."

"You, too."

Vel and the cart moved on to the lift and down toward sub-levels, sparking unintelligible comments along the way whenever the doors opened and granted others a glimpse of her cargo. Each time, those outside opted to wait for the next lift. Alira and her unsuspecting driver rode all the way down to the disposal level, where Vel guided the cart out. Dim lighting lined walls damp from high humidity in the salt-laden air. Her only memory of this section of the base came from Bellamy's disjointed mind, or flashes that seeped through Rook's restraint. They were nearing the caverns. That's how they disposed of bodies. Bellamy's words rang in her ears. *Gulls have to eat, you know.* Crude, perhaps, but similar to what the unammi did with their dead.

Eli flashed in her mind. "Now."

Alira rolled off the cart as gently as she could, stopped by the wall, and matched her dermal patterns to the new background, holding her breath. Carpet tiles, nudged by her movement, slid off the opposite side by Vel's feet. Cursing, the crewman stopped the cart and reloaded them before she moved on.

When she was gone, Alira drew a shaky breath. The stench of blood and the tang of salt clung, cloying, in her nostrils. The voices edged in, crowded her thoughts. Her surroundings shifted, wavered as if breathing in and out. Everything around her took on an overbright sheen.

Eli appeared before her in the corridor, and she frowned. Wouldn't others see him?

"Focus," he hissed.

The internal babble faded into a background hum, but her surroundings continued to shimmer and move as if they were breathing.

Fine. But she'd need to get off base. She couldn't do it while she was camouflaged. She'd need a human face. An ident.

He disappeared. Alira shook her head, squinted at her surroundings, and looked over her shoulder. No one in sight. Probably all the activity on base was happening on the tenth floor. She frowned. Maybe Vel would serve. How well known was she? Disgust rose in Alira's throat, oily and sickening, at the thought of another harvest. No. She wasn't killing anyone else. But she didn't have to kill them to mimic them for a short time, just long enough to get off base. As long as she didn't run into friends or acquaintances, she'd be fine.

But Vel had already been called to the admiral's office once. What if she had to go there again?

Alira squirmed. Which way? She scurried in the direction Vel had gone. Ahead and to the left, someone whistled a melody, and Alira followed the sound around the corner. She stopped and crouched low. Vel approached from the other direction without the cart. She'd made her delivery then. Alira eased out of the trip zone and waited.

Vel crossed an intersecting corridor a few meters away and exchanged comments with someone out of sight but did not stop. Seconds later, she passed so close, Alira felt the breeze of her wake. It was only then Alira realized she'd been holding her breath. She closed her eyes, let it out and tried to relax.

The whistler started up again, and she moved toward him, slowing as she neared. At the next corner, she stopped and leaned out to see the source. A man. From the look of his cart, a gardener. He shuffled between his cart and a small storage room, whistling that patchy tune. When he went into the closet again, Eli appeared behind him, pointing.

Alira sprinted to the door, glanced at the ceiling, up in the corners, everywhere she might find a camera. No way to tell if this would be surveilled. She'd have to take that chance. She turned her attention to the human inside, stepped in behind him and dropped her camouflage. As he turned, shock spreading over his face, she reached into his body and constricted the blood flow to his brain. The fright melted away. His eyelids sagged. His figure slumped. His legs buckled. She dropped Rook's chain and ident, caught his toppling form, and gently laid him on the floor. He would have a headache and a small gap in his memory when he woke, but he would live.

A search of his pockets turned up few items, among them his ident. Adam Sato. She stared at the photo in the poor light, then peered at his face. This photo was old. More gray colored his dark hair, more lines crinkled the folds around his eyes. She lifted his eyelids to check color, examined his hands and skin, then shifted, paying special attention to the dirt beneath his nails, the leathery, sun-weathered skin, the scuffed boots. No way to match the real Adam's usual stride or gait. In fact, without a holovid to compare Alira's efforts, his doppelgänger could only hope he'd done well enough to convince the human's fellow crewmen.

Adam closed the gardening closet behind him, abandoned the gardening cart, and put Rook's ident and neck chain in his pockets as he headed toward the lift. Sparkles glinted on the breathing walls. Adam's breath quickened. His balance hiccupped, and he stumbled against the wall. Voices rose in his mind, clamoring for attention until Eli's touch once again soothed them into submission.

"How many more times can you do that?" Adam wondered aloud.

Eli did not respond.

Adam shook his head and stepped into the lift. He made it all the way to the main level without seeing another soul.

"Adam!" a younger man called as Adam stepped out into the main level corridor.

Adam's jaw tightened. His fingers curled into fists. He turned toward the sound and forced a small smile. "Yeah."

"Where ya going? I thought we were playing tonight."

"That's right," he said. "Just running an errand."

"You want me to take you?" The younger man winked. "I know how you hate the transports."

Adam waved him away. "Thanks, but no. Go ahead and start without me."

The man frowned. "Start without you?"

A knot formed in Adam's belly. "Yeah. You know, set everything up so when I get there we can begin."

"What are you talking about?" The man's frown deepened. He cocked his head to one side. "You feeling okay?"

Adam sighed. "It's a long story. I'll tell you when I get back. I have to go." He left the man staring in the corridor and navigated the maze to the front gate. No one else stopped him, and he breathed a small sigh of relief under the night sky.

On the street, the nearest transport stop waited straight ahead, at the other end of the base. Closer, yes, but also a greater risk of seeing someone he—or, rather, the real Adam—knew. He turned instead to the right and began walking. Pelarr never got completely dark. Besides Zebalu's three moons, a plethora of lamps warmed the nighttime streets with golden pools of illumination. City coffers prospered when locals and visitors alike were encouraged to spend more of their credits, and they did that best in an inviting, safe place. Oh, the city held its shadows, but along this main beat just shy of the beaches, the illusion of security held strong.

Yet the night sky belied the mirage of light in Adam's field of vision. People and visuals shimmered brighter than they should in his eyes. He winced at their garish, exaggerated faces

it isn't real... it isn't real...

and struggled to maintain a steady pace and blend in. He needed someplace safe to hide until he could regain self-control. *If* he could. Bellamy was in Alira's head now. His knees almost buckled at the thought of facing that beast. Would she best Alira? Break her? Destroy her? Could Eli help without pushing Alira over the edge? How long was too long in contact with Eli's bridge?

Adam continued walking. He stared straight ahead, ignoring what he thought were stares and pointing fingers. He was imagining it. He had to be.

A hoverbus passed, slowed, then stopped at the transport station ahead. Adam broke into a jog and caught up just as the last riders were stepping on or off. He climbed up onto the rear access and took the closest seat he could find. As slow as these things ran, he'd be on it for a while. He turned away from his fellow travelers and watched the city pass. Trees and parks and buildings and industrial centers…Pelarr was just like New Canaan in so many ways. He remembered his arrival there, his first trip on the transport, arriving at Nyros' flat.

> *nyros!*

Grief wrenched his gut, rose to tighten his throat. He forced it down

> *not here. not now.*

and tried to relax.

Pedestrians passed on one side as the transport traversed the streets. New travelers got on or old ones got off at each station. Adam ignored them. Their attention would only frighten him, awaken his internal confusion, raise new fears.

The noise of other travelers joined the voices in his head until he could not distinguish his own thoughts from their running commentary. Sparkles shimmered along the seat in front of him, the floor at his feet, the humans nearby, even the passing scenery. He rubbed his temple

> *shut up.*

as his focus slipped further away by the minute.

At some point, he got off the transport and switched to one going south, toward the landport. His body worked on autopilot, and he focused only on holding his shape and getting to his destination. With every passing block, it got harder. By the time he arrived at the port, it was hard to hold a thought. What was he doing here?

Oh yes. Alira's ship. He frowned. Adam's ident wouldn't grant access.

> *lockers.*

A shaky memory flashed in his mind of a visual, dreamy and surreal, lockers in long rows and Bellamy around the corner.

But no, Bellamy was dead now, a member of his multitudes.

He shook his head, ignored the stares, real or imagined, from others around him, and pushed forward. His head swiveled, looking for—

There. Adam cut across the concourse and dove into the unattended bay of storage bins. Which one?

He ducked down one of the rows until he could stand out of sight from passersby, and stopped, eyes closed.

which one?

Images rose and faded on the screen of his closed lids, visuals from Alira's experiences behind one or another of her faces. How long since she'd come here? It had to be three, no, four weeks. He remembered the ship, that it was registered to someone…else…not Alira, not any of her idented personas. He searched through the memories until he came to those from the landport. Adam straightened. His breathing deepened. Yes. Yes!

He opened his eyes and followed the pass-through down three rows, then turned left. Five banks of bins down on the right. Number 729516. He glanced around for watching eyes. No one nearby. He couldn't help the surveillance cams. Hopefully, they wouldn't be able to tell which ident card he used. He fumbled in his pockets, withdrew Rook's ident and swiped it over the access. The door popped open.

There, alone in the storage bin, lay a diminutive receptacle, flat black, beautiful in its simplicity. Adam forced himself to act naturally

define "naturally" in this circumstance.

and not glance around again. With his finger, he drew a rufesh seed on the surface to bring up the keypad. The combination and the identification of his DNA opened the case. Adam withdrew the ident for Zachary Moss. His fingers clicked the box closed and slid it along with the Moss card into his pocket.

Adam gazed a moment longer at his own ident and that of Captain Rook before leaving them in the locker and closing its door. Now it would require landport security to discover the contents of this bin. He could only hope it would be a long time before that need arose. Alira hadn't killed this Adam, but she didn't wish him dead either. If his ident and Rook's were found together, Hannah would start asking questions the real Adam would never be able to answer. If enough time passed before colonial or Cartel security had any need to review surveillance vids from this time period, Alira would be long gone, and the real Adam would have an alibi. At least Alira wouldn't have doomed him by choosing his face.

Back in the main corridors, Adam blinked in the glare and winced at the garish colors, lurched in the direction of the concourse where Alira's ship awaited. His head swam with vague recollections of port corridors filled with other travelers and stumbling past the hatch into the *Cepheid* before the voices rose screaming in his mind and everything else went black.

chapter 70

Pelarr, Zebalu
Landport Station, Concourse F27

RIZZO LOCKED DOWN HER SHIP, stalked into the concourse, and turned right. A quick port check on approach had shown her the docking location of the *Cepheid*. Now to find it in this labyrinth of arrivals and long-term docking slips. Perhaps she should have memorized a layout before leaving the *Kris Cross*. Nothing looked quite the same as she remembered. Corpgov had made changes since the last time she was here, but then when wasn't corpgov mucking around with what already worked just fine?

She clenched her jaw, watching for the concourse she sought while alert for signs of trouble as she went. Various non-metal knives sat ready at her waist, ankle, cleavage, and thigh. A stunner snugged tight at her right hip, while a tranquer rode the left. She was ready for whatever might happen. Her trips to Zebalu were rare for a reason. It couldn't be said that Rizzo lived a drama-free life. Not even close. Yet treading into Bellamy's territory risked conflict Rizzo would rather avoid.

This situation warranted that chance. Not strictly for Alira's benefit, but for that of her people. Images of the ruined city on Iridos flashed through Rizzo's mind. How many had survived that holocaust? Where were they now?

She passed a set of windows. Outside, ground crews worked to maintain docked ships. The gray sky spat its first fat drops of precipitation down on their heads, making them scramble for cover. Moisture dotted the plaz, joining into rivulets that trickled toward the ground.

Just ahead, she spied the docking slip she sought. She glanced around. Had Bellamy already been alerted to her presence? If not, it wouldn't be long. Rizzo picked up her pace and turned in at the slip.

Outside the hatch, she hesitated. No way to know what awaited her inside. Baldric's communique echoed in her memory. *You have no idea the damage she can do in an instant.* Whatever that meant, Rizzo had a clear recollection of the last time she'd struggled with this unammi. Skilled as Rizzo was in a fight, she'd been outmatched. Which is why she intended to capitalize on the element of surprise as much as possible. She had no intention of sacrificing herself in this effort. Not if it could be helped.

Of course, she'd come unannounced to New Canaan, too, and Alira had still gotten the best of her.

Rizzo took a slow breath. *Here we go.*

She entered the override, stepped onto the ship, and closed the hatch behind her as quietly as possible. In the small craft's dim passageway, air hung stale and thick. Her nostrils flared at the stench. Not death. Not decay. Just the reek of sweat and bodily waste.

She pulled a knife and stood still, listening. Nothing. She crept to the intersection, ears perked for any sound. The plan was to deliver her target unharmed, but plans were made to change.

Muscles in her legs flexed to step out into the open until she heard something. A voice. Mumbled words. Coming from the right, toward the rear of the ship. She glanced around the corner. The way was clear, and she eased out, creeping toward the sound.

The *Cepheid*'s small size would have made short work of a search, but she didn't have to go far. At the rear of the ship, in one of the bunk rooms, Alira huddled in the corner, curled into a squat. Her arms wrapped around herself, her body rocking so that each forward motion bumped her head into a bloody patch on the wall. Her normally bright skin had dulled, the colors muted and wan. She mumbled unintelligibly, seeming unaware of anyone else's presence.

The admiral's lips drew tight against her teeth. She squinted at this pathetic creature before her, recognizable only in the loosest sense. She should kill the poor thing, end her suffering. Instead, Rizzo drew the tranquer, pointed it at her target, and pulled the trigger.

Alira flinched, the colors in her skin buzzing across the surface in a momentary frenzy before settling again to a dull display. A few seconds later, she fell onto her side, her head cocked against the wall at an odd angle.

It took only a moment to confirm that she was truly out and, for the most part, physically sound. Rizzo stared into the slack, bloody face for a moment, then sat back on her heels. So much for her initial plan. No way she could move the unammi through the station to the *Kris* now. Not in this shape. They'd be forced to take their leave of Zebalu on the *Cepheid*. She'd have to send someone after her ship while en route.

"As if my life weren't complicated enough," she muttered. She moved Alira's unconscious form to the bottom bunk, left her with a whispered apology, and locked the door behind her.

chapter 71

Nöbetchi Mountains
Southernmost Tip of Syrinaia, Harajüd

THRACE WATCHED THE OTHER SHIP come in low, then rise up to meet the face of the cliff. The ledge on which she stood was the only flat space for kilometers and offered barely enough space for two such craft. She stepped into the mouth of the cave while the *Cepheid* landed, and its pilot powered down.

She closed her eyes, willing her heart to slow. By some miracle, her hands hung quiet at her sides.

Botha joined her. "This will be a bitter fruit, my friend. I hope you are ready to swallow it."

She cast him a sidelong glance, then looked again at the ship. "I guess we'll see."

Before them, Rizzo leaned out of the opening hatch and gestured. They hurried forward to follow. Inside, she led them down the length of the ship and gestured to the rearmost quarters.

Thrace hesitated. "Is it bad?"

Rizzo hesitated, her gaze locked on Thrace's face. "Yes."

Thrace's chest hitched, caught, and she swung her attention to the indicated chamber. She didn't want to see, but she couldn't judge the extent of damage from out here in the passageway. She took a deep breath and stepped inside.

On the bottom bunk, Alira's thin body contorted on the blanket. A bruise darkened almost half of her forehead and part of her scalp, a raw, sutured cut off-center in its shadow. The fact that it had not healed itself gave Thrace an idea of how bad her i'shin's situation really was.

Alira's lips moved, even in this state. Thrace leaned close but couldn't make out the words. She wanted to reach out, gather her damaged lover in her arms, tell her everything would be made right. But that might be a lie. Thrace had no way of knowing whether Alira would survive this. If present appearances offered any clue, the odds were not good.

She pulled a piece of irolium from her pocket and lay it on the bunk in front of her i'shin. Would it be too late? Was Alira not only mad, but dimmed?

Thrace straightened and gestured toward the door. Botha and the admiral followed her out. In the corridor, she leaned against the wall and sighed.

"Was she like that when you found her?" she asked Rizzo.

"Yes."

"What happened to her head?"

"She'd been rocking, bumping it against the wall, for maybe a day or more before I reached her. I patched it. Cleaned her up." Rizzo opened her mouth, closed it again as if deciding whether to say more. "This is bad, but it was worse when I got to the ship. She'd been unwashed, sitting in her own excrement."

Thrace shrank away from the news as if Rizzo had slapped her face. Nearby, Botha raised his hands to his head and turned away.

Rizzo's gaze went from Thrace to Botha before she shook her head. "No offense, but you should kill her."

Botha winced.

Thrace squinted at Rizzo. "What did you say?"

"It sounds harsh," Rizzo said, her expression flat, "but I don't know if you can help her at this point. Would she want to live this way?"

Botha turned to Thrace. "You are a healer. Can you not—"

"No." Thrace said. Was she denying her own ability? or the fact that Alira needed healing in the first place? Could she even be healed? "This is beyond my skill. Alira—" Her voice broke, and she stopped. Were Alira standing with them now, instead of lying on that bed, she would be capable.

Botha touched her arm. "You should take her home. She can heal among her people, surely."

Thrace shook her head. "She can't return there. Not ever. They didn't want her when she was whole. They'd never accept her now. She's too alien. The best they would offer is mitigation, not healing."

"Mitigation?" Rizzo asked.

Thrace waved a hand. "Long story. I'll tell you sometime." She turned a gray gaze on Botha. "What about you?"

Botha's eyes widened. "What about me?"

"You could help her."

Botha shook his head. "Her harvests are a boulder too big for my boat, Thrace. If I take her on, she will sink us both."

"I don't believe that for a minute," Thrace said. "Your experience and wisdom might be the only thing that can pull her out of this hole."

He looked away, still shaking his head.

"What if she were a human, from your village?" Thrace pressed. "Would you try it then?"

Botha's hard gaze snapped to her face. He glared at her a moment before he spoke. "You are an animal in pain," he said a moment later. "So, I will forgive that bite."

"Let's move this to the galley," Rizzo said. She nodded toward the way they'd come, and they retreated to sit around the small table.

She stared at Thrace. "What's wrong with her?"

Thrace lifted her hands before her face as if to pull the explanation out of her head. "She…" Thrace paused, then sighed. "Alira absorbs the memories and personalities of anyone who dies in her presence."

Rizzo swore under her breath. "That's why she thought she could take Skalar's place. And Rook's."

Thrace nodded. "Yes."

"But it didn't work the way she expected."

"No."

Rizzo's brown face twitched. "How many?"

"How many has she harvested?"

"Yes."

Thrace shook her head. "I don't know. Dozens. Too many." She sighed. "The unammi believe that not all harvesters live through the gift. Some, like Alira, manifest a sickness."

Something shifted in Rizzo's expression. "That's what you think is wrong with her?"

Thrace sagged in her seat. Answer enough in itself, but she shook her head. "I don't know. I hope not. I don't want to accept—" She looked away.

In the hush that followed, Thrace's heartbeat thrummed in her ears. She imagined she could hear Alira's voice at the far end of the ship. She listened, taking small comfort in that fantasy.

"Is this sickness always fatal?" Rizzo asked.

"As far as I know, yes. But I'm not sure whether our healers really tried to help the others who died..." Thrace cleared her throat. It did nothing to dislodge the lump lodged there. "They just assumed it was over and did what they could to comfort those afflicted until the end."

Botha leaned forward. "Why do you drag her behind your boat," he said, his words soft, "if she can never climb back in with you? She is suffering. Let her go."

Thrace's chin came up and she glared at him and at Rizzo. "Because Alira isn't like the others. She is a fighter. She's been through things they never would have survived, and she's still here. I don't know what pushed her past her limit, but I can't just give up without even trying to help her."

Thrace peered at Botha. She could convince him. Reach into his emotions and find the weakness she could exploit to make him decide in Alira's favor. As well as she knew Botha, she wouldn't have to dig far. That friendship, though, that mutual respect built over time and shared experiences, deterred Thrace. No. She would not tamper with her friend's honest response.

"Will you at least try?" Thrace asked.

"Wait." Rizzo pointed at Thrace. "I thought you said she was dangerous. Even deadly."

Thrace sighed, nodded. "Yes. She can be. But if we keep her on the tranq, just enough to keep her calm, she shouldn't be a problem."

"But you don't know for sure." Rizzo shot a look at Botha. "Think hard, Baba. Your village won't want to lose you."

Thrace smiled despite the circumstance. *Baba.* Father. Botha had that effect on everyone. He would either agree or not.

Botha looked from Thrace to Rizzo to the ceiling above them. He spread his hands and muttered something unintelligible under his breath as if speaking to someone not there.

At last, Botha nodded. "I told your woman when she wore Skalar's face that I would help her if I could. I will keep my word."

Thrace closed her eyes, heaved a breath, then looked up once more. "Thank you, Botha."

"But," he said, "not in Bregaina. Children and elders need no beasts in their midst. Find me another place. A safe place. Private. Secure."

"I might have an idea," Rizzo said. "I'll see if it's an option." She rose and walked toward control.

Thrace clasped her hands together and nodded to Botha. "Thank you. I know if anyone can save her, it's you."

He nodded, his gaze sharp as a blade. "If that is what you believe, I will do my best. But you need to know that if I am the only one who can help her, and I find that she is beyond my rope, I will put her down like any other suffering animal."

A sharp pain pierced Thrace's chest and radiated out and up into her throat, quivering there long enough to make her cough. She took a deep breath, her gaze locked on Botha's face. He was right, but oh how his truth stung!

"If she is beyond your rope, my friend, comm me," Thrace said. "I will put her down myself."

chapter 72

New Canaan, Harajüd
Consortium Trader Base, Admiral Baldric's Office

RAIN POUNDED THE WINDOW, BLURRING Thrace's view. She stared out anyway, as if she could see details of the city, glimpse the bay through the downpour. Botha and Alira had left with Rizzo and a hold full of fresh supplies two days ago, one day after Skalar's—Alira's—thirty-day deadline. The hollow in Thrace's gut radiated up through her torso, tugged at her bones, pounded in her head. From the cave mouth, she'd watched *Cepheid* depart, dropping over the lip of the ledge to hug the surface as only an expert pilot could do. Long after the ship had disappeared into the distance, she'd stared at the spot where she'd seen it last.

When she finally left, she'd gone straight to Skalar's residence for one last visit. Despite the short time Galen and Alira had been at this charade, that home held a lot of memories both happy and unpleasant. Now it sat empty and forlorn. An unfamiliar dark stain marred one wall near the bar—a remnant of Skalar's rage, perhaps. Echoes of their last confrontation there had unsettled her, pushing Thrace out the door sooner than she'd planned, still mulling the irrevocable step ahead of her. HHU would no doubt seize the house and its land. Thrace hadn't decided, yet, how she felt about that.

A message had awaited her on the base, word from Rizzo that her contacts had learned Bellamy was dead. The timing was such that Thrace had to wonder if Alira'd had anything to do with it, but surely she wouldn't have done something so foolish. Would she? Botha would have said Alira stuck her head in the jakkal's mouth once too often, but unless—until— she survived this trial, they would never know.

Now, Thrace blinked at the rain. Alira might be gone, but Thrace still had a decision ahead of her. What to do about Iridos?

It galled her to imagine slaves working the tunnels, reportedly without suits or meds for the radiation, being mistreated or killed in the temple cavern. Even with Bellamy dead, Rizzo had said, Hannah would probably continue what her predecessor had started. Thrace's hands hung fisted at her sides. That was the unammi city, built by the Founders and their descendants. The ruins now stood in testament to what had happened there, a memorial to Galen's ancestors, and for those lost in the attack. The very granules of dust in the winds held the elements of his people. How dare the humans violate that grave? Scrape it raw? Where was their decency? Their respect for the beloved dead?

Rizzo had been as appalled by the idea of looters on the unammi's homeworld, but she'd pointed out that the Consortium couldn't protect the integrity of the site forever. Even without the Cartel's desecration, it was only a matter of time until someone else found the ruins and laid claim to the resources in the habitable zone.

"You should decide," she'd said, "whose presence there would upset you and your people least. Make sure it's someone who can annex it and make the claim stick."

But when Thrace offered it to the Syndicate, Rizzo had refused. Give it to any faction, she'd said, and there'll be a fight. Even if she was right, Thrace didn't have to like it.

Lips puckered, she laid her forehead against the window. Only a few of the colonial worlds had the means to claim Iridos and enforce their stake. Zebalu was one, but Thrace couldn't see how that would be better than the Cartel, as tied together as those organizations were. Saacharis was another. Rizzo had made a face at that suggestion but would not explain her reticence.

That left Harajüd. In the long run, this choice offered benefits to Thrace and the Consortium the other options would not. It would buy her favor with the HHU board of directors and security. Having this colony coordinating the operations on Iridos would make it easier for Thrace to keep tabs on her home world. She would have to make friends with Chief Downing, but she'd already begun that process. It also meant the faction's hematium orders could be filled faster, since the ready supply would be kept on Harajüd after she turned over their current stock.

And she *would* turn it over. Just like she had handed Harlan the ALT game and the bolt of silk and the gemstones. Because alliances were based on giving as well as taking. Skalar—or Alira's parody of him, anyway— had never understood that.

Thrace sighed. It was no choice, really.

"TICS, comm Chief Harlan Downing of the Harajüd Corporation." The conversation she was about to initiate could set back the efforts she'd already made toward better relations with HHU, but it also might convince the skeptical security chief that she was sincere. Eventually.

Either way, it couldn't be avoided.

"Downing." His reply came voice only. "Go."

"Chief, Admiral Baldric. I have something for you. Can you come?" She waited a moment, two.

"I'm busy. Can it wait?" he said at last.

"I'm afraid not. It's urgent."

"What's going on?"

"Not on the comm, Chief."

He expelled a heavy breath. "Very well. I'm ten minutes away. Downing out."

Thrace nodded as if he could see her. Once disconnected from the chief, she spoke again. "TICS, record communique to Spencer Kilbee."

What would Tiral and the others say about Alira's status? Thrace still danced around the edge of acceptance that it might be permanent. Rakalesh's disappointment, should that be the case, would be difficult to deflect. Alira never had sent those requested genetic samples.

Thrace blinked. Recording had started. "Kilbee, please load all remaining hematium on your faction hauler and deliver it to the main Consortium base in New Canaan as soon as possible. I'll explain everything when you arrive. Comm me when you're a day away so I can ensure adequate crew on hand to unload. Baldric out."

She'd considered turning over the unammi ships, too. It would sweeten the pot for Downing, and Thrace would need all the incentive she could muster to make him take this offer on her terms. Beyond keeping a few for shuttling supplies from the outpost to Earth, neither the Consortium nor the unammi would need those ships now, anyway. But she'd decided against it in the end. The Syndicate's proprietary tech threaded through each of those boats, making them a potential risk to Rizzo's business if they ended up in another colony's hands. If Thrace decided later to unload them, she could always offer them to Rizzo.

"TICS, locate Captain Cohen. Send her to my office immediately." Thrace turned to the window. Rain fell even harder now, turning the view into a melted blob that blurred and ran down the plaz. The thought of handing Iridos over to anyone was enough to make her ill. If—when—Harajüd House sent workers to the city, Galen could never go there again. No unammi survivors could. Somehow, Thrace had imagined it would always be her people's fallback. Yes, it was contaminated. But after several generations, that would ebb enough so they could rebuild the city. If they wanted to.

She shook her head. Stupid of her. The unammi would make Earth their home, and that was that. Iridos was no longer their haven. Now it would fall prey to the scavengers. At least she could have some say in that.

The chime sounded.

"Come."

Mira entered, then frowned. "You don't look so good. What's wrong?"

Thrace offered her a thin smile and sat behind her desk. "Harlan Downing is on his way here."

"Again? What did we do this time?"

"I called him." Thrace gestured at a chair. "I'm going to turn Skalar in."

Mira collapsed, more than sat, in the seat. "Seriously?"

"Seriously."

The captain nodded, her features a mask of confusion. "Okay. What for? Anything in particular? Or everything in general?"

Thrace pressed her lips together. "For Iridos."

Mira's face went slack. "But…they…we…" She stopped, shook her head. "Ma'am, that'll incriminate a lot of other faction crew. Captain Ronan, for one. You know he's on the fence right now. We need him on our side."

"Downing can demand other names all he wants. He won't get them from me, and he won't get them from Skalar."

The clouds in her second's expression did not clear. "But why? I thought we were going to run the hematium as if the squibs were still alive. If you hand over Iridos, we'll be buying it from the House, just like before."

Thrace leaned forward, elbows on her desk, hands lightly clasped before her. "First of all," she said, "natives to Iridos are—were—called 'unammi,' not 'squibs.' I may not intend to walk the straight and narrow letter of the law, but I will not tolerate racism. My officers will afford the respect and dignity due any intelligent species. You, as my second, will set an example in that regard. Am I clear?"

She could feel Mira trying to understand this unexpected non sequitur, but in the end the captain nodded. "Of course, ma'am. Sorry about that."

A chirp sounded.

"Admiral Baldric," the gate officer said via comm, "Chief Downing to see you, ma'am."

"Thank you. Send him up with an escort. Baldric out." Thrace looked at Mira. "Second, the Cartel has been sending slaves to mine the hematium on Iridos. Children."

Mira's lip curled as if she'd smelled something putrid. "Children?"

"They aren't even medicating them against the radiation. Seems it's cheaper to replace them. I don't intend to stand by and allow that to continue. What Skalar did there is bad enough. I find the destruction of that city and the total annihilation of the unammi a horrific, inexcusable act deserving of justice."

"But he only did it because he—"

"The fact is that he did it to prove a point," Thrace said. "But that's irrelevant. Genocide is never an acceptable course of action. The Consortium will no longer conduct business in that way."

"Wow." Mira ran a hand over her face. "You really are making big changes."

"We can be better, Mira. Better than before. Better than Skalar. But we can't do it by perpetuating his reprehensible tactics. If this is a deal breaker for you, then you don't belong on my crew. There's the door."

Mira shook her head. "No, ma'am. I'm on board. These changes are along the same lines as what you did for Kisle. I can get behind that."

"Good." Thrace's skin prickled. "He's here. And he's angry." Her lips drew into a tight line.

Mira stood just as the chime sounded. "You want me to leave?"

"On the contrary. I want you to observe and spread the word among the crew of what goes on here. I want them to know my people come first."

"No problem, ma'am."

"Come," Thrace called, then stood to greet her annoyed guest. "Chief Downing. I trust you are well."

"Well enough," he said. "What's this about?"

"Won't you sit?"

"I hope this won't take that long."

Thrace nodded. "Suit yourself." She lowered herself into her chair and took a deep breath. "I've just learned that Iridos was bombarded with LADRAS missiles."

"Bom—what?" Harlan's head tilted forward, a frown darkening his already perplexed face.

"The city on Iridos was utterly destroyed. The unammi people were slaughtered. Skalar was responsible."

"Wh—wh—" Harlan stammered. He blinked hard a few times, shaking his head. "Why? No, wait. Let me guess. He wanted the hematium."

"Yes."

"Any survivors?"

Thrace hesitated. Lying apparently would be a regular part of her new life. She should have seen that coming. "We found none."

"Bastard!" Harlan shouted, pacing away before whirling toward her. "When?"

"Five months ago."

"Five *months?*" he said. "That can't be right! We've heard from the Iridosians since then. They said they didn't want any more contact with the humans, that they'd be…delivering future shipments by drone." His words slowed as the truth dawned on him, and he shoved his fingers through his thinning hair, standing it on end like weeds. "That was Skalar."

Thrace nodded.

He shouted a word Thrace didn't recognize. Shock and rage radiated from him in waves.

"No wonder we haven't gotten any response from our latest order. The board's going nuts," he said, his voice hoarse, raspy. "I seem to remember you suddenly coming on the scene a few months ago, Baldric. Where were you when this all went down?"

"I was on Rubene at the time of the attack," Thrace said.

"Sure you were."

She shrugged. "I lived there for months. Check my purchase and lease records with Rubene Holding. They'll confirm."

"Uh huh. What were you doing on Rubene?"

"Conducting business for Skalar."

He stepped closer. "What kind of business?"

Thrace allowed a slow smile to spread across her face. "Legitimate."

He huffed in apparent disgust. "Where's Skalar now?"

"I honestly don't know." Thrace sighed. "When I found out what he'd done, I vowed to turn him in. He ran."

"Why would he do that? Why didn't he just kill you?"

Her smile returned. "He tried."

"But he's still alive?"

"He was the last time I saw him." She leaned back in her chair. "I don't know his status now."

Harlan paced away again. When he turned, he flung his hands out to the sides in frustration. "Where's the hematium? If that's why he flattened the city, I'm sure he didn't leave empty-handed."

"The Consortium has it," she said with a nod. "My people have been instructed to load it up and bring it to Harajüd with all haste. As soon as it arrives, I'll let you know."

"Where is it?"

"En route."

"You people are all alike," Harlan said, his mouth contorted, jaw tight, eyes narrow. "Okay. You said Skalar was responsible, but we both know he doesn't get his hands dirty with wetwork like that. And it wasn't no small boat that did that kind of damage, not with LADRAS—which is illegal, in case you didn't know. I want the names of everyone on the ship that killed Iridos."

"I'm afraid I can't do that, Chief," Thrace said. She tilted her head to peer at him. "You shouldn't even ask, and you know it."

Here it comes.

"My ass," he yelled. "It's my job to investigate crime. Flattening a goddamn planet is reason enough!"

"You are familiar with the contract between Harajüd Corporation and the Consortium, I take it."

"So?"

"Then you know that if Consortium crew break corporate law outside their home base and within any colony's territory, their faction aegis is forfeit. They become answerable to that colony's security forces."

"You're goddamn right they do."

"However," Thrace said, her tone calm, "Iridos and Iridosian space are not colonial territory. Therefore, no colony can claim jurisdiction or seek prosecution against the perpetrators."

His expression went blank, then reverted to rage. "Then why the hell are you even telling me about Skalar?" Harlan yelled even louder than before. He jabbed a finger at her. "I don't care what the damn contract says. I want those names. If you won't give 'em to me, I'll make your life hell. I'll make it so goddamn hard for the Consortium to do business you'll rue this day."

"That is your prerogative, of course," she said, lifting her hands before her in a gesture of surrender. "But I feel compelled to advise you that I don't have to keep this information to myself. I could easily make it public knowledge, in which case every colony with the capability will be on Iridos' doorstep as fast as their ships will carry them."

His face reddened. "That so? Thrace Baldric," he said, advancing on her desk, "you're under arrest—"

Thrace touched the door control. The panel hissed aside, and Harlan's security escort stepped in. "Everything okay, Admiral?"

Harlan's advance halted, his face a grimacing mask. He glared at her, his jaw working as if he were chewing rocks.

"I guess that depends on Chief Downing," she said, smiling at her guest. "I told you, Chief, I want to improve relations between HHU and the Consortium. I'd hoped this revelation and the subsequent opportunity it holds would help pave the way. Instead, you're clearly upset. I'm sorry about that, but I will protect my people."

Harlan ran a hand over his face, pulling it down into a contorted mask.

"You can fight me if you like," Thrace said. "But it seems to me HHU would be better served to keep this news private until its own ships can 'discover' the ruins on Iridos and claim the resources for Harajüd colony." She spread that slow smile again. "Of course, the choice is yours."

chapter 73

Haven, Danua
<u>Clan Trader Base, Brig</u>

KNØFA STARED AT THE VIDSCREEN, watching the prisoner pace inside the isolated cell. This little shit was not what he'd expected in that cave. No siree. He touched the comm.

"Good morning," he said. Tsurin always admonished him about forgetting the pleasantries. Said it made him seem more normal if he engaged in the niceties, even if he didn't understand why. "I do believe you're feeling better today. That's excellent. It means we can get started sooner than I'd expected."

The prisoner hesitated, looked around as always, then resumed its trek.

Knøfa nodded almost imperceptibly. "That's okay. You don't have to talk yet. We can get to that later. I just wanted you to know how glad I am we found you that day. You turned out to be a jackpot. More than I'd dared to hope. I had plans for you all along, but now…" He smiled, nodding again. "Now that I've seen your capabilities, I'm fairly excited to see where you can take us. Admiral Tsurin—she's the one you met in the cave—wants to improve the Clan's reach. Mark my words, you're going to be key in that process."

He could hardly wait for the lab to get started. Tsurin's squeamishness about human feelings and dignity didn't apply here. Since this prisoner wasn't human, she surely would approve the tests. Of course, they'd have to keep the squib medicated. It got too agitated otherwise and had already sent one crewman to his quarters with nightmares. A frown shadowed Knøfa's brow as he watched the little blue and white alien pacing in its tight space. What did all those other colors mean, anyway?

He shrugged. Didn't matter. He and the lab crew would figure it out along the way. He turned off the comm and left the watchbox without acknowledging the crewman guarding their treasure. Tsurin would surely want a report. It'd been a whole day.

He walked through the corridors to the lift, then up to medical where he pushed through the door.

The doctor on duty turned. "Sir."

Knøfa stopped at the foot of the bed, his eyes roving over the equipment in front of him, hardware hooked up to Tsurin—breathing for her, pumping her heart, keeping her brain active, flushing her kidneys, feeding nourishment into her veins. She, who had always been a giant in his mind, looked so small beneath all those tubes and attachments.

"Report," Knøfa said to the doctor.

The man winced. "There's been no change, sir. I wish I had better news."

"She's been like this almost a week. Did you at least find out what's wrong?"

"Unfortunately," the man said.

Knøfa turned a chilled stare on him. "Yes or no?"

The doctor's shoulders sagged. "Yes, sir."

"Tell me."

"Her brain is damaged—"

"You already knew that. Why is it damaged? What caused it?"

The doctor looked at his patient. "There's no way to know. Scans look like something cut through her brain stem, sir. She has no way to function as normal, no means to communicate with us or even be aware of us."

"Someone cut into her brain?" Knøfa frowned. "How is that possible? She was only out of our sight for five minutes. She wasn't bleeding when I found her, just unconscious."

"No, sir," the doctor said. "I didn't find any evidence of external incisions, only the internal ones. I don't know how it was done. I can't explain it. I just know that the cuts are clean, surgical, even cauterized."

Knøfa frowned, pursed his lips and stared at his admiral. "How long before she's up and around again?"

The other man's hesitation drew Knøfa's glare. "Well?"

"Sir," the doctor said, shaking his head, "I'm afraid this is as good as she's going to get."

"Ridiculous. With all this technology, all this equipment, you must be able to repair the damage and heal her," Knøfa said. "If you need to call in favors with Danuagov, make it happen. Whatever it takes. Whatever it costs. Just do it."

The doctor grimaced. "We've run every test we know, every scan there is. She doesn't respond to outside stimulation, even painful ones. There's no detectable neurological activity. No brainstem reflex. Without the ventilator, she wouldn't breathe. Her heart wouldn't beat. Given those criteria, and the fact that there is clear damage to her brain, it is my belief that she will not recover, sir. You said yourself it's been over a week with no change. That doesn't bode well."

"You don't know her very well, then. Anything is possible. Tsurin never retreated from a fight. She's not going to start now. Keep trying."

The doctor shook his head, a sympathetic look in his eyes. He reached toward Knøfa as if to touch his arm but stopped short. "Sir, I'm sorry, but Admiral Tsurin's brain is dead. This is all that's left of her. She's gone."

Knøfa grabbed the doctor's outstretched hand and yanked him around until his back was snugged up against Knøfa's belly. With the other hand, Knøfa pulled his knife and slowly slit the doctor's throat. Blood sprayed across the admiral's bed.

He dropped the convulsing doctor and called another of the med staff without turning. The med tech who appeared at his side blanched at the quivering doctor and the spraying blood but said nothing.

Knøfa pointed. "Get that out of here. I want a team in here to clean up the mess and change the admiral's bed. She shouldn't be laying on wet sheets."

The tech nodded with jerky movements and turned to carry out his orders.

"One other thing," he said before she left. "Let the other medical staff know that I will hear no negative word about the admiral's recovery."

Eyes wide, the woman nodded.

Knøfa jerked his chin toward the door. "Go."

When she was gone, he stepped to Tsurin's side. "You'll be happy to know," he told her, "that we got that shipment out of the barrens before the fly-by. The last of the merchandise was delivered yesterday, ahead of schedule. I even made a bigger profit than we expected by raising the price. Told the clients it was a hazardous duty expense."

He brushed a strand of lank hair from her face. The shine it had held a week ago was gone, along with her bad jokes. He missed both.

"You'll never guess what I found out earlier today about our prisoner. That 'child' who'd scavenged our shipment wasn't even human. I don't know how it got here without anyone knowing, or why it was hiding in our caves, but I'll find out. When I do, I'll let you know. I'm more interested, though, in how it made itself look human. And there's more. Turns out it can heal itself and affect people around it. That's probably what happened to you."

His throat thickened as if he'd swallowed too big a bite of food, and he coughed.

"Doesn't matter, though. We have it in isolation, so it can't hurt anyone else. And while you're resting and getting better, I'm going to begin the experiments we talked about. I know what you said about testing humans, but you never objected to using animals, so I figure you'll be okay with this." He paused. What would she say, if she could? When she could? Would she approve of his plan?

"I'm looking forward to seeing what turns up. Imagine if we could figure out how it changes shapes, or what makes it flash those colors, or how it heals itself! You wanted to jack up the Clan's influence. This is a sure way to do that."

He paused a moment, watching for any reaction. Nothing.

"I know you didn't believe this would be worth it, but you'll see I was right. Maybe…" He paused. It wouldn't do to upset her. But what if annoying her pushed her to recover faster? Maybe if he pissed her off, she'd want to kick his ass. "Maybe it was you holding us back, your reluctance to cross arbitrary ethical constraints. Did you ever think of that?" He shrugged. "I trust you. I always have, so I've done things your way. But for now, we're going to do things my way, see if I was right. We'll never know unless we try. If it turns out you were right, I'll stop. Retreat to your boundaries. You have my word."

Behind him, the door slid open, and he heard the crew enter. He leaned closer. "I know you don't approve of slackers, so I'm going to work now. The crew will clean you up, get you some dry sheets. I'll report later."

He turned, pushing past the waiting workers, and left the room.

Did you enjoy this book?

Please leave a rating and/or comment wherever books are reviewed
and help others find and enjoy it, as well!

Sign up for Drema's newsletter!

You'll get articles, occasional sneak peaks at upcoming stories, project
updates, garden pictures, and cat news. You'll also be the first to receive
announcements about upcoming book releases, cover reveals, special
promotions, and other juicy tidbits from Niveym Arts.

https://niveymarts.com/newsletter

Want to follow Drema's process on her indie publishing journey?
Subscribe to Drema's blog and/or follow her on social media.

Blog:	https://www.dremadeoraich.com
Facebook:	https://www.facebook.com/NiveymArtsLLC
Instagram:	https://www.instagram.com/dremadeoraich
BlueSky:	https://bsky.app/profile/dremadeoraich.bsky.social

Acknowledgments

Book Two in this series was a long time coming, and I owe thanks to a number of people for helping me to bring it to your hands:

To my beloved beta readers Ann, Becky, John, Lillith, Lily, Mary Lou, Michael, Stephanie, and Vince for helping me identify plot holes, rough spots, and readability issues and who, by now, might be able to quote lengthy passages from the book as well as I can. I couldn't do this without you!

To my friends and associates whose gatherings I missed so that I could finish "that next draft." Thanks for being patient with me!

To Susan Posey, for Spanish-English translation, and to Thea Wallace of Lingo Whiz CC, for Afrikaans-English translation. Thanks for honing my rough Google translate versions of these beautiful languages into realistic words and phrases correct for the story's context.

To my editor, Lauran Strait, who helped me smooth out all the unnecessary kinks, and who helped me decide which kinks were worth keeping.

To my proofreader, Stephanie Brannock, for helping me make the story look great on the page.

To Francis and the team at 100Covers who once again designed the perfect cover from my garbled concept notes.

And most especially to B, for all the things, all the time, every day, everywhere. Thank you, Silly Man. I love you!

About the Author

Drema Deòraich is an award-winning author of speculative fiction that sometimes asks big questions. Her short stories have been published in numerous online journals, as well as a few semi-professional zines.

Her debut novel *Entheóphage*, a medical sci-fi/climate fiction novel, was published in 2022, and received the Literary Titan Gold Book Award in November of 2024. "Phagey" (as it is affectionately known by its fans) has become a subject of book club discussions in many places, including the club "Reading Between the Wines," of Lexington, North Carolina. (Thanks, Carol and friends!) Her second novel, *Fallen*, first book in the science fantasy trilogy, The Founder's Seed, was released on May 1, 2024. *Broken*, Drema's third release, continues the Founder's Seed saga.

Drema currently lives in Southeast Virginia with her husband, two cats, and all her other characters. When time and mosquitoes permit, Drema works on transforming the lawn around their small home into more welcoming habitat for birds, butterflies, bees, and other wildlife. She also blogs about writing, ideas from Life that inspire her, environmental issues, ways to live more sustainably, and whatever else captures her fancy. Follow her writing posts at www.dremadeoraich.com, and her environmental posts at www.niveymarts.com.

Currently, Drema is hard at work on the third book in the Founder's Seed trilogy with a projected release date in the Summer of 2025. When not writing, she helps her legal-eagle boss save the world one case at a time, pets her husband's cats, or spends time in Nature, surrounded by flora and fauna.

Also by Drema Deòraich

Entheóphage
https://books2read.com/Entheophage

Fallen
The Founder's Seed Trilogy, Book 1
https://books2read.com/Fallen-The-Founders-Seed-1

~ • ~

Recent Short Releases

"Jane Doe #7" (a dark sci-fi novelette in three parts)
Part One: https://lukevans.substack.com/p/jane-doe-7
Part Two: https://lukevans.substack.com/p/jane-doe-7-9b0
Part Three: https://lukevans.substack.com/p/jane-doe-7-4fe

~ • ~

Coming Soon:

Driven
The Founder's Seed Trilogy, Book 3
(Summer of 2025)

Coming Short Releases:
"Deer In Headlights" (dark speculative fiction/ecofiction novelette)
coming to State of Matter in November
https://stateofmatter.in

Appendix A

Characters List

Alira (ah-LEE-rah)—Unammi. Has multiple human personae.

Amadi Patel—See Patel, Amadi.

Bailey Madden—See Madden, Bailey.

Baldric, Thrace (BAHL-drihk, THRAES)—Human persona of Galen. Captain and second in command in The Consortium Trader faction.

Bardo (BAR-doh)—Human. Admiral of The Order Trader faction. Childhood friend of Rizzo.

Bellamy (BEH-lah-mee)—Human. Admiral of The Cartel Trader faction.

Bohmer (BOH-mur)—Human. Lieutenant who first served under Commander Walker. Now serves under Captain Ronan.

Botha (BOI-tah)—Human. Beloved elder in the village of Bregaina on the colony world Bejami. Called Baba by some outside his village.

Braithwaite, Jukka (BRAYTH-wayt, JOO-kuh)—Human. Captain and head of security in The Syndicate Trader faction.

Cesar (say-ZAHR)—Unammi. Killed in the Fall of Iridos. Now lives on as one of Alira's harvests.

Chandra (SHAHN-druh)—Human. Gardener for Admiral Bellamy.

Cohen, Kisle—Human. Mira Cohen's brother.

Cohen, Mira—Human. Commander in The Consortium Trader faction.

Companion—Other. The ethereal multifaceted entity that represents the hive mind of all the Iri, everywhere. Appears to Alira as Guide and Advisor. Only she can see him/them in this manifestation. See also entry for Iri in the Glossary.

Crow—Human. Deceased. Now lives on as one of Alira's harvests.

Dawa, Tenzin (DAH-wah, TEHN-zihn)—Former human persona of Galan. Now abandoned.

Doe—Human. Captains the *Coriolis* for The Cartel Trader faction.

Downing, Harlan (DOW-neeng, HAR-lehn)—Human. Security chief for Harajüd House, Unlimited.

Dupré, Hannah (doo-PREE, HA-nuh)—Human. Captain and second in command of The Cartel Trader faction.

Edanor (EH-duh-nor)—Unammi. Pilot for The Consortium. Stationed at the outpost.

Eli—see Sullivan, Elias.

Enzo (EHN-zoh)—Human. Lieutenant serving in The Consortium Trader faction. Crewed with Vandana Walker until that Captain's incarceration.

Esther (EH-stur)—Human persona of Ijydin. Now used by Alira.

Galen (GAY-lehn)—Unammi. Alira's lover and partner. Has used multiple human personae in the past but is currently using only Thrace Baldric.

Georgeanne (a.k.a. George)—Human. Admiral of The Federation Trader faction.

Guide—Human. Name given to spiritual mentors and teachers in the Bindhu faith.

Hannah Dupré—See Dupré, Hannah.

Harlan Downing—See Downing, Harlan.

Henri (awn-REE)—Human. Deceased. Past Admiral of The Clan Trader faction. Admiral Tsurin's predecessor and mentor.

Ijydin (ee-JEE-dihn)—Unammi. Killed as a result of the attack on Iridos. Now lives on as one of Alira's harvests.

Jammer—Human. Lieutenant junior grade in The Cartel Trader faction. Comms specialist on the *Coriolis*.

Jarod (JAH-rahd)—Human. Metalworker employed by The Consortium Trader faction. It was Jarod's discovery of special hematium properties that led to the Fall of Iridos. (See Book 1, *Fallen*).

Jax—Human. Manager at Bahtya Gaming House. Employed by The Consortium Trader faction.

Jude (JOOD)—Human. Commander of the *Sea Star* for The Cartel Trader faction.

Jukka—See Braithwaite, Jukka.

Kilbee, Spencer (KILL-bee, SPEHN-suhr)—Human persona of Tiral.

Kisle Cohen—See Cohen, Kisle.

Knøfa (NEW-fuh)—Human. Captain and second in command of The Clan Trader faction.

Logan Roucharde—See Roucharde, Logan.

Lourdes (LOR-dehs)—Human. The woman who purchased young Turizomi (later known as Rizzo) from The Cartel, raised and educated her, then set her free.

Lurien (LOO-ree-ehn)—Unammi. Alira's mother. Killed in the Fall of Iridos.

Luther Michels—See Michels, Luther.

Madden, Bailey (MA-dehn, BAY-lee)—Human. Captain and second in command in The Syndicate Trader faction.

Malcolm Skalar—See Skalar, Malcolm.

Michels, Luther (MI-kulz, LOO-ther)—Human. Vice Chair of Saacharis Aggregate Mining.

Mira Cohen—See Cohen, Mira.

Moss, Zachary—Human persona of Ijydin, then of Alira. Not currently in use.

Nyros (NEE-rohs)—Unammi. Alira's brother. Killed by Crow. Now lives on as one of Alira's harvests.

Patel, Amadi (pah-TEHL, ah-MAH-dee)—Human persona of Ijydin, then of Alira. Not currently in use.

Rakalesh (rah-KAY-lehsh)—Unammi. One of the surviving unammi councilors.

Reyes, Thomas (RAY-ehz, TAH-muhs)—Human. Manager of the Gauri Metalb Mine on the colony world Saacharis.

Ripley—Human. Lieutenant commander who first served under Commander Walker. Now serves under Captain Ronan.

Rizzo (RIH-zoh)—Human. Known to a rare few by her childhood name of Turizomi. Admiral of The Syndicate Trader faction.

Ronan (ROH-nuhn)—Human. Captains the *Treasure Chest* for The Consortium Trader faction.

Rook—Human. Captain in The Cartel Trader faction.

Roucharde, Logan (roo-SHARD, LOH-guhn)—Human. Chairman of the board of directors for Harajüd House, Unlimited.

Rugrat—See Skalar, Amelia.

Sa'abah (sah-AH-bah)—Human. Captain and head of security in The Consortium Trader faction.

Skalar, Amelia (skah-LAHR, ah-MEE-lee-uh)—Human. Also known as Rugrat. Malcolm Skalar's little sister. Deceased.

Skalar, Malcolm (skah-LAHR, MAL-cuhm)—Human. Admiral of The Consortium Trader faction. Deceased. Now lives on as one of Alira's harvests.

Spencer Kilbee—See Kilbee, Spencer.

Sullivan, Elias (SUH-lih-vuhn, ee-LI-uhs)—Human. First Founder of Iridos. Also the human face of the Companion when communicating with Alira. Called Eli by Alira, and Elisul by the other unammi.

Tenzin Dawa—See Dawa, Tenzin.

Thomas Reyes—See Reyes, Thomas.

Thrace Baldric—See Baldric, Thrace.

Tiral (tee-RAHL)—Unammi. Pilot and outcast. Has multiple human personae. Most common one is Spencer Kilbee.

Trumo (TROO-moh)—Unammi. A youngling in one of Alira's classes before The Fall of Iridos, one with whom she feels a strong kinship.

Tsurin (TSOOR-ihn)—Human. Admiral of The Clan Trader faction.

Turizomi (too-rih-ZOH-mee)—Human. Admiral Rizzo's birth name. This is not common knowledge.

Vandana Walker—See Walker, Vandana.

Virgil (VER-juhl)—Human. Deceased. Past Admiral of The Cartel Trader faction. Admiral Bellamy's predecessor and mentor.

Walker, Vandana (WAHL-kur, van-DA-nuh)—Human. Commander in The Consortium Trader faction.

Appendix B

Glossary

adjustment—A physical process administered by unammi healers at a new frem's Rite of Decision; its intention is to nudge the brain/mind/persona in order to help the new frem be content with their chosen role and to serve without doubt.

aes (AY-ehs) *Unameze* — Are. Can also be and often is merged with another part of the sentence (most often the adverb which qualifies or gives focus to the verb).

Aes te nalya (AY-es teh NAH-lee-yah) *Unameze*—We are one.

Aggregate—Refers to Saacharis Aggregate Mining, the corporate governing body on the colony world Saacharis.

ALT game—ALT Stands for Alternate Life Track. A virtual reality gaming system that employs a digital cerebral access device that manipulates alpha patterns in the brain so that the player can actually believe they are some*where*, some*one,* some*when,* or even some*thing* else. Highly controversial and illegal in all twelve colony worlds because the game is so addictive and, in numerous cases, causes psychosis in the player.

ama (AH-mah) *Unameze*—Genetic dam. Mother.

amornae (ah-MOOR-nay)—Blue mushroom indigenous to Zebalu. Spores from this "blue love" mushroom intoxicate by stimulating oxytocin and increasing libido. Used to make sexual enhancement recreationals. Highly illegal due to its addictive properties, and because quantity for a recreational dose is so close to that of a fatal dose.

annulus tree (AHN-yoo-luhs)—Tall, flexible trees with bands of annuli, or fibrous tissue left behind on the trunk when each layer of branching leaflets sprouts forth in the tree's upward growth. Mature trees have a band of tissue, then a rosette of flexible branches that go all the way around the trunk, then another band of tissue, and another rosette of branches, etc. Can grow up to 30 meters high. Native to Harajud.

arpë (AHR-peh)—Non-venomous python indigenous to Bejami's equatorial jungles, especially near Bregaina. Anaconda-sized. Eats whatever it can catch and swallow.

Arzu Aslan (AHR-zoo AH-slahn)—Pleasure house/brothel in New Canaan on Harajüd.

Baba (BAH-bah)—Father. A term of respect used by many humans as an honorific for tribal and village elders.

Bahtya Gaming House (BAH-tee-ah)—Business owned/operated by The Consortium Trader faction in New Canaan, Harajüd.

bala (BAH-lah)—Indigenous to Bejami. A tall (127-130 cm) wading bird found along equatorial riverbanks and deltas. Feeds on fish, crustaceans, and reptiles found in water or marshy areas. Bright green feathers on back and wings, sky blue belly and undertail, reed-yellow legs. Long sinuous neck is iridescent blue-green. Face is black with bright red crest feathers that lay flat along the neck most of the time and stand up when courting or fighting. Long, spear-like bill. Bright red eyes. Nests in inland trees.

Bantali Sea (bahn-TAH-lee)—Body of water just off the coast of Pelarr on the colony world Zebalu.

barrens, the—Regions common to certain latitudes both north and south on the colony world Danua. Characteristics include cold, temperamental weather; rocky, hilly terrain; minimal stunted scrub; scattered caverns and barrows; and a few hardy wildlife species.

Bejami (beh-JAH-mee)—One of twelve colony worlds. Governed by the Bejami Trust. Not a planet; this colony world is a moon in orbit around a gas giant in the Emlacha star system (same as Rubene), though the Bregainans call the star Lynju. Bejami is home to the Mandoslóna prison continent. No spaceport. Single landport located in the capital city of Bel-rhoven.

Bel-Rhovan (behl-ROH-vahn)—Bejami's capital city. Smaller than most cities on other worlds. Bejami prefers to keep settlements small, but Bel-Rhovan comes close to breaking that rule/precept. Many tourist attractions here. Located on the continent of Dórucuin in the northern hemisphere.

bh'tati (buh-TAH-tee)—Native to Bejami. Oceanic fruit of enormous seaweed forests in Dairnen Bay on the west coast of Dórucuin. Savory, salty, juicy. Center of the fruit is eaten raw or in stews. Pulp from layer between edible center and rubbery skin is used in pigments for tattoos, paints, dyes, etc. Rubbery skin is soaked in other fruit juices and allowed to ferment. Makes an alcoholic mead-like drink. (See úta.)

Bindhu (BIHN-doo)—Human spiritual practice. The word bindhu means dot, or point. In metaphysical terms, Bindhu is held to be the point at which creation begins and the point at which the many becomes the One. Beliefs consist mainly of peaceful coexistence. Varying levels include paths to suit most practitioners: Ashaan Path encourages rigorous training of the body and mind until it is a finely honed instrument/weapon; Shidara Path espouses asceticism and withdrawal from daily life; and Tuchani Path explores sexuality as a route to enlightenment. All paths teach meditation. Bindhu practice expects this as a daily regimen.

bismuth (BIZ-muhth)—High-density metal often produced as a by-product of refining lead, copper, tin, and other ores. However, it also occurs naturally in small quantities. The Gauri Metalb mine on Saacharis, however, holds the raw metal ore in abundance. Brittle, often mixed with other metals to make it more useful. Highly valued in various industries.

Bregaina (breh-GAY-nuh) — Second largest village on Bejami. This is Botha's home. All buildings situated on platforms raised above the delta so that the tide can ebb and flow beneath them.

burrit (BUR-riht)—Indigenous to Saacharis. Small mammal with large pale eyes, snub nose, large ears that lay flat against its head, stumpy tail. Range in color from pale tan to pale grey; none are dark. Shy of people, but active during the day, even in city parks. Lives in a hole in the ground but can climb trees if threatened.

Cartel, The—Trader faction located on the colony world Zebalu. Run by Admiral Bellamy and her second in command, Captain Hannah Dupré.

Cepheid (SEE-fee-ihd)—Small interstel-capable transport ship. Four-person crew, tiny hold. No stealth. Looks weathered, unremarkable. Registered to a non-existent person named Lyla Ravish, but off the record belongs to The Consortium.

charsten (SHAR-stehn)—Indigenous to Danua. Cattle with long, silky fur prized for its use in textiles.

Charter, Intercolonial Charter—An agreement drawn up and signed by governing bodies of all twelve colony worlds. Initially drafted and confirmed by the first three colonies to be settled in Earth Year 2687, the Charter governs the vast majority of interrelations between the colonies, as well as what is acceptable and legal on any one of those worlds, including (but not limited to): ecological sustainability, intercolonial time measures (standard day/week/month/year), weaponry, languages, the sanctity of the contract, citizenship, rights and privileges due all citizens, responsibilities of all citizens, medical and other systems of law, population growth, extradition, governance, etc.

Chimaera Public House (ki-MEE-rah)—Busy public house located in Pelarr on the colony world Zebalu. Owned and operated by the Zebalu Association.

ciotta (chee-OH-tah)—Indigenous to Saacharis. Short, stubby, gnarled cross between a shrub and a tree. Thrives in the low light of Saacharis; would die in brighter light of other colony worlds. Leaves are long, flat, droopy, yellowish-green, and numerous.

Clan, The—Trader faction located on the colony world Danua. Run by Admiral Tsurin and her second in command, Knøfa.

comm—Communique. Communication between two locations. Message can be recorded and sent over interstel distances, or it can be live, real-time exchange intraplanet. Can be verbal, holovisual, or both. Can also be text only, but this is rare.

Consortium, The—Trader faction located on the colony world Harajüd. Run by Admiral Skalar (human persona of unammi Alira) and second in command, Thrace Baldric (human persona of unammi Galen).

Coriolis, The (kor-ee-OH-lihs)—Cartel ship, scout class.

corpgov—Human slang term. Refers to corporate governments on the colony worlds. Sometimes morphs into similar slang tied to a specific world, like Danuagov.

Corsair, The (kor-SEHR)—Cartel ship, cargo class.

Cuthars gulls (KOO-thurz)—Indigenous to Zebalu. Large black seabirds with gray wingtips and facial accents. Cliff-nesters who seldom travel further inland than the coast. Mostly suited to sea life, though they take advantage of plentiful fish and aquatic life near the cliffs in the equatorial zone, especially shellfish that attach themselves to the rocks at the tideline. Cuthars like to ride the winds just off the cliff face.

Dagons Pub (DAY-guhnz)—Upscale public house located in New Canaan, Harajüd. Owned and operated by The Consortium Trader faction.

Danua (DAN-yoo-ah)—One of twelve colony worlds. Governed by Danua Textiles. Located in the Restelys star system. Three small moons. Home to The Danua Clan Trader faction, run by Admiral Tsurin and her second-in-command, Captain Knøfa. Temperate equatorial zones, skirted north and south by rocky barrens, rolling hills, and polar zones. One spaceport. One landport.

¡Déjame respirar! (Spanish)—Let me catch my breath!

diamina (di-ah-MEE-nah)—Precious stone similar to diamonds in appearance, but slightly different chemical composition. Found only on Levyron. Both diamina mines on that world sit on land owned by The Order Trader faction, but are worked by Levyron corpgov, for a price. Diamina dust is sometimes used in artwork, as well as in high-end computer components.

Dórucuin (DOR-oo-koon)—One of three lands on a single supercontinent on Bejami. Its name means Land of Two People. Home to Bel-Rhovan and Bregaina.

Duakela (doo-AH-keh-luh)—Largest non-polar continent on Zebalu. Located in the southern hemisphere. Its name means Two Heads. Home to Zebalu's capital city of Pelarr.

Earth (URth)—Homeworld of humans. Located in the Sol star system. One moon, which houses the Consortium's secret outpost. Abandoned centuries ago, after other colony worlds had been settled, when ecological and environmental destruction gave rise to a lethal plague that rendered the biosphere uninhabitable by humans. Those humans left behind after the planetary quarantine was established did not survive. Now clear of infectious agents, and home to the surviving unammi.

En ou vriende stel die hart gerus (Afrikaans)—Old friends ease the heart. Familiar Bejami greeting, informal.

Estoy en eso (Spanish)—I'm working on it.

Fall of Iridos, The—A term used by unammi survivors to refer to the attacks on Iridos by the Consortium's armada. The majority of their population was killed during or as a result of the attacks. The unammi's city was destroyed, and the survivors all eventually evacuated.

Fashere (fah-SHEER)—One of twelve colony worlds. Governed by Fashere Enterprises. Located in the Jaunuit star system. Two small moons. One spaceport. One landport.

Federation, The—Trader faction located on the colony world Rubene. Run by Admiral Georgeanne (a.k.a. George) and her second in command, Captain Claudio.

Founder's Daughter—An unammi female conceived through a union of the high councilor and Eli Sullivan (the Founder). Sullivan donated seed generations ago, which was preserved in a sealed vault encrusted with irolium that genetically alters its DNA. Only a Founder's Daughter can harvest those who die in her presence. Founder's Daughters can absorb the memories and knowledge (but not the gifts) of those who die within their presence. Also called a soul harvester. See harvest.

frem (FREHM) *Unameze*—Adult in service to the unammi; the opposite of youngling.

fryt (FREET)—Indigenous to Bejami. Large brown water snake common along the wetlands on the western coast of Dórucuin. Long sinuous fins along the top of its body, and in strategic locations along the bottom, as well as along its tail. Burrows deep into the mud when the tide is out. Once a fryt is snug in its burrow, it's almost impossible to lure or dig it out.

Gadney (GAD-nee)—One of twelve colony worlds. Governed by the Gadney Farm League. Located in the Biziar star system. One small moon. One spaceport. One landport.

Gauri Metalb (GOW-ree meh-TAHLB)—Bismuth mine on the colony world Saacharis. Located on the continent of Metaliven. Owned by The Syndicate Trader faction. Leased by Saacharis Aggregate Mining.

ghostnet—A stealth-based, illegal tracking program installed into another organization's computer system. The ghostnet tracks recordings, purchases and sales, decisions, private memos and communiques, and all other activity of the targeted system, and therefore is privy to sensitive and secure information without the affected organization's knowledge.

Haar voorganger (Afrikaans)—Her predecessor.

Harajüd (hah-RAH-joohd)—One of twelve colony worlds. Governed by Harajüd House, Unlimited (HHU). Located in the Lakaya star system. Seven moons, all small, icy; the largest holds medical isolation facilities under a dome. Largest and most affluent of all the colonies. Home to The Consortium Trader faction. One of the first three exoplanets to be settled by colonists from Earth. Five space ports, as well as one space-based shipbuilding port and one space-based repair station. Two land ports.

harvest, the—Iridosian special skill granted only to Founder's Daughters, one in each generation, always a genetic female. This individual harvests or absorbs the memories and personalities of those who die in their presence. The harvest is seen as sacred. Not all harvesters survive; some are driven mad by their harvests. Some refer to a harvest or to harvested souls as a reaping.

harvesting sickness—The gradual loss of identity in an unammi harvester when she cannot control the harvests, and the absorbed personalities take her over.

Haven—Capital city of the colony world Danua. Located on the continent of Storelandsør.

hematium (heh-MAH-tee-uhm)—Metal found only on Iridos; holds very unique qualities, like the ability to shed a radioactive charge, which make it essential in contemporary shipbuilding. Highly valuable to the colonies.

HHU—Refers to Harajüd House, Unlimited, the corporate governing body on the colony world Harajüd. Sometimes called "the House."

hologen (HAH-loh-gehn)—Holographic generator used to project an image. Can be sized to fit the purpose; small for in-office or in-home use, large for commercial purposes, industrial-sized when necessary to project large, sweeping images.

holovid (HAH-loh-vihd)—Holographic video or visual.

hoverbus—Large public transports that do not make physical contact with the ground in order to move. Intracity transport only; limited to short-distance travel. Free passage to any traveler. Ground-bound. Motors make a deep thrumming sound.

interstel craft—Interplanetary and interstellar flight capable. Smaller and most mid-size vessels can dock at landports. Larger ships may only dock at spaceport.

Iri (IH-ree) *Unameze*—Subquantum beings that lived in the surface of the caverns on Iridos, as well as many other places in other realms, other worlds. It is thought that they are hive-based entities, and that they and those with whom they find a connection, like the unammi, live in symbiotic relationship. On Iridos, that symbiosis produced irolium stones, which introduced special qualities into the unammi. (See irolium) The Iri appear to Alira in multiple forms as Guide and Advisor. See entry for Companion in Appendix A, Characters List.

Iridos (IH-rih-dohs)—The original homeworld of the unammi. Now abandoned. See Fall of Iridos.

irolium (ih-ROH-lee-uhm)—A blue stone that encrusted several caverns on Iridos before The Fall. The stone emits low-level, non-thermal magnetic radiation. This crystal is the source of unammi special gifts. Salvaged after The Fall and transported with the surviving unammi to their new city on Earth.

i'shin (ee-SHEEN) *Unameze*—Familiar pet name for a beloved friend or lover, either gender. A shortened combination of "my heart."

jakkal (jah-KAHL)—Indigenous to Bejami. Medium-sized canine-type mammal. Travel, hunt, and live in social packs. Females make the rules. Young are raised by all.

jumper—Personal transports. Atmospheric craft capable of flight within a single planet's atmosphere. Not interstel capable. More functional than stylish. Makes a small whining sound.

Juveltranstør, The (JOO-vuhl-trans-tewr)—Clan ship, cargo class.

Kaiken, The (KI-kehn)—Syndicate ship, recon class.

kata (KAH-tah)—A series of movements and body postures inherent to training in martial arts. Can also be practiced for spiritual and meditative effect.

kinders (Afrikaans)—Children.

kris—A type of knife.

Kris Cross, The—Syndicate ship, command class. Sometimes referred to as the Kris.

Labrys, The (LA-brihs)—Syndicate ship, cargo class.

LADRAS (LAH-druhs)—Stands for Limited Area Dispersal Radiation System. LADRAS missiles are illegal, as are all radioactive weapons, by the terms of the Interplanetary Charter. See Charter.

lênask (leh-NASK)—Indigenous to Bejami. Large omnivorous primate. Lives in the trees among equatorial jungles. Sharp canine teeth, long, strong limbs. Will eat anything, including humans. Will also eat its own, if they are mortally injured or born with challenges that make them unlikely to survive. Screeches in whooping cries as it attacks. Sometimes hunts in packs.

Levyron (leh-VI-ruhn)—One of twelve colony worlds. Governed by the Levyron Institute. Located in the G'laudis star system. One small moon, which holds a biohazards medical facility beneath a dome. Home to The Order Trader faction. Levyron has an axial tilt of 157°, and a retrograde rotation. Visible in the night sky is the Finbeck Galactic Arm, which extends beyond Levyron, the farthest reach of human habitation in this section of the galaxy. One spaceport. One landport.

libidinorr (lih-BEE-deh-noor)—Recreational drug created from leaves of the nofasa shrub. Mood alterative. Greatly enhances libido. Heightens physical senses. Mind-expanding. Produced and sold by The Federation Trader faction. See nofasa.

lumenettes (loo-mih-NEHTZ)—Wispy strands of lighting made to be worn in the hair and on clothing. Although lumenettes are sometimes found on other worlds, they are most common to inhabitants of Saacharis.

Mandoslóna (man-duh-SLOH-nuh)—A prison continent established on Bejami. Bordered in the north by jungles filled with voracious predators, and on the East, South, and West by vicious riptides and frigid waters. Home to life-sentenced prisoners from all twelve colony worlds.

Mari Bay (MAH-ree)—Large bay located on Harajüd between the Syrinaia coastline and Shamashu.

medfac (MEHD-fak)—Refers to a medical facility.

Mirovia, The (mih-ROH-vee-uh)—Cartel ship, command class.

mitigant—An unammi frem who has proven to be problematic to unammi society in one way or another and has undergone the process of mitigation.

mitigation—A physical process undertaken by healers on Iridos to reprogram a frem's entire brain. Its purpose is to fix frem who cannot adjust to a life of service, or whose mental and neural connections go awry due to some unforeseen problems in their physical makeup. It is also used to adjust those who become problematic in unammi society, a tool to bring them into line with social expectations so that they do not foster discontent in others.

Mjolnir Island (MYOHL-neer)—Large island on the colony world Danua. Located off the eastern coast of Landetorr in the southern hemisphere. Northern half is in the fertile latitudes. Southern half is in the barrens.

muil—(MWEEL) Indigenous to Bejami. Small wading bird found along shorelines in equatorial regions; eats insects, small fish, crustaceans, worms, etc. Nests in large ground colonies just inland of the marsh. Small-bodied, stands up to 38 cm tall. Dull greenish grey backs and heads, pale grey bellies, mottled faces. Brownish yellow legs and bills, orange eyes.

muñara (moo-NYAH-rah) *Unameze*—Communion. Shared mind/awareness.

muñise tree (moo-NYEE-suh) *Unameze*—Found only on Iridos. Tall, stately. Sturdy trunks with crusty, scale-like exterior surface (thicker on the windward side) to withstand sand and wind. All limbs are found at the top quarter of the tree, above the winds, and all angle up.

Nalena t'staani (nah-LAY-nah tih stah-AH-nee) *Unameze*—One is All. Proper response to "Aes te nalya."

nanopanel—Large plaz panel chemically treated and infused with nanotech. Can be clear, like a window, or be set to project colored pattern displays, specific scenes from historical or contemporary vistas, or any visual that the programmer or user can adequately define.

Na'Staani (nah stah-AH-nee) *Unameze*—Respected All. Refers to the Great Mind, The All, The Universe, the unammi concept of All-That-Is, or the Divine.

netzyl—(NEHT-zul)—An unflattering, slang term for someone who causes problems or whose actions generate upheaval. A troublemaker.

New Canaan (noo KAY-nahn)—Capital city on the colony world Harajüd. Located on the west coast of Syrinaia near the equator. Largest city on any colony world. Tourist city, numerous attractions, abundant industries.

Nidahn (nee-DAHN)—Intended to be the thirteenth colony. Settled last in the exodus from Earth, but quarantined when a plague ship made it there from Earth very early in its settlement. All the settlers died before they could sign the Charter, thus Nidahn was never a full colony world.

Nie alweer nie (Afrikaans)—Not again.

niveym (nih-VAY-uhm) *Unameze*—Indigenous to Iridos. Large, delicate white bird on Iridos. Never comes down to the ground due to the surface winds. Lives its entire life in and above the very tall muñise trees. Wings are exceptionally long and powerful. Seen as a symbol of freedom and the act of rising above turmoil.

nofasa (no-FAH-suh)—Hardy shrub indigenous to edges of the equatorial jungle on Bejami. Thick branches and foliage. Fast-growing. Berries and bark eaten by some smaller mammals and birds. Leaves harvested by locals for Bejami corpgov, who export the product to The Federation Trader faction. See libidinorr.

Nöbetchi Mountains (nuh-BAYT-chee)—Also called The Sentinels. Ragged mountain chain at the southernmost tip of Syrinaia, near the southern polar region. Many caves.

obsequiem (uhb-SEH-kwee-uhm)—A non-lethal gas used in the colonies (both Trader faction and corpgov settings) to enforce compliance. Those affected by minimal to medium quantities are more open to suggestion and easily led. Heavy gassing causes those affected to lose consciousness.

Order, The—Trader faction located on the colony world Levyron. Run by Admiral Bardo and his second in command, Captain Izra.

outpost, the—Secret base owned/operated by the Consortium Trader base. Located on the moon of old Earth.

ørkhund (OORK-huhnd)—Indigenous to Danua. Small canine mammals, four-legged, large-eared, bright-eyed. Usually brownish in color to blend in with barrens soil/rocks/primary grasses. Native to Danua's barrens. Can be found in every barrens zone with slight variations in appearance and behavior. Also called a barrens hound. Often dig dens in the foothills, but can sometimes be found in hillier, more rocky areas where caves are possible. Ørkhunds are the primary predator in the barrens, but shy of humans. Territorial.

Pelarr (pee-LAHR)—Capitol city of the colony world Zebalu. Located on the northern coast, near the western end of Duakela.

Pepita Public House (peh-PEE-tah)—Upscale public house on Saacharis. Owned and operated by The Syndicate Trader faction.

Phejoss (feh-JAHSS)—One of twelve colony worlds. Governed by The Phejoss Society. Located in the Nagapo star system. Luxury resort world, habitable only in the fringes of the large volcanic regions. No moon. One small spaceport. Two small landports.

Pirate's Cove—Cliffside location of the waterborne ship docks for The Cartel Trader faction in Pelarr, Zebalu.

plaz—A non-toxic, plastic-like polymer used in place of glass in the colony worlds. Far more pliable and versatile, more shatter-resistant, more easily constructed and transported, more heat- and cold-resistant than glass. Used in windows, doors, furniture, artwork, anywhere glass could be used. Few things in the colonies are still made from glass, Admiral Skalar's drinkware among them.

pui (POO-ee)—Native to Zebalu. Thick, thorny shrub that produces a sweet-tart fruit the size of a strawberry.

pyshta (PEESH-tah)—Indigenous to Bejami. Small, water-reliant mammals who live along the riverbanks and at the deltas in warm climates. Feed on marsh tubers, small mollusks and crustaceans, muil eggs, and fryt when they can catch them.

Ranafta (rah-NAF-tah)—One of twelve colony worlds. Governed by the Ranafta Wildlife Preserve. Located in the Alama star system. One large moon, one small moon, minor ring system. Ranafta is home to many of the animals brought from old Earth, most of which have increased in size given the larger environment in which they are left to thrive. Two space ports. Two land ports.

reap, reaping—See harvest.

recreational(s)—Herbal or pharmaceutical substances used for recreational purposes. Mostly legal in all twelve colonies. Only a few are banned for serious safety reasons or perhaps because the botanical substances necessary to produce them are endangered.

Rubene (roo-BEE-nuh)—One of twelve colony worlds. Governed by Rubene Holding Company. Located in the Emlacha star system (same as Bejami). No moon. Home to The Federation Trader faction. One of the first three exoplanets to be settled by colonists from Earth. This is a green world, focused even more heavily than other colonies on sustainability and ecosystem-friendly practices. One spaceport. Two landports.

rufesh (ROO-fehsh) *Unameze*—Indigenous to Iridos. Opportunistic epiphyte that entangles tubers in the root systems of other plants and trees on Iridos. Lost to the unammi since The Fall.

rusucre tree (ROO-seh-cur)—Indigenous to Saacharis. Tallest trees on this world, but trunk and branches are thickly twisted and contorted. Bark is as pale greyish-yellow as their leaves, which appear as thicker, overlapping scales that grow in thumb-sized-thick tails at the ends of the branches and hang, willow-like, from the tree. Small seed cones hang near the end of the tail, and glow when ripe. Every centimeter of surface on this odd-looking tree is utilized in gathering light.

Saacharis (sah-KAH-rihs)—One of twelve colony worlds. Governed by Saacharis Aggregate Mining. Located in the Nadisa star system. Two moons. Sometimes dark on the planet's surface for hours when one or another eclipses the star; when both moons join in the eclipse, temperatures on the planet can drop significantly. Home to The Syndicate Trader faction. One of the first three exoplanets to be settled by colonists from Earth. Nadisa is larger and brighter than Sol of Old Earth. Yet the planet's thick upper atmosphere reflects back much of the harmful radiation and heat. Thus the surface of Saacharis is dimmer, darker than other colonies. Two large spaceports. Two landports.

Salisbury (SAHLZ-buhr-ee)—A city on the colony world of Harajüd.

sanitile (SA-nih-tiyl)—Sound-absorbent tiling used in flooring and ceiling for many buildings within the colonies. Sanitile is treated in such a way that it is resistant to infectious organisms or substances. Easy to keep clean, sanitary.

Sea Star, The—Cartel ship, cargo class.

season—Unammi measure of time on Iridos, used to denote a complete circuit of the planet around its star. Still used by unammi elders, even though they are no longer living on Iridos.

sedolyn (SEH-doh-lihn)—Indigenous to Harajüd but farmed on several colony worlds. Recreational. Safe herbal relaxant made from leaves and flowers of the *sedolinis* plant. Usually smoked but can be ingested in food or drink. Mild, not sleep-inducing.

seedstones—Bits of stone embedded or encrusted with irolium, brought from Iridos and attached to cavern and tunnel surfaces in the new unammi city on Earth in the hope of establishing a new colony of Iri and thus irolium on Earth and elsewhere the unammi might settle.

Seifugi (SEE-foo-gee)—City at the estuary on Laguna Dosit, continent of Curluci on the colony world Saacharis. Much coming and going here, by air, land, and sea. Favorite transport spot for illegal goods or people on the run.

Shamashu Island (SHA-mah-shoo)—Large island off the coast of New Canaan, Harajüd.

Shemonaea (sheh-moh-NAY-uh)—One of twelve colony worlds. Governed by The Shemonaea Fellowship of Seekers. Located in the Sakĕdris star system. No moon. First colonial world established and settled by colonists from other Charter worlds; organized for the specific purpose of retreating from civilization. No spaceport. One landport.

Shidara (shih-DAH-ruh)—See Bindhu.

shisté (shis-TAY)—A light, dry wine from Gadney. Obtained from the nectar of a rare native flower whose blooms last one solar day for one season per solar year, the wine is only produced during that brief period. Aging requires several solar years, and storage requirements during that time are stringent, else the wine will spoil. Understandably, the fermented beverage is available only in limited quantities and is therefore quite expensive.

shuttle—Small version of a passenger carrier. Ferries passengers and travelers back and forth between the spaceport and the landport, or from one planetary city to another. Cannot be rented. Passage available to anyone who can pay, or who is being transported by corpgov for work or other official purposes.

silk beetle—Indigenous to Danua. Beetle-like insects that produce silky fibers. Highly prized for their contribution to the production of famous silks and other expensive textiles.

skimmer—Small personal craft same size and class as a small jumper. Faster, sleeker, more elite. Stylish, functional, greater capacity for speed and distance. Limited to atmospheric travel. Quieter than a jumper.

Sot (Afrikaans)—Fool.

squib—Derogatory term used by some humans to describe an unammi.

standard time—Colonial measure of time created to standardize business practices between the various colony worlds, which all have varying natural day, week, month, and year lengths. Hours, minutes, and seconds remain the same as Earth time measures.
    One standard day = 30 hours.
    One standard week = 6 standard days.
    One standard month = 30 standard days (5 standard weeks).
    One standard year = 15 standard months (75 standard weeks).

Storelandsør (stoh-reh-LAHN-sewr)—One of two lands located on the largest continent on Danua. Its name means Great Land to the South. Home to Haven.

stunner—up-close weapon. Smaller versions must touch the target. More expensive (and illegal) ones can fire from short distances. Depending on the setting, the weapon can simply stop the target or render it unconscious.

sukabo (soo-KAH-bo)—Indigenous to Zebalu. A fungus that grows only along the northern coastline bordering the Gulf of Busala, as well as on two islands in that Gulf. Quite expensive due to their rarity and because they are protected by law. Produces feelings of ecstasy that last for hours. Highly addictive. Illegal to pick, eat, or sell.

Syndicate, The—Trader faction located on the colony world Saacharis. Run by Admiral Rizzo and second in command, Captain Bailey.

Syrinaia (seer-ih-NAY-uh)—Continent on Harajüd, contained almost entirely in the southern hemisphere. Home to the Nöbetchi Mountains and New Canaan.

TICS (tihks)—Tachyon interlink control system. Used for inter- and intraplanetary communications, computer controls, personal memo systems, and numerous other purposes. Voice activated/controlled.

Treasure Chest, The—Consortium ship, large cargo class. Captained by Ronan.

Tuneloras (too-NELL-oh-rah)—Capital city on the colony world of Saacharis. Located on the continent of Metaliven. Entire city is grungy. Dark. Large.

Ulykkevik (yoo-LEE-kah-vihk)—Large bay on Danua. Surrounded by the northern peninsula of Landetorr on the north, east, and south, and an arc of unnamed, uninhabited islands on the west. There is a crater in the bay's basin where divers found ruins that predate the human colonies. That whole area has been ruled strictly off-limits by Danua Textiles.

Un momento (Spanish)—One minute; give me a minute.

unammi (oo-NAH-mee) *Unameze*—The Iridosians' name for themselves.

úta (OO-tah)—Mead-like alcoholic beverage made from oceanic fruit on Bejami. See bh'tati.

Vagabond, The—Spencer Kilbee's ship, small cargo class. Old, but well-maintained.

visaug (VIH-zawg)—Visual augmentation gear standard in human space suits.

VR—Virtual reality.

Wanneer geestenote ontmoet, is daar vreugde (Afrikaans)—When spirits meet, there is joy. Traditional Bejami greeting, formal.

youngling—Unammi term for offspring; children.

Zebalu (zeh-BAH-loo)—One of twelve colony worlds. Governed by The Zebalu Association. Located in the Rasuka star system. Three moons, one large with some atmosphere. Medical facilities located there under a dome. Home to The Cartel Trader faction. Three spaceports. Two landports.

Zebalu Association—The corporate governing body on colony world Zebalu.

Zekes Pub—Public house in New Canaan, Harajüd. Owned/operated by Harajüd House, Unlimited.